16

STORY AND ART BY
NORIYUKI KONISHI

ORIGINAL CONCEPT AND SUPERVISED BY LEVEL-5 INC.

7

YO-KAI WATCH™
Volume 16
VIZ Media Edition

Story and Art by Noriyuki Konishi
Original Concept and Supervised by LEVEL-5 Inc.

Translation/Tetsuichiro Miyaki
Lettering/John Hunt
Design/Kam Li

YO-KAI WATCH Vol. 16
by Noriyuki KONISHI
© 2013 Noriyuki KONISHI
©LEVEL-5 Inc.
Original Concept and Supervised by LEVEL-5 Inc.
All rights reserved.
Original Japanese edition published by SHOGAKUKAN.
English translation rights in the United States of America,
Canada, the United Kingdom, Ireland, Australia and New Zealand
arranged with SHOGAKUKAN.

Printed in the U.S.A.

Published by VIZ Media, LLC
P.O. Box 77010
San Francisco, CA 94107

10 9 8 7 6 5 4 3 2 1
First printing, January 2021

YO-KAI WATCH™

16

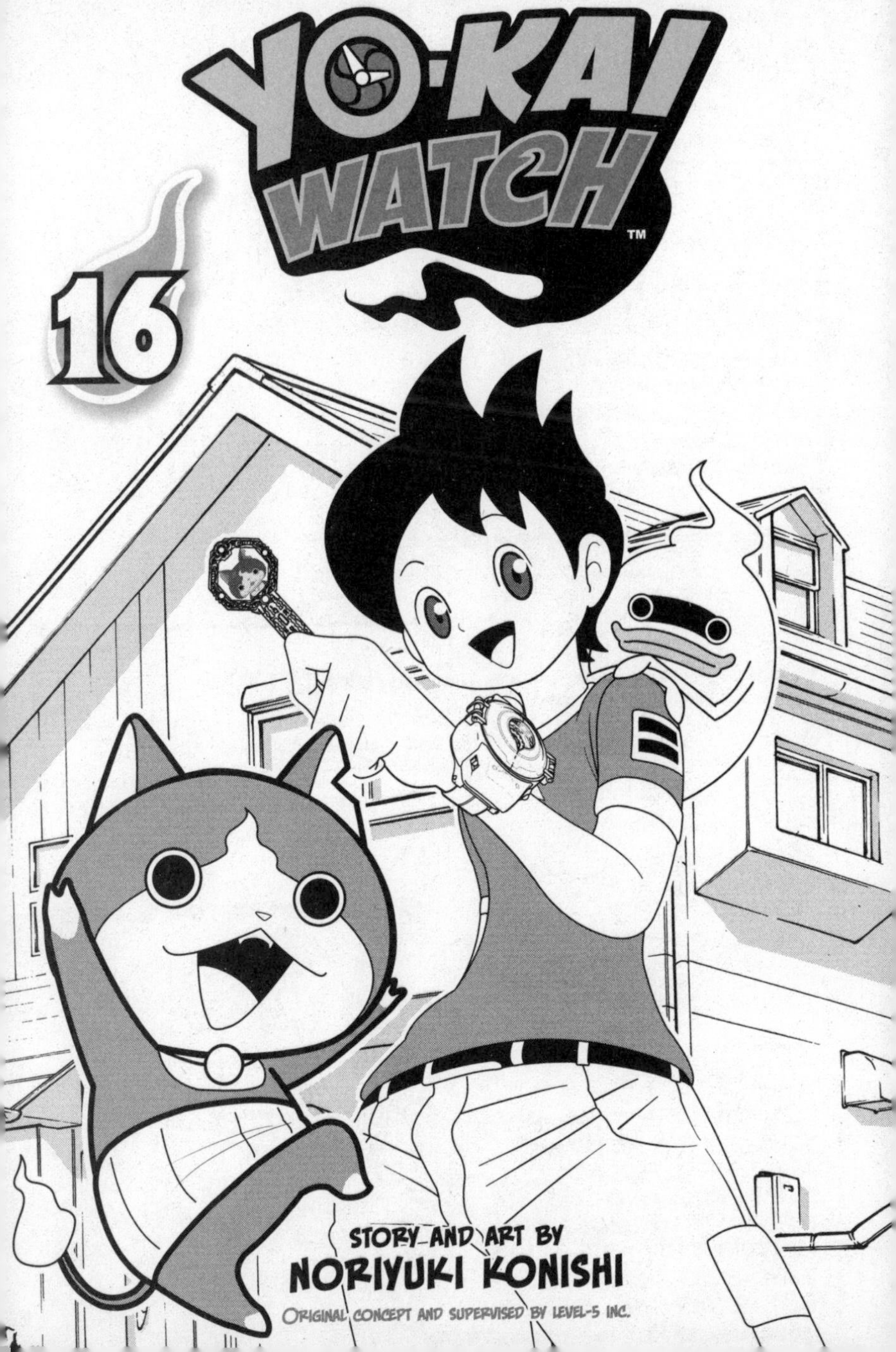

STORY AND ART BY

NORIYUKI KONISHI

ORIGINAL CONCEPT AND SUPERVISED BY LEVEL-5 INC.

CHARACTER INTRODUCTION

NATHAN ADAMS

AN ORDINARY ELEMENTARY SCHOOL STUDENT. WHISPER GAVE HIM THE YO-KAI WATCH AND HE'S USED IT TO MAKE A BUNCH OF YO-KAI FRIENDS!

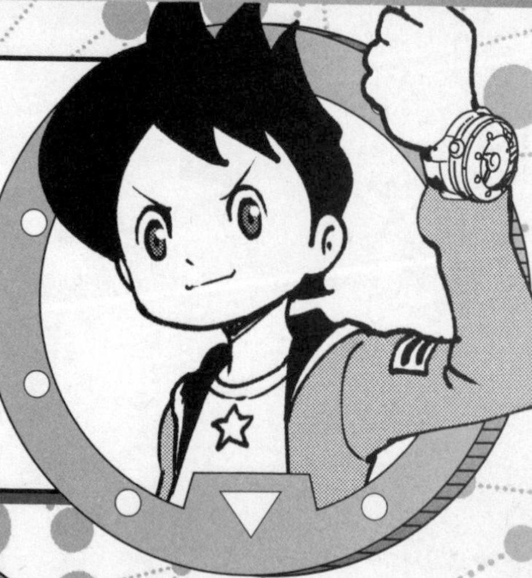

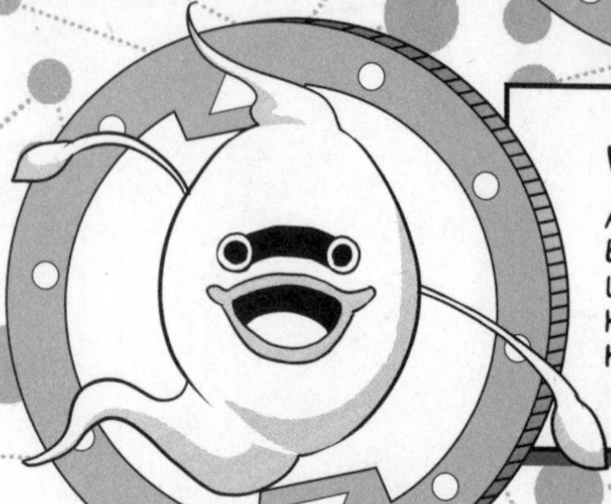

WHISPER

A YO-KAI BUTLER FREED BY NATE, WHISPER USES HIS EXTENSIVE KNOWLEDGE TO TEACH HIM ALL ABOUT YO-KAI!

JIBANYAN

A CAT WHO BECAME A YO-KAI WHEN HE PASSED AWAY. HE IS FRIENDLY, CAREFREE, AND THE FIRST YO-KAI THAT NATE BEFRIENDED. HE'S BEEN TRYING TO FIGHT TRUCKS, BUT HE ALWAYS LOSES.

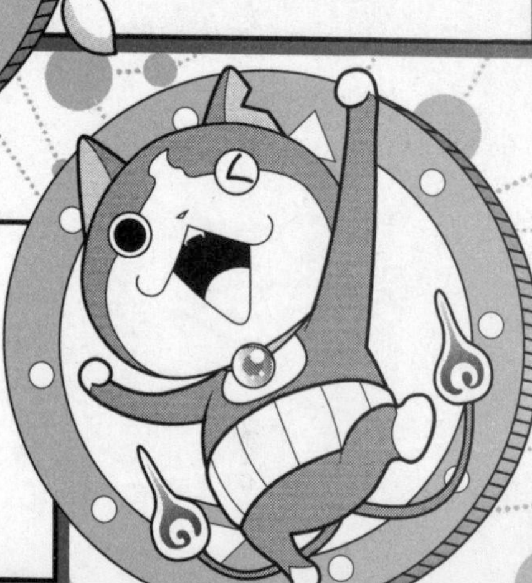

BARNABY BERNSTEIN
NATE'S CLASSMATE.
NICKNAME: BEAR.
CAN BE MISCHIEVOUS.

EDWARD ARCHER
NATE'S CLASSMATE.
NICKNAME: EDDIE.
HE ALWAYS WEARS
HEAPHONES.

KATIE FORESTER
THE MOST POPULAR
GIRL IN NATE'S CLASS.

TABLE OF CONTENTS

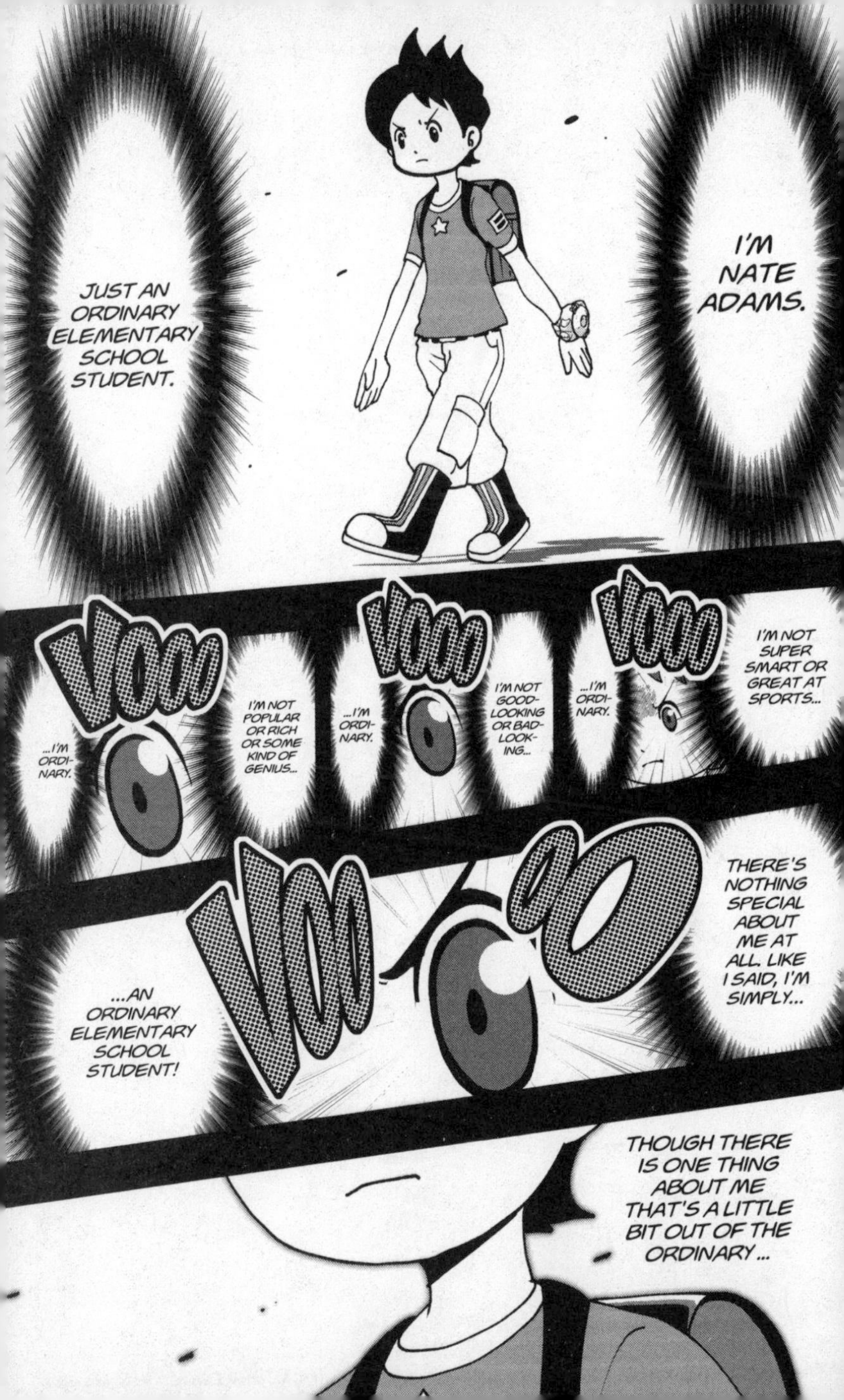
I'M NATE ADAMS.
JUST AN ORDINARY ELEMENTARY SCHOOL STUDENT.
I'M NOT SUPER SMART OR GREAT AT SPORTS...
VOOO
...I'M ORDINARY.
I'M NOT GOOD-LOOKING OR BAD-LOOKING...
VOOO
...I'M ORDINARY.
I'M NOT POPULAR OR RICH OR SOME KIND OF GENIUS...
VOOO
...I'M ORDINARY.
THERE'S NOTHING SPECIAL ABOUT ME AT ALL. LIKE I SAID, I'M SIMPLY...
VOOOO
...AN ORDINARY ELEMENTARY SCHOOL STUDENT!
THOUGH THERE IS ONE THING ABOUT ME THAT'S A LITTLE BIT OUT OF THE ORDINARY...

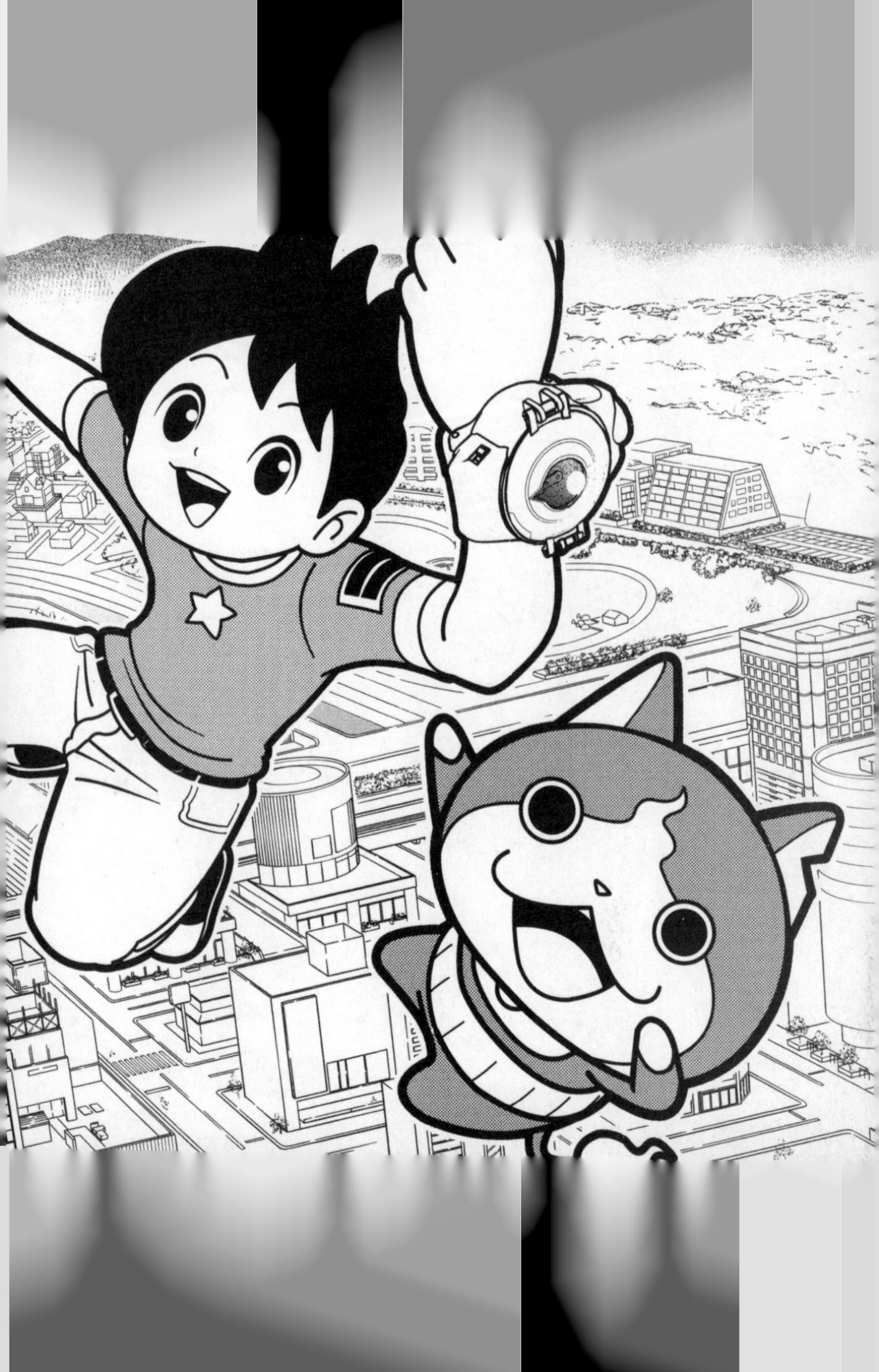

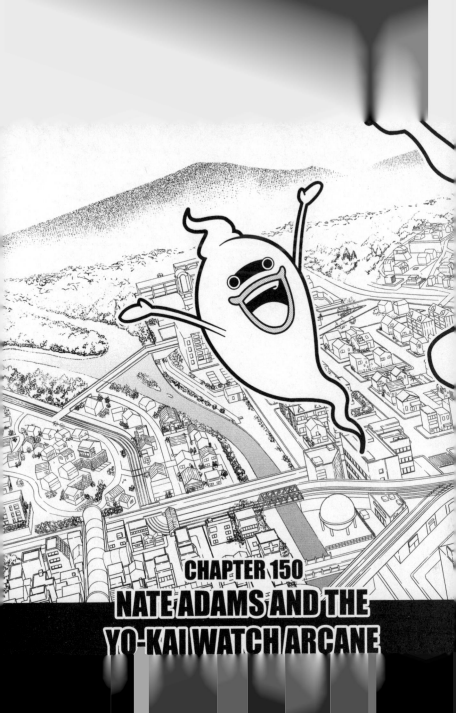

CHAPTER 150
NATE ADAMS AND THE
YO-KAI WATCH ARCANE

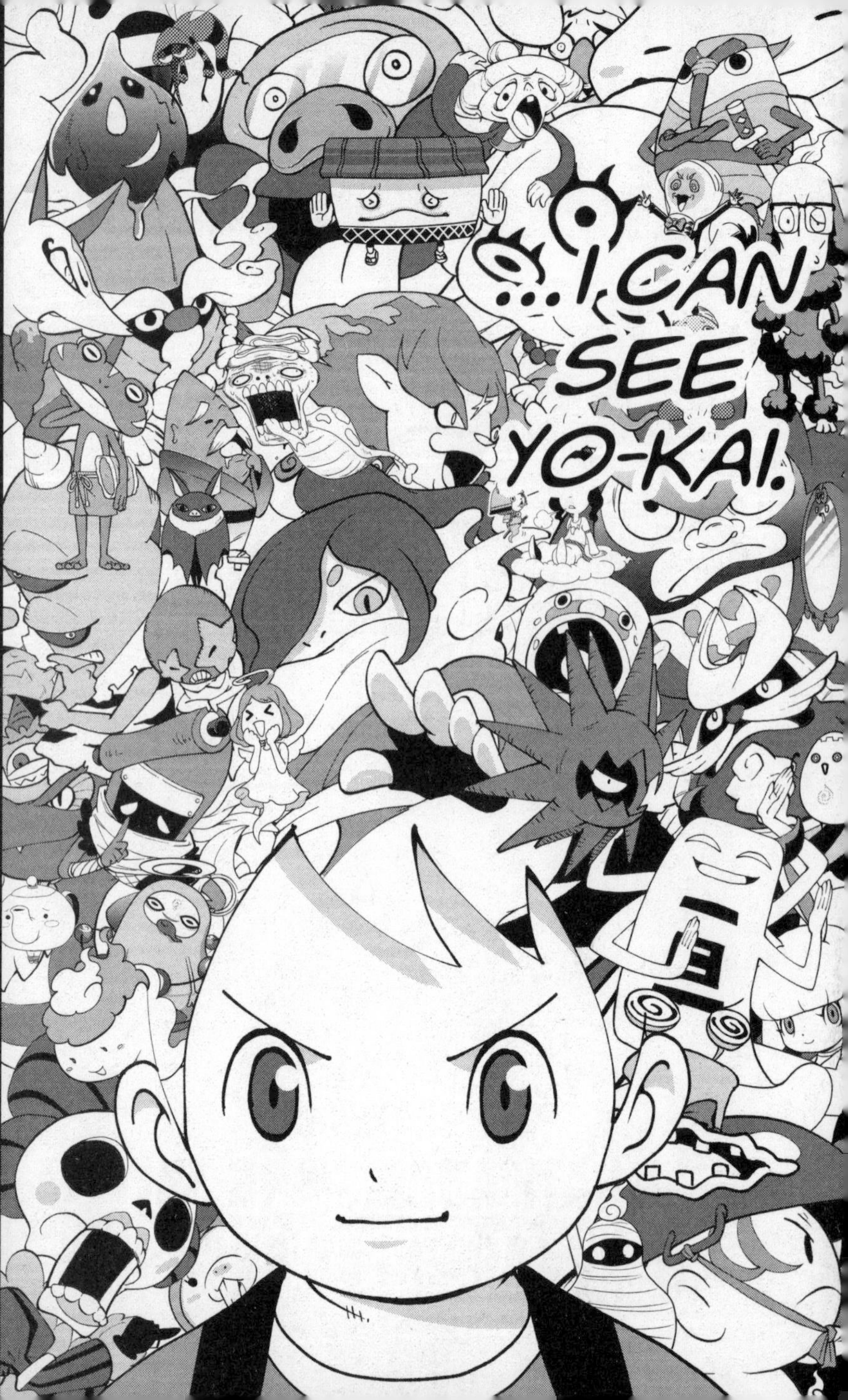
I CAN SEE YO-KAI!

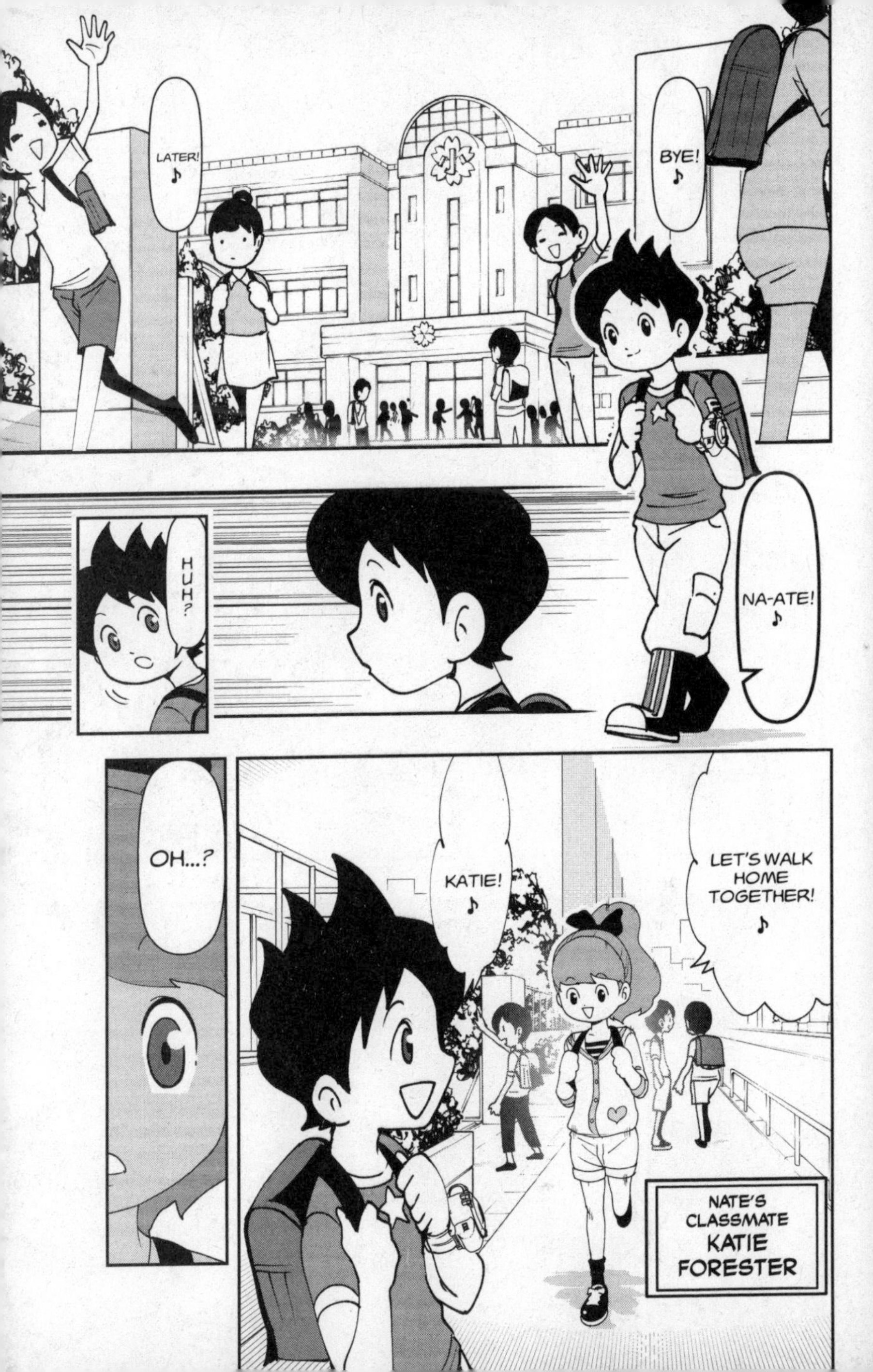
BYE! ♪
LATER! ♪
NA-ATE! ♪
HUH?
LET'S WALK HOME TOGETHER! ♪
KATIE! ♪
NATE'S CLASSMATE KATIE FORESTER
OH...?

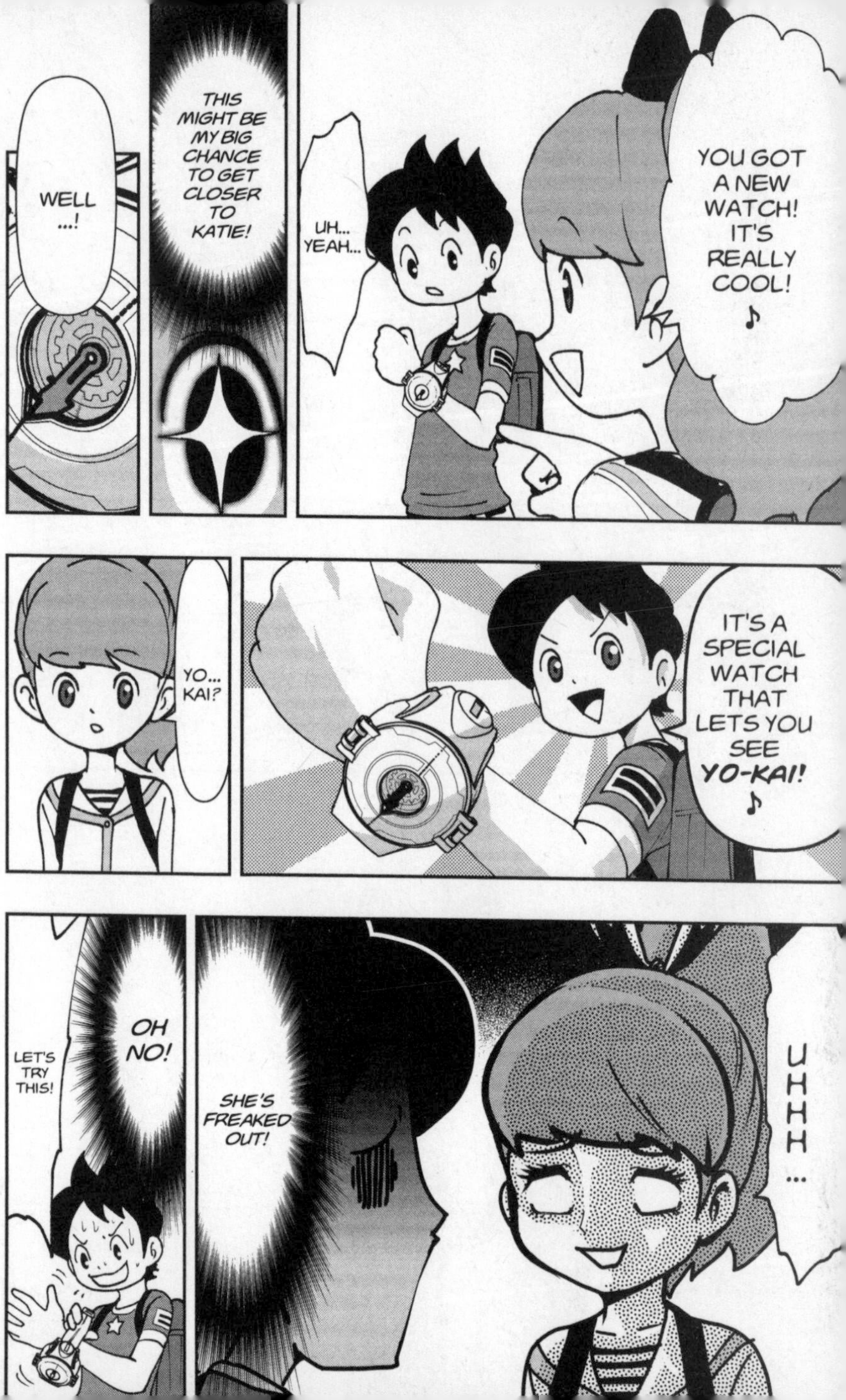
YOU GOT A NEW WATCH! IT'S REALLY COOL! ♪
UH... YEAH...
THIS MIGHT BE MY BIG CHANCE TO GET CLOSER TO KATIE!
WELL ...!
IT'S A SPECIAL WATCH THAT LETS YOU SEE *YO-KAI!* ♪
YO... KAI?
UHHH ...
OH NO!
SHE'S FREAKED OUT!
LET'S TRY THIS!

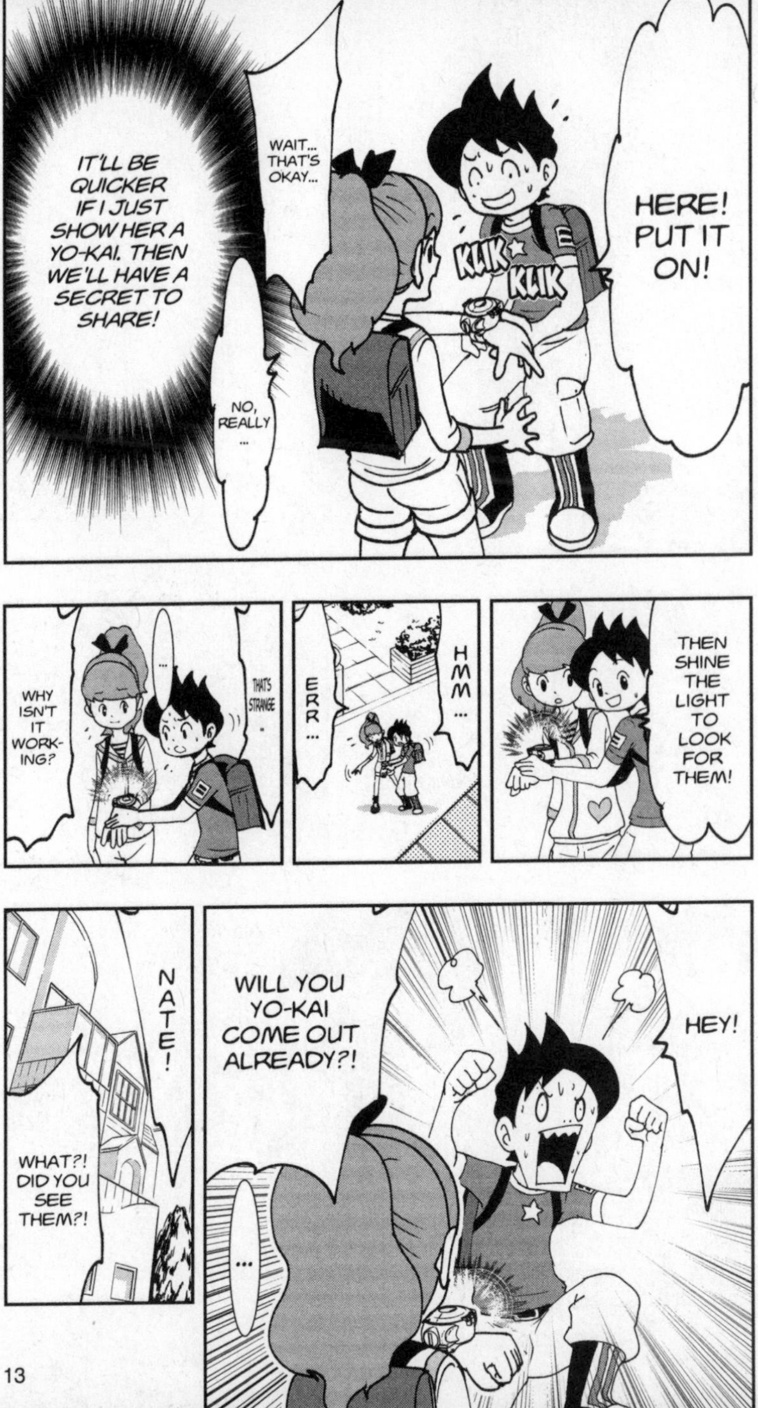
HERE! PUT IT ON!
KLIK KLIK
WAIT... THAT'S OKAY...
IT'LL BE QUICKER IF I JUST SHOW HER A YO-KAI. THEN WE'LL HAVE A SECRET TO SHARE!
NO, REALLY ...
THEN SHINE THE LIGHT TO LOOK FOR THEM!
HMM ...
ERR ...
THAT'S STRANGE.
...
WHY ISN'T IT WORKING?
HEY!
WILL YOU YO-KAI COME OUT ALREADY?!
...
NATE!
WHAT?! DID YOU SEE THEM?!

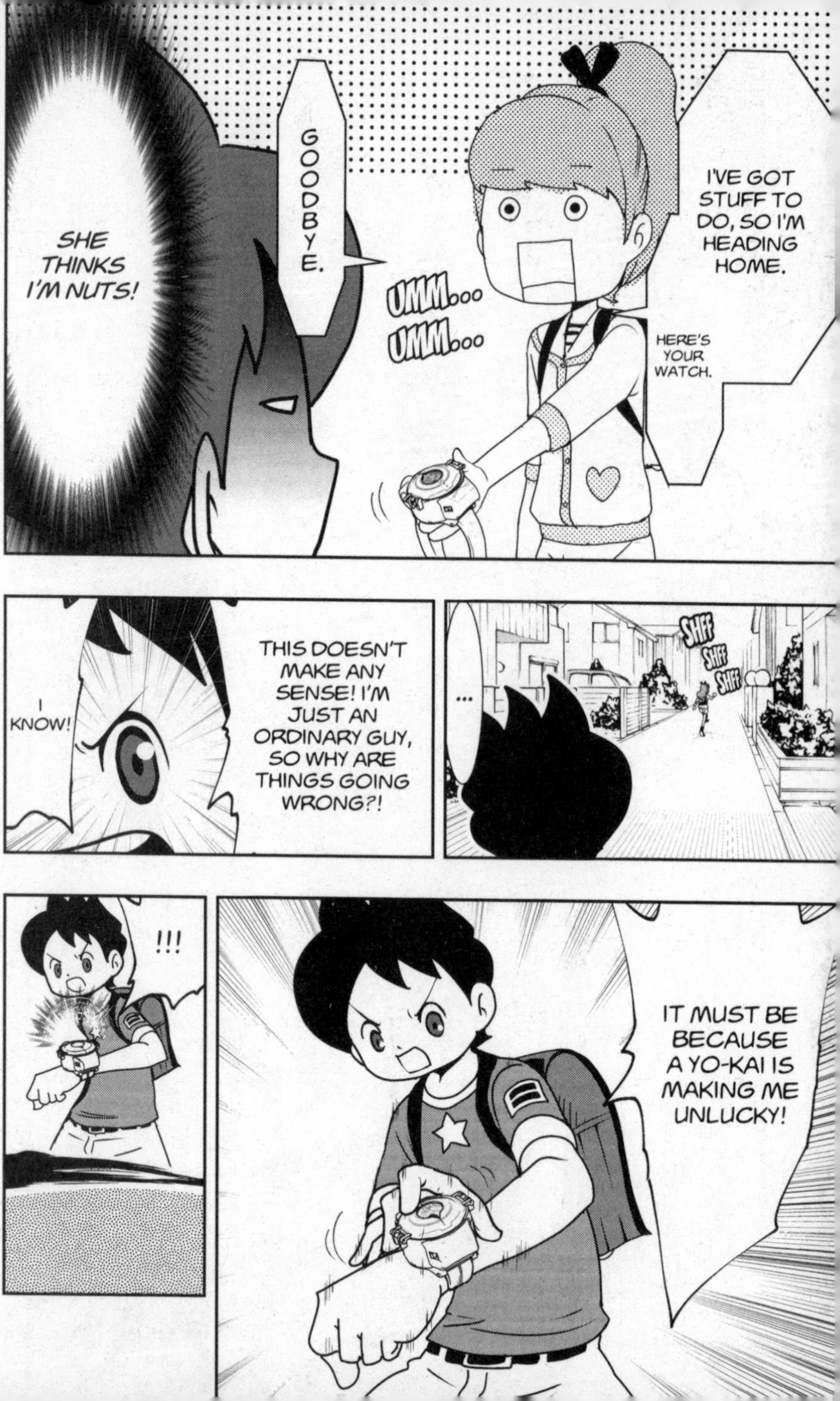
I'VE GOT STUFF TO DO, SO I'M HEADING HOME.
HERE'S YOUR WATCH.
UMM...
UMM...
GOODBYE.
SHE THINKS I'M NUTS!
SHFF
SHFF
SHFF
...
THIS DOESN'T MAKE ANY SENSE! I'M JUST AN ORDINARY GUY, SO WHY ARE THINGS GOING WRONG?!
I KNOW!
IT MUST BE BECAUSE A YO-KAI IS MAKING ME UNLUCKY!
!!!

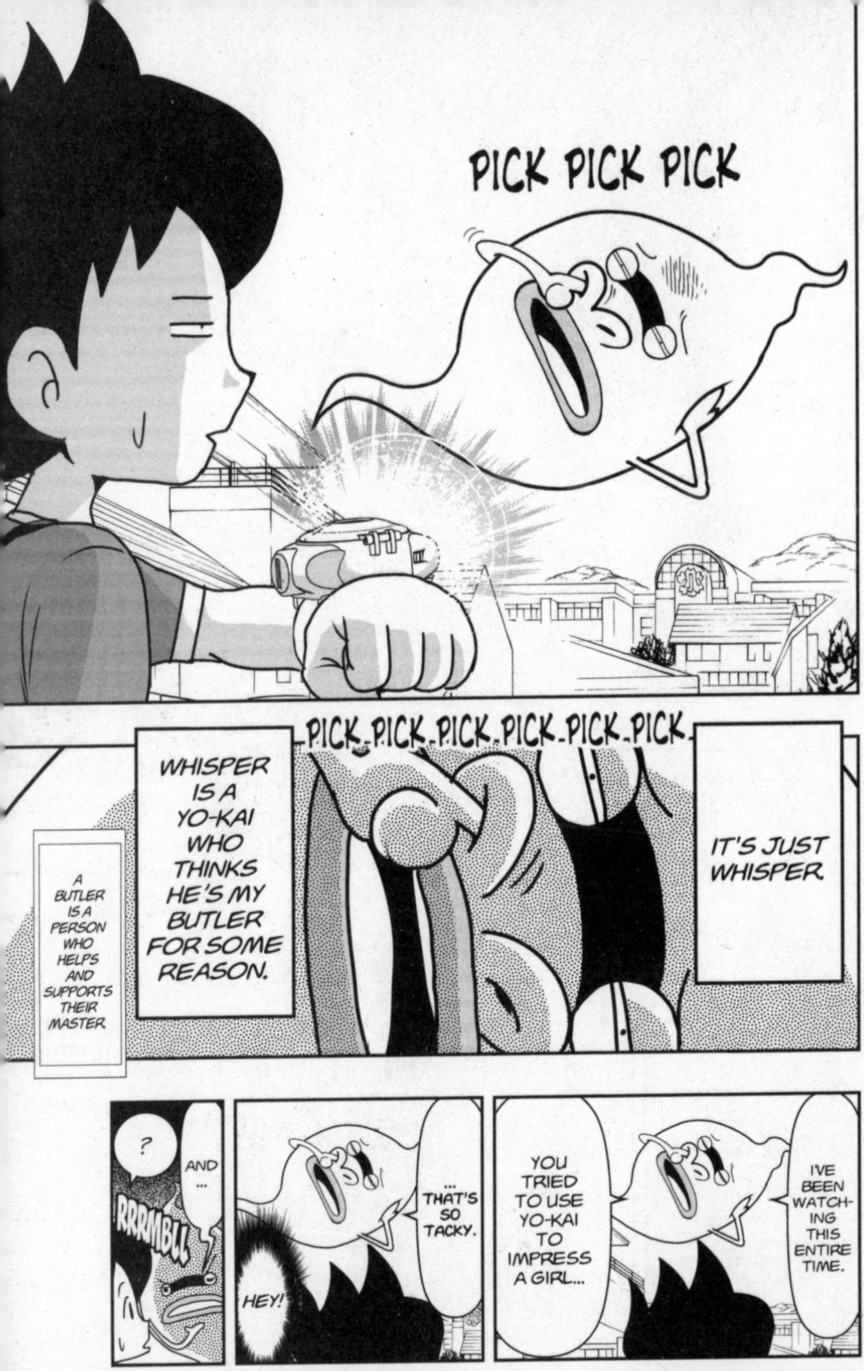
PICK PICK PICK
PICK PICK PICK PICK PICK PICK
IT'S JUST WHISPER.
WHISPER IS A YO-KAI WHO THINKS HE'S MY BUTLER FOR SOME REASON.
A BUTLER IS A PERSON WHO HELPS AND SUPPORTS THEIR MASTER.
I'VE BEEN WATCHING THIS ENTIRE TIME.
YOU TRIED TO USE YO-KAI TO IMPRESS A GIRL...
... THAT'S SO TACKY.
HEY!
AND ...
?
RRRMBLL

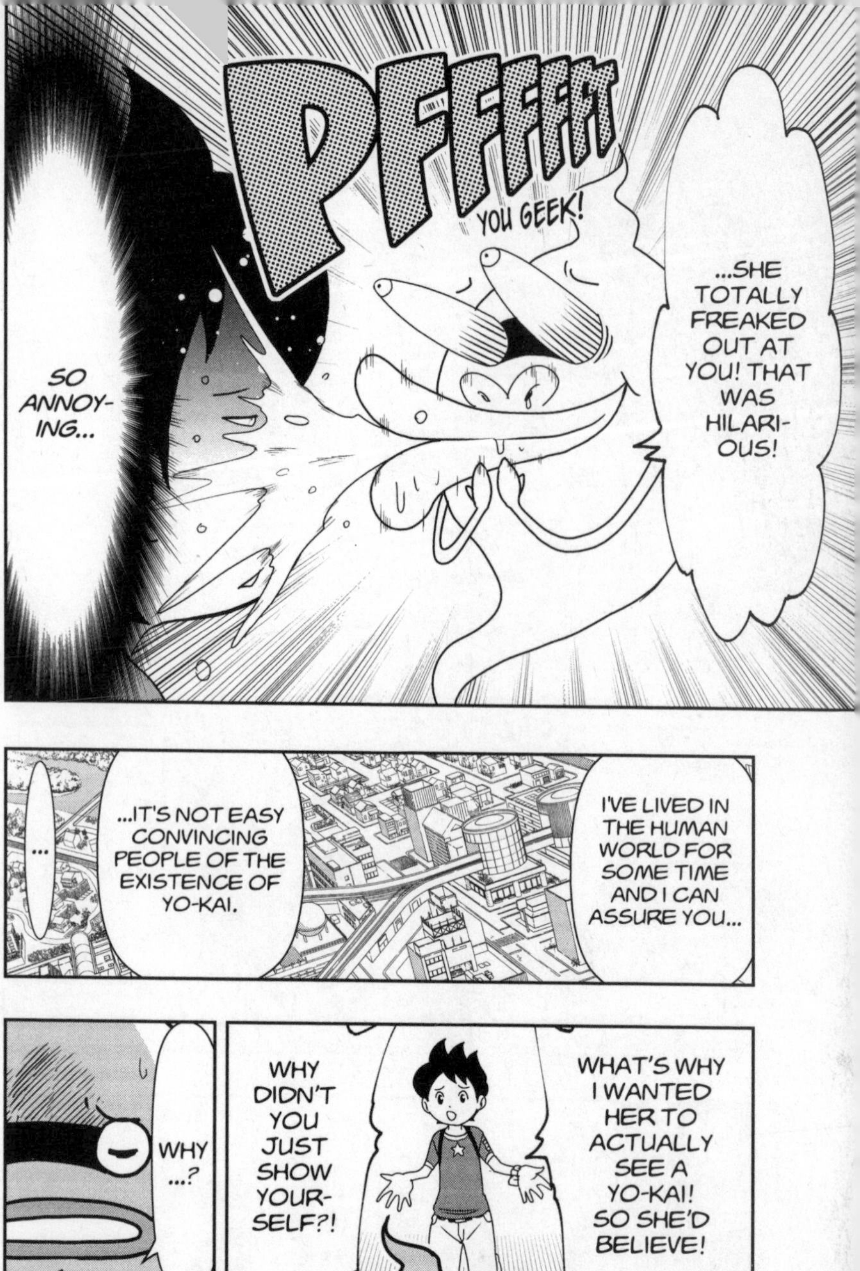
...SHE TOTALLY FREAKED OUT AT YOU! THAT WAS HILARIOUS!
PFFFRT
YOU GEEK!
SO ANNOYING...
I'VE LIVED IN THE HUMAN WORLD FOR SOME TIME AND I CAN ASSURE YOU...
...IT'S NOT EASY CONVINCING PEOPLE OF THE EXISTENCE OF YO-KAI.
...
WHAT'S WHY I WANTED HER TO ACTUALLY SEE A YO-KAI! SO SHE'D BELIEVE!
WHY DIDN'T YOU JUST SHOW YOURSELF?!
WHY ...?

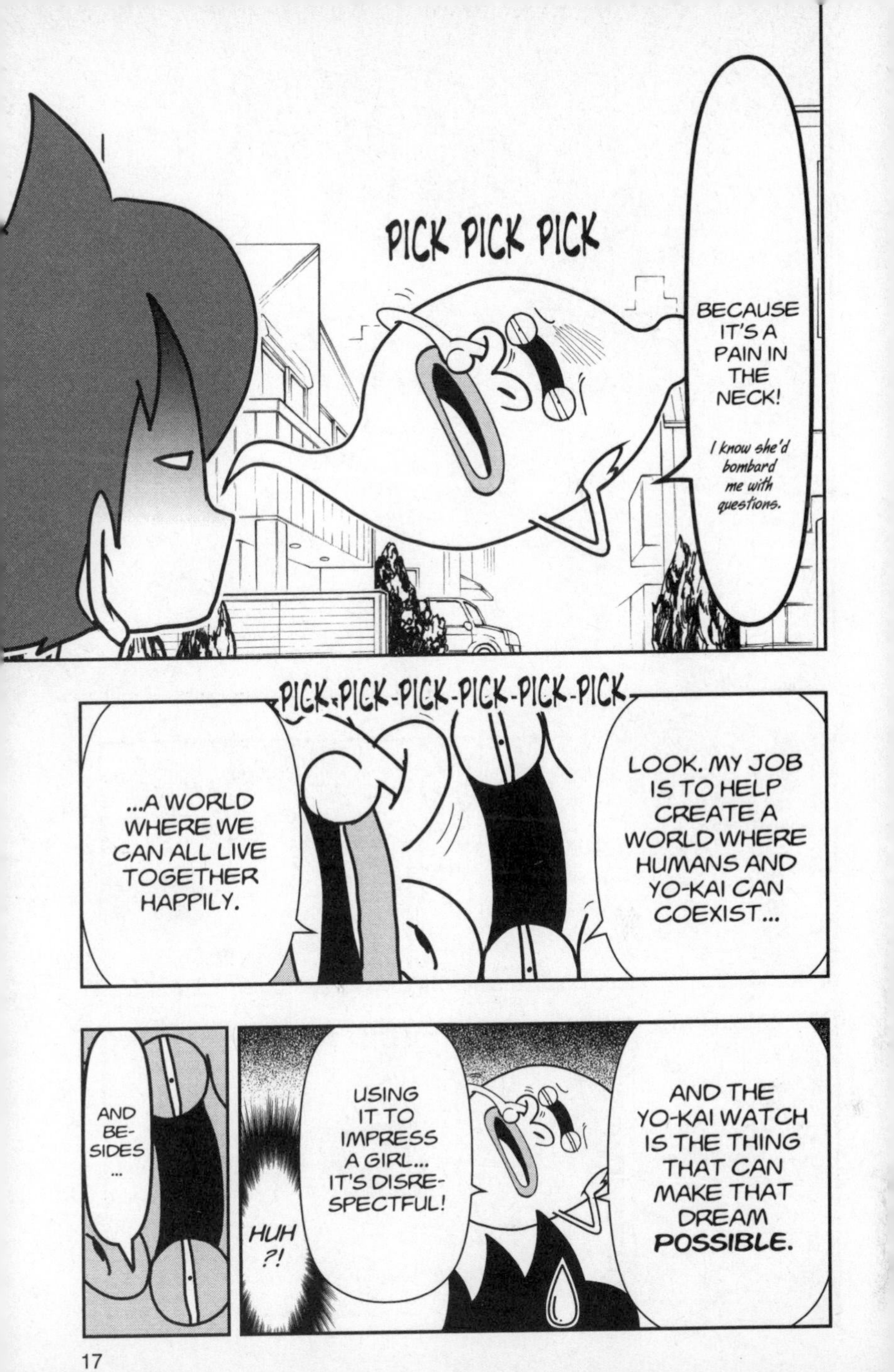
BECAUSE IT'S A PAIN IN THE NECK!
I know she'd bombard me with questions.
PICK PICK PICK
PICK-PICK-PICK-PICK-PICK-PICK
LOOK. MY JOB IS TO HELP CREATE A WORLD WHERE HUMANS AND YO-KAI CAN COEXIST...
...A WORLD WHERE WE CAN ALL LIVE TOGETHER HAPPILY.
AND THE YO-KAI WATCH IS THE THING THAT CAN MAKE THAT DREAM **POSSIBLE.**
USING IT TO IMPRESS A GIRL... IT'S DISRE-SPECTFUL!
HUH ?!
AND BE-SIDES ...

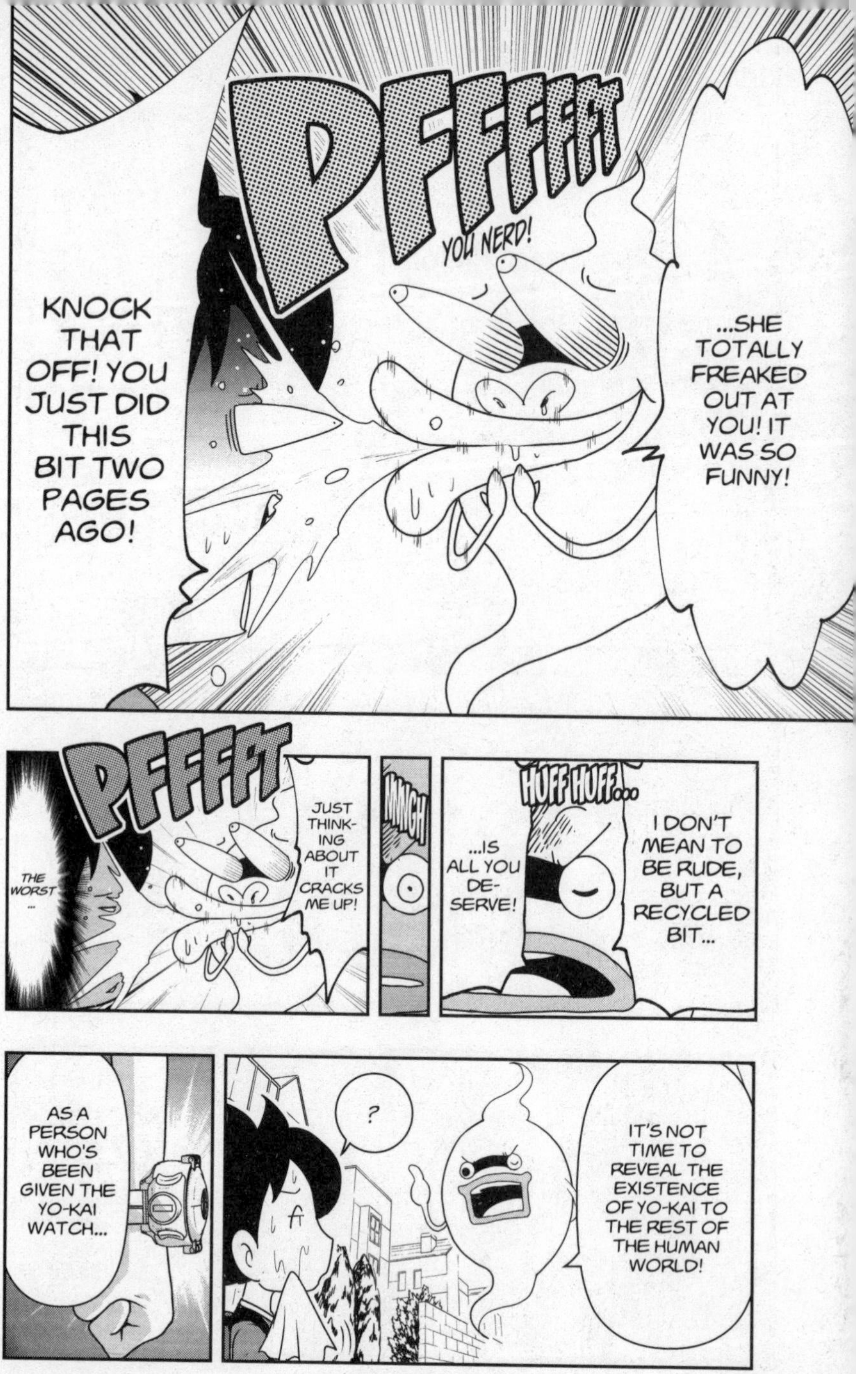
...SHE TOTALLY FREAKED OUT AT YOU! IT WAS SO FUNNY!
PFFFFFT
YOU NERD!
KNOCK THAT OFF! YOU JUST DID THIS BIT TWO PAGES AGO!
HUFF HUFF...
I DON'T MEAN TO BE RUDE, BUT A RECYCLED BIT...
...IS ALL YOU DE-SERVE!
MMGH
PFFFFT
JUST THINK-ING ABOUT IT CRACKS ME UP!
THE WORST...
IT'S NOT TIME TO REVEAL THE EXISTENCE OF YO-KAI TO THE REST OF THE HUMAN WORLD!
?
AS A PERSON WHO'S BEEN GIVEN THE YO-KAI WATCH...

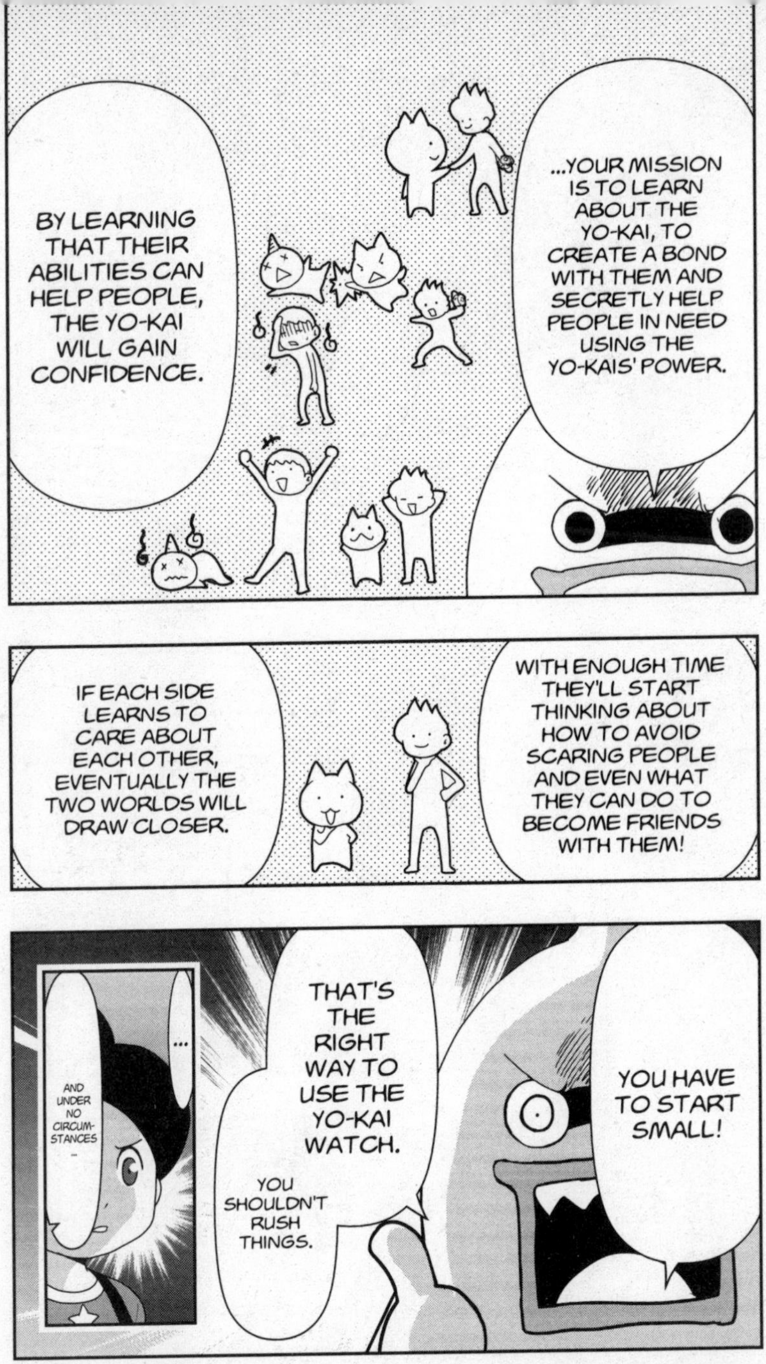
...YOUR MISSION IS TO LEARN ABOUT THE YO-KAI, TO CREATE A BOND WITH THEM AND SECRETLY HELP PEOPLE IN NEED USING THE YO-KAIS' POWER.
BY LEARNING THAT THEIR ABILITIES CAN HELP PEOPLE, THE YO-KAI WILL GAIN CONFIDENCE.
WITH ENOUGH TIME THEY'LL START THINKING ABOUT HOW TO AVOID SCARING PEOPLE AND EVEN WHAT THEY CAN DO TO BECOME FRIENDS WITH THEM!
IF EACH SIDE LEARNS TO CARE ABOUT EACH OTHER, EVENTUALLY THE TWO WORLDS WILL DRAW CLOSER.
YOU HAVE TO START SMALL!
THAT'S THE RIGHT WAY TO USE THE YO-KAI WATCH.
YOU SHOULDN'T RUSH THINGS.
...
AND UNDER NO CIRCUMSTANCES ...

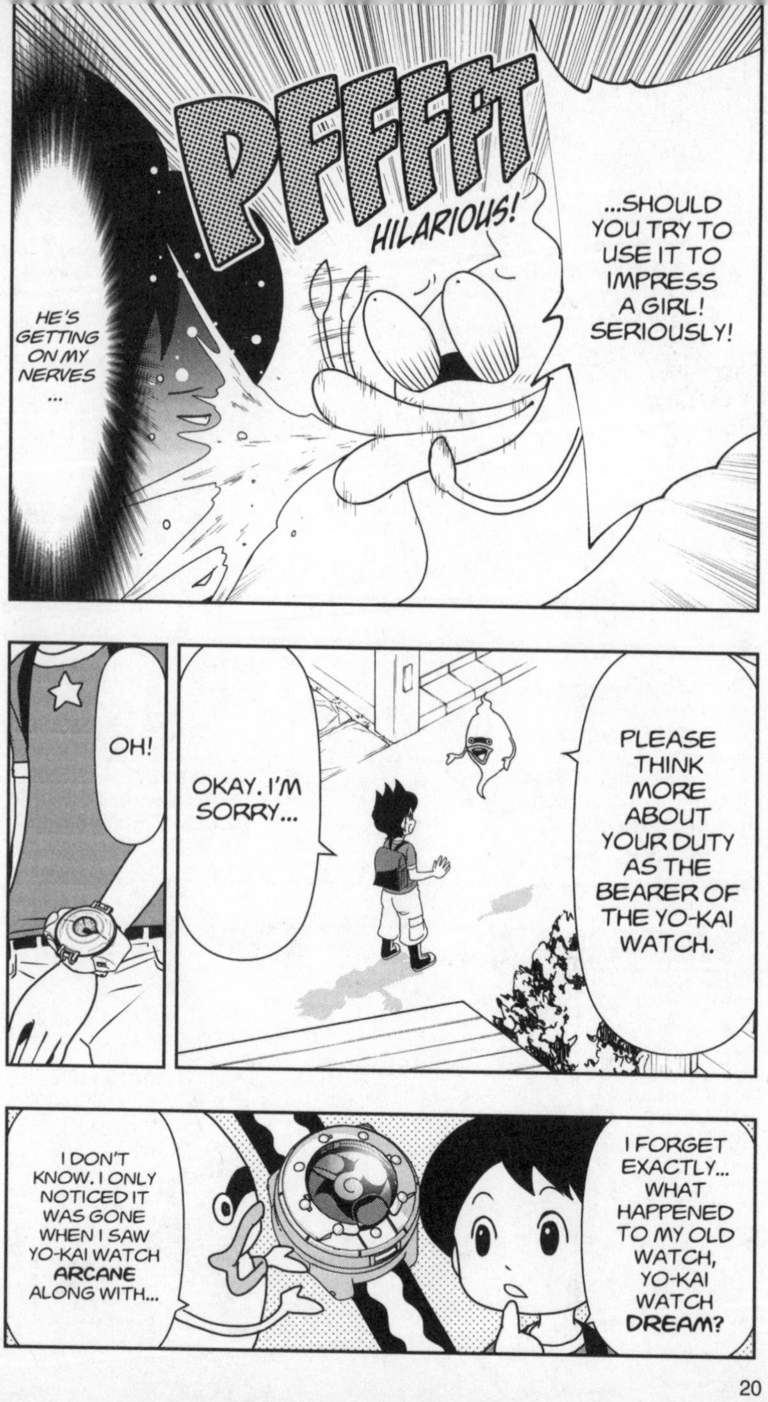
PFFFFT
HILARIOUS!
...SHOULD YOU TRY TO USE IT TO IMPRESS A GIRL! SERIOUSLY!
HE'S GETTING ON MY NERVES ...
PLEASE THINK MORE ABOUT YOUR DUTY AS THE BEARER OF THE YO-KAI WATCH.
OKAY. I'M SORRY...
OH!
I FORGET EXACTLY... WHAT HAPPENED TO MY OLD WATCH, YO-KAI WATCH **DREAM**?
I DON'T KNOW. I ONLY NOTICED IT WAS GONE WHEN I SAW YO-KAI WATCH **ARCANE** ALONG WITH...

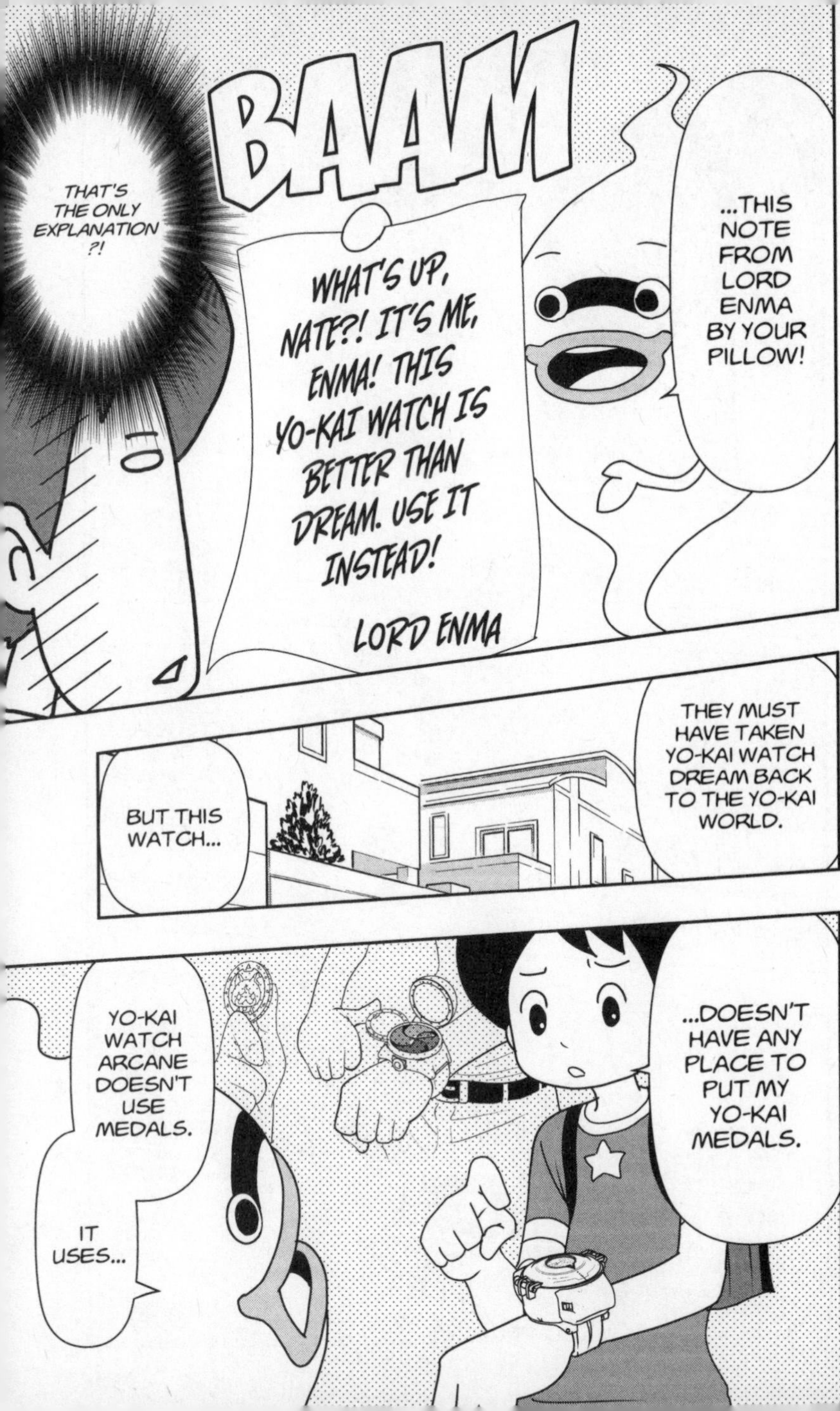
...THIS NOTE FROM LORD ENMA BY YOUR PILLOW!
BAAM
WHAT'S UP, NATE?! IT'S ME, ENMA! THIS YO-KAI WATCH IS BETTER THAN DREAM. USE IT INSTEAD!
LORD ENMA
THAT'S THE ONLY EXPLANATION ?!
THEY MUST HAVE TAKEN YO-KAI WATCH DREAM BACK TO THE YO-KAI WORLD.
BUT THIS WATCH...
...DOESN'T HAVE ANY PLACE TO PUT MY YO-KAI MEDALS.
YO-KAI WATCH ARCANE DOESN'T USE MEDALS.
IT USES...

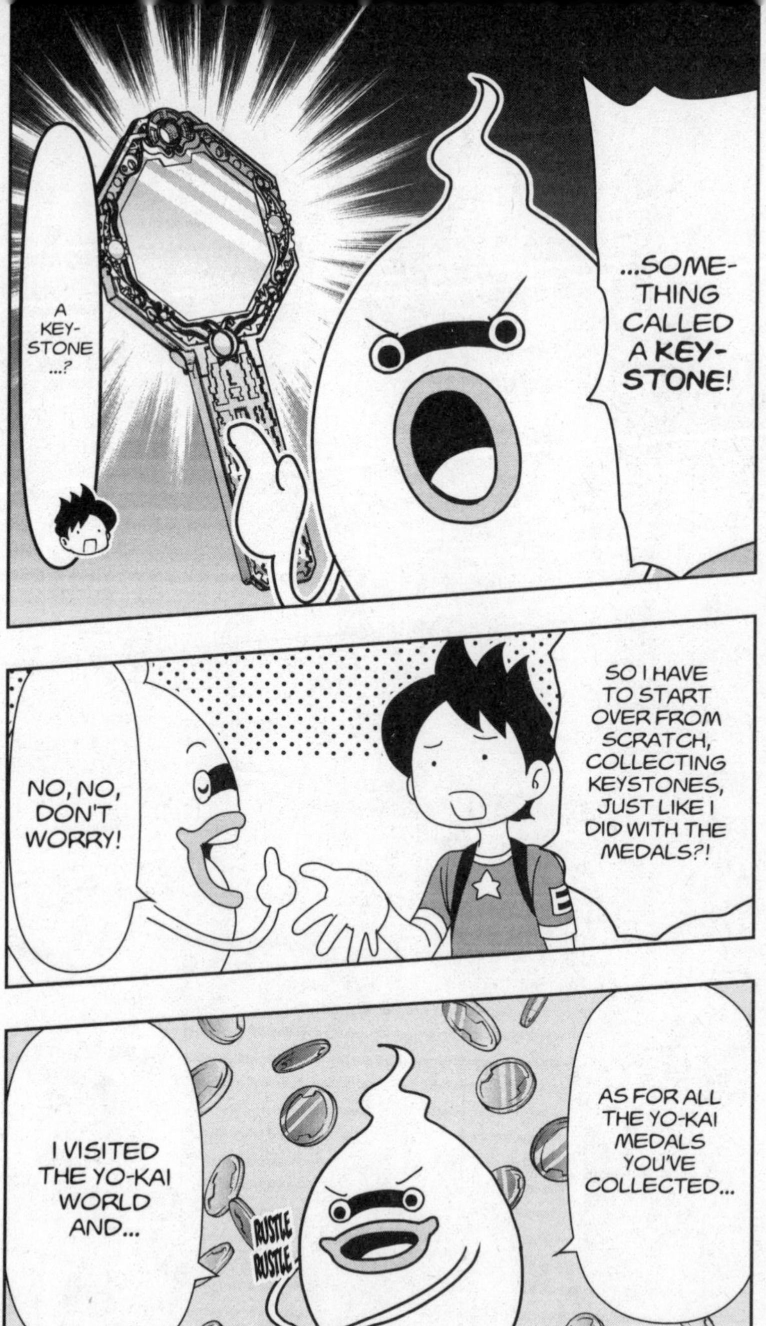
...SOME-THING CALLED A **KEY-STONE**!
A KEY-STONE ...?
SO I HAVE TO START OVER FROM SCRATCH, COLLECTING KEYSTONES, JUST LIKE I DID WITH THE MEDALS?!
NO, NO, DON'T WORRY!
AS FOR ALL THE YO-KAI MEDALS YOU'VE COLLECTED...
RUSTLE RUSTLE
I VISITED THE YO-KAI WORLD AND...

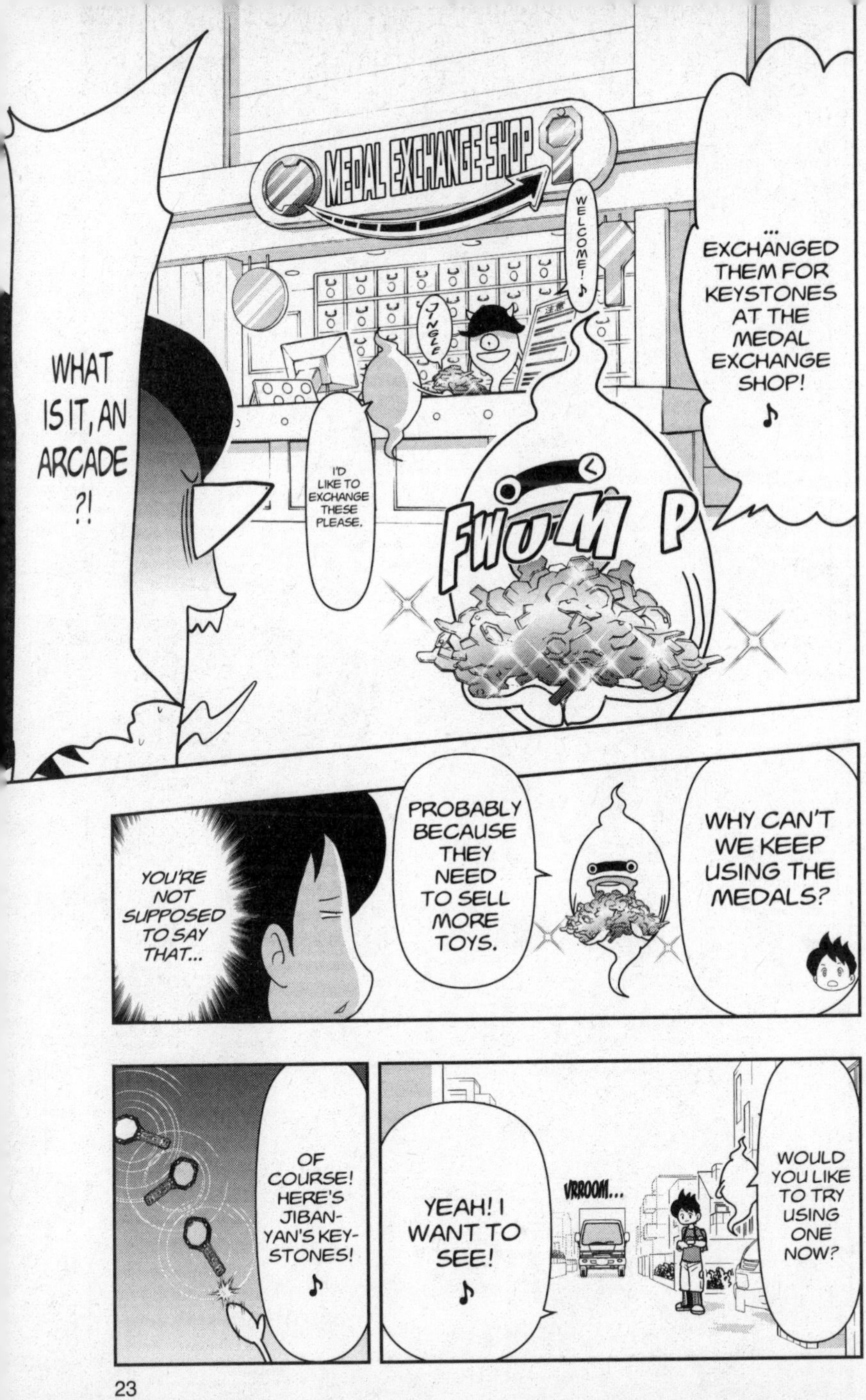
...EXCHANGED THEM FOR KEYSTONES AT THE MEDAL EXCHANGE SHOP! ♪
MEDAL EXCHANGE SHOP
WELCOME! ♪
JINGLE
I'D LIKE TO EXCHANGE THESE PLEASE.
FWUMP
WHAT IS IT, AN ARCADE?!
WHY CAN'T WE KEEP USING THE MEDALS?
PROBABLY BECAUSE THEY NEED TO SELL MORE TOYS.
YOU'RE NOT SUPPOSED TO SAY THAT...
WOULD YOU LIKE TO TRY USING ONE NOW?
VRROOM...
YEAH! I WANT TO SEE! ♪
OF COURSE! HERE'S JIBANYAN'S KEYSTONES! ♪

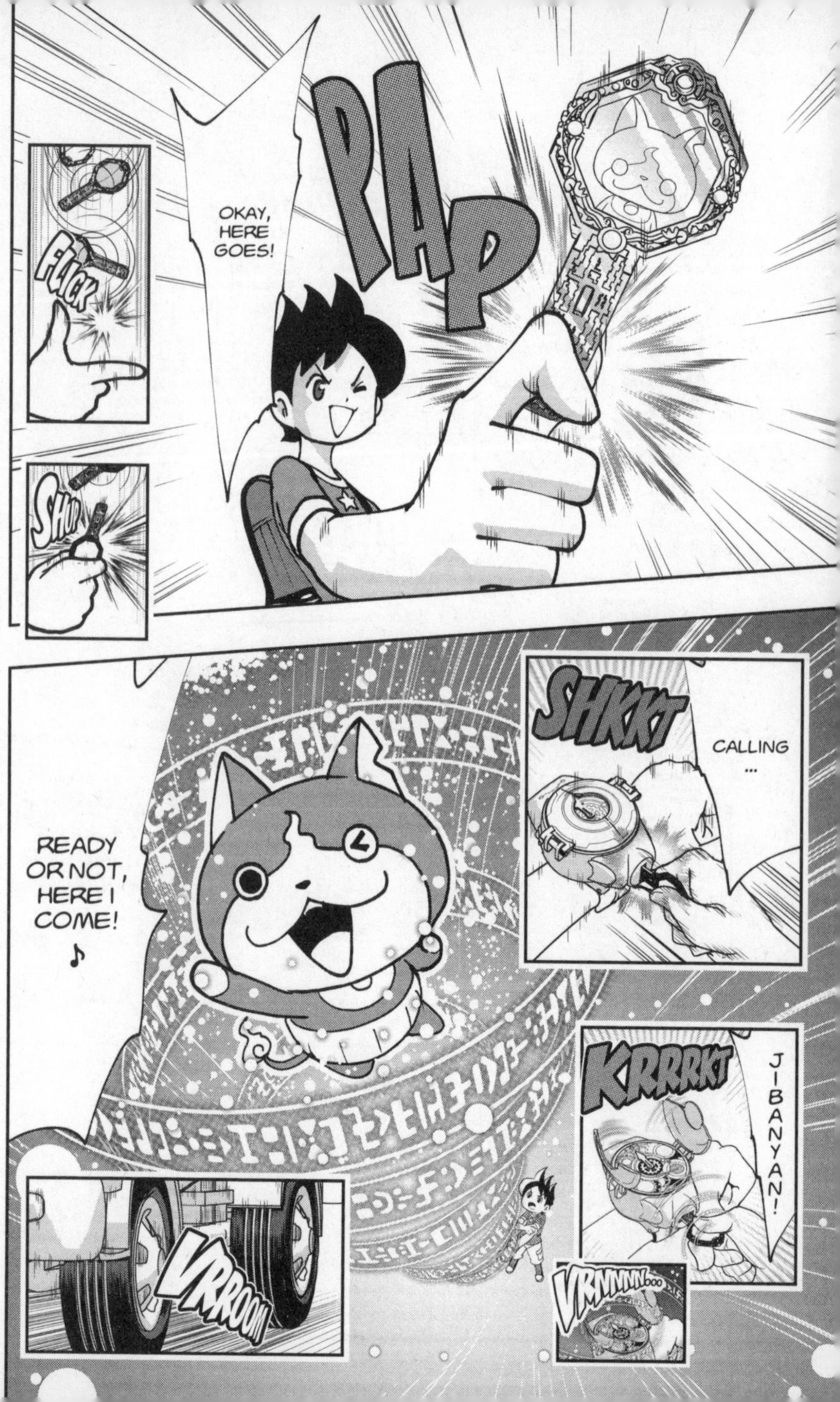
OKAY, HERE GOES!
RAP
FLICK
SHUP
SHKKT
CALLING ...
KRRRKT
JIBANYAN!
VRNNNN...
READY OR NOT, HERE I COME! ♪
VRROOM

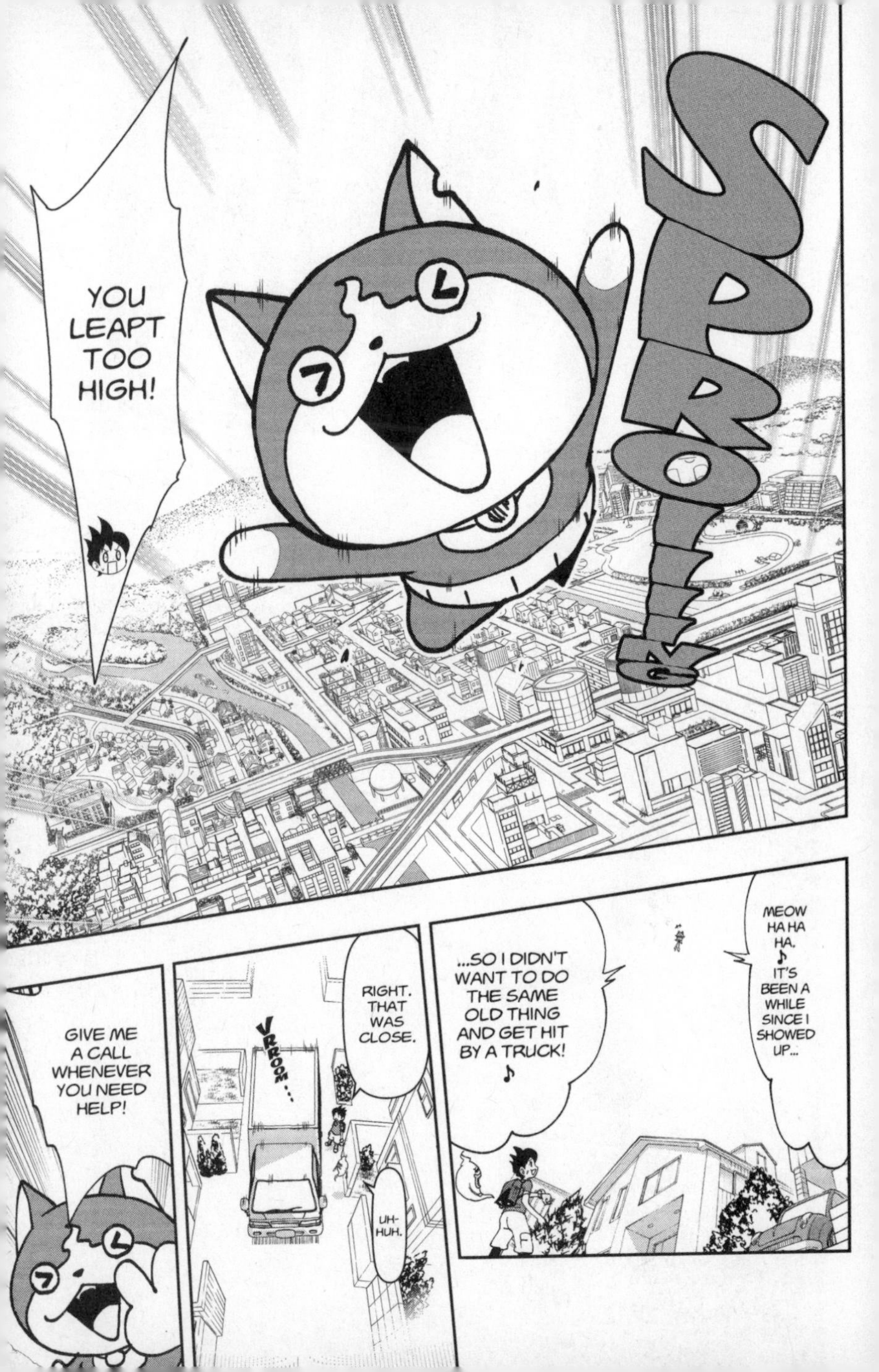
SPROING
YOU LEAPT TOO HIGH!
MEOW HA HA HA. ♪ IT'S BEEN A WHILE SINCE I SHOWED UP...
...SO I DIDN'T WANT TO DO THE SAME OLD THING AND GET HIT BY A TRUCK! ♪
RIGHT. THAT WAS CLOSE.
VRROOM...
UH-HUH.
GIVE ME A CALL WHENEVER YOU NEED HELP!

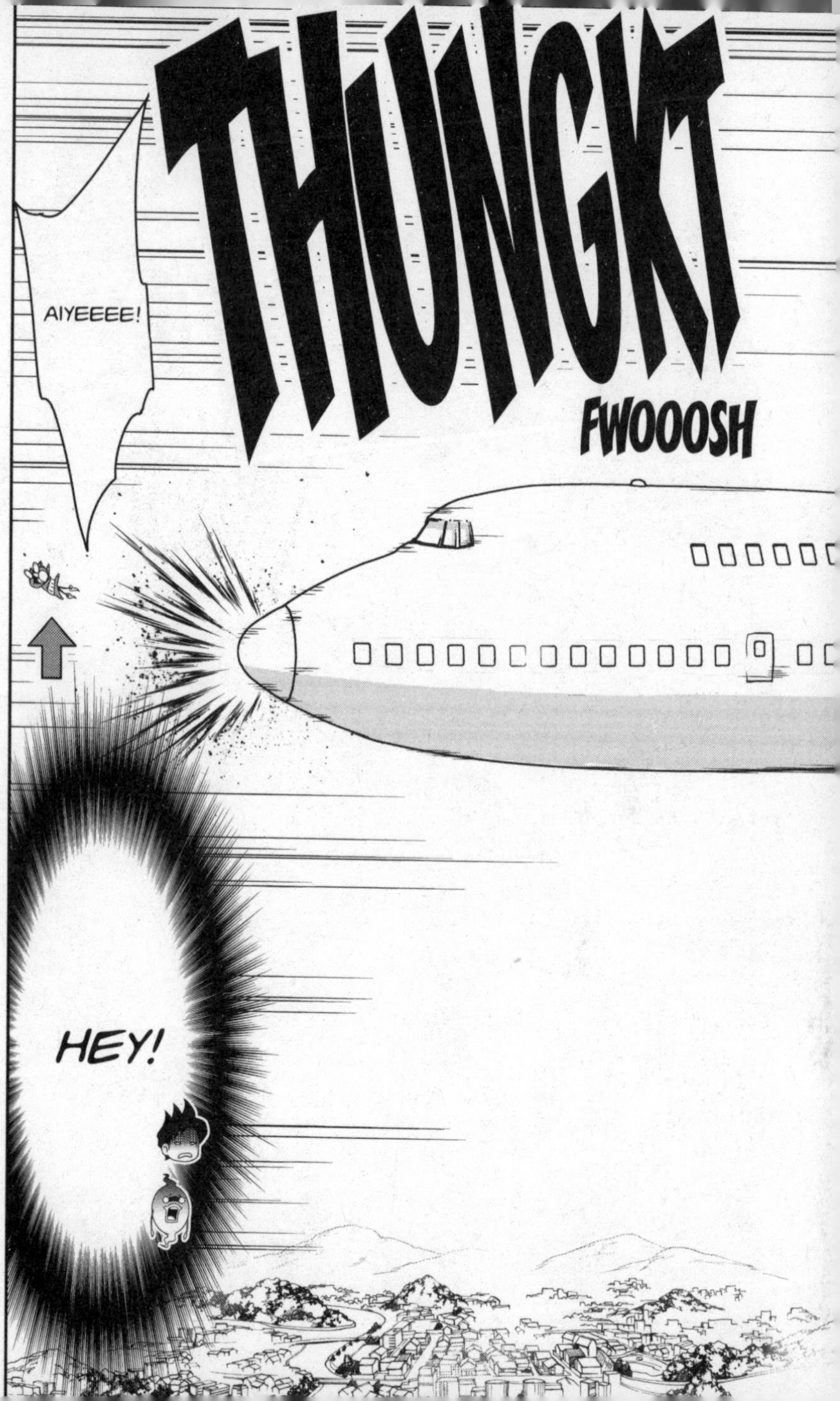
THUNGKT
FWOOOSH
AIYEEEE!
HEY!

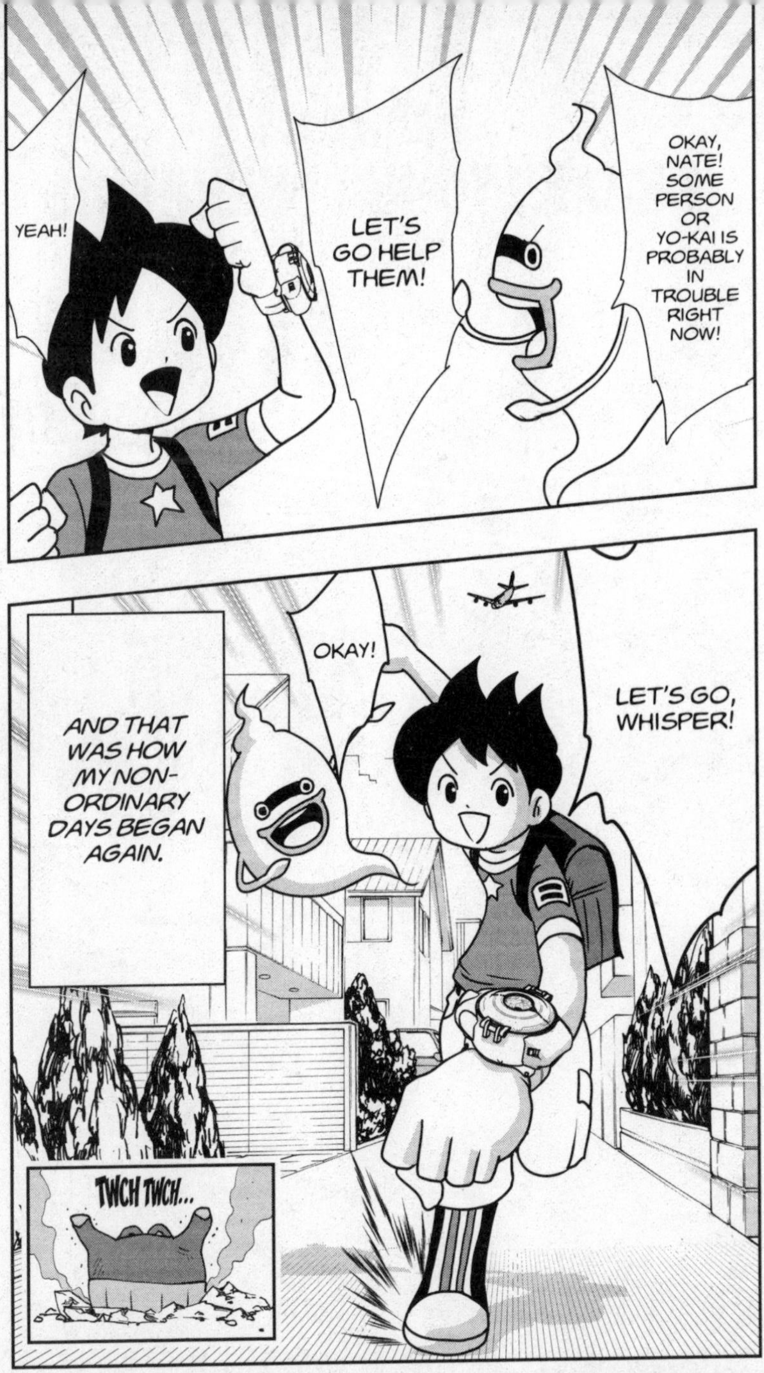
OKAY, NATE! SOME PERSON OR YO-KAI IS PROBABLY IN TROUBLE RIGHT NOW!
LET'S GO HELP THEM!
YEAH!
LET'S GO, WHISPER!
OKAY!
AND THAT WAS HOW MY NON-ORDINARY DAYS BEGAN AGAIN.
TWCH TWCH...

CHAPTER 151
CRANKY YO-KAI PUNKUPINE

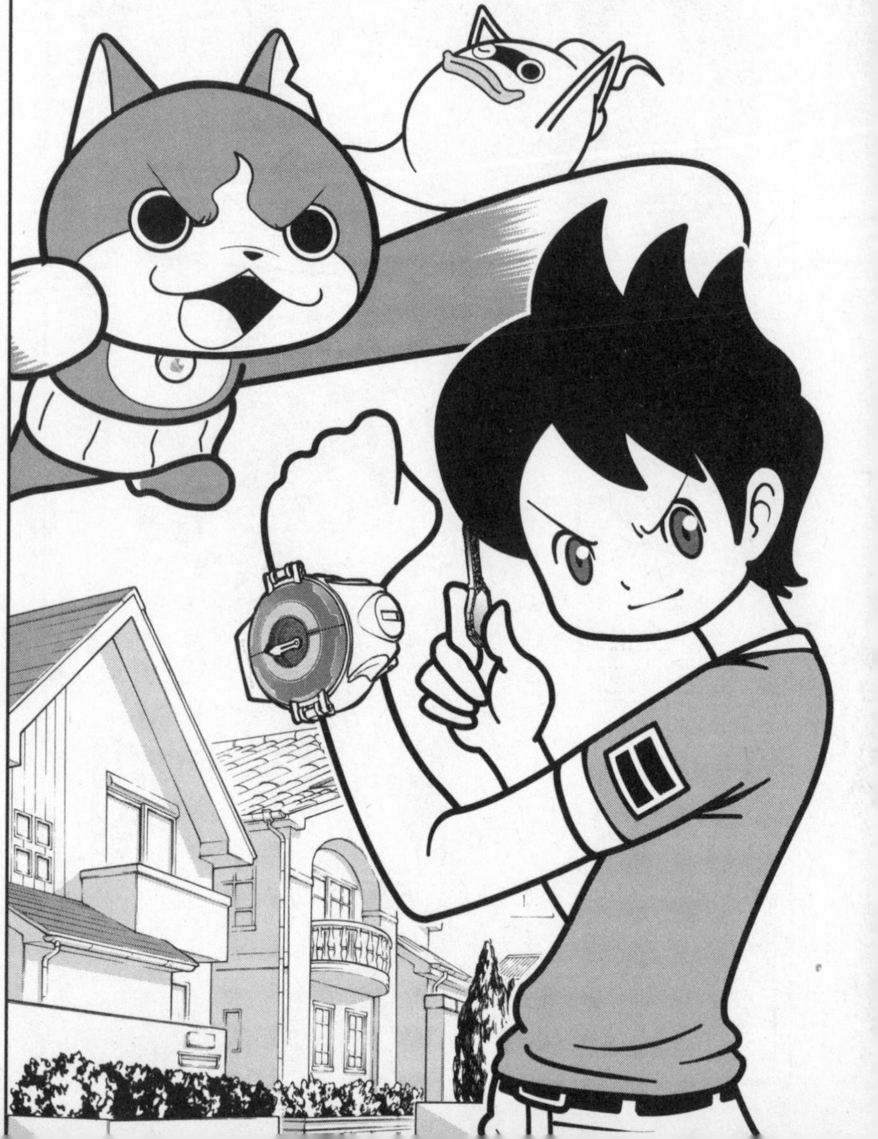

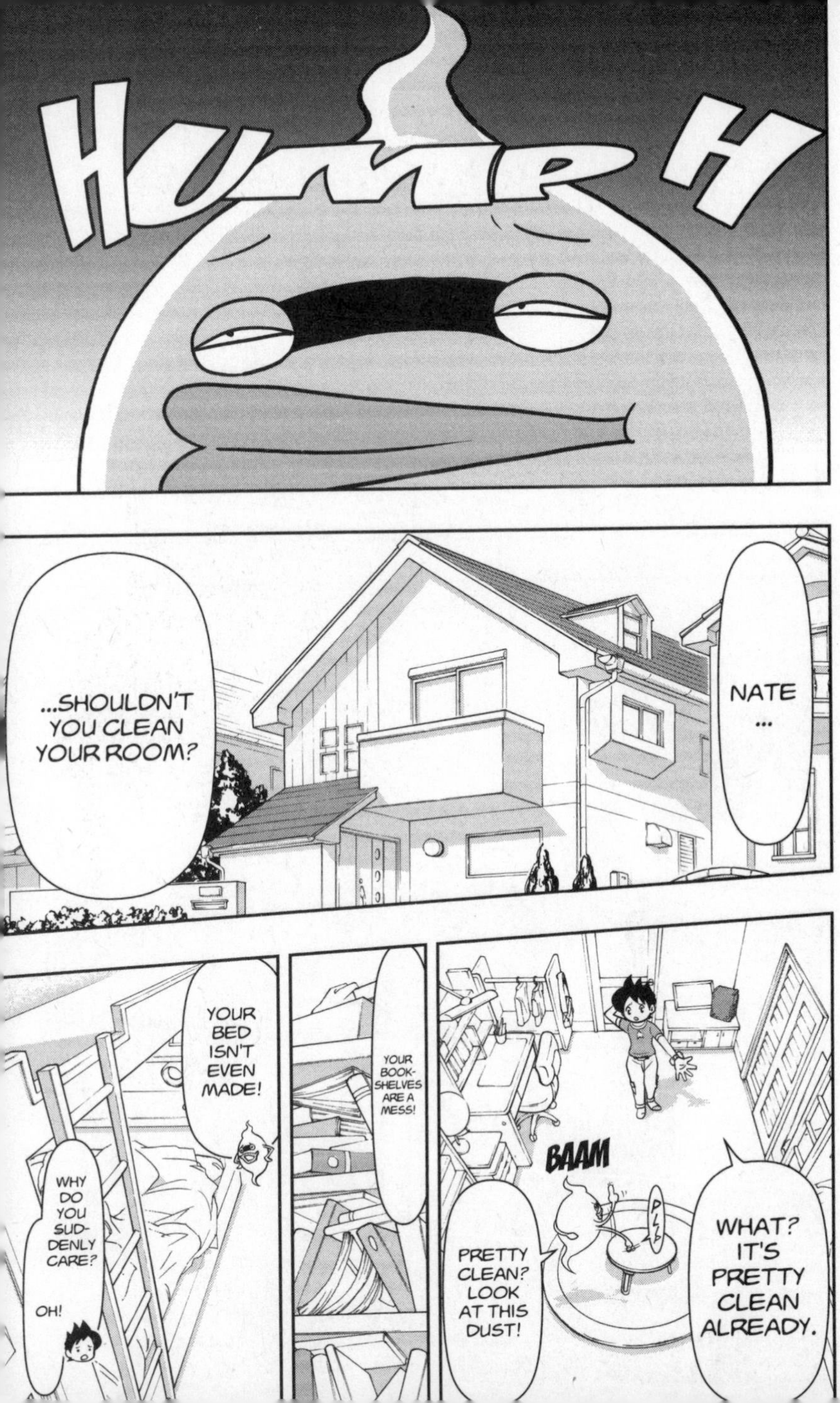
HUMPH
NATE ...
...SHOULDN'T YOU CLEAN YOUR ROOM?
WHAT? IT'S PRETTY CLEAN ALREADY.
BAAM
PRETTY CLEAN? LOOK AT THIS DUST!
YOUR BOOK-SHELVES ARE A MESS!
YOUR BED ISN'T EVEN MADE!
WHY DO YOU SUD-DENLY CARE?
OH!

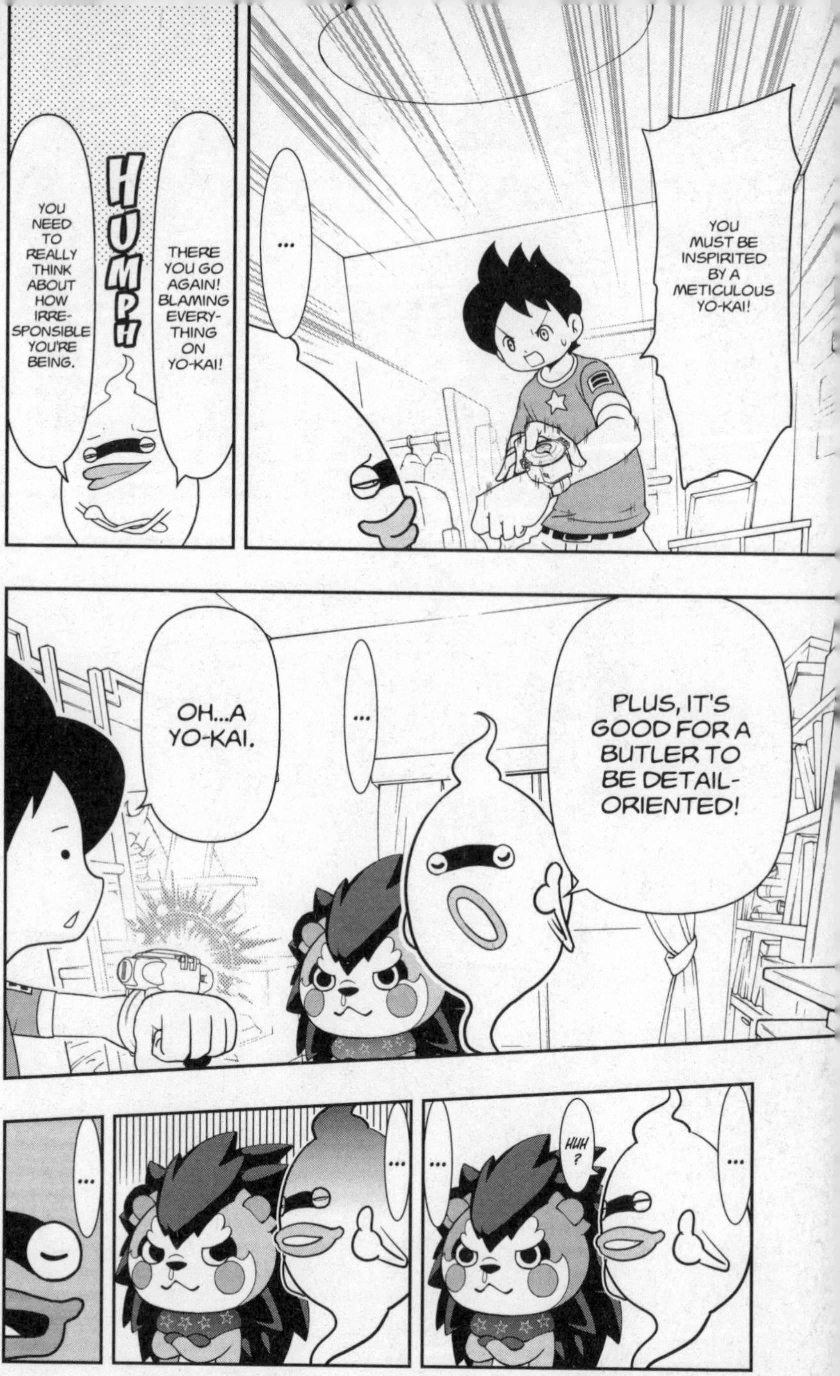
YOU MUST BE INSPIRITED BY A METICULOUS YO-KAI!
...
THERE YOU GO AGAIN! BLAMING EVERY-THING ON YO-KAI!
HUMPH
YOU NEED TO REALLY THINK ABOUT HOW IRRE-SPONSIBLE YOU'RE BEING.
PLUS, IT'S GOOD FOR A BUTLER TO BE DETAIL-ORIENTED!
...
OH...A YO-KAI.
...
HUH?
...
...
...

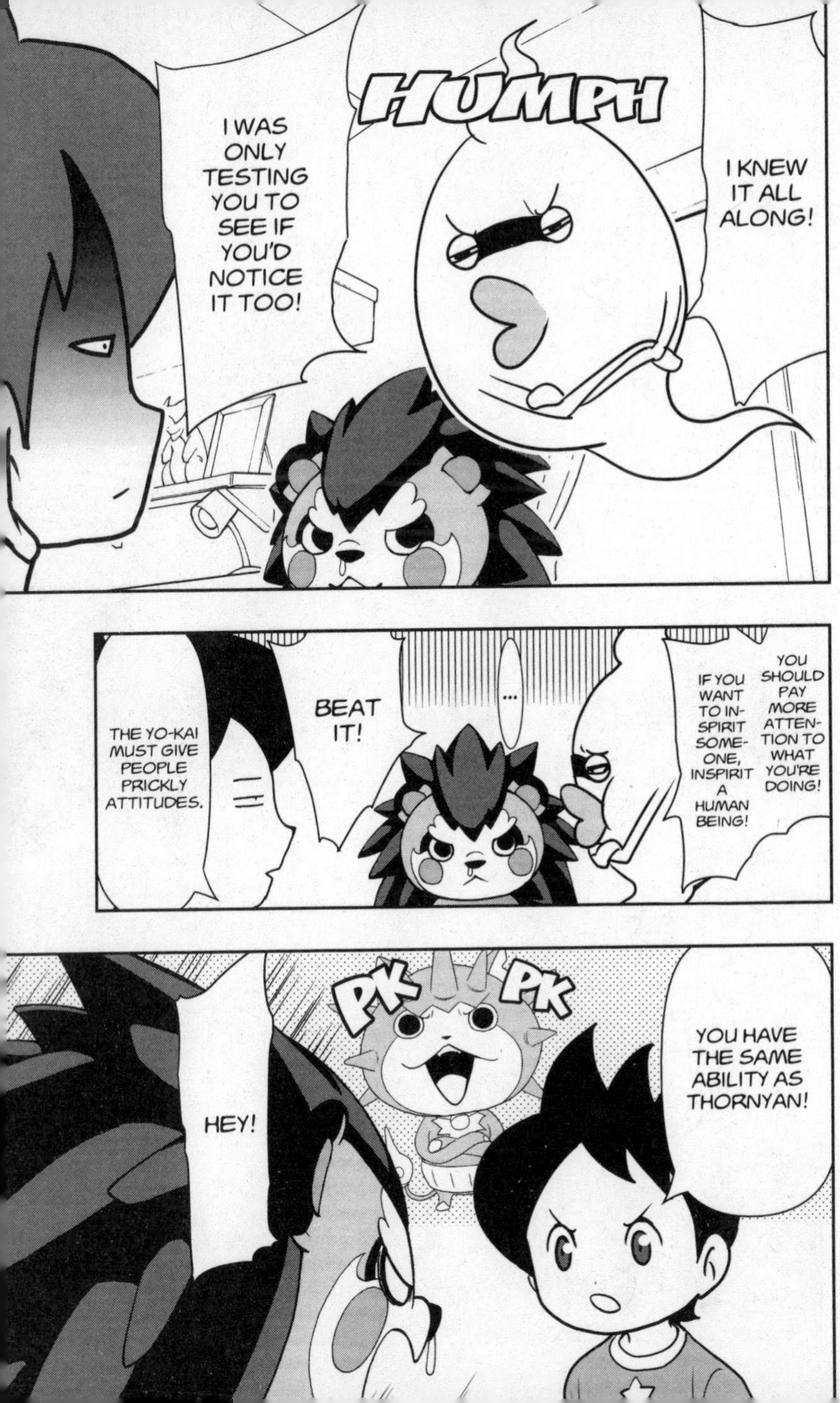
HUMPH
I KNEW IT ALL ALONG!
I WAS ONLY TESTING YOU TO SEE IF YOU'D NOTICE IT TOO!
YOU SHOULD PAY MORE ATTEN-TION TO WHAT YOU'RE DOING!
IF YOU WANT TO IN-SPIRIT SOME-ONE, INSPIRIT A HUMAN BEING!
...
BEAT IT!
THE YO-KAI MUST GIVE PEOPLE PRICKLY ATTITUDES.
YOU HAVE THE SAME ABILITY AS THORNYAN!
PK PK
HEY!

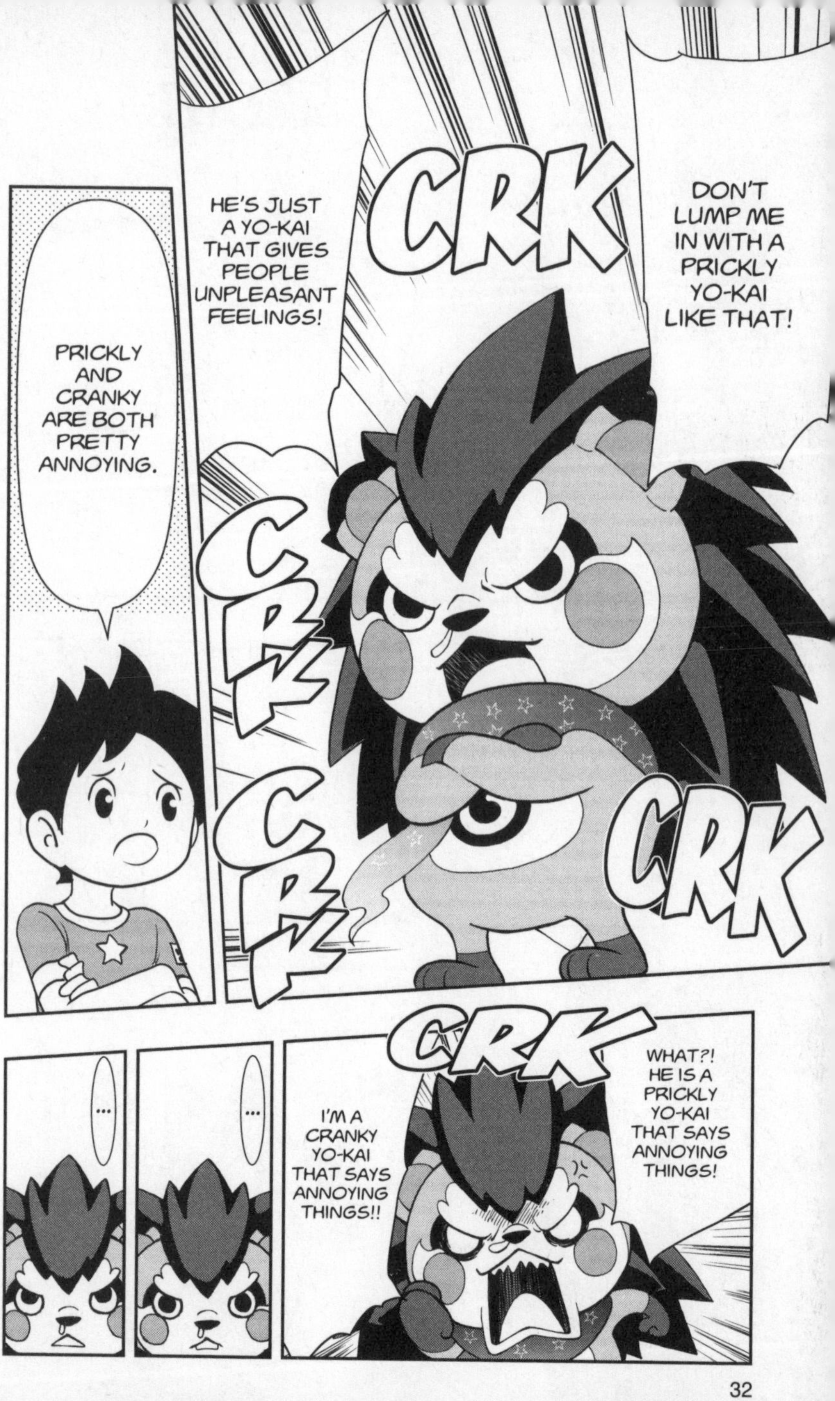
DON'T LUMP ME IN WITH A PRICKLY YO-KAI LIKE THAT!
CRK
HE'S JUST A YO-KAI THAT GIVES PEOPLE UNPLEASANT FEELINGS!
CRK
CRK
CRK
PRICKLY AND CRANKY ARE BOTH PRETTY ANNOYING.
CRK
WHAT?! HE IS A PRICKLY YO-KAI THAT SAYS ANNOYING THINGS!
I'M A CRANKY YO-KAI THAT SAYS ANNOYING THINGS!!
...
...

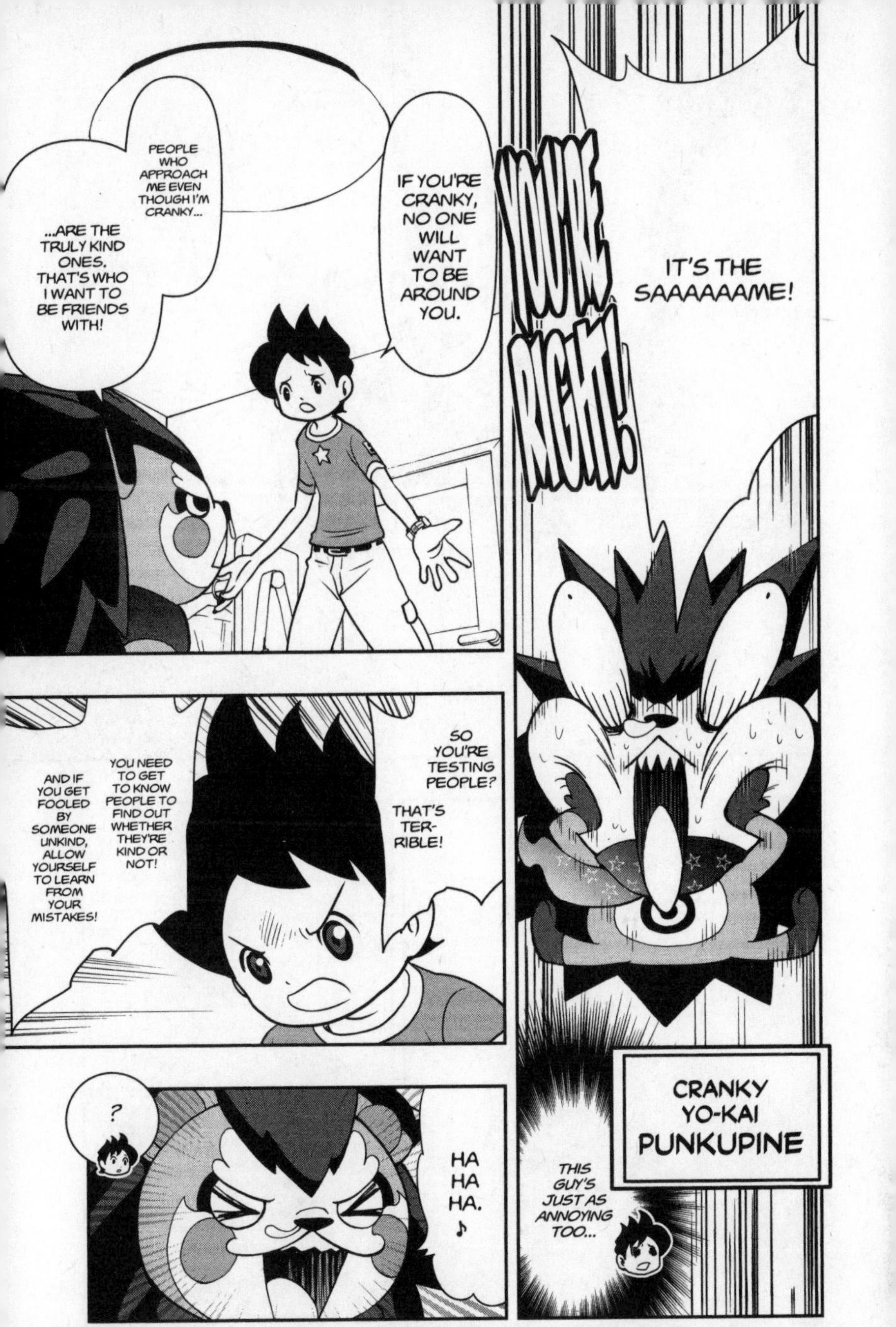
IF YOU'RE CRANKY, NO ONE WILL WANT TO BE AROUND YOU.
PEOPLE WHO APPROACH ME EVEN THOUGH I'M CRANKY...
...ARE THE TRULY KIND ONES. THAT'S WHO I WANT TO BE FRIENDS WITH!
SO YOU'RE TESTING PEOPLE?
THAT'S TER-RIBLE!
YOU NEED TO GET TO KNOW PEOPLE TO FIND OUT WHETHER THEY'RE KIND OR NOT!
AND IF YOU GET FOOLED BY SOMEONE UNKIND, ALLOW YOURSELF TO LEARN FROM YOUR MISTAKES!
?
HA HA HA. ♪
YOU'RE RIGHT!
IT'S THE SAAAAAAME!
CRANKY YO-KAI PUNKUPINE
THIS GUY'S JUST AS ANNOYING TOO...

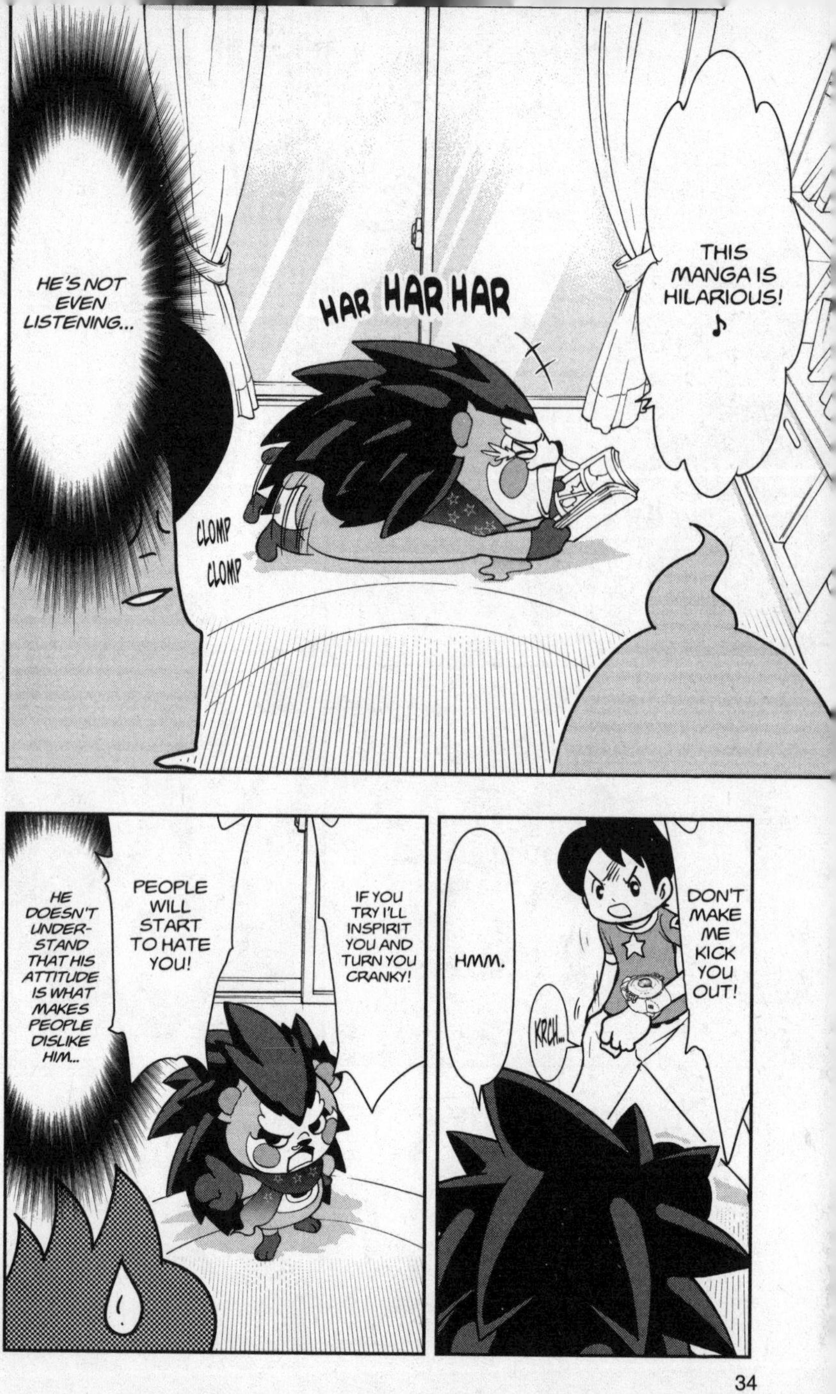
THIS MANGA IS HILARIOUS! ♪
HAR HAR HAR
CLOMP CLOMP
HE'S NOT EVEN LISTENING...
DON'T MAKE ME KICK YOU OUT!
KRCH...
HMM.
IF YOU TRY I'LL INSPIRIT YOU AND TURN YOU CRANKY!
PEOPLE WILL START TO HATE YOU!
HE DOESN'T UNDER-STAND THAT HIS ATTITUDE IS WHAT MAKES PEOPLE DISLIKE HIM...

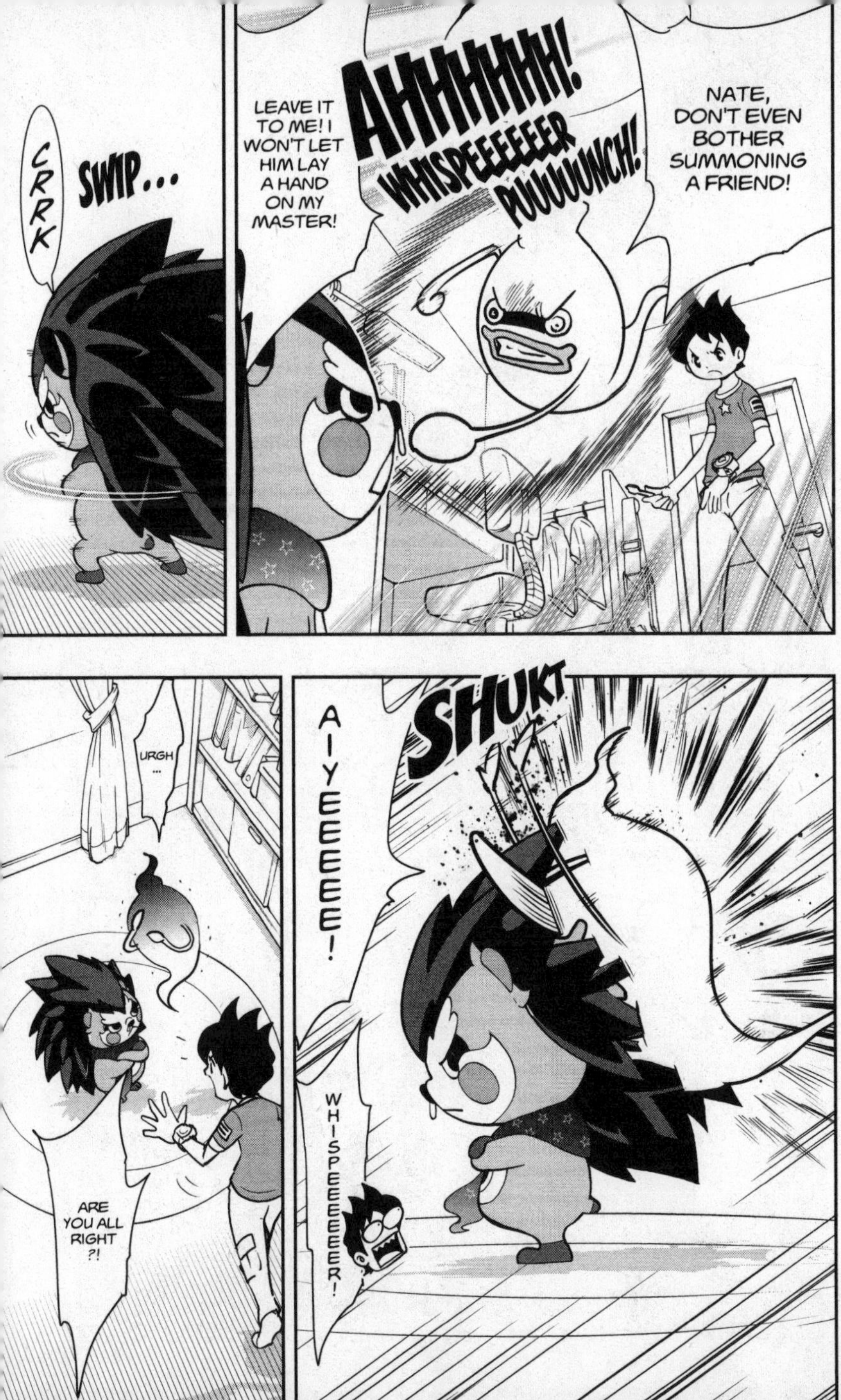
NATE, DON'T EVEN BOTHER SUMMONING A FRIEND!
AHHHHHHH! WHISPEEEEEER PUUUUUNCH!
LEAVE IT TO ME! I WON'T LET HIM LAY A HAND ON MY MASTER!
CRRK
SWIP...
SHUKT
AIYEEEEEE!
WHISPEEEEEER!
URGH...
ARE YOU ALL RIGHT?!

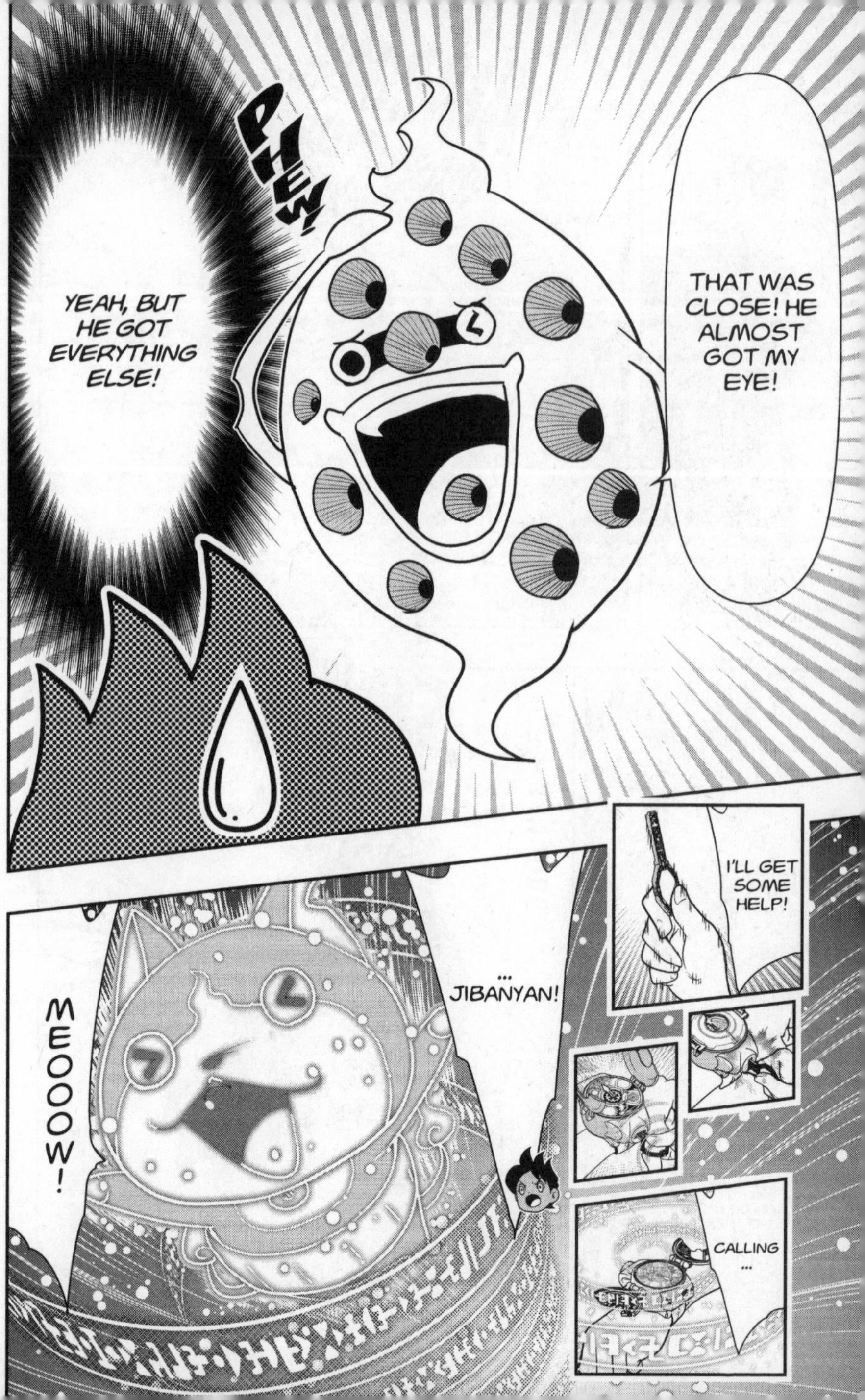
THAT WAS CLOSE! HE ALMOST GOT MY EYE!
PHEW!
YEAH, BUT HE GOT EVERYTHING ELSE!
I'LL GET SOME HELP!
CALLING ...
... JIBANYAN!
MEOOOOW!

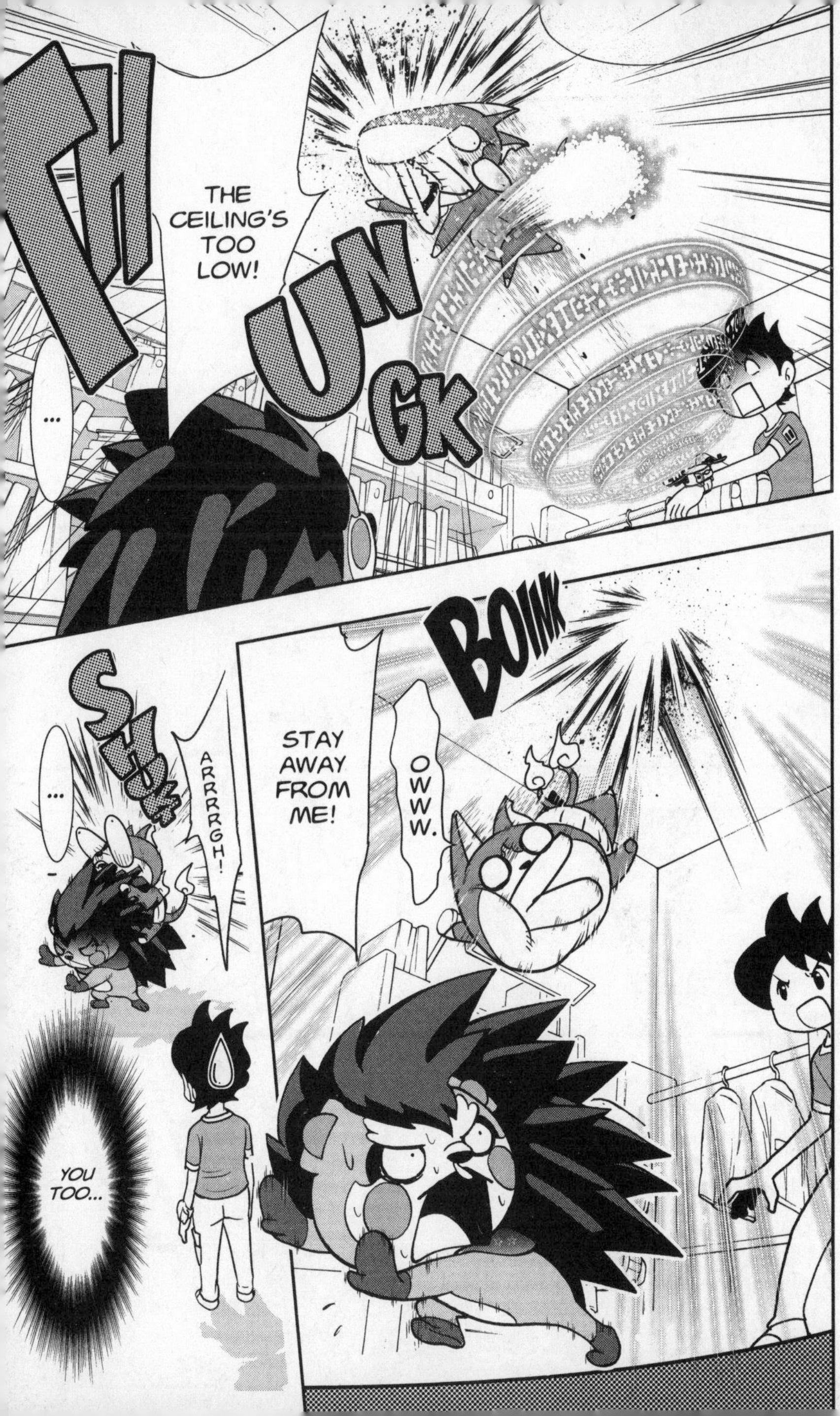
THE CEILING'S TOO LOW!
...
BOINK
OWWW.
STAY AWAY FROM ME!
ARRRRGH!
...
YOU TOO...

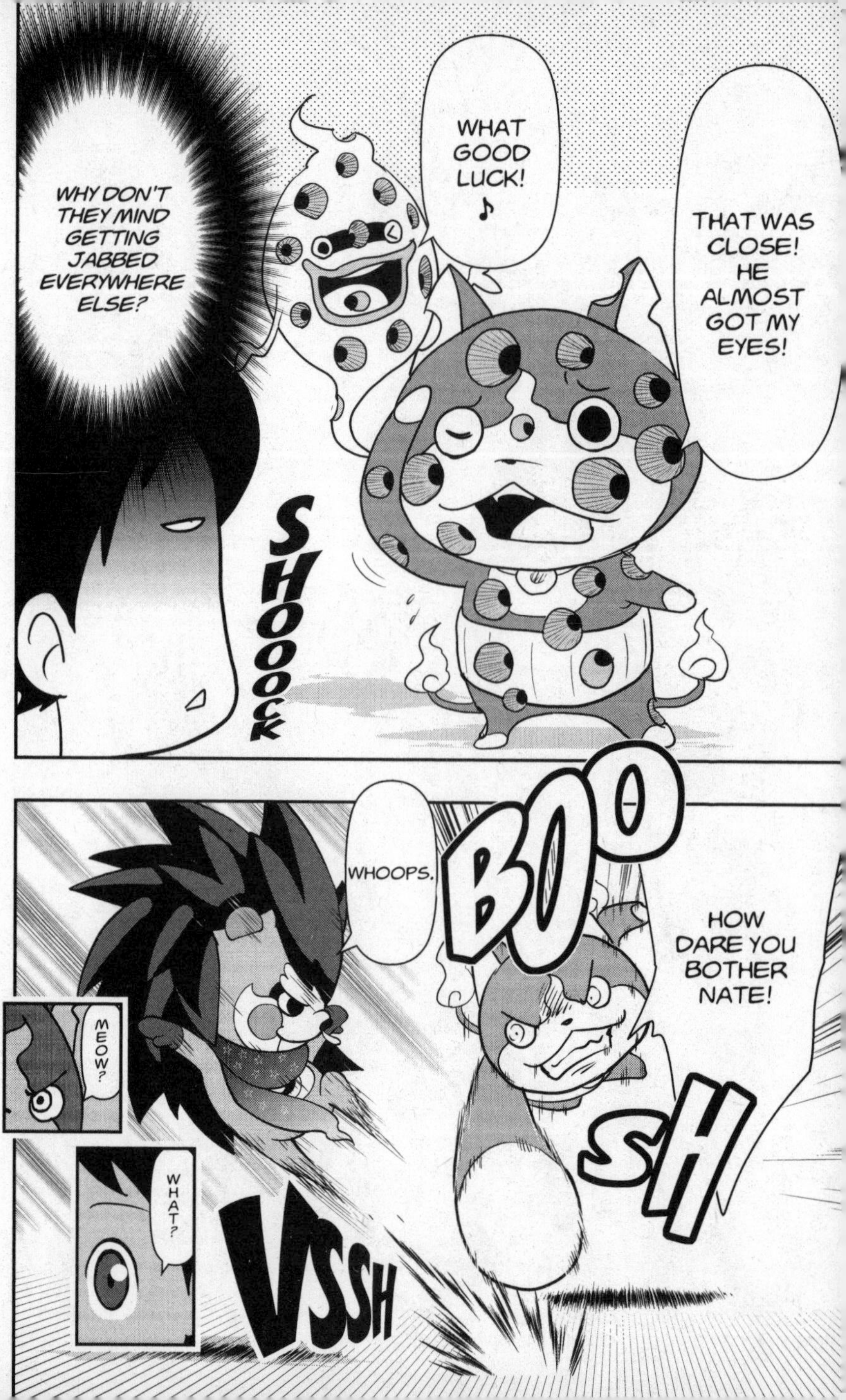
THAT WAS CLOSE! HE ALMOST GOT MY EYES!
WHAT GOOD LUCK! ♪
SHOOOOCK
WHY DON'T THEY MIND GETTING JABBED EVERYWHERE ELSE?
HOW DARE YOU BOTHER NATE!
BOO
WHOOPS.
SH
VSSH
MEOW?
WHAT?

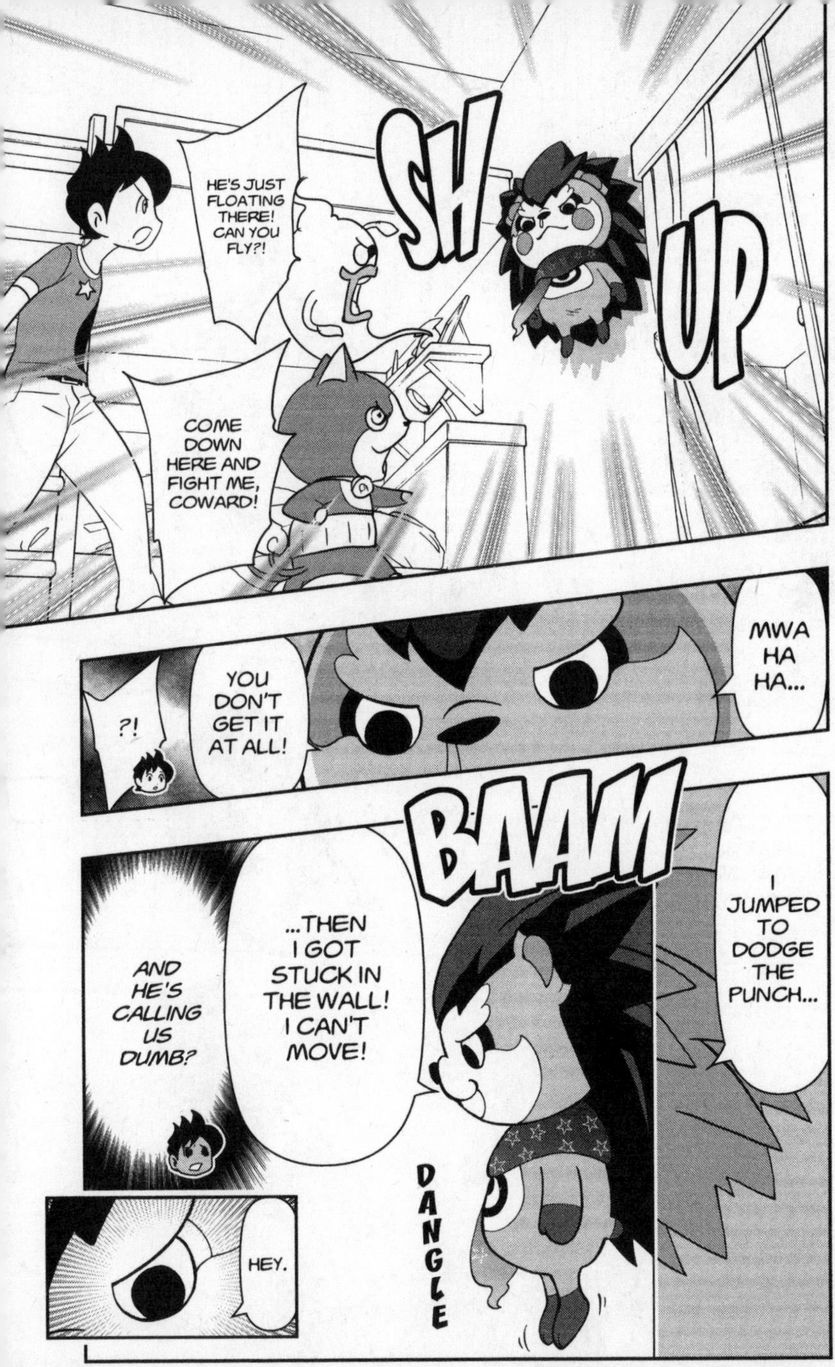
SH UP
HE'S JUST FLOATING THERE! CAN YOU FLY?!
COME DOWN HERE AND FIGHT ME, COWARD!
MWA HA HA...
YOU DON'T GET IT AT ALL!
?!
BAAM
I JUMPED TO DODGE THE PUNCH...
...THEN I GOT STUCK IN THE WALL! I CAN'T MOVE!
DANGLE
AND HE'S CALLING US DUMB?
HEY.

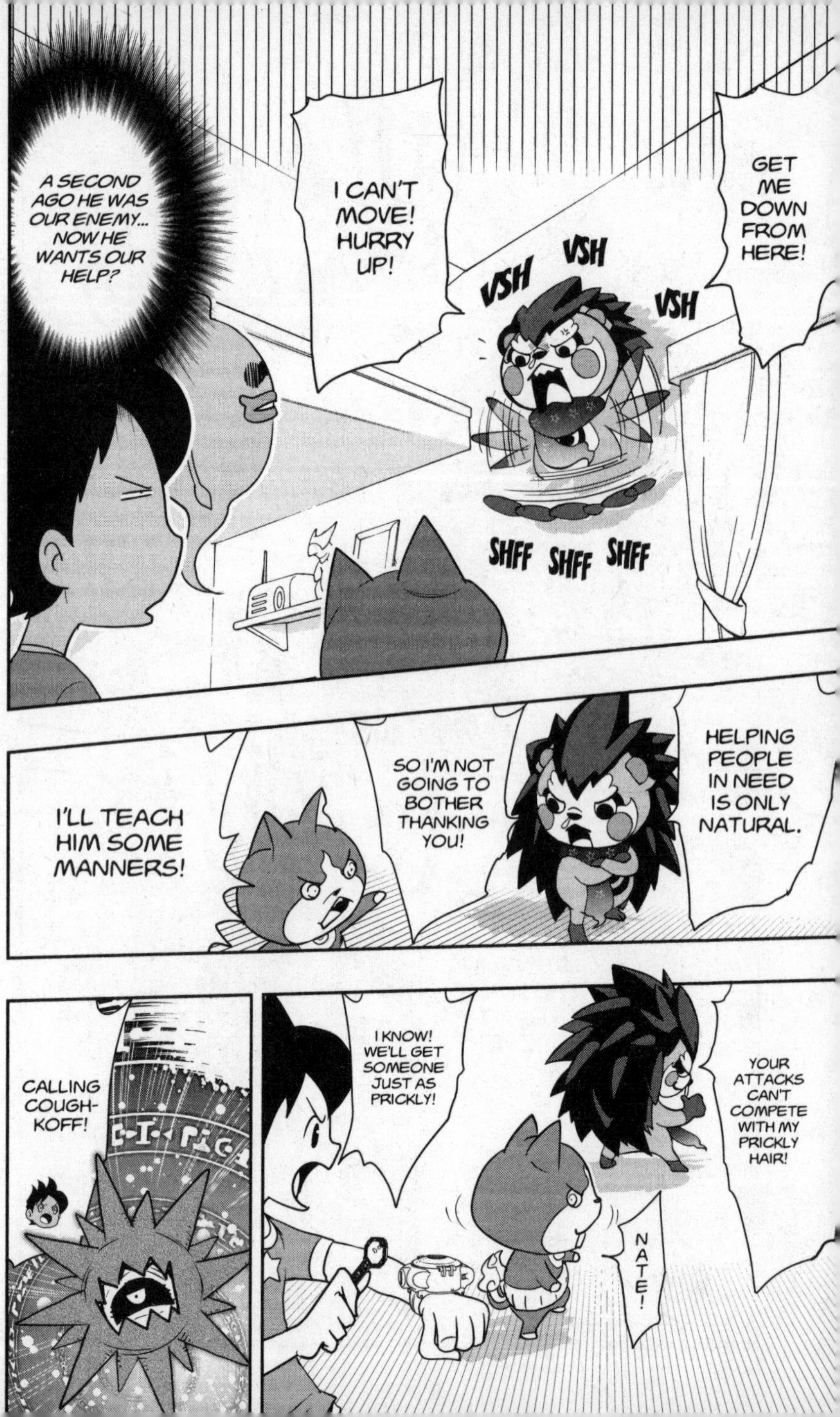
GET ME DOWN FROM HERE!
I CAN'T MOVE! HURRY UP!
VSH VSH VSH
SHFF SHFF SHFF
A SECOND AGO HE WAS OUR ENEMY... NOW HE WANTS OUR HELP?
HELPING PEOPLE IN NEED IS ONLY NATURAL.
SO I'M NOT GOING TO BOTHER THANKING YOU!
I'LL TEACH HIM SOME MANNERS!
YOUR ATTACKS CAN'T COMPETE WITH MY PRICKLY HAIR!
NATE!
I KNOW! WE'LL GET SOMEONE JUST AS PRICKLY!
CALLING COUGH-KOFF!

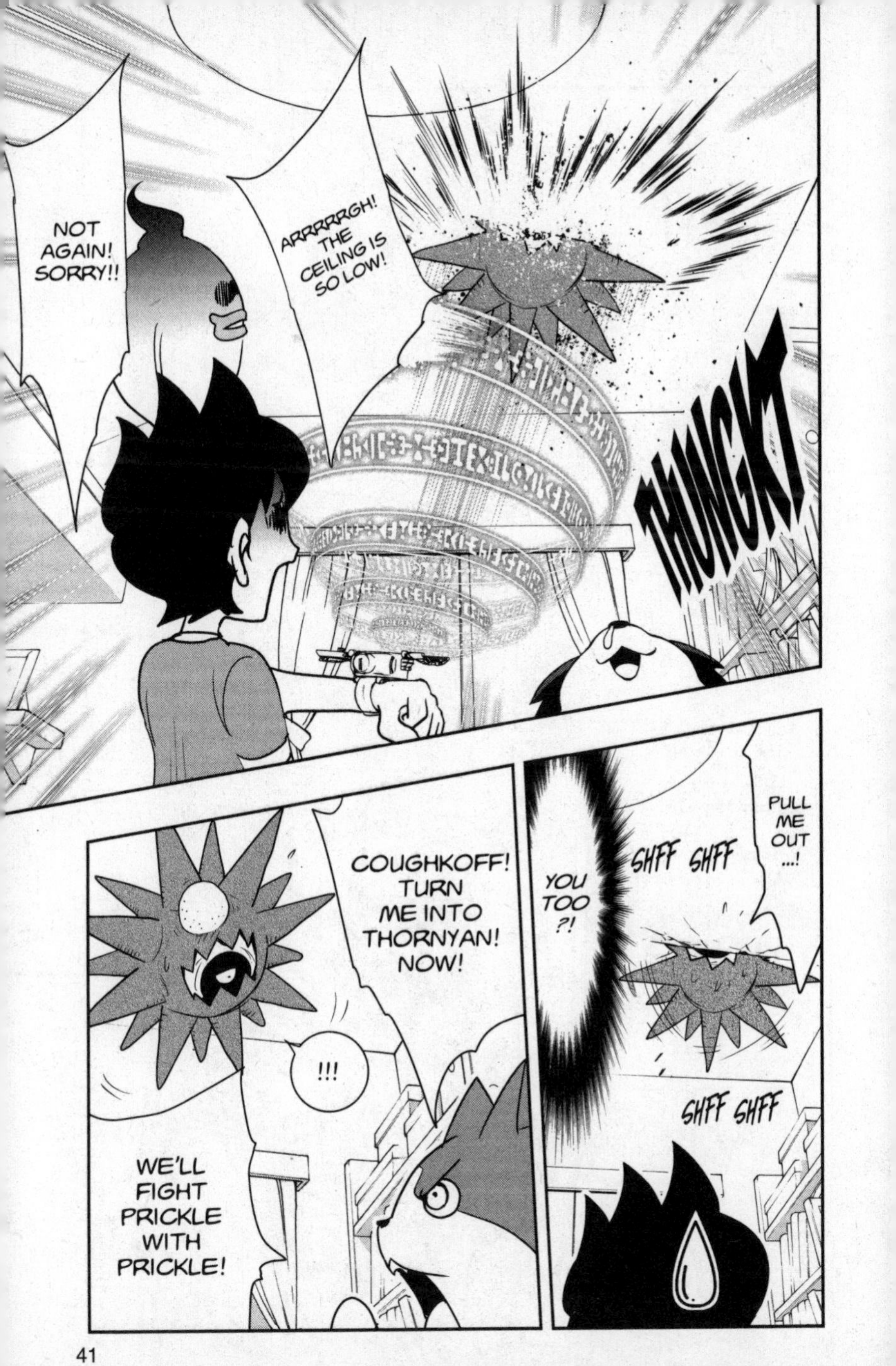

ARRRRRGH! THE CEILING IS SO LOW!
NOT AGAIN! SORRY!!
THUNGK!
PULL ME OUT ...!
SHFF SHFF
YOU TOO ?!
SHFF SHFF
COUGHKOFF! TURN ME INTO THORNYAN! NOW!
!!!
WE'LL FIGHT PRICKLE WITH PRICKLE!

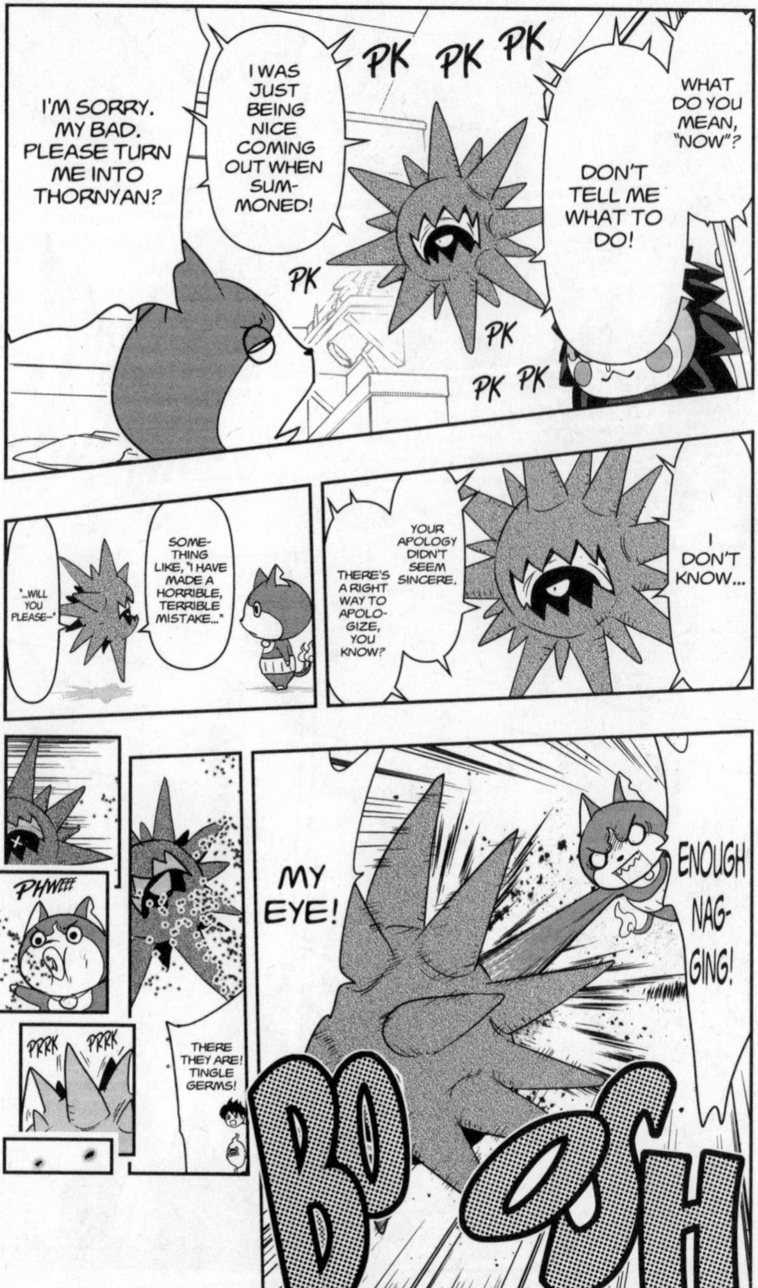
WHAT DO YOU MEAN, "NOW"?
DON'T TELL ME WHAT TO DO!
PK PK PK
I WAS JUST BEING NICE COMING OUT WHEN SUM-MONED!
I'M SORRY. MY BAD. PLEASE TURN ME INTO THORNYAN?
PK
PK
PK PK
I DON'T KNOW...
YOUR APOLOGY DIDN'T SEEM SINCERE.
THERE'S A RIGHT WAY TO APOLO-GIZE, YOU KNOW?
SOME-THING LIKE, "I HAVE MADE A HORRIBLE, TERRIBLE MISTAKE..."
"...WILL YOU PLEASE—"
ENOUGH NAG-GING!
MY EYE!
BOOSH
THERE THEY ARE! TINGLE GERMS!
PHWEEE
PRRK PRRK

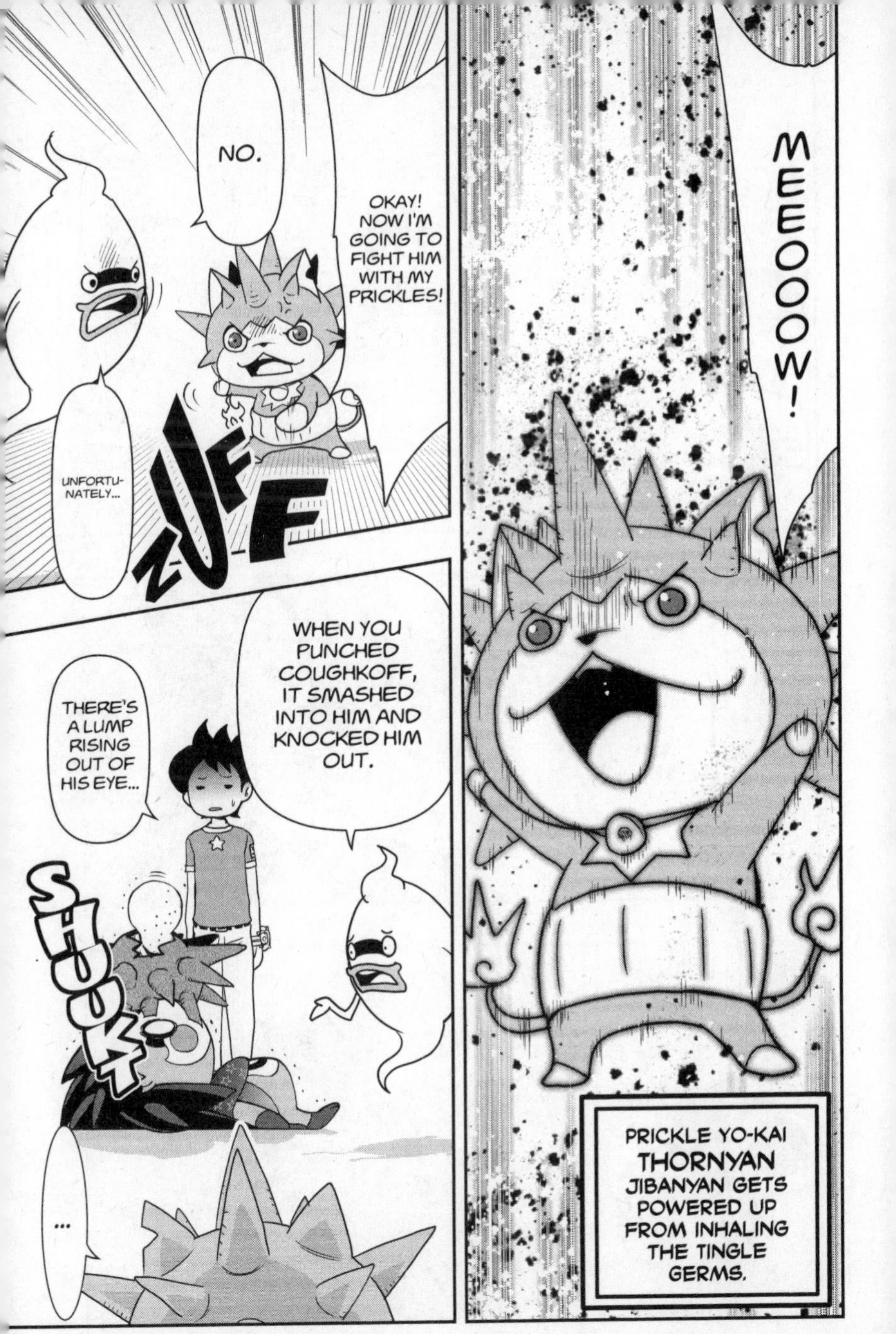
MEEOOOW!
PRICKLE YO-KAI THORNYAN JIBANYAN GETS POWERED UP FROM INHALING THE TINGLE GERMS.
OKAY! NOW I'M GOING TO FIGHT HIM WITH MY PRICKLES!
NO.
UNFORTU-NATELY...
ZUFF
WHEN YOU PUNCHED COUGHKOFF, IT SMASHED INTO HIM AND KNOCKED HIM OUT.
THERE'S A LUMP RISING OUT OF HIS EYE...
SHOUK
...

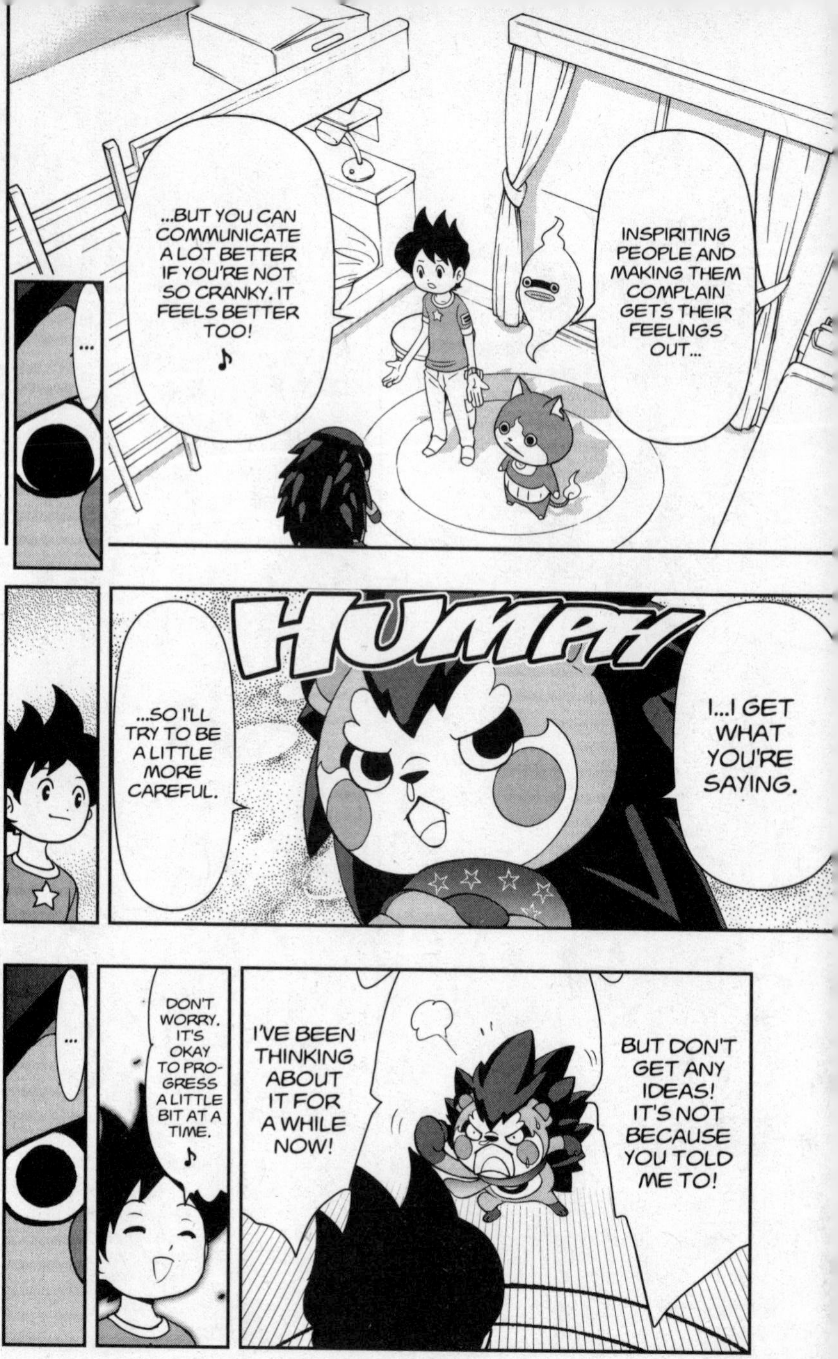
INSPIRITING PEOPLE AND MAKING THEM COMPLAIN GETS THEIR FEELINGS OUT...
...BUT YOU CAN COMMUNICATE A LOT BETTER IF YOU'RE NOT SO CRANKY. IT FEELS BETTER TOO! ♪
...
HUMPH
I...I GET WHAT YOU'RE SAYING.
...SO I'LL TRY TO BE A LITTLE MORE CAREFUL.
BUT DON'T GET ANY IDEAS! IT'S NOT BECAUSE YOU TOLD ME TO!
I'VE BEEN THINKING ABOUT IT FOR A WHILE NOW!
DON'T WORRY. IT'S OKAY TO PRO-GRESS A LITTLE BIT AT A TIME. ♪
...

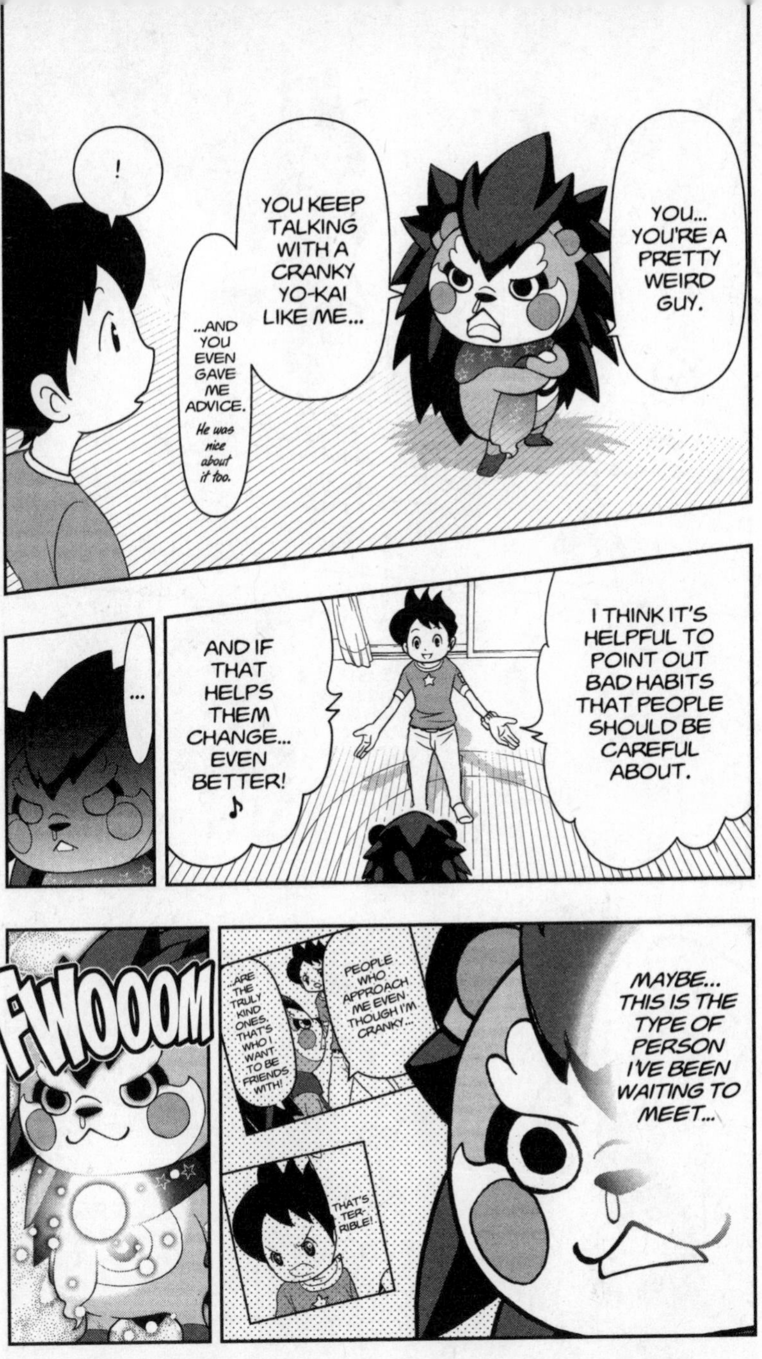
YOU... YOU'RE A PRETTY WEIRD GUY.
YOU KEEP TALKING WITH A CRANKY YO-KAI LIKE ME...
...AND YOU EVEN GAVE ME ADVICE.
He was nice about it too.
!
I THINK IT'S HELPFUL TO POINT OUT BAD HABITS THAT PEOPLE SHOULD BE CAREFUL ABOUT.
AND IF THAT HELPS THEM CHANGE... EVEN BETTER! ♪
...
MAYBE... THIS IS THE TYPE OF PERSON I'VE BEEN WAITING TO MEET...
PEOPLE WHO APPROACH ME EVEN THOUGH I'M CRANKY...
...ARE THE TRULY KIND ONES. THAT'S WHO I WANT TO BE FRIENDS WITH!
THAT'S TER-RIBLE!
FWOOOM

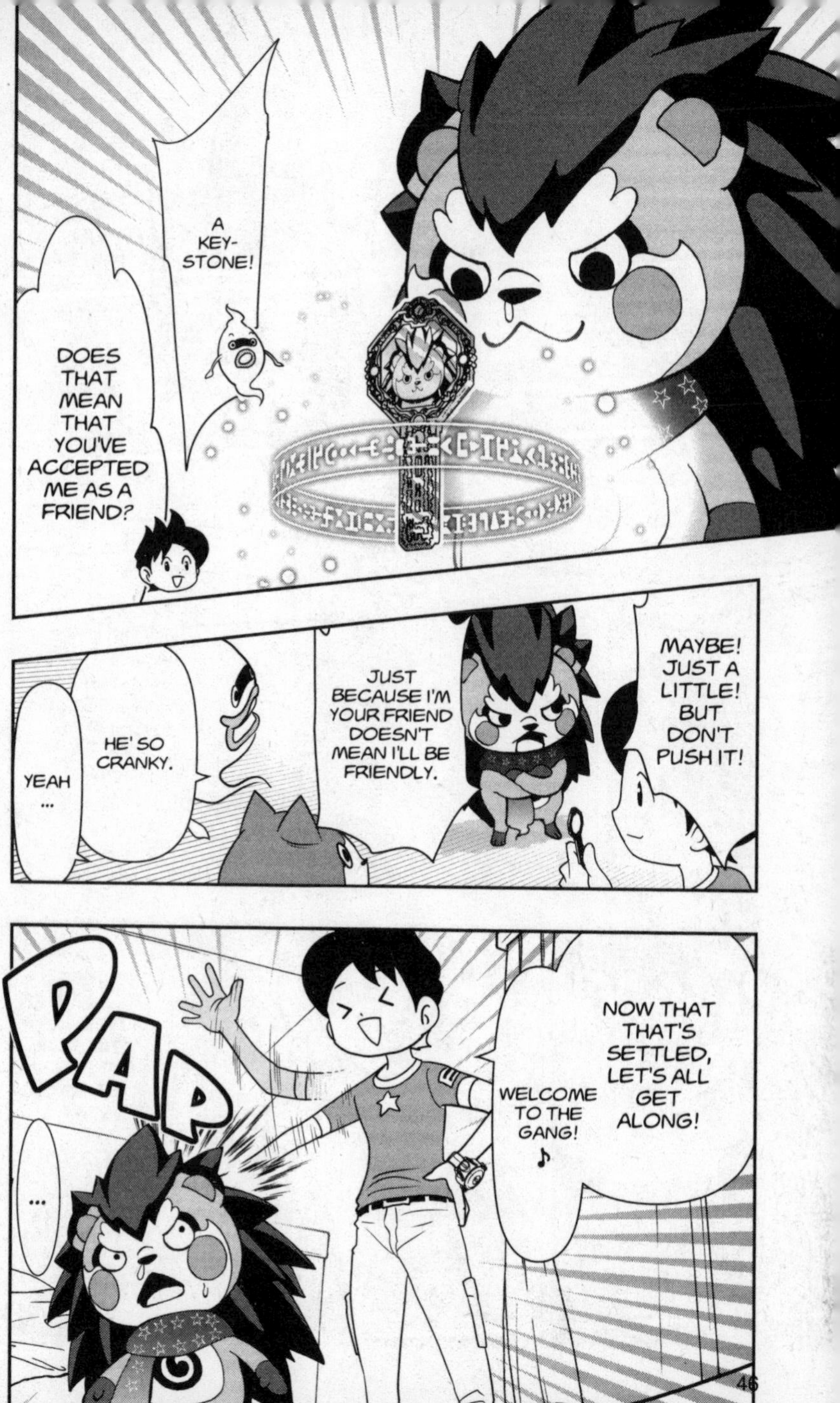
A KEY-STONE!
DOES THAT MEAN THAT YOU'VE ACCEPTED ME AS A FRIEND?
MAYBE! JUST A LITTLE! BUT DON'T PUSH IT!
JUST BECAUSE I'M YOUR FRIEND DOESN'T MEAN I'LL BE FRIENDLY.
HE' SO CRANKY.
YEAH ...
NOW THAT THAT'S SETTLED, LET'S ALL GET ALONG!
WELCOME TO THE GANG! ♪
DAP
...

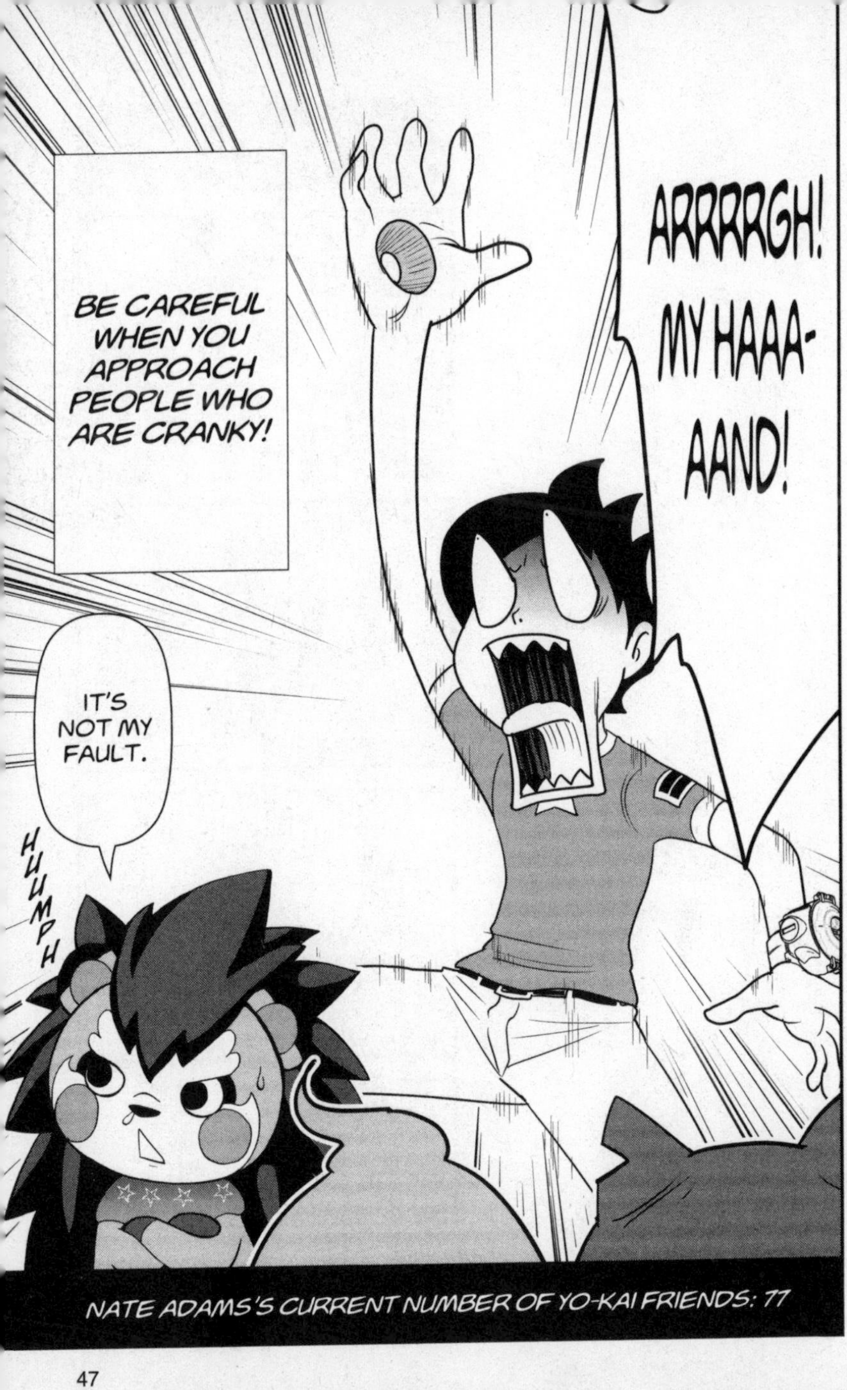
ARRRRGH! MY HAAA-AAND!
BE CAREFUL WHEN YOU APPROACH PEOPLE WHO ARE CRANKY!
IT'S NOT MY FAULT.
HUUMPH
NATE ADAMS'S CURRENT NUMBER OF YO-KAI FRIENDS: 77

THORNYAN LEARNS HIS LESSON

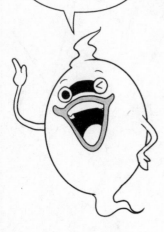

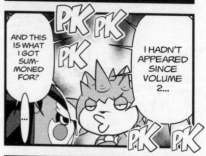

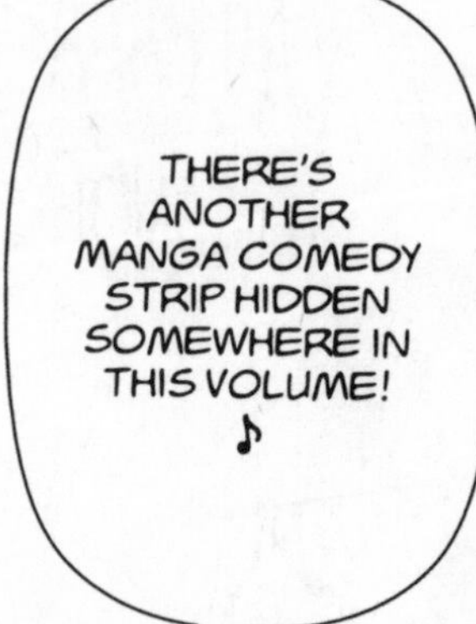

I HADN'T APPEARED SINCE VOLUME 2...
PK PK PK
AND THIS IS WHAT I GOT SUMMONED FOR?
...
PK PK
IF IT WASN'T FOR ME, YOU WOULDN'T HAVE SHOWN UP AT ALL!
HUMPH
YOU SHOULD BE THANKING ME!
...
YOU'RE RIGHT...
GLAD YOU UNDERSTAND!
I WAS BEING TOO PRICKLY ...
I'M SORRY.
FORGIVE ME...
SHUKT
ARRRRRGH!

THERE'S ANOTHER MANGA COMEDY STRIP HIDDEN SOMEWHERE IN THIS VOLUME! ♪

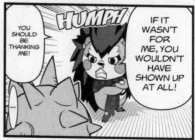

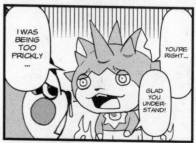

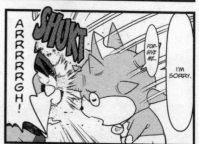

CHAPTER 152
TIMID APOLOGY YO-KAI SORRYPUS

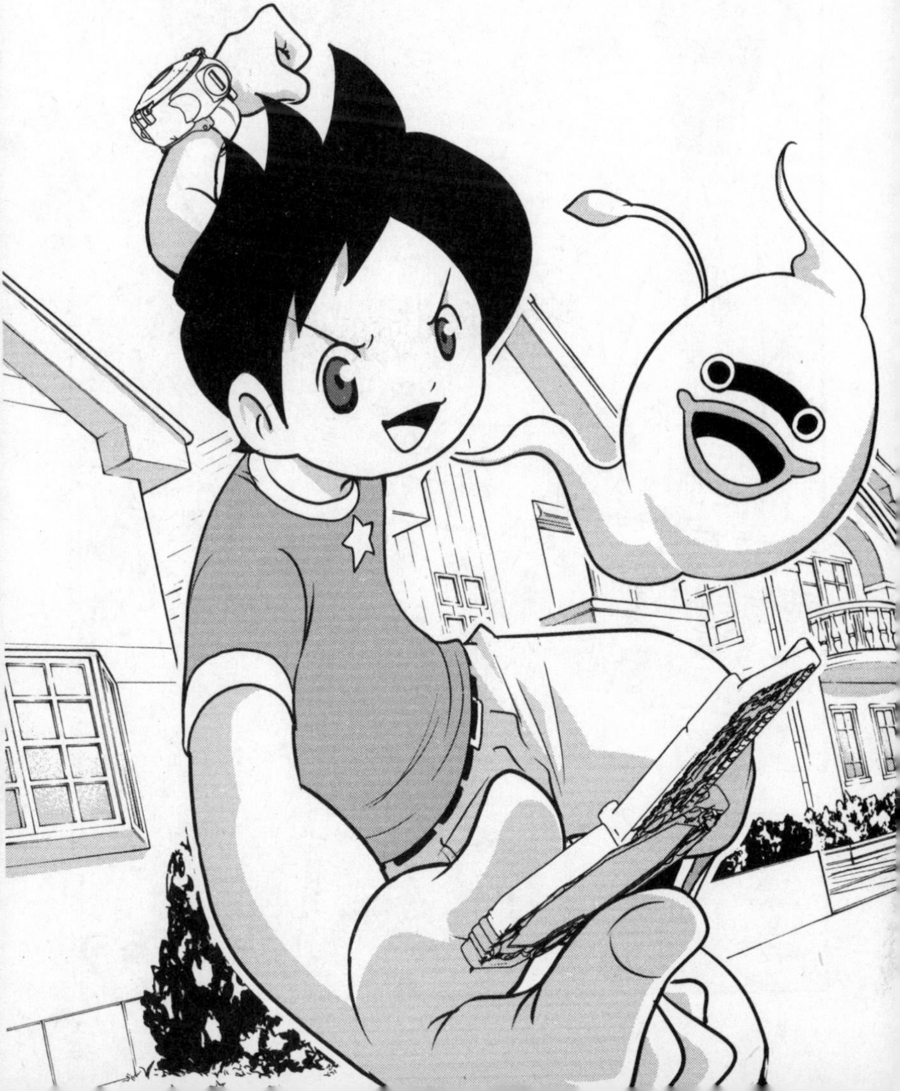

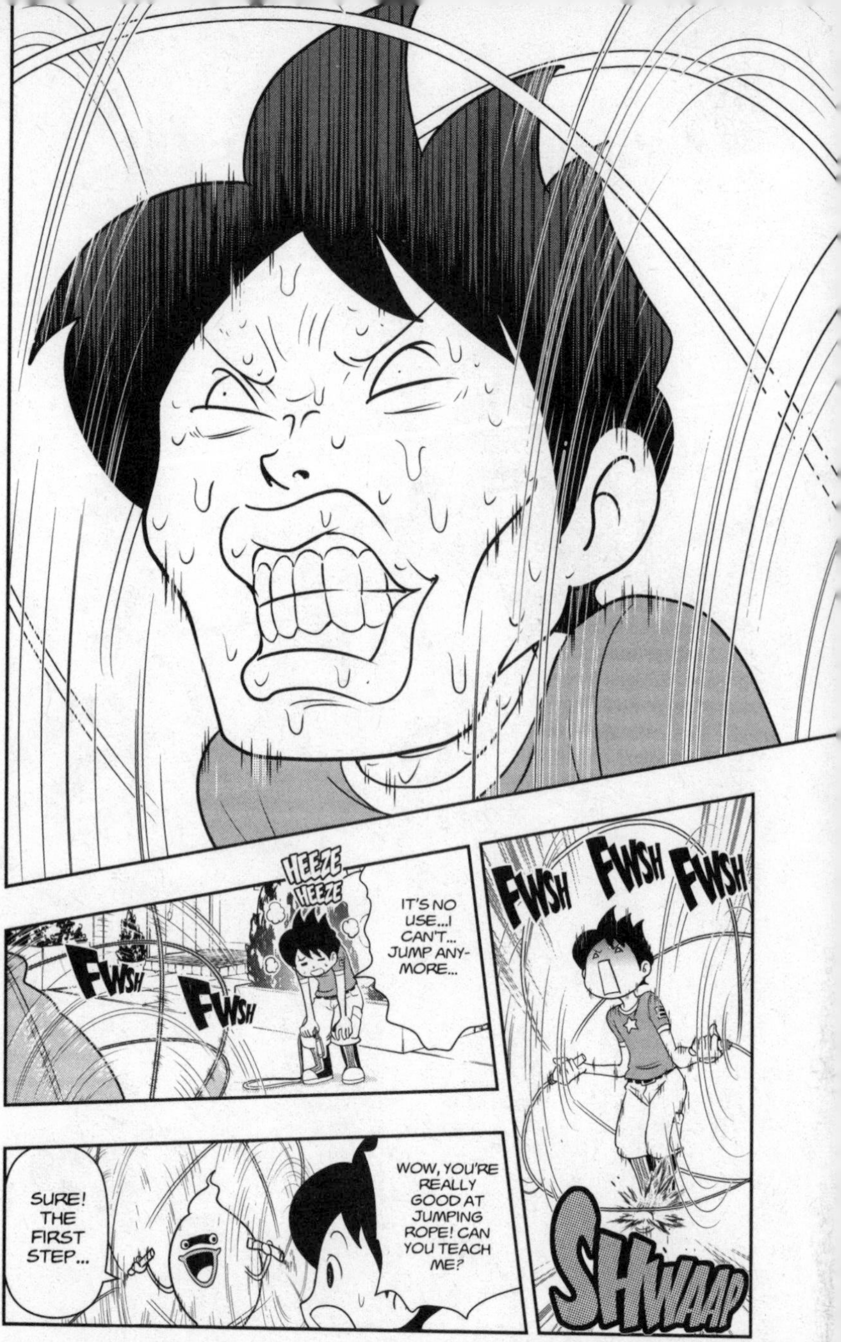
FWSH FWSH FWSH
SHWAAP
HEEZE HEEZE
IT'S NO USE...I CAN'T... JUMP ANY-MORE...
FWSH
FWSH
WOW, YOU'RE REALLY GOOD AT JUMPING ROPE! CAN YOU TEACH ME?
SURE! THE FIRST STEP...

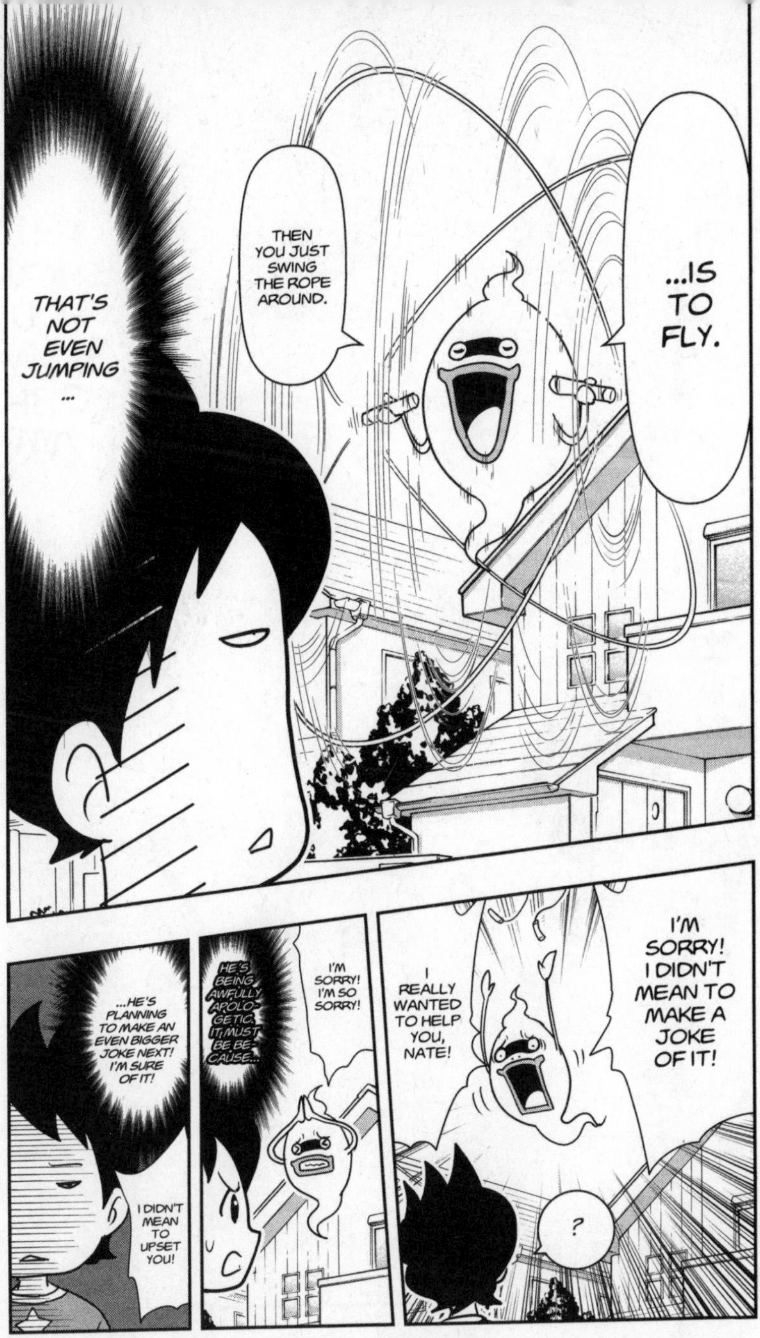
...IS TO FLY.
THEN YOU JUST SWING THE ROPE AROUND.
THAT'S NOT EVEN JUMPING ...
I'M SORRY! I DIDN'T MEAN TO MAKE A JOKE OF IT!
I REALLY WANTED TO HELP YOU, NATE!
?
I'M SORRY! I'M SO SORRY!
HE'S BEING AWFULLY APOLO-GETIC. IT MUST BE BE-CAUSE...
...HE'S PLANNING TO MAKE AN EVEN BIGGER JOKE NEXT! I'M SURE OF IT!
I DIDN'T MEAN TO UPSET YOU!

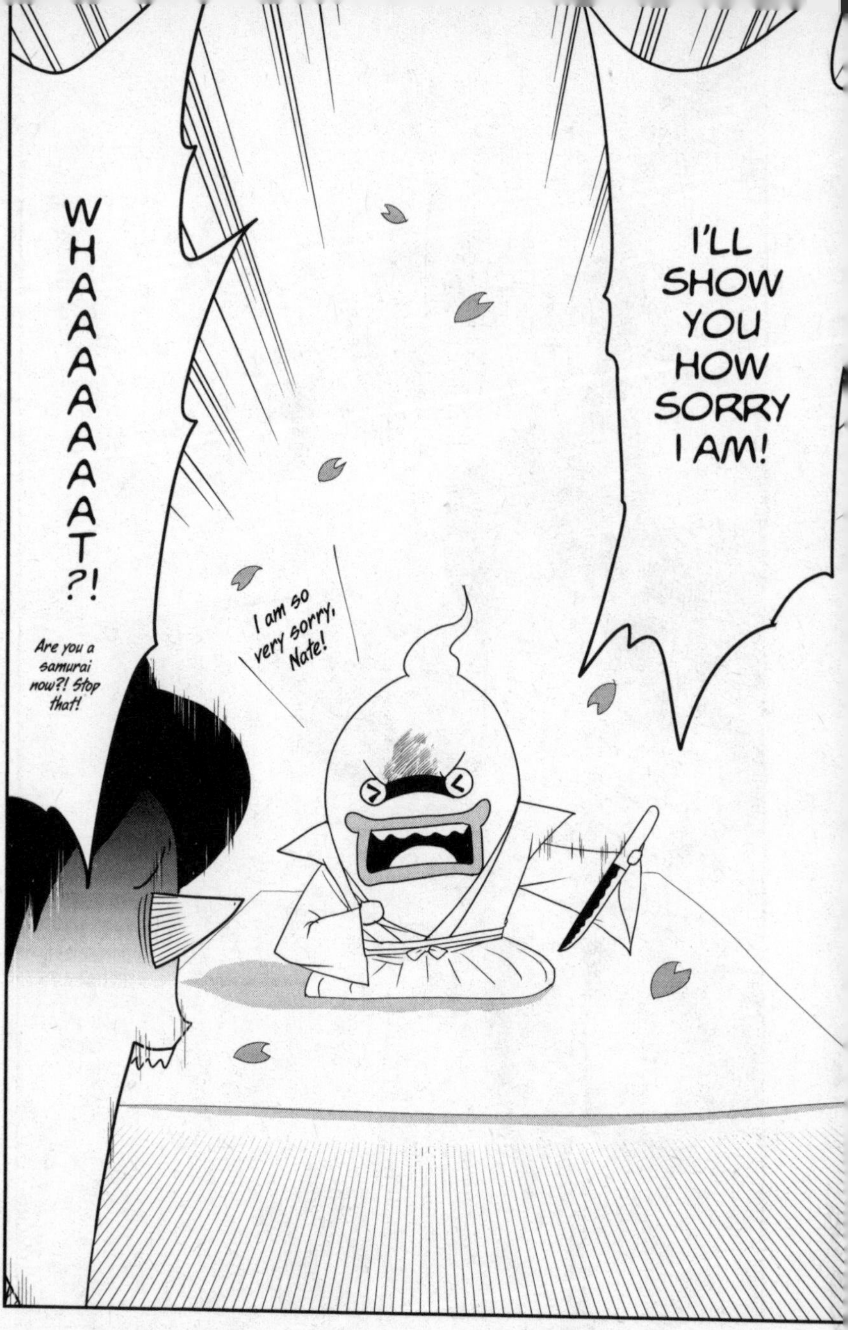
I'LL SHOW YOU HOW SORRY I AM!
I am so very sorry, Nate!
WHAAAAAAAAAT?!
Are you a samurai now?! Stop that!

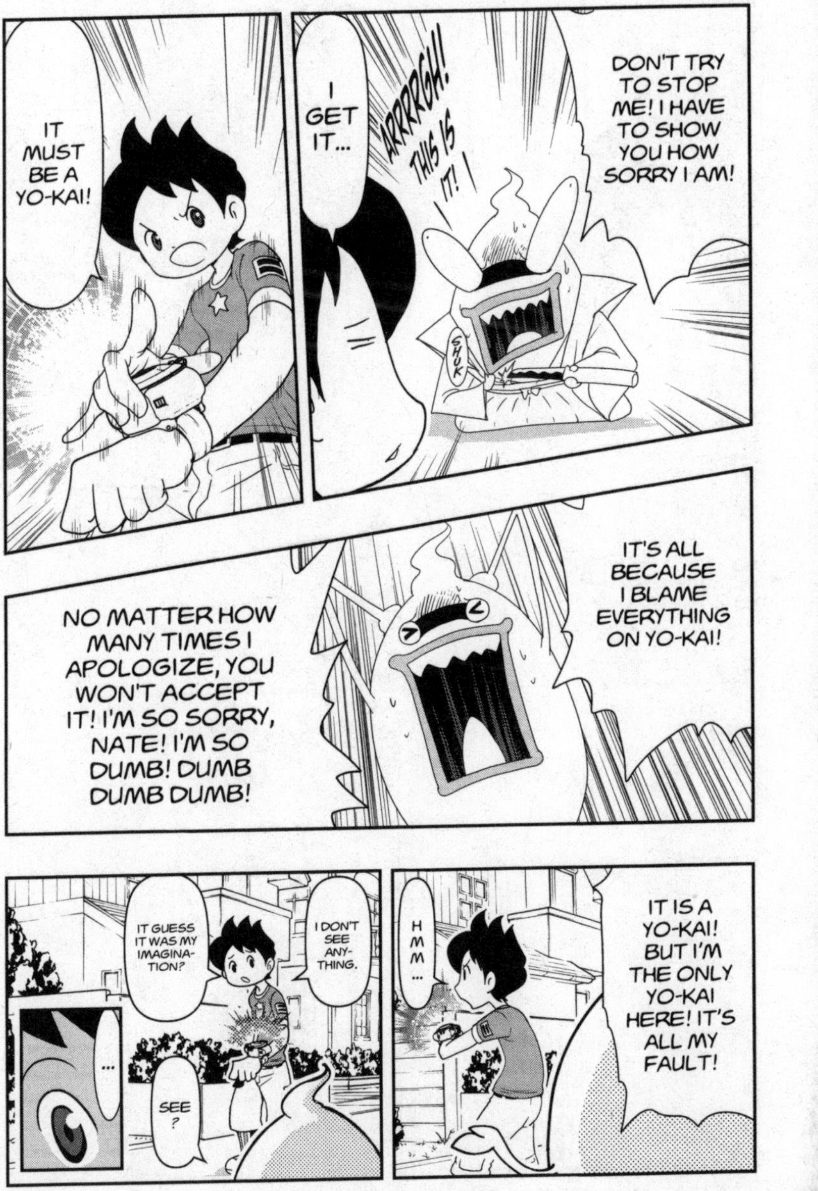
DON'T TRY TO STOP ME! I HAVE TO SHOW YOU HOW SORRY I AM!
ARRRRGH! THIS IS IT!
I GET IT...
SHUK
IT MUST BE A YO-KAI!
IT'S ALL BECAUSE I BLAME EVERYTHING ON YO-KAI!
NO MATTER HOW MANY TIMES I APOLOGIZE, YOU WON'T ACCEPT IT! I'M SO SORRY, NATE! I'M SO DUMB! DUMB DUMB DUMB!
IT IS A YO-KAI! BUT I'M THE ONLY YO-KAI HERE! IT'S ALL MY FAULT!
HMM...
I DON'T SEE ANYTHING.
IT GUESS IT WAS MY IMAGINATION?
SEE?
...

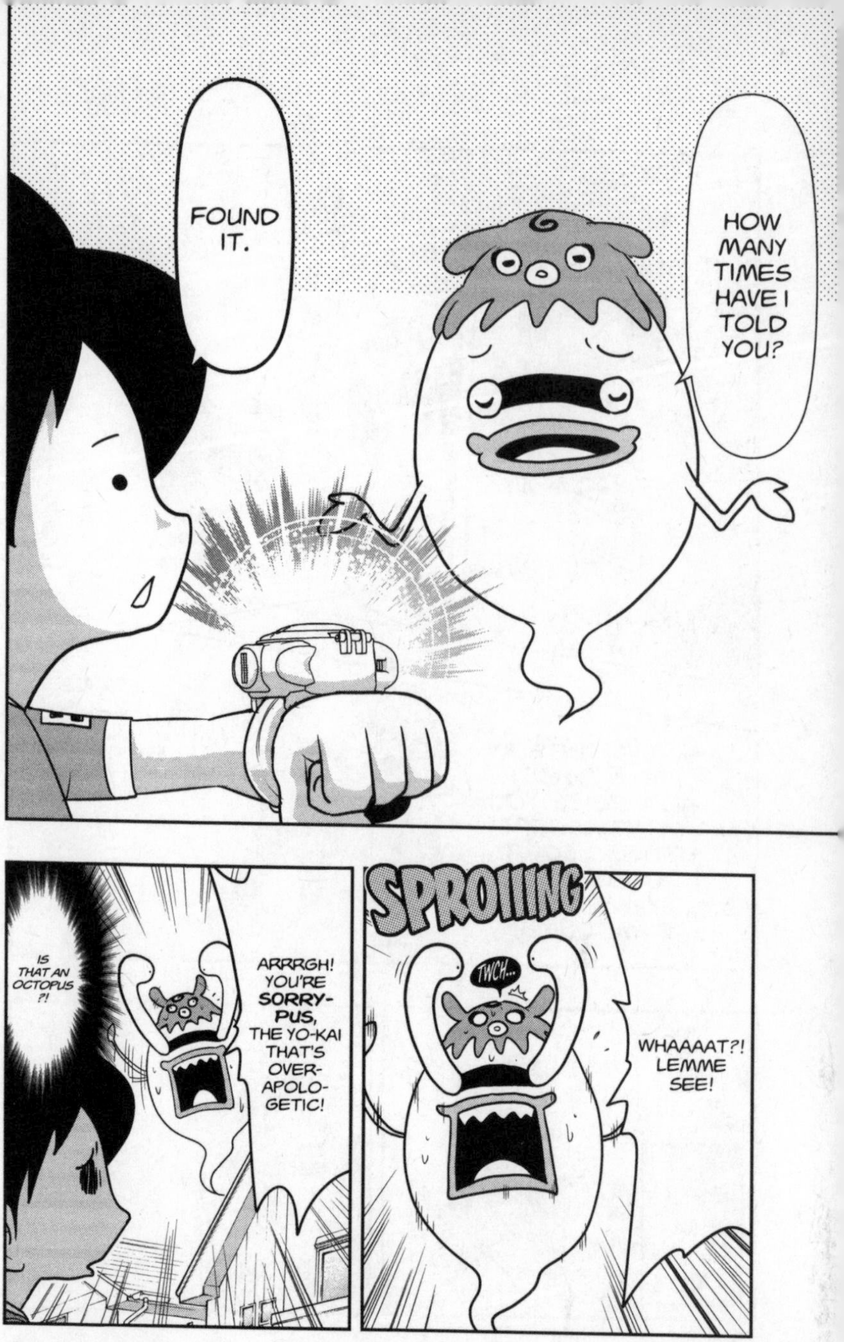
HOW MANY TIMES HAVE I TOLD YOU?
FOUND IT.
SPROIIING
TWCH...
WHAAAAT?! LEMME SEE!
ARRRGH! YOU'RE SORRYPUS, THE YO-KAI THAT'S OVER-APOLOGETIC!
IS THAT AN OCTOPUS ?!

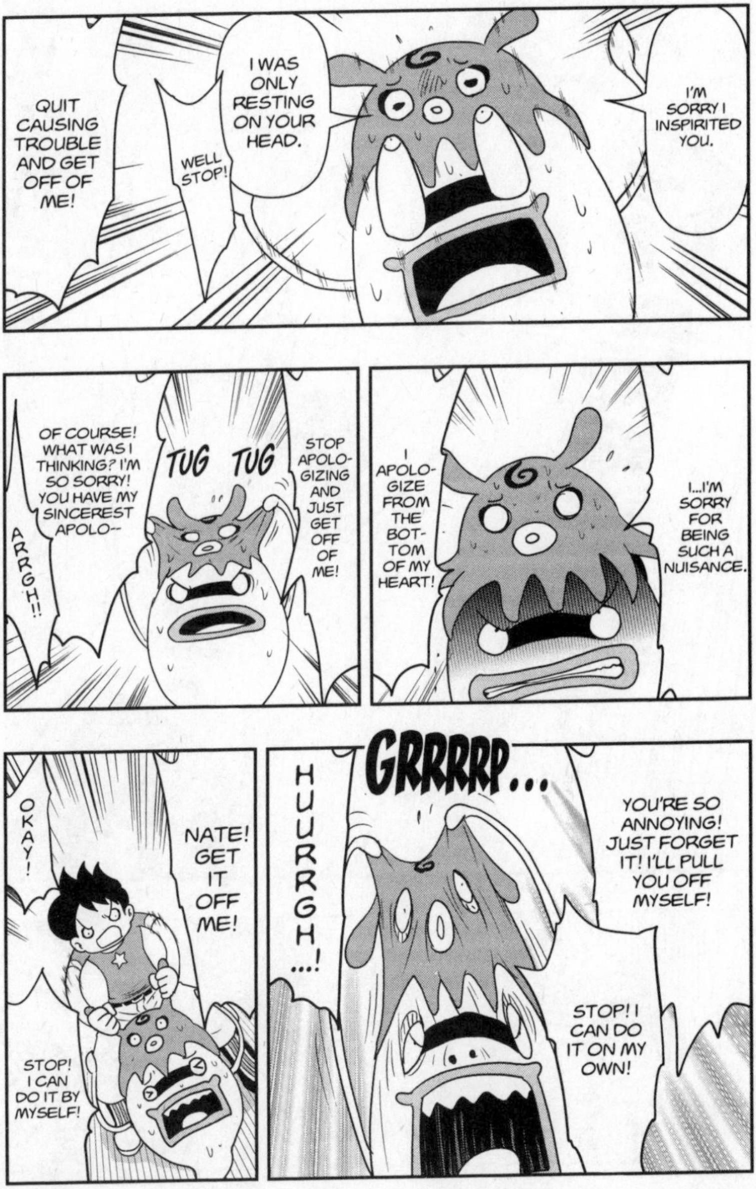
I'M SORRY I INSPIRITED YOU.
I WAS ONLY RESTING ON YOUR HEAD.
WELL STOP!
QUIT CAUSING TROUBLE AND GET OFF OF ME!
I...I'M SORRY FOR BEING SUCH A NUISANCE.
I APOLOGIZE FROM THE BOTTOM OF MY HEART!
STOP APOLOGIZING AND JUST GET OFF OF ME!
TUG TUG
OF COURSE! WHAT WAS I THINKING? I'M SO SORRY! YOU HAVE MY SINCEREST APOLO--
ARRGH!!
GRRRRP...
YOU'RE SO ANNOYING! JUST FORGET IT! I'LL PULL YOU OFF MYSELF!
HUURRGH...!
STOP! I CAN DO IT ON MY OWN!
NATE! GET IT OFF ME!
OKAY!
STOP! I CAN DO IT BY MYSELF!

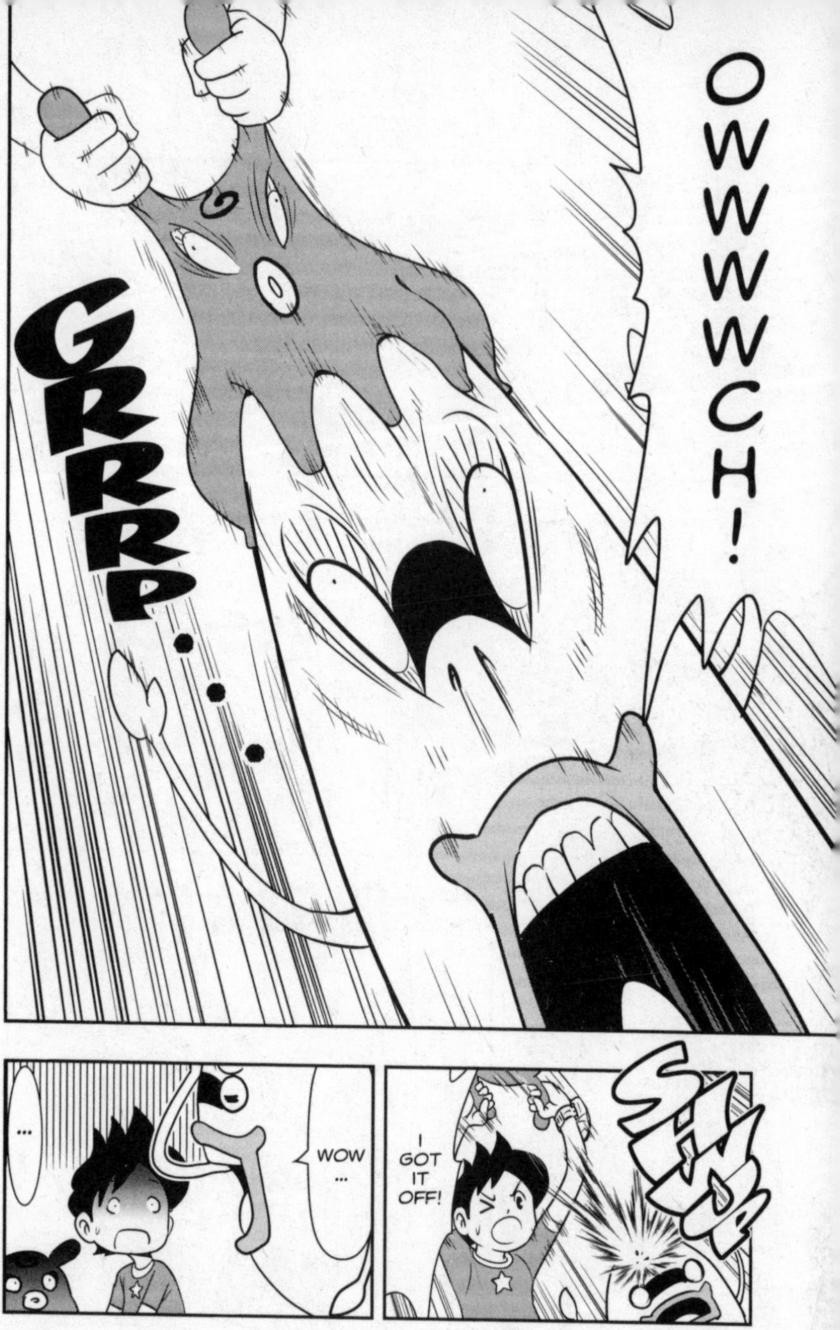
OWWWWCH!
GRRRP...
SHWUP
I GOT IT OFF!
WOW ...
...

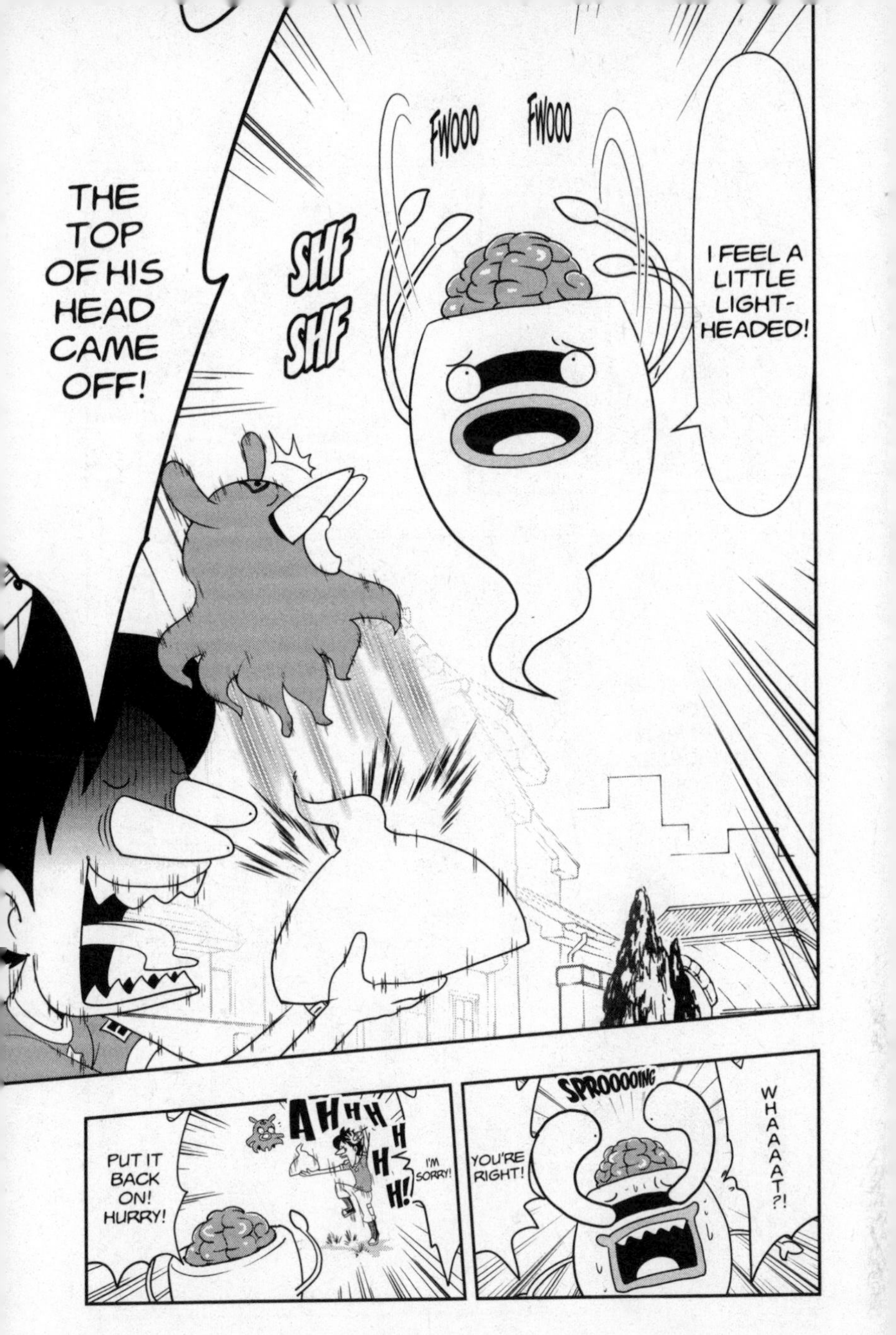
I FEEL A LITTLE LIGHT-HEADED!
FWOOO FWOOO
SHF SHF
THE TOP OF HIS HEAD CAME OFF!
WHAAAAAT?!
SPROOOOING
YOU'RE RIGHT!
I'M SORRY!
AHHHHHH!
PUT IT BACK ON! HURRY!

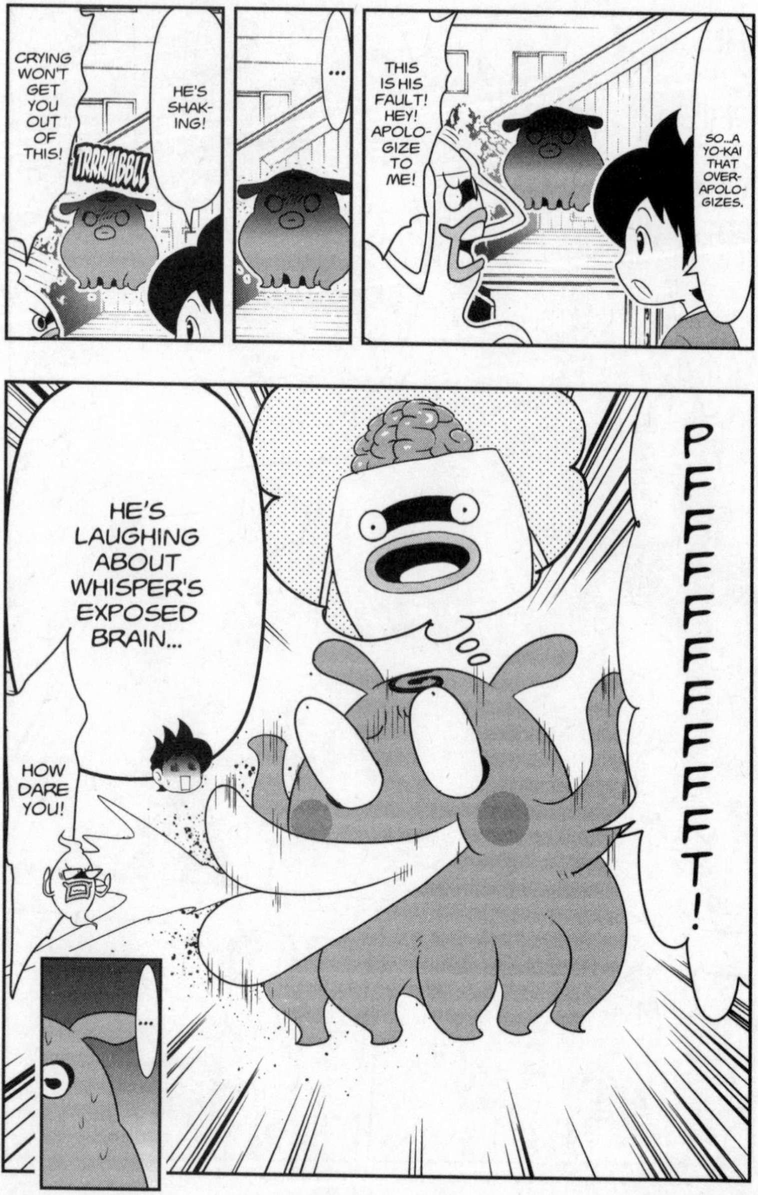
SO...A YO-KAI THAT OVER-APOLOGIZES.
THIS IS HIS FAULT! HEY! APOLOGIZE TO ME!
...
HE'S SHAKING!
CRYING WON'T GET YOU OUT OF THIS!
TRRRMBBLL
PFFFFFFFFFT!
HE'S LAUGHING ABOUT WHISPER'S EXPOSED BRAIN...
HOW DARE YOU!
...

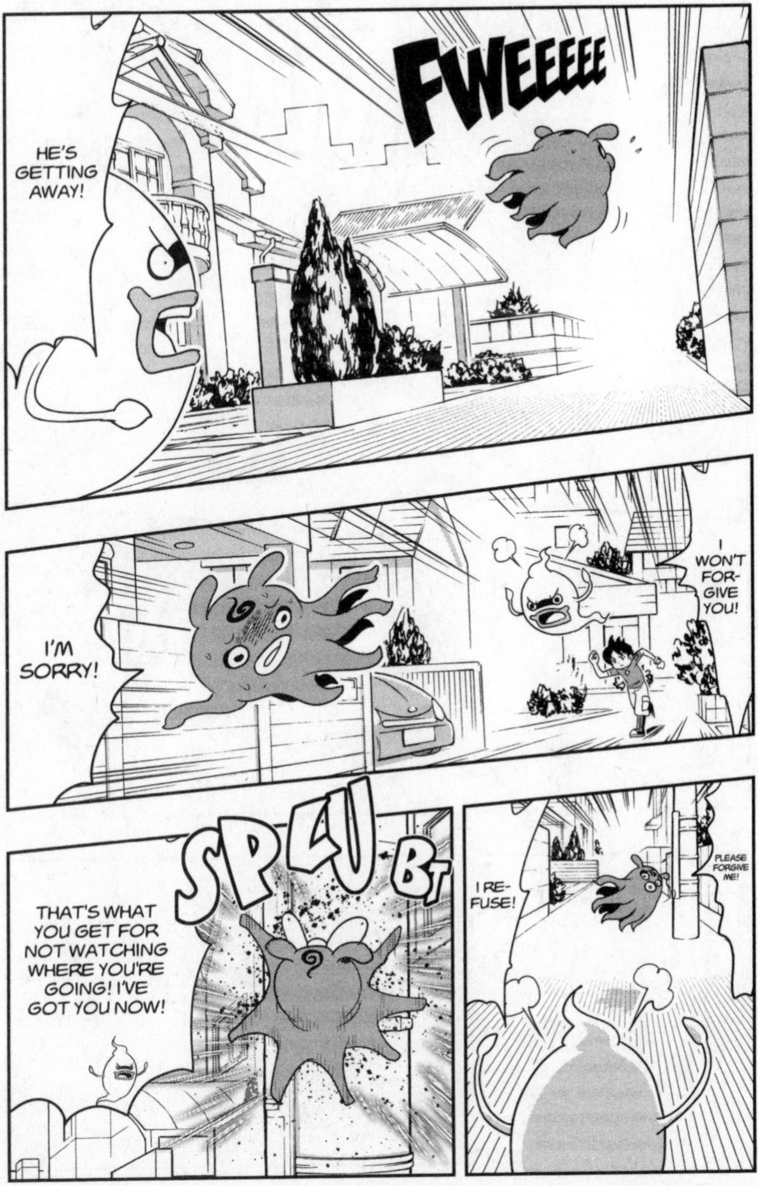
FWEEEEE
HE'S GETTING AWAY!
I WON'T FOR-GIVE YOU!
I'M SORRY!
PLEASE FORGIVE ME!
I RE-FUSE!
SPLUBT
THAT'S WHAT YOU GET FOR NOT WATCHING WHERE YOU'RE GOING! I'VE GOT YOU NOW!

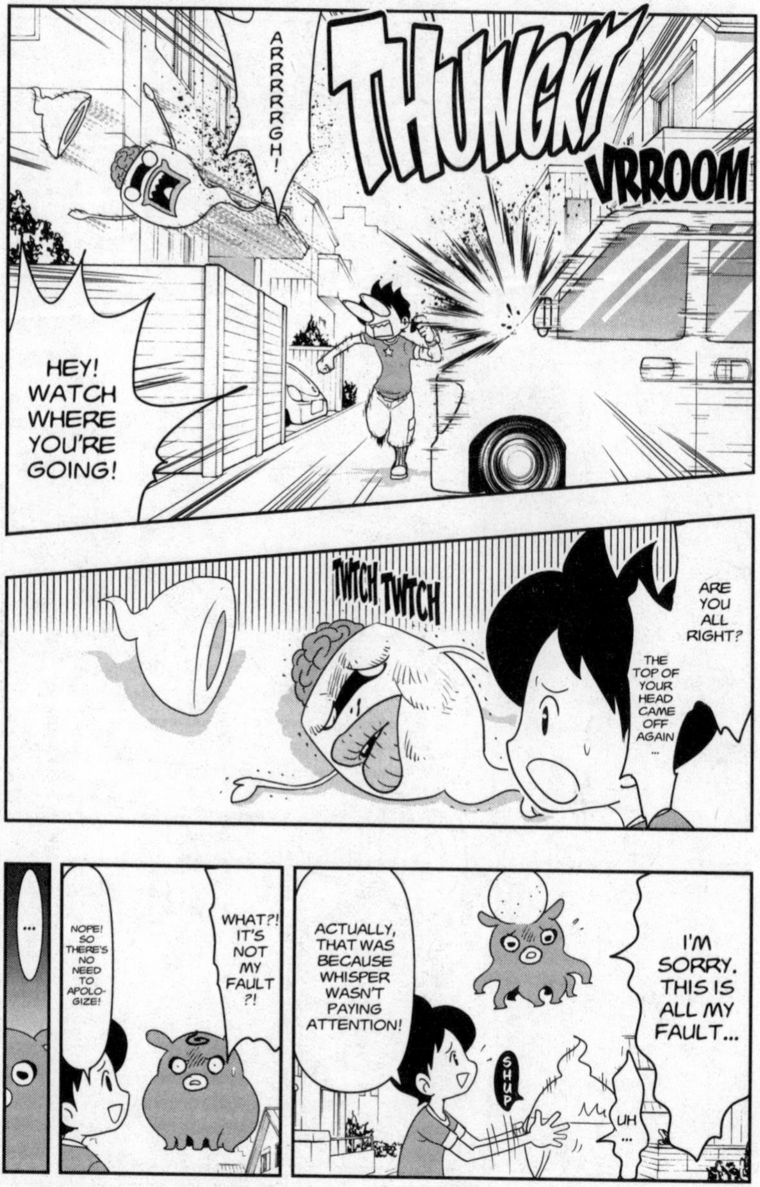
THUNCK!!
VRROOM
ARRRRRGH!
HEY! WATCH WHERE YOU'RE GOING!
ARE YOU ALL RIGHT?
THE TOP OF YOUR HEAD CAME OFF AGAIN...
TWITCH TWITCH
I'M SORRY. THIS IS ALL MY FAULT...
UH...
SHUP
ACTUALLY, THAT WAS BECAUSE WHISPER WASN'T PAYING ATTENTION!
WHAT?! IT'S NOT MY FAULT?!
NOPE! SO THERE'S NO NEED TO APOLOGIZE!
...

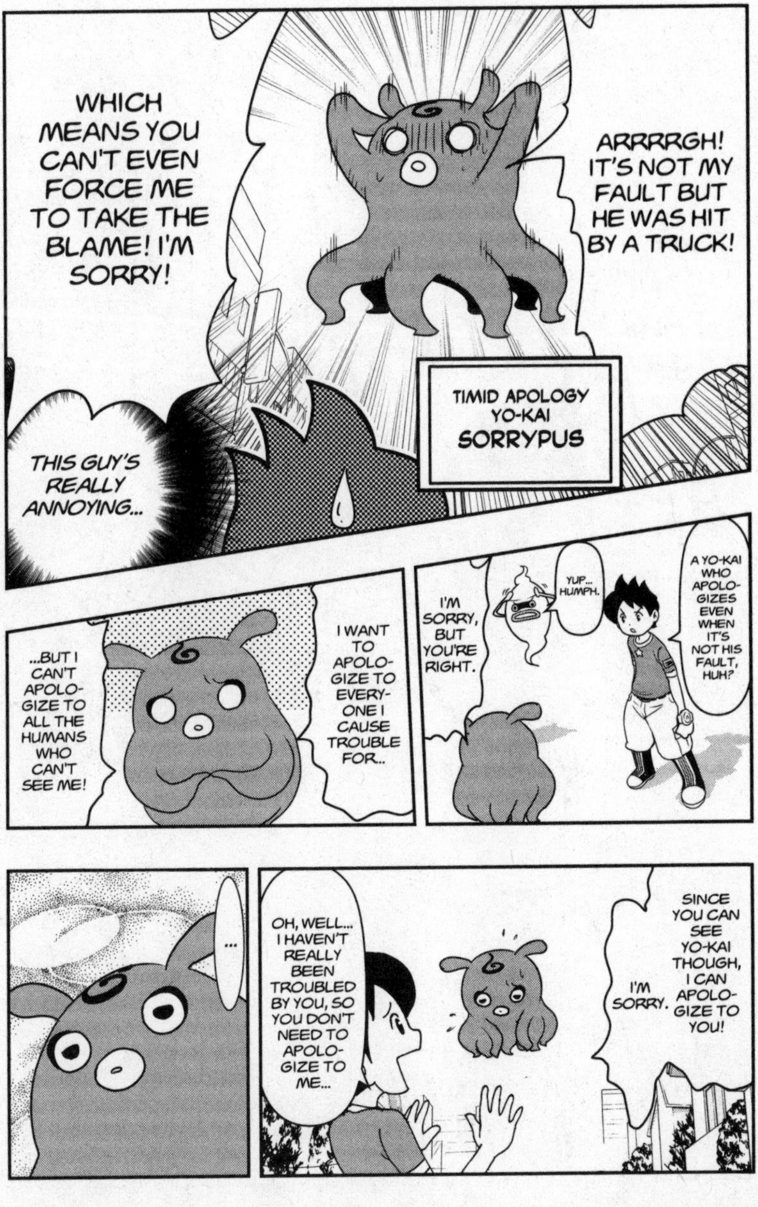
ARRRRGH! IT'S NOT MY FAULT BUT HE WAS HIT BY A TRUCK!
WHICH MEANS YOU CAN'T EVEN FORCE ME TO TAKE THE BLAME! I'M SORRY!
TIMID APOLOGY YO-KAI SORRYPUS
THIS GUY'S REALLY ANNOYING...
A YO-KAI WHO APOLOGIZES EVEN WHEN IT'S NOT HIS FAULT, HUH?
YUP... HUMPH.
I'M SORRY, BUT YOU'RE RIGHT.
I WANT TO APOLOGIZE TO EVERYONE I CAUSE TROUBLE FOR...
...BUT I CAN'T APOLOGIZE TO ALL THE HUMANS WHO CAN'T SEE ME!
SINCE YOU CAN SEE YO-KAI THOUGH, I CAN APOLOGIZE TO YOU!
I'M SORRY.
OH, WELL... I HAVEN'T REALLY BEEN TROUBLED BY YOU, SO YOU DON'T NEED TO APOLOGIZE TO ME...
...

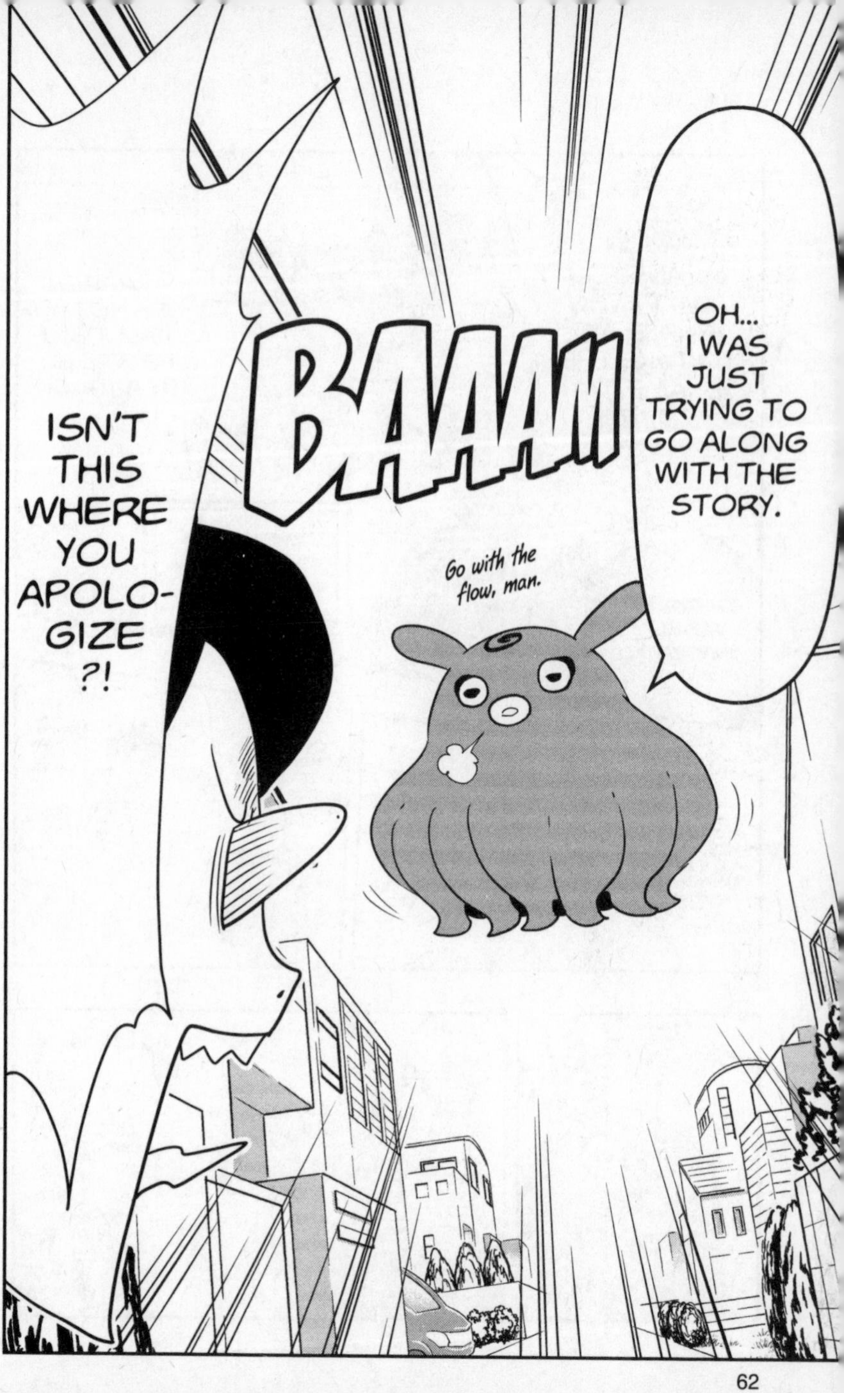
OH... I WAS JUST TRYING TO GO ALONG WITH THE STORY.
BAAAM
Go with the flow, man.
ISN'T THIS WHERE YOU APOLOGIZE ?!

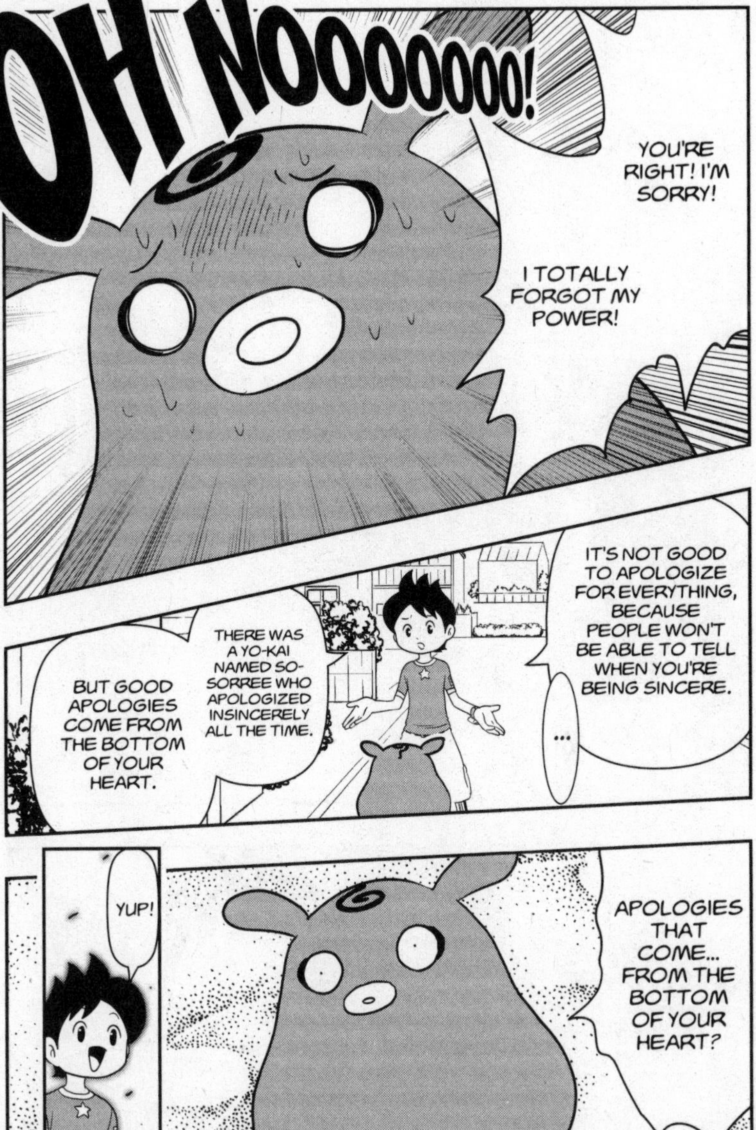
OH NOOOOOO!
YOU'RE RIGHT! I'M SORRY!
I TOTALLY FORGOT MY POWER!
IT'S NOT GOOD TO APOLOGIZE FOR EVERYTHING, BECAUSE PEOPLE WON'T BE ABLE TO TELL WHEN YOU'RE BEING SINCERE.
...
THERE WAS A YO-KAI NAMED SO-SORREE WHO APOLOGIZED INSINCERELY ALL THE TIME.
BUT GOOD APOLOGIES COME FROM THE BOTTOM OF YOUR HEART.
APOLOGIES THAT COME... FROM THE BOTTOM OF YOUR HEART?
YUP!

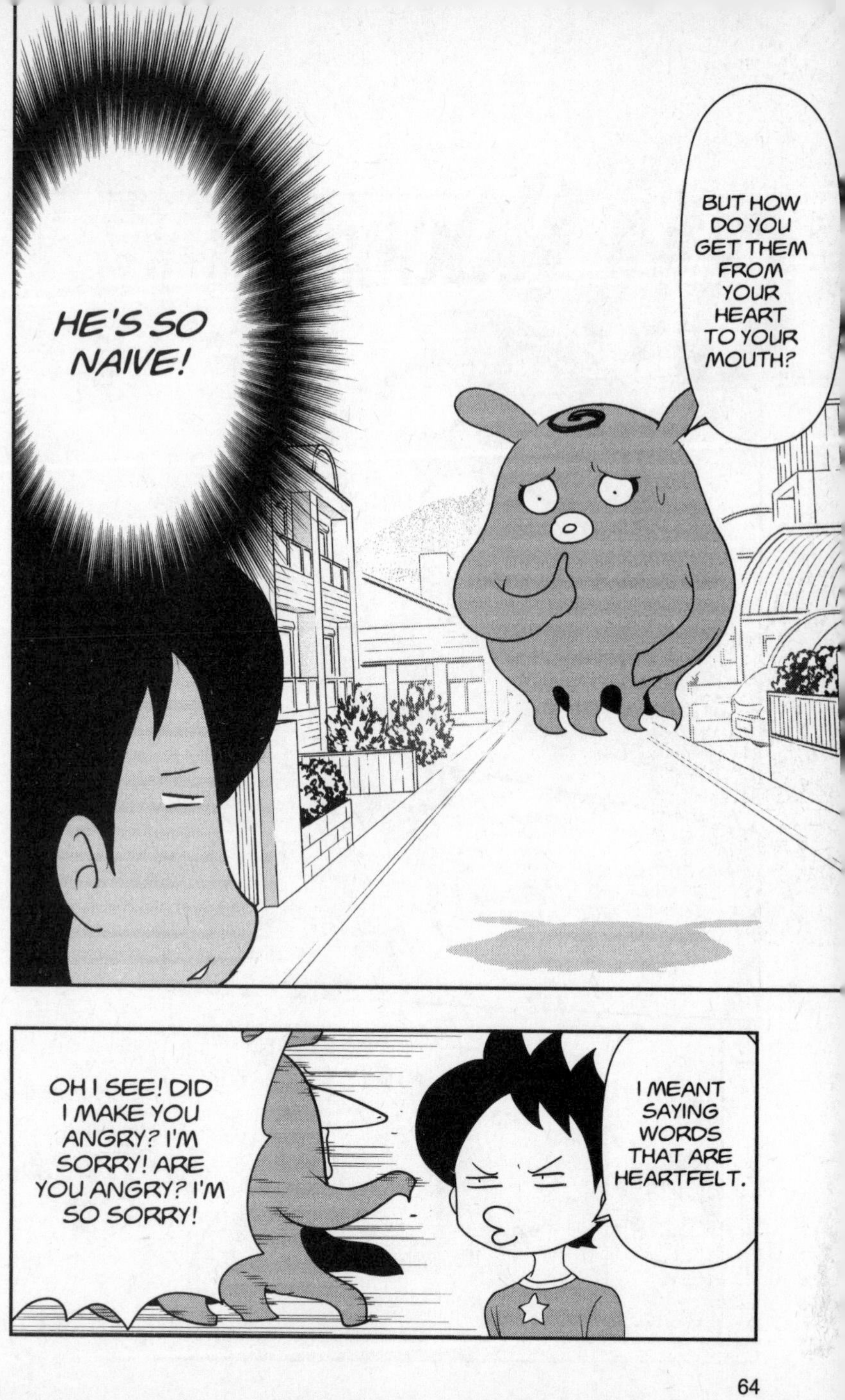
BUT HOW DO YOU GET THEM FROM YOUR HEART TO YOUR MOUTH?
HE'S SO NAIVE!
I MEANT SAYING WORDS THAT ARE HEARTFELT.
OH I SEE! DID I MAKE YOU ANGRY? I'M SORRY! ARE YOU ANGRY? I'M SO SORRY!

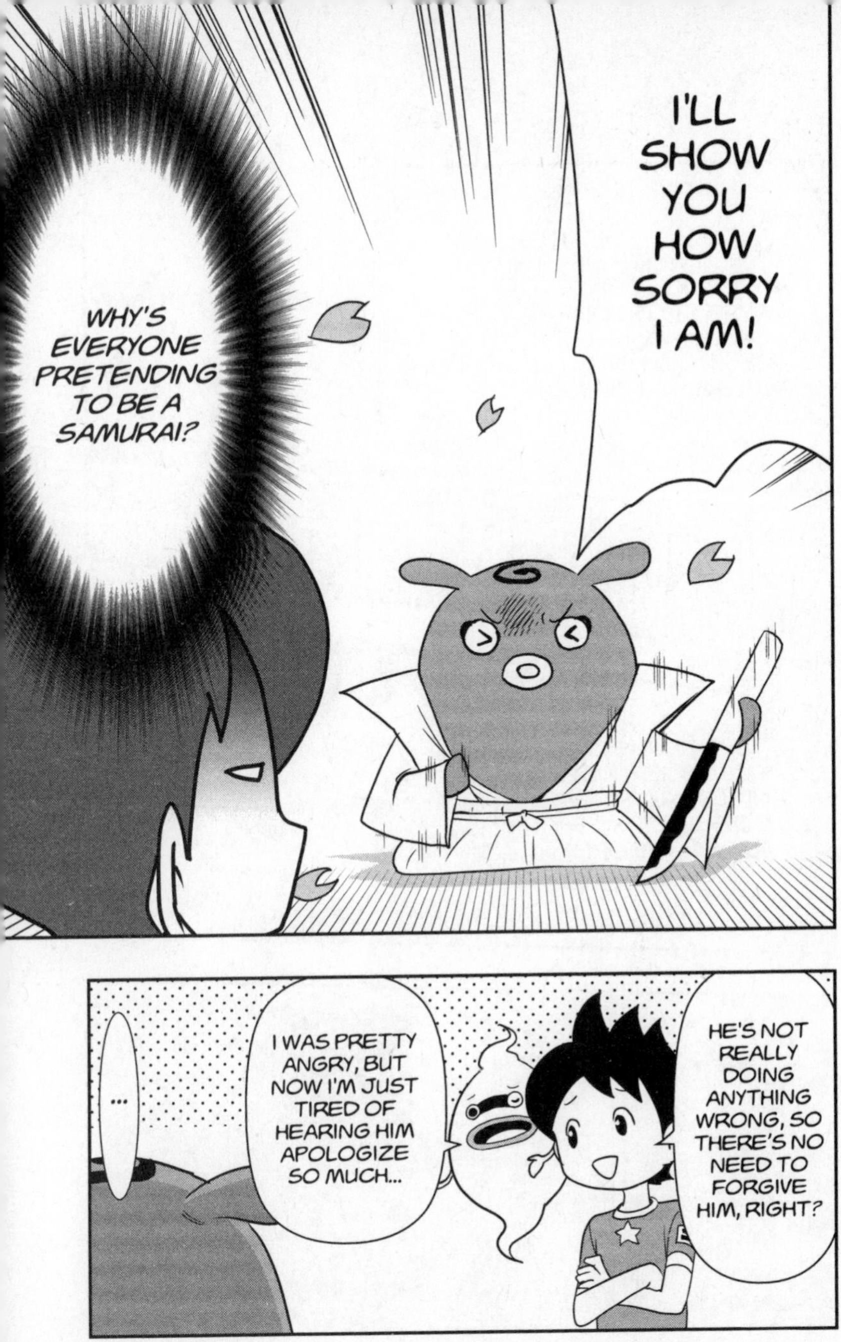
I'LL SHOW YOU HOW SORRY I AM!
WHY'S EVERYONE PRETENDING TO BE A SAMURAI?
HE'S NOT REALLY DOING ANYTHING WRONG, SO THERE'S NO NEED TO FORGIVE HIM, RIGHT?
I WAS PRETTY ANGRY, BUT NOW I'M JUST TIRED OF HEARING HIM APOLOGIZE SO MUCH...
...

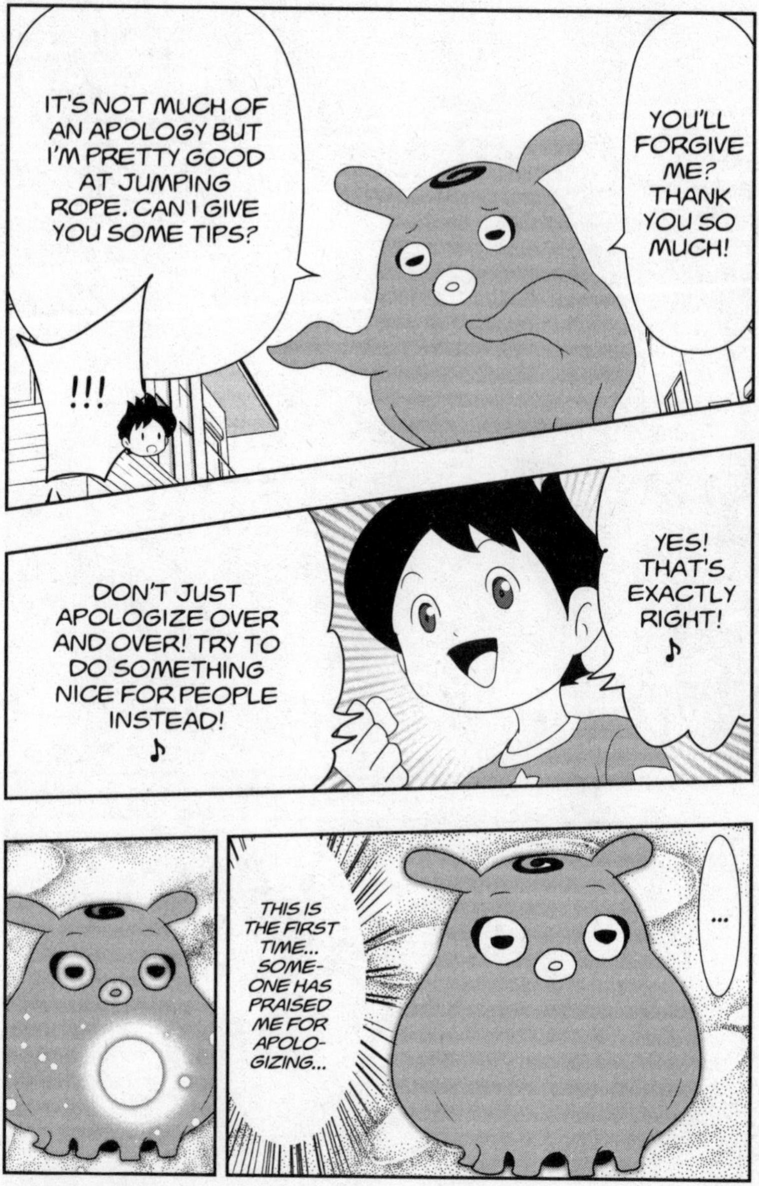
YOU'LL FORGIVE ME? THANK YOU SO MUCH!
IT'S NOT MUCH OF AN APOLOGY BUT I'M PRETTY GOOD AT JUMPING ROPE. CAN I GIVE YOU SOME TIPS?
!!!
YES! THAT'S EXACTLY RIGHT! ♪
DON'T JUST APOLOGIZE OVER AND OVER! TRY TO DO SOMETHING NICE FOR PEOPLE INSTEAD! ♪
...
THIS IS THE FIRST TIME... SOME-ONE HAS PRAISED ME FOR APOLO-GIZING...

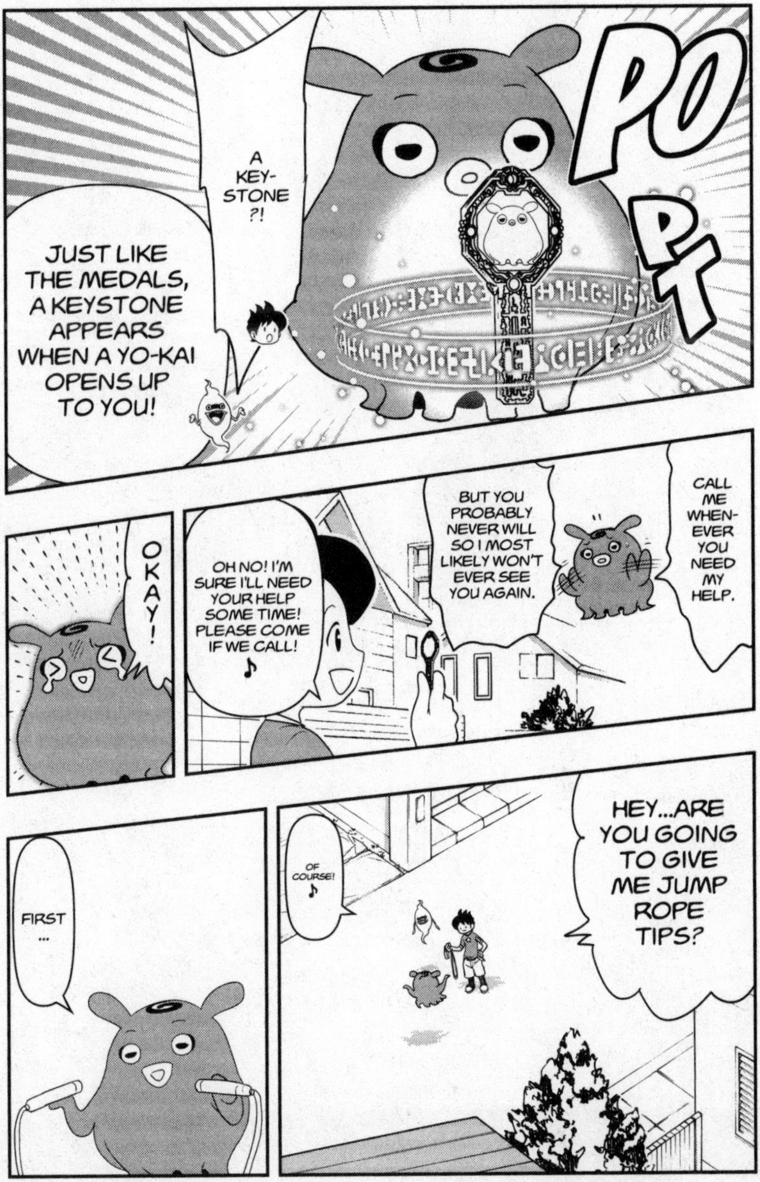
POPT
A KEY-STONE ?!
JUST LIKE THE MEDALS, A KEYSTONE APPEARS WHEN A YO-KAI OPENS UP TO YOU!
CALL ME WHEN-EVER YOU NEED MY HELP.
BUT YOU PROBABLY NEVER WILL SO I MOST LIKELY WON'T EVER SEE YOU AGAIN.
OH NO! I'M SURE I'LL NEED YOUR HELP SOME TIME! PLEASE COME IF WE CALL! ♪
OKAY!
HEY...ARE YOU GOING TO GIVE ME JUMP ROPE TIPS?
OF COURSE! ♪
FIRST...

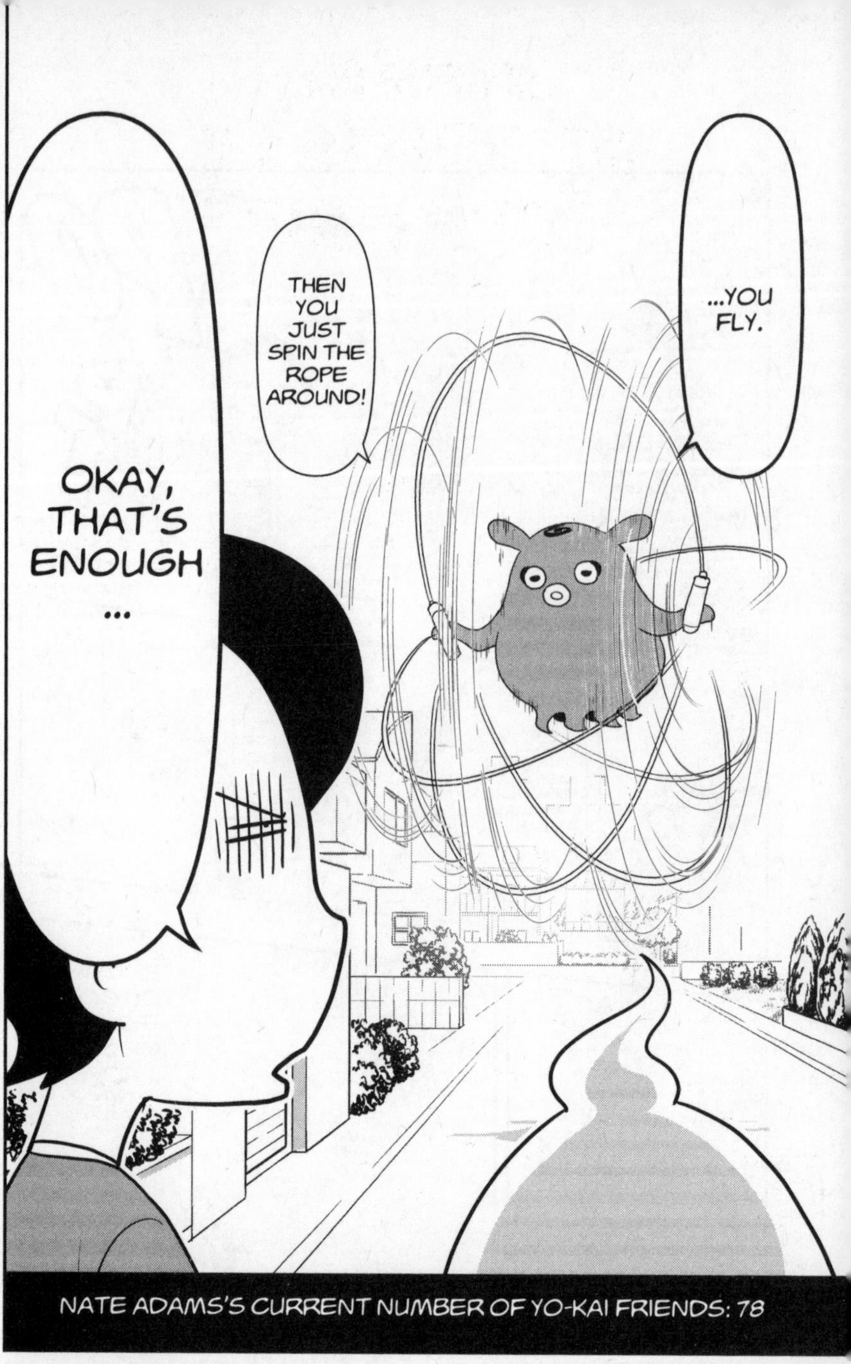
...YOU FLY.
THEN YOU JUST SPIN THE ROPE AROUND!
OKAY, THAT'S ENOUGH ...
NATE ADAMS'S CURRENT NUMBER OF YO-KAI FRIENDS: 78

CHAPTER 153
CITY LOVER YO-KAI MOLAR PETITE

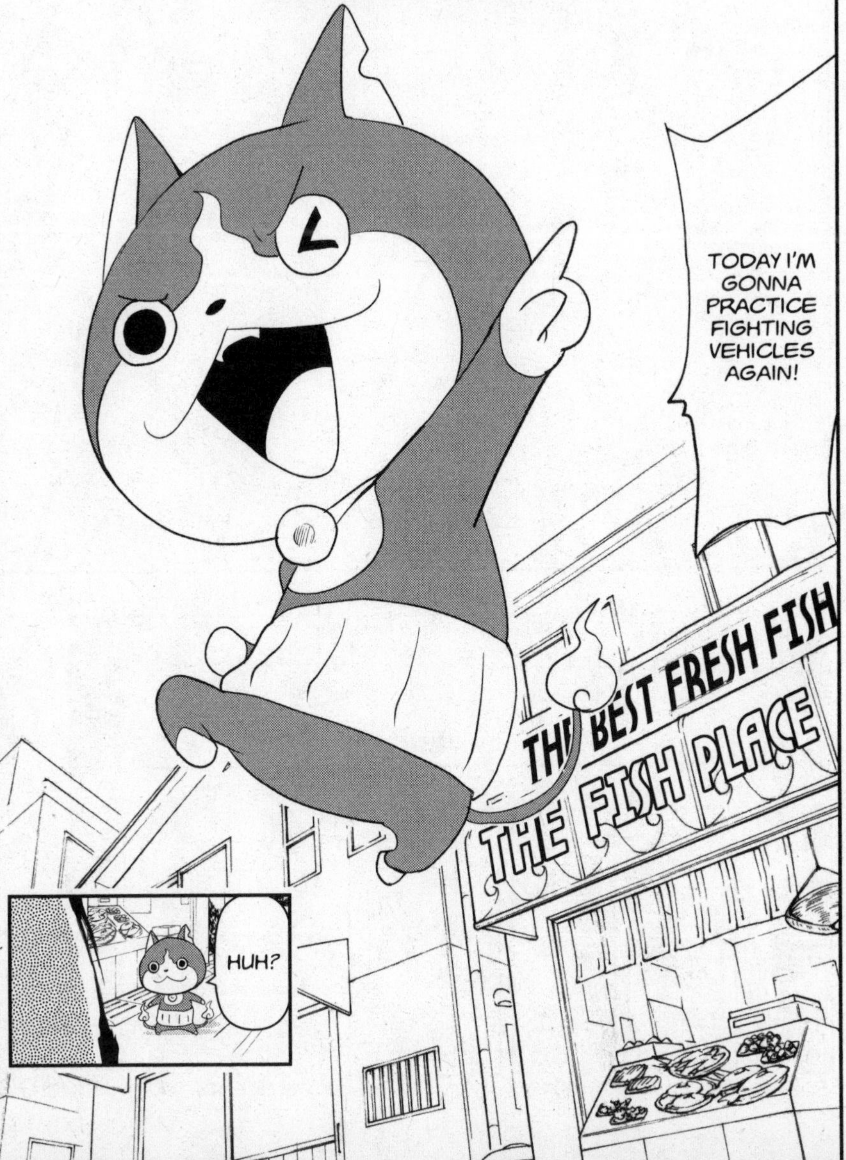
TODAY I'M GONNA PRACTICE FIGHTING VEHICLES AGAIN!
BEST FRESH FISH
THE FISH PLACE
HUH?

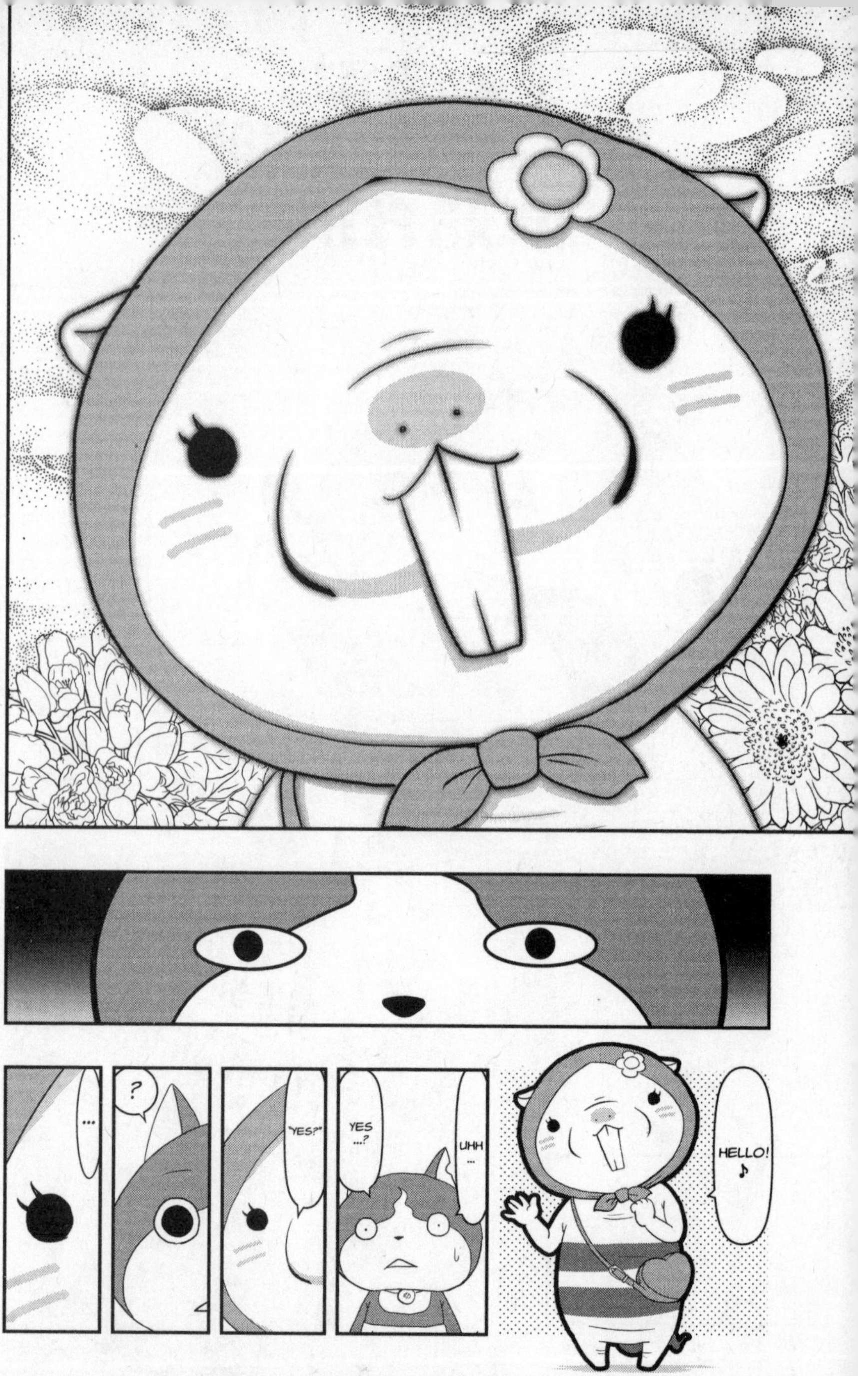
HELLO! ♪
UHH ...
YES ...?
"YES?"
?
...

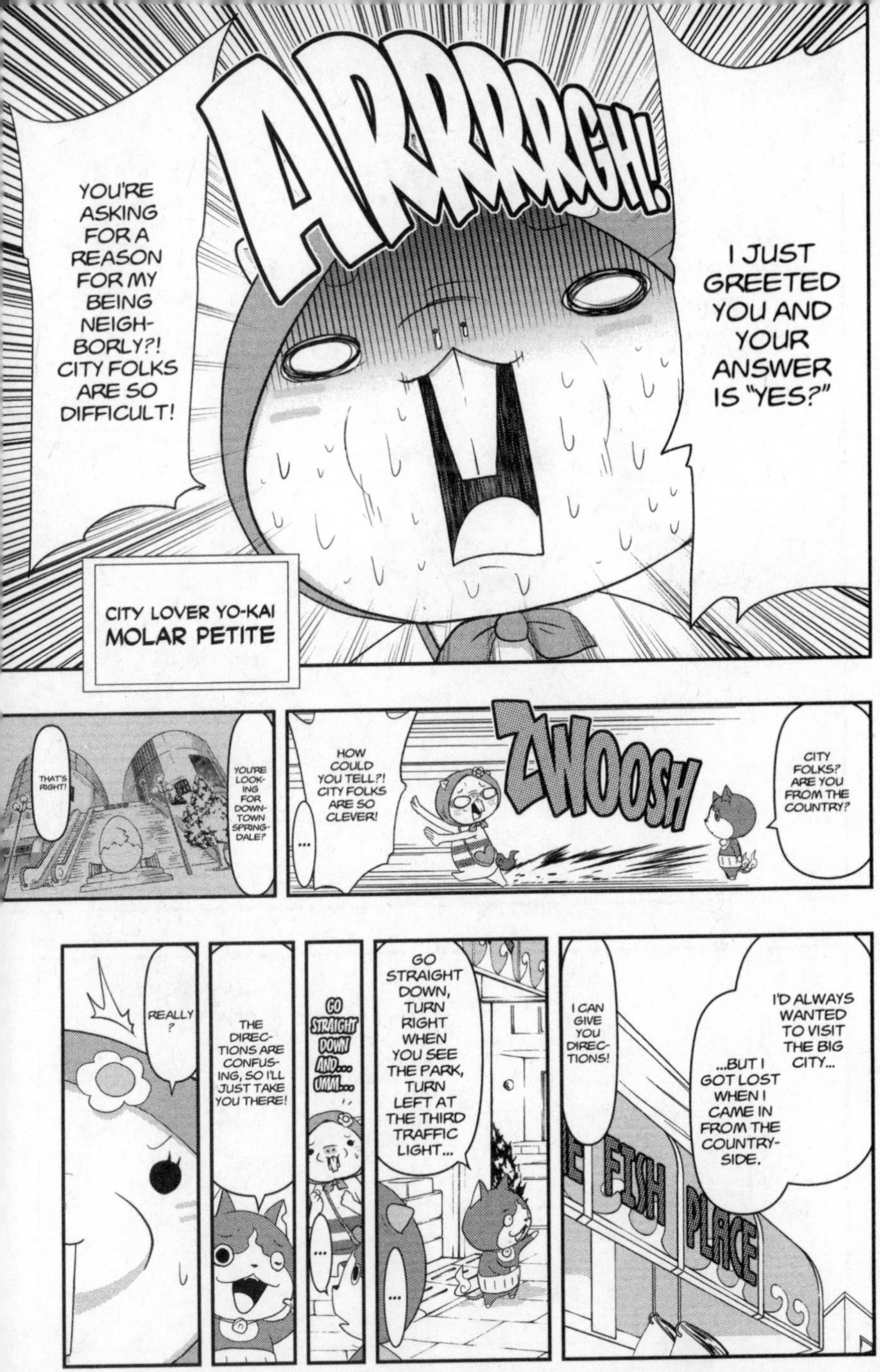
I JUST GREETED YOU AND YOUR ANSWER IS "YES?"
ARRRRGH!
YOU'RE ASKING FOR A REASON FOR MY BEING NEIGHBORLY?! CITY FOLKS ARE SO DIFFICULT!
CITY LOVER YO-KAI MOLAR PETITE
CITY FOLKS? ARE YOU FROM THE COUNTRY?
ZWOOSH
HOW COULD YOU TELL?! CITY FOLKS ARE SO CLEVER!
...
YOU'RE LOOKING FOR DOWNTOWN SPRINGDALE?
THAT'S RIGHT!
I'D ALWAYS WANTED TO VISIT THE BIG CITY...
...BUT I GOT LOST WHEN I CAME IN FROM THE COUNTRYSIDE.
I CAN GIVE YOU DIRECTIONS!
FISH PLACE
GO STRAIGHT DOWN, TURN RIGHT WHEN YOU SEE THE PARK, TURN LEFT AT THE THIRD TRAFFIC LIGHT...
...
GO STRAIGHT DOWN AND... UMM...
...
THE DIRECTIONS ARE CONFUSING, SO I'LL JUST TAKE YOU THERE!
REALLY?

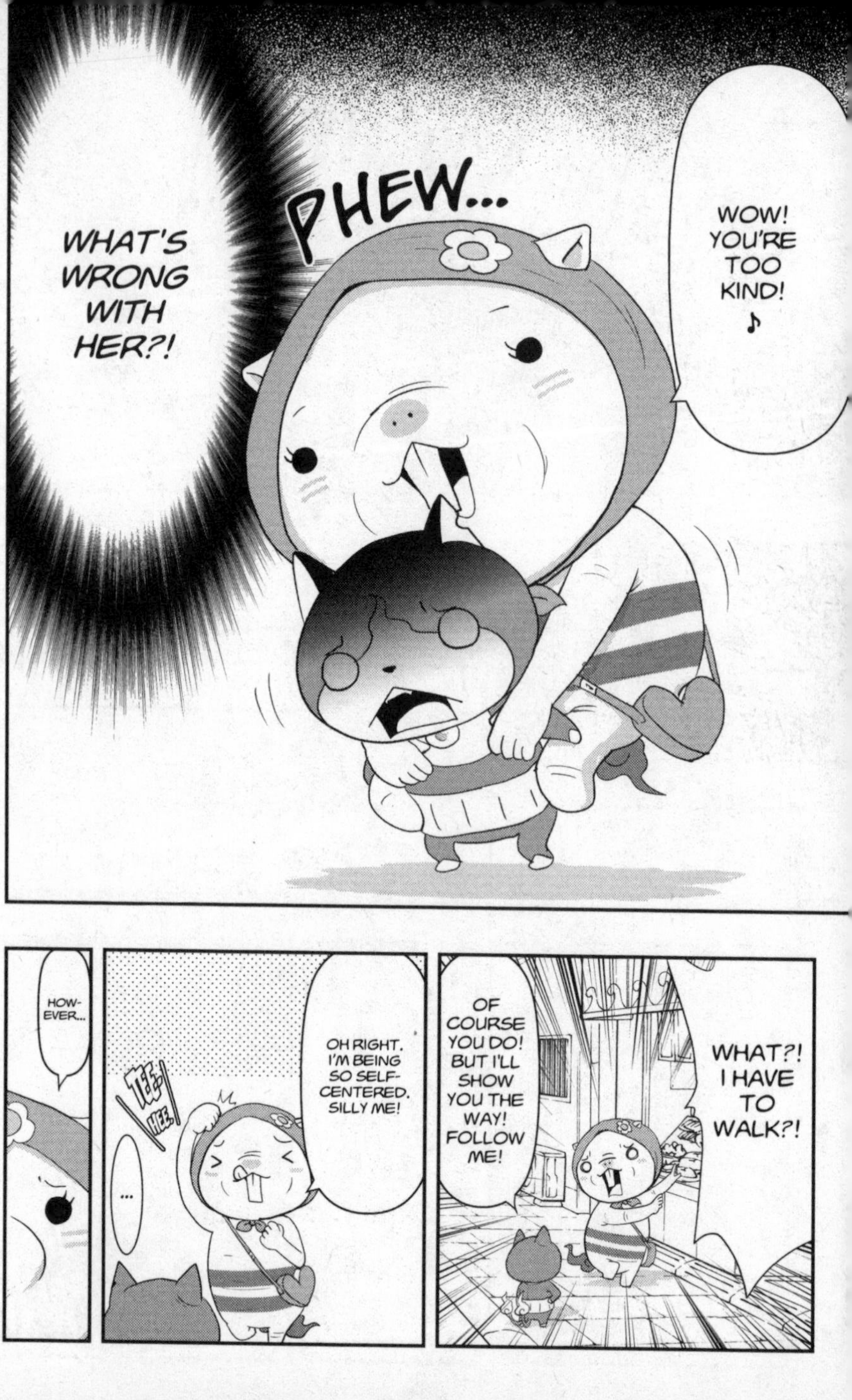
WOW! YOU'RE TOO KIND! ♪
PHEW...
WHAT'S WRONG WITH HER?!
WHAT?! I HAVE TO WALK?!
OF COURSE YOU DO! BUT I'LL SHOW YOU THE WAY! FOLLOW ME!
OH RIGHT. I'M BEING SO SELF-CENTERED. SILLY ME!
TEE HEE
...
HOW-EVER...

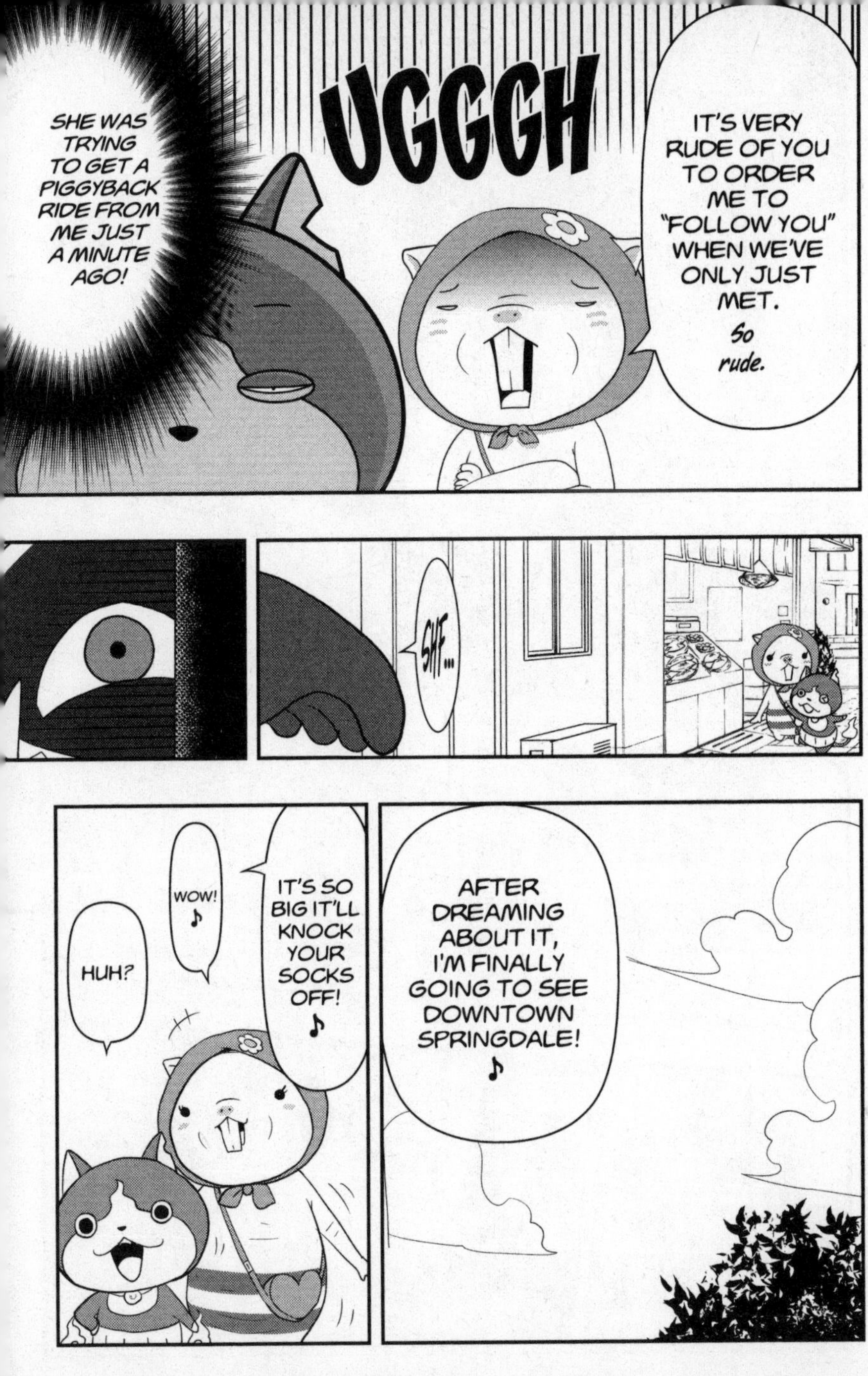
IT'S VERY RUDE OF YOU TO ORDER ME TO "FOLLOW YOU" WHEN WE'VE ONLY JUST MET.
So rude.
UGGGH
SHE WAS TRYING TO GET A PIGGYBACK RIDE FROM ME JUST A MINUTE AGO!
SHF...
AFTER DREAMING ABOUT IT, I'M FINALLY GOING TO SEE DOWNTOWN SPRINGDALE! ♪
IT'S SO BIG IT'LL KNOCK YOUR SOCKS OFF! ♪
WOW! ♪
HUH?

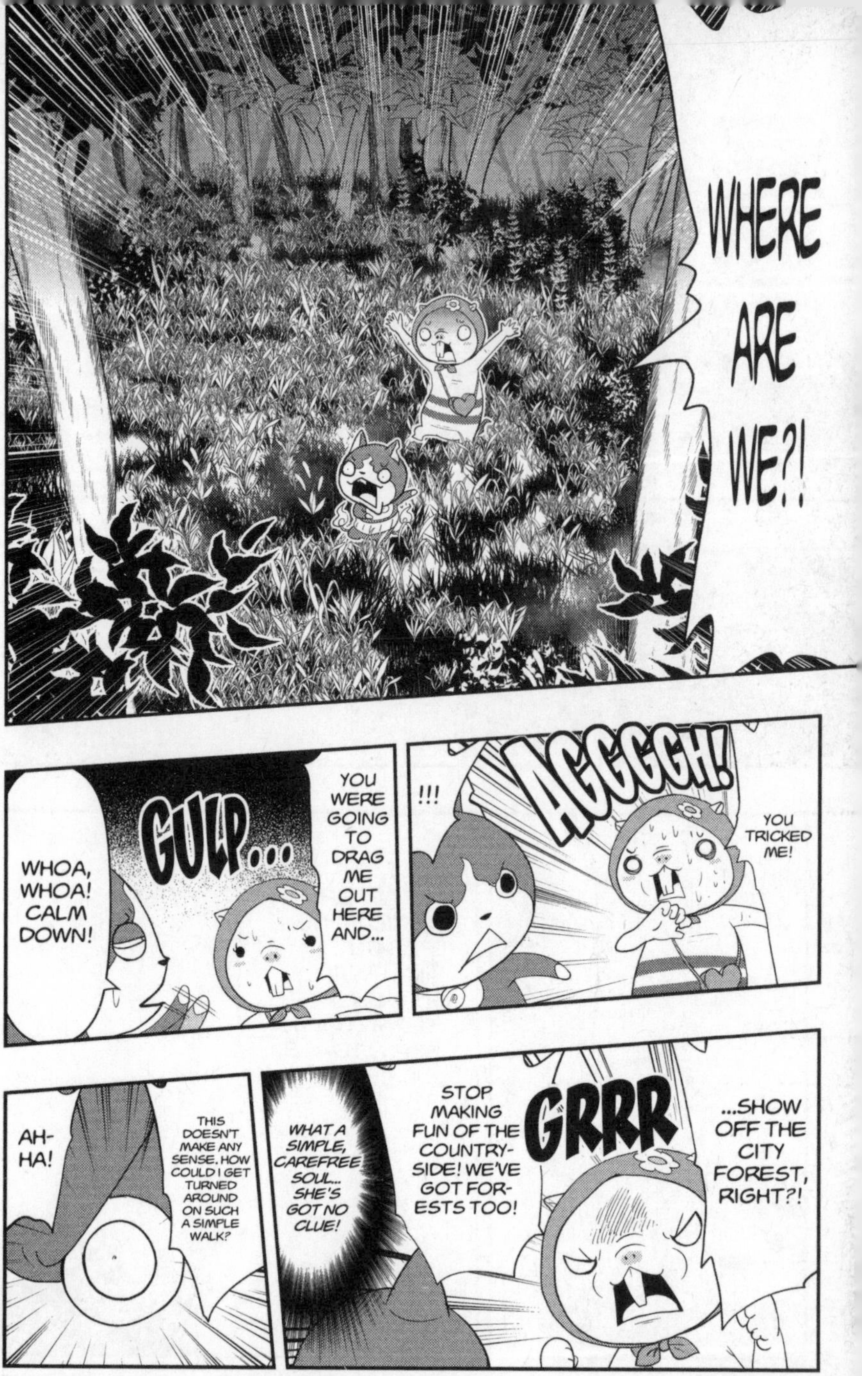
WHERE ARE WE?!
AGGGGH!
YOU TRICKED ME!
!!!
YOU WERE GOING TO DRAG ME OUT HERE AND...
GULP...
WHOA, WHOA! CALM DOWN!
...SHOW OFF THE CITY FOREST, RIGHT?!
GRRR
STOP MAKING FUN OF THE COUNTRY-SIDE! WE'VE GOT FOR-ESTS TOO!
WHAT A SIMPLE, CAREFREE SOUL... SHE'S GOT NO CLUE!
THIS DOESN'T MAKE ANY SENSE. HOW COULD I GET TURNED AROUND ON SUCH A SIMPLE WALK?
AH-HA!

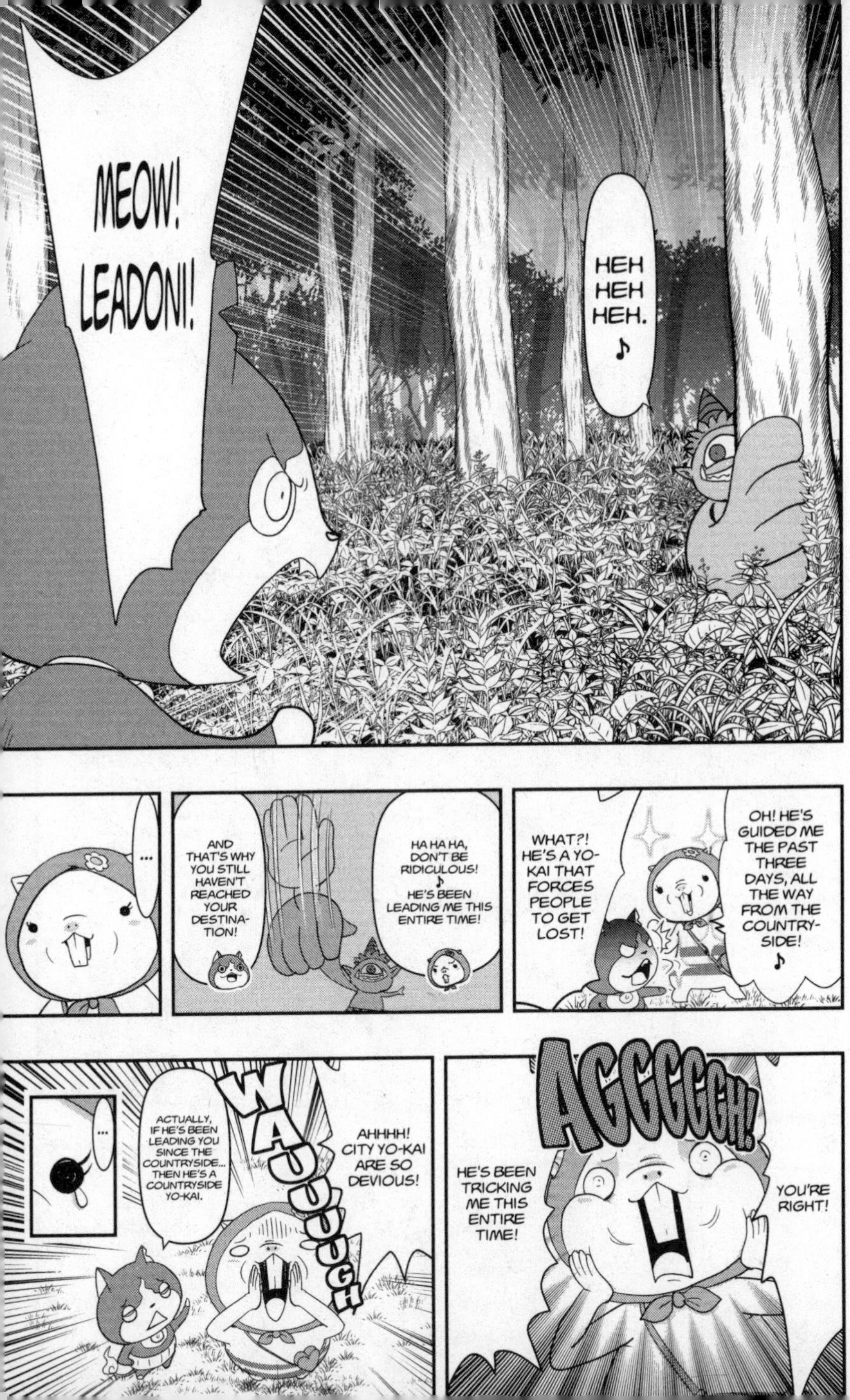
HEH HEH HEH. ♪
MEOW! LEADONI!
OH! HE'S GUIDED ME THE PAST THREE DAYS, ALL THE WAY FROM THE COUNTRY-SIDE! ♪
WHAT?! HE'S A YO-KAI THAT FORCES PEOPLE TO GET LOST!
HA HA HA, DON'T BE RIDICULOUS! ♪ HE'S BEEN LEADING ME THIS ENTIRE TIME!
AND THAT'S WHY YOU STILL HAVEN'T REACHED YOUR DESTINATION!
...
AGGGGGH!
YOU'RE RIGHT!
HE'S BEEN TRICKING ME THIS ENTIRE TIME!
AHHHH! CITY YO-KAI ARE SO DEVIOUS!
WAUUUUGH
ACTUALLY, IF HE'S BEEN LEADING YOU SINCE THE COUNTRYSIDE... THEN HE'S A COUNTRYSIDE YO-KAI.
...

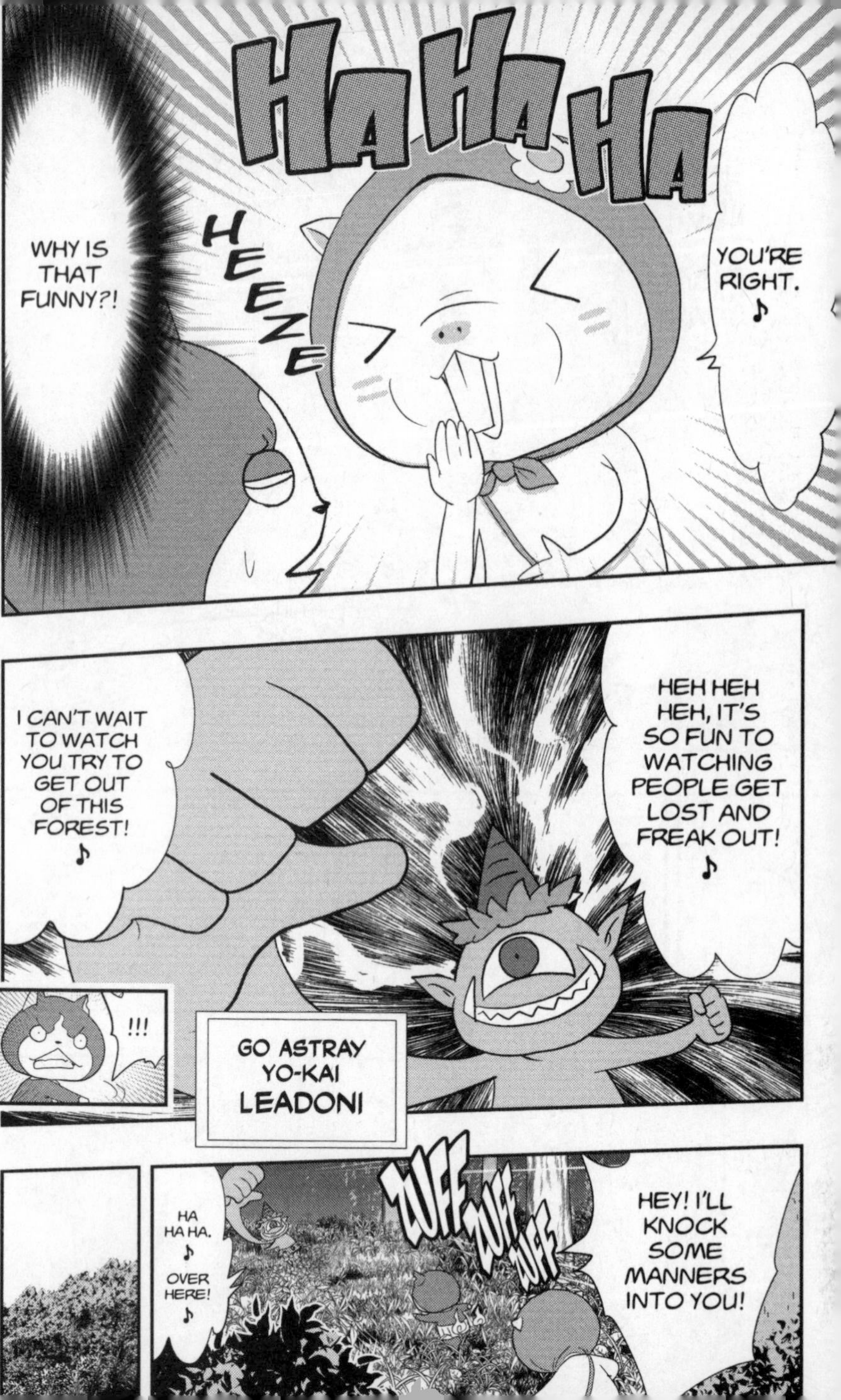
HA HA HA HA
YOU'RE RIGHT. ♪
HEEZE
WHY IS THAT FUNNY?!
HEH HEH HEH, IT'S SO FUN TO WATCHING PEOPLE GET LOST AND FREAK OUT! ♪
I CAN'T WAIT TO WATCH YOU TRY TO GET OUT OF THIS FOREST! ♪
GO ASTRAY YO-KAI LEADONI
!!!
HEY! I'LL KNOCK SOME MANNERS INTO YOU!
ZUFF ZUFF ZUFF
HA HA HA. ♪
OVER HERE! ♪

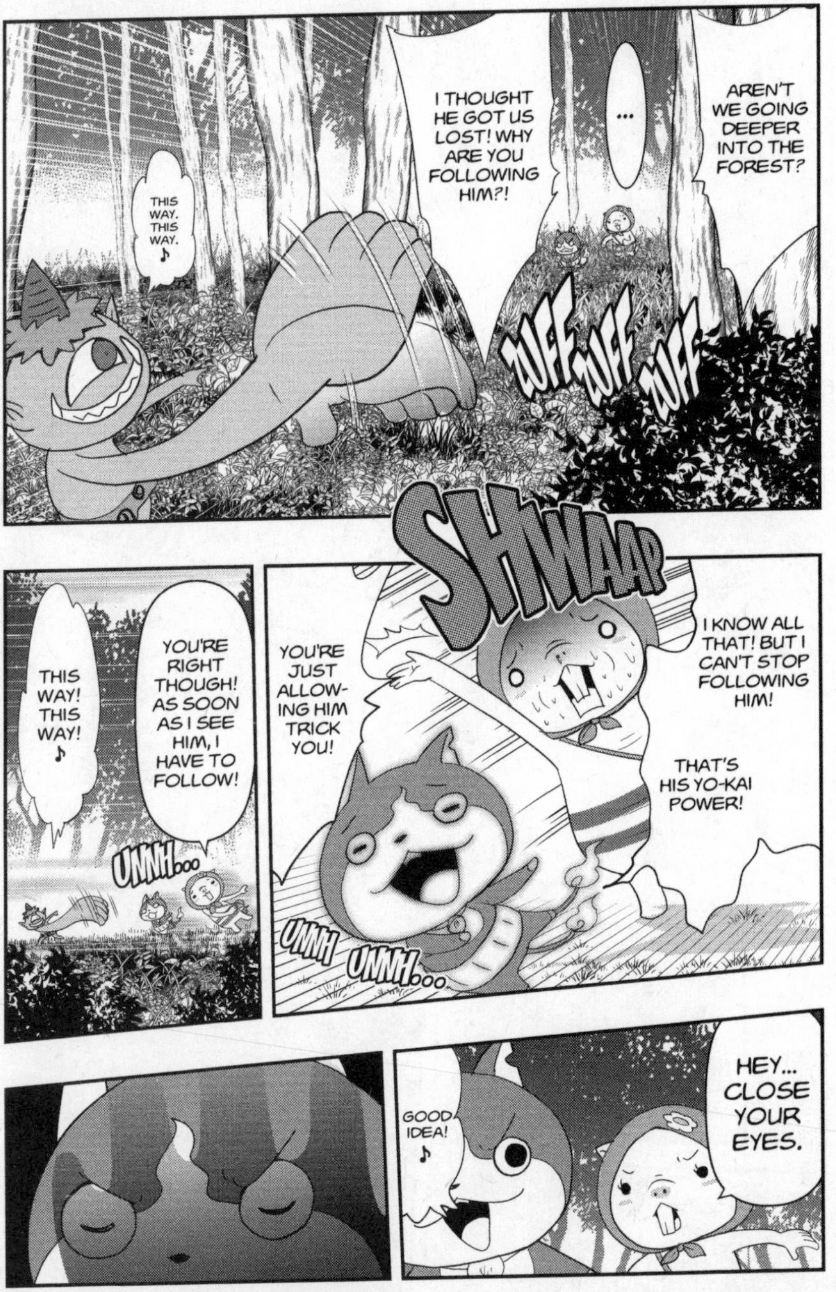
AREN'T WE GOING DEEPER INTO THE FOREST?
...
I THOUGHT HE GOT US LOST! WHY ARE YOU FOLLOWING HIM?!
THIS WAY. THIS WAY. ♪
ZUFF ZUFF ZUFF
SHWAAP
I KNOW ALL THAT! BUT I CAN'T STOP FOLLOWING HIM!
YOU'RE JUST ALLOW-ING HIM TRICK YOU!
THAT'S HIS YO-KAI POWER!
UNNH UNNH...
YOU'RE RIGHT THOUGH! AS SOON AS I SEE HIM, I HAVE TO FOLLOW!
THIS WAY! THIS WAY! ♪
UNNH...
HEY... CLOSE YOUR EYES.
GOOD IDEA! ♪

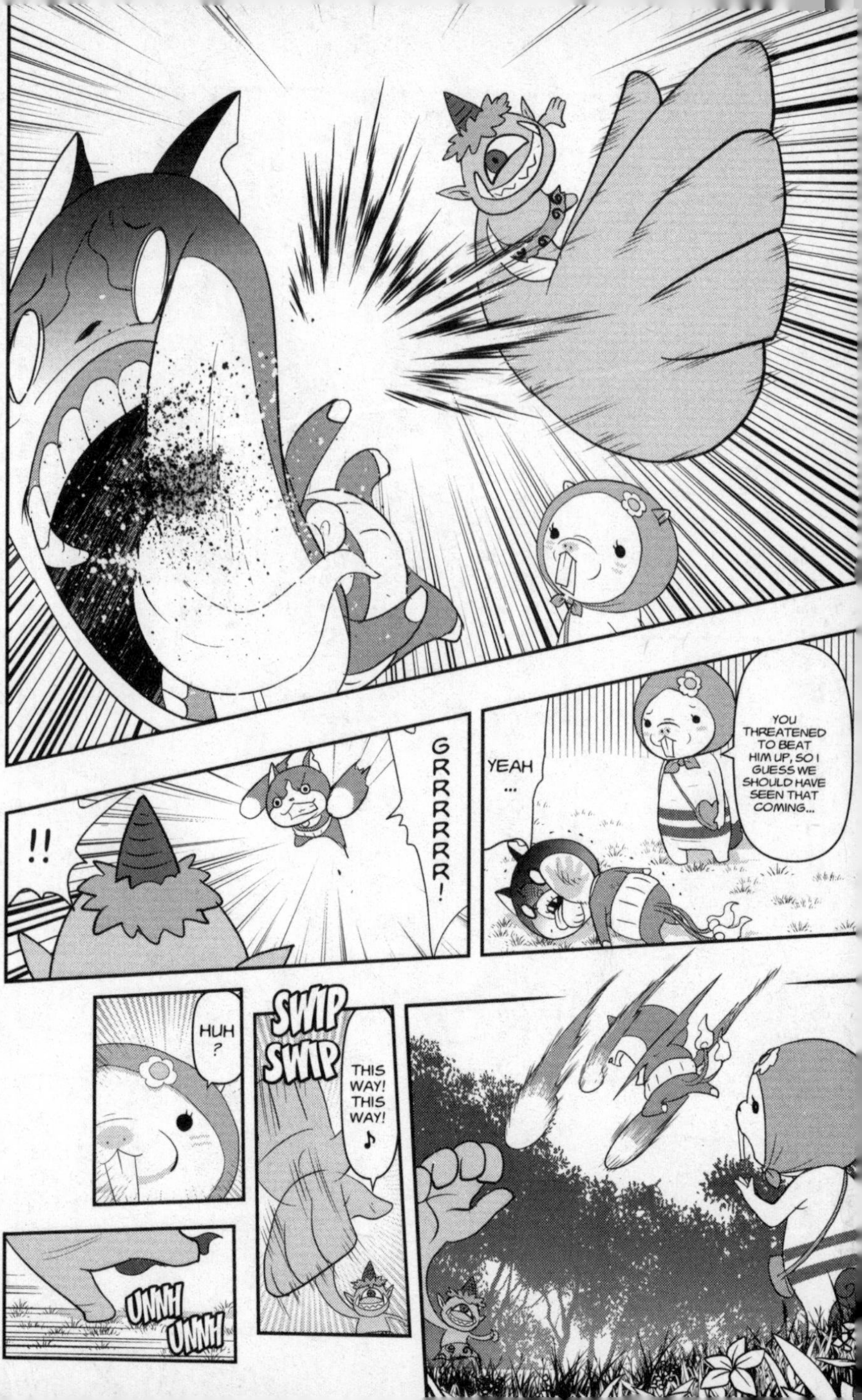
YOU THREATENED TO BEAT HIM UP, SO I GUESS WE SHOULD HAVE SEEN THAT COMING...
YEAH ...
GRRRRRR!
!!
SWIP SWIP
THIS WAY! THIS WAY! ♪
HUH ?
UNNH UNNH

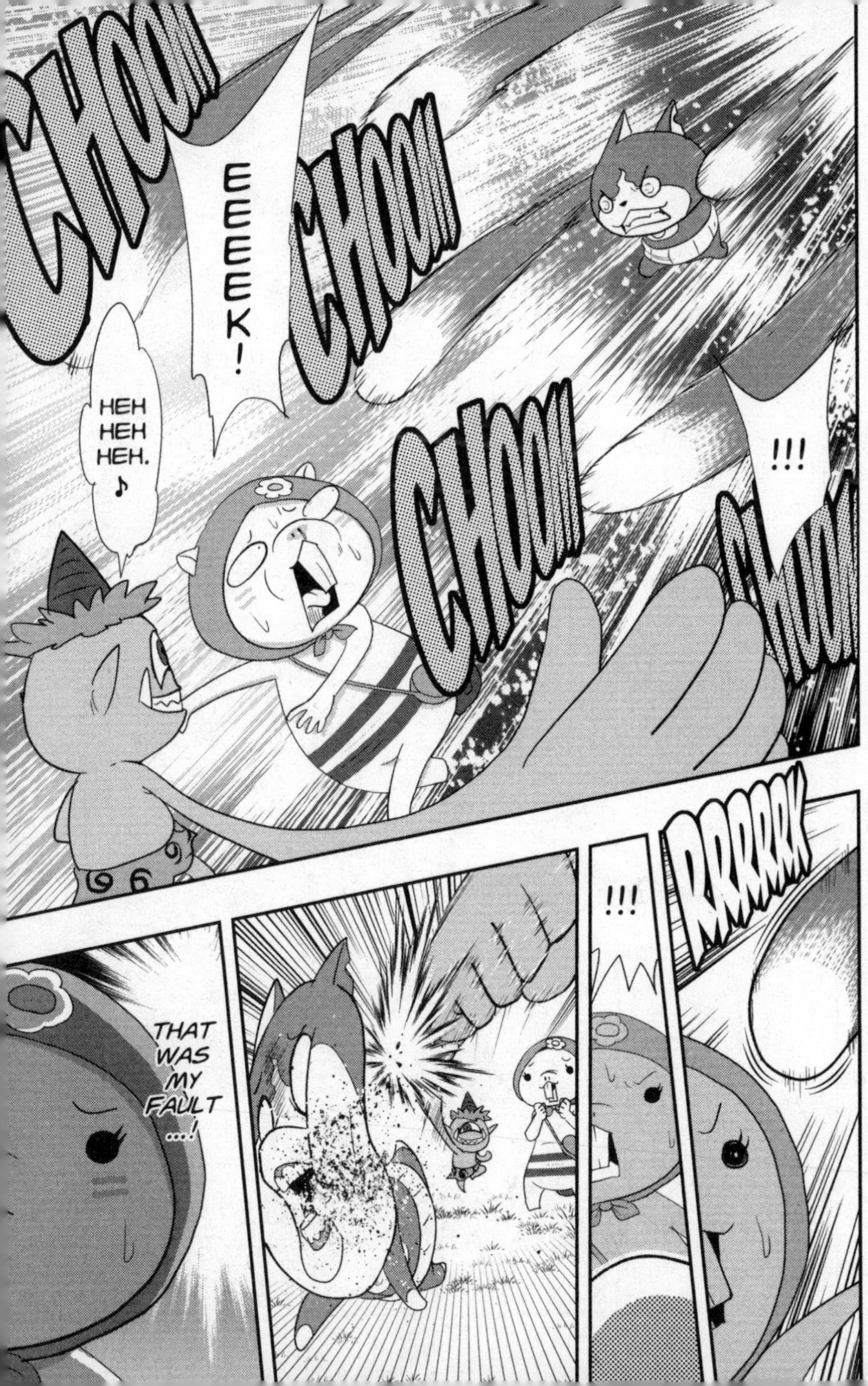
!!!
CHOO!!
CHOO!!
EEEEEK!
HEH HEH HEH. ♪
CHOO!!
RRRRRK
!!!
THAT WAS MY FAULT ...!

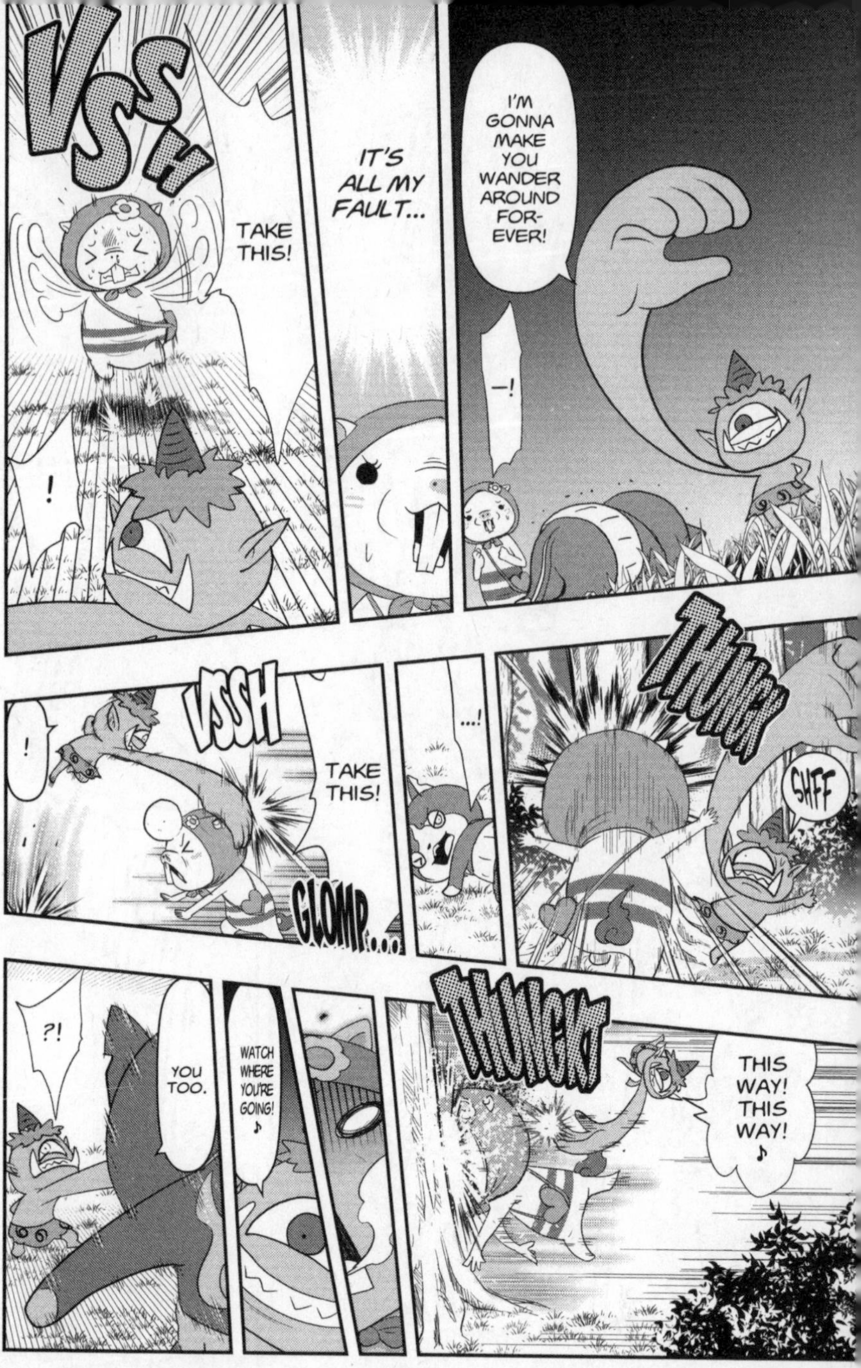
I'M GONNA MAKE YOU WANDER AROUND FOR-EVER!
—!
IT'S ALL MY FAULT...
VSSH
TAKE THIS!
!
THUNK
SHFF
...!
VSSH
TAKE THIS!
!
GLOMP...
THUNCK!
THIS WAY! THIS WAY! ♪
WATCH WHERE YOU'RE GOING! ♪
YOU TOO.
?!

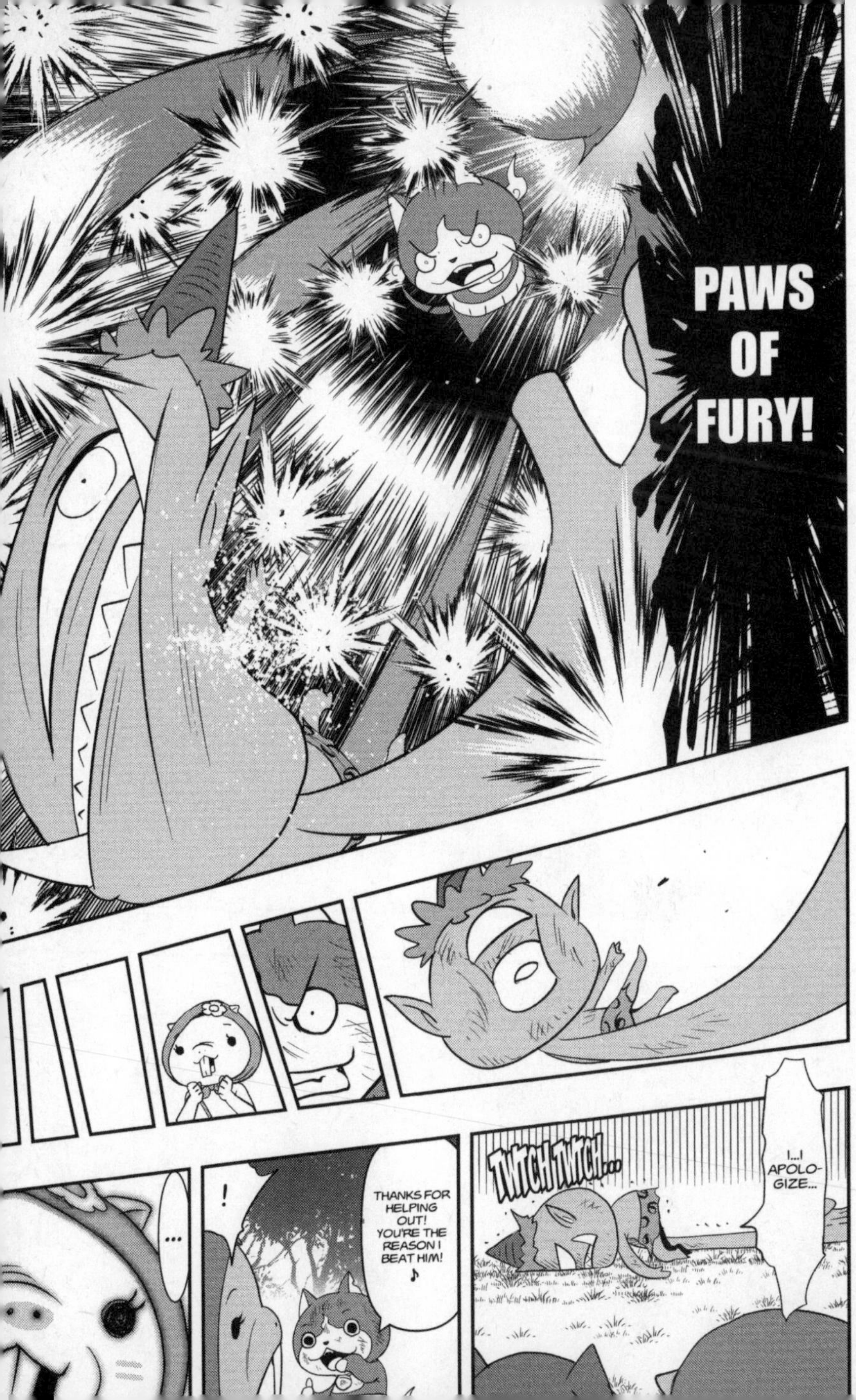
PAWS OF FURY!
I...I APOLO-GIZE...
TWITCH TWITCH...
THANKS FOR HELPING OUT! YOU'RE THE REASON I BEAT HIM! ♪
!
...

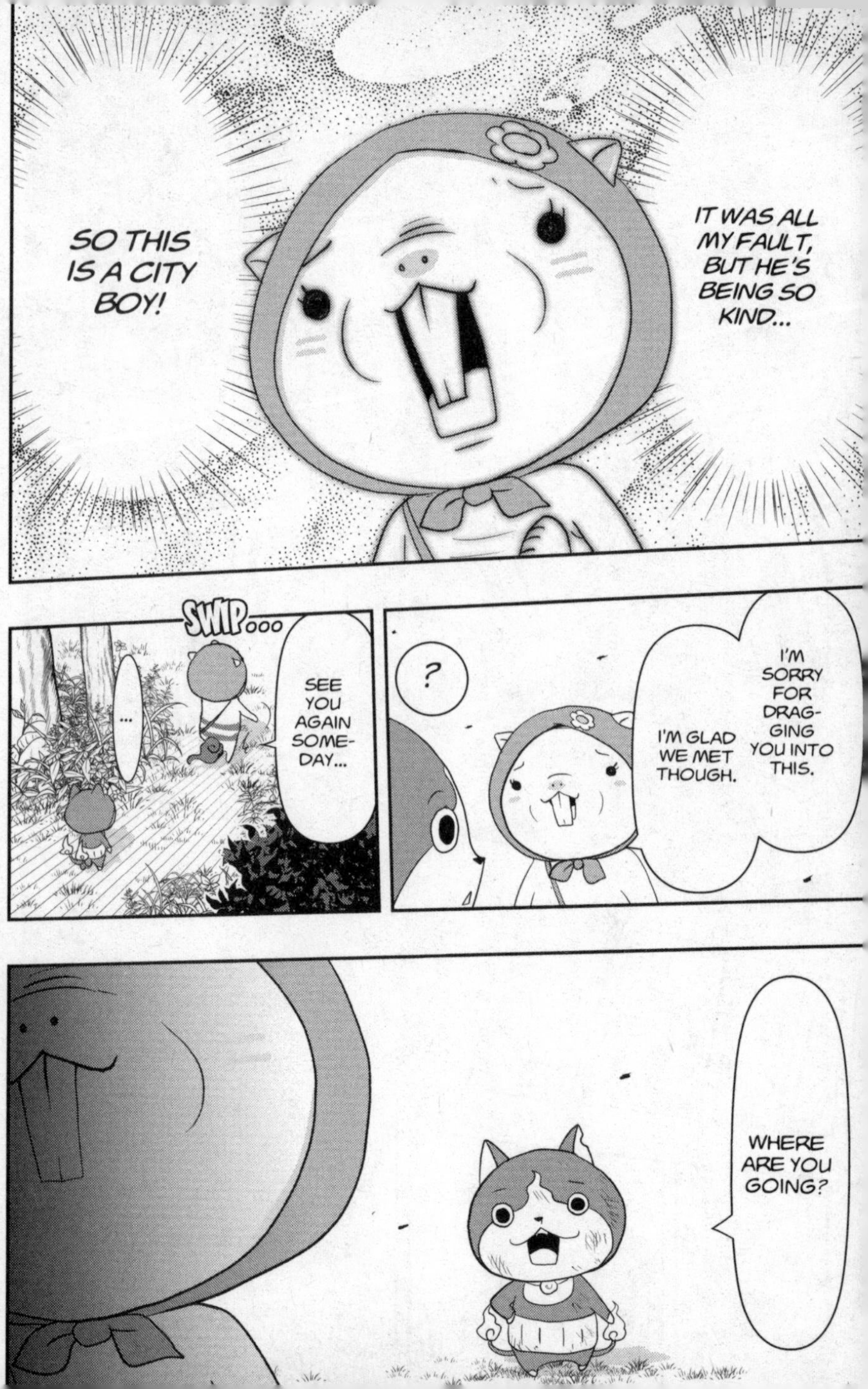
IT WAS ALL MY FAULT, BUT HE'S BEING SO KIND...
SO THIS IS A CITY BOY!
I'M SORRY FOR DRAG-GING YOU INTO THIS.
I'M GLAD WE MET THOUGH.
?
SEE YOU AGAIN SOME-DAY...
SWIPooo
...
WHERE ARE YOU GOING?

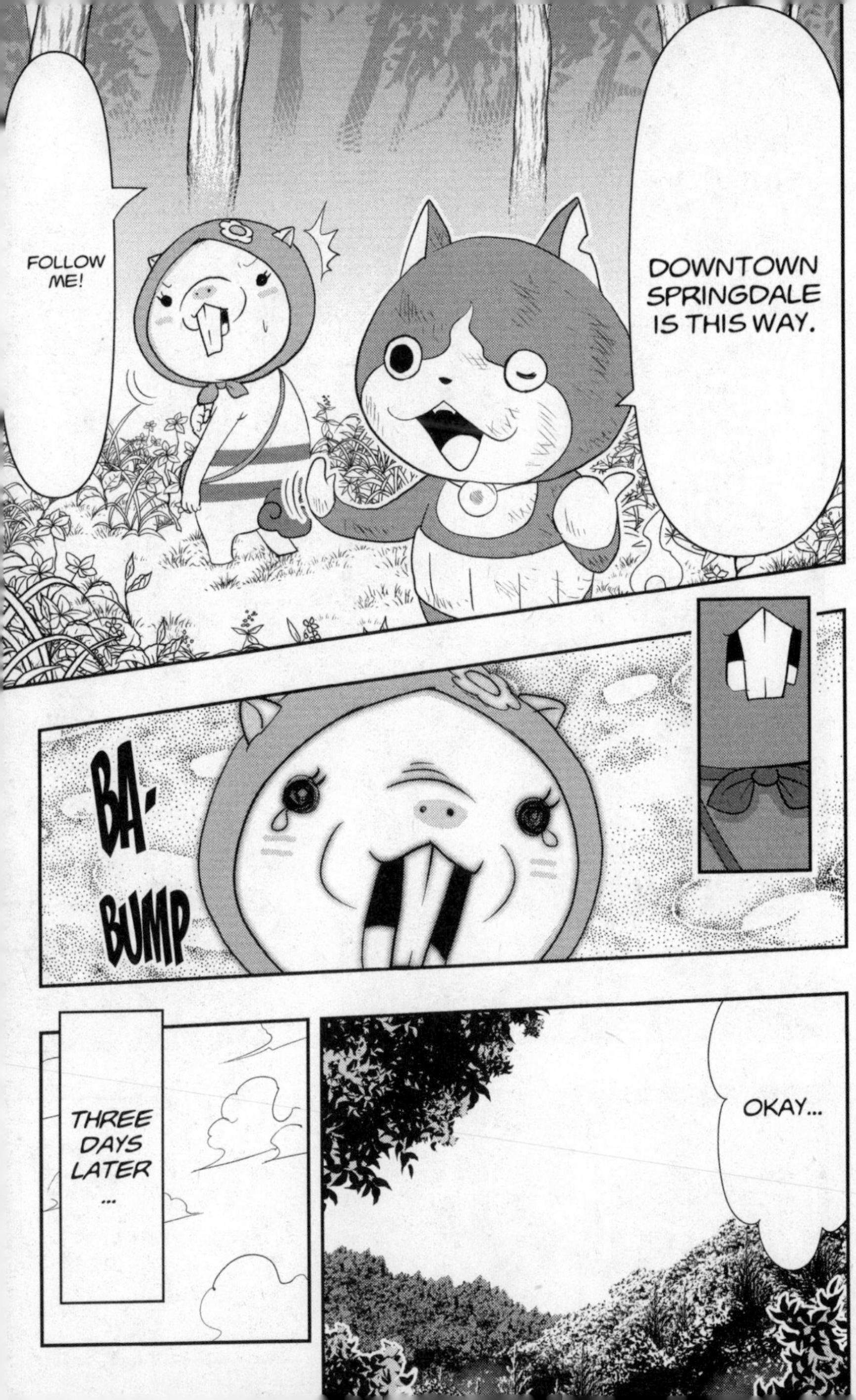
DOWNTOWN SPRINGDALE IS THIS WAY.
FOLLOW ME!
BA-BUMP
OKAY...
THREE DAYS LATER ...

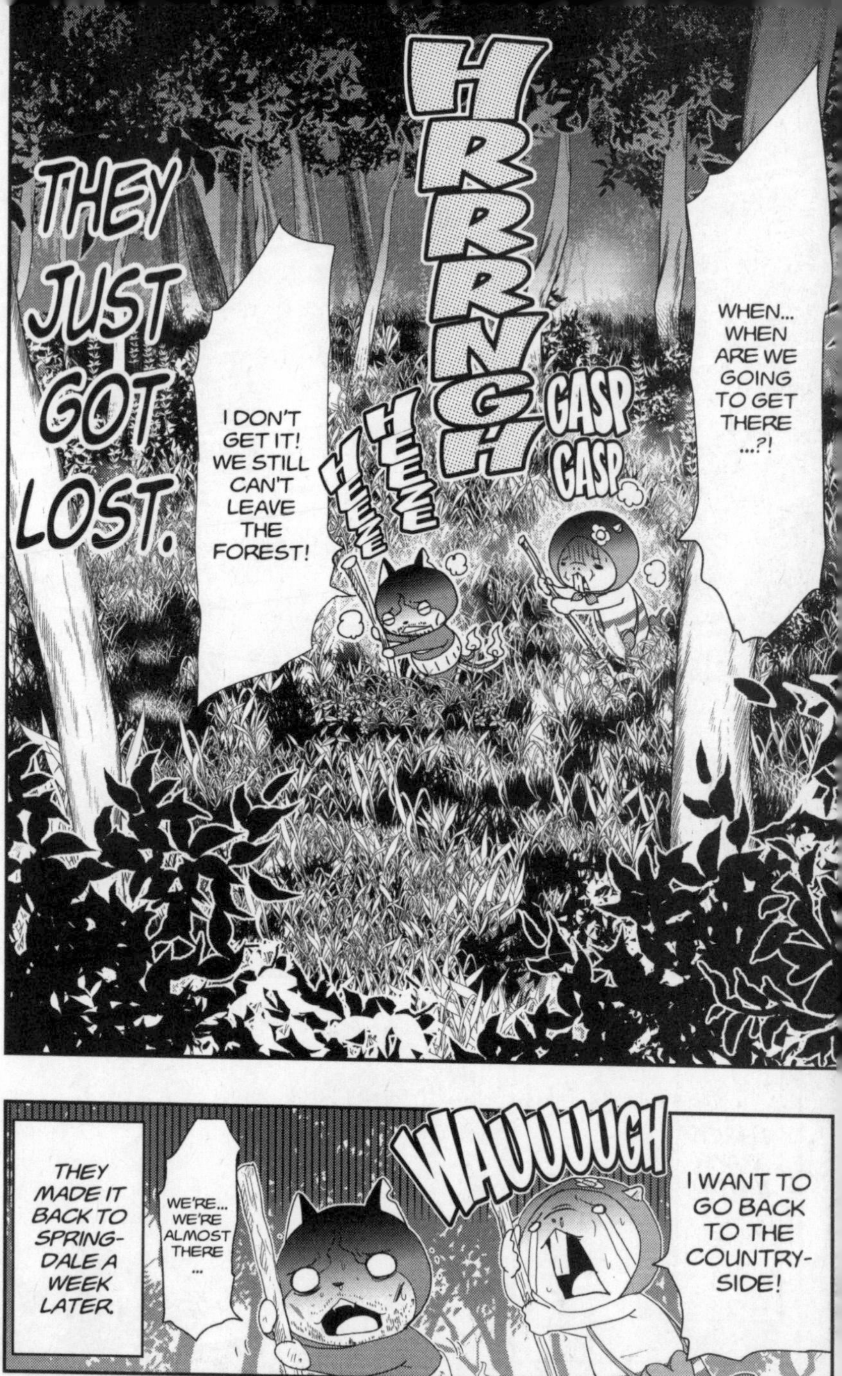
WHEN... WHEN ARE WE GOING TO GET THERE ...?!
GASP GASP
HRRNGH
HEEZE HEEZE
I DON'T GET IT! WE STILL CAN'T LEAVE THE FOREST!
THEY JUST GOT LOST.
I WANT TO GO BACK TO THE COUNTRY-SIDE!
WAUUUUGH
WE'RE... WE'RE ALMOST THERE ...
THEY MADE IT BACK TO SPRING-DALE A WEEK LATER.

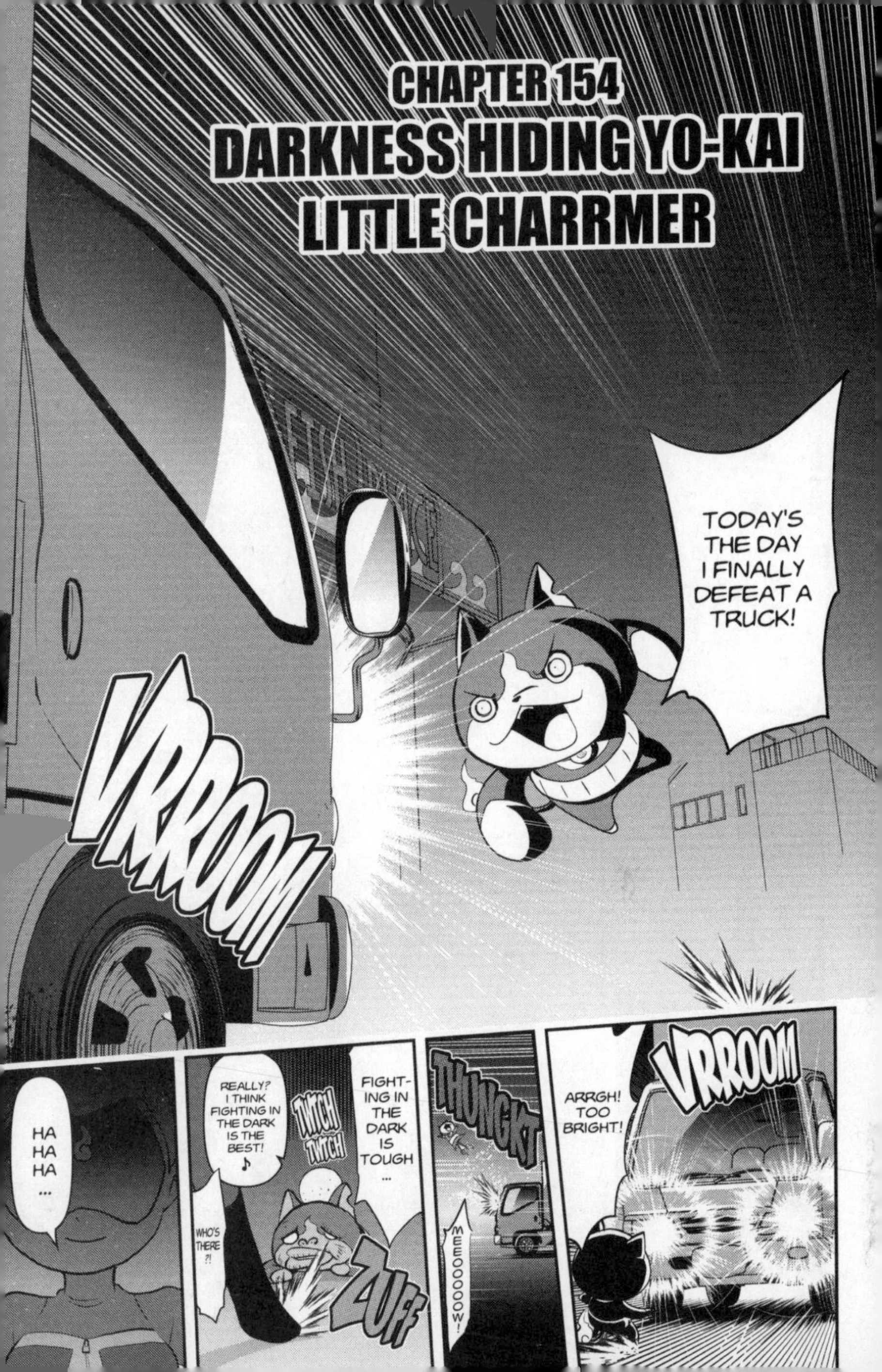
CHAPTER 154
DARKNESS HIDING YO-KAI
LITTLE CHARRMER
TODAY'S THE DAY I FINALLY DEFEAT A TRUCK!
VRROOM
VRROOM
ARRGH! TOO BRIGHT!
THUNGKT
MEEOOOOOW!
FIGHT-ING IN THE DARK IS TOUGH ...
TWITCH TWITCH
REALLY? I THINK FIGHTING IN THE DARK IS THE BEST! ♪
WHO'S THERE ?!
ZUFF
HA HA HA ...

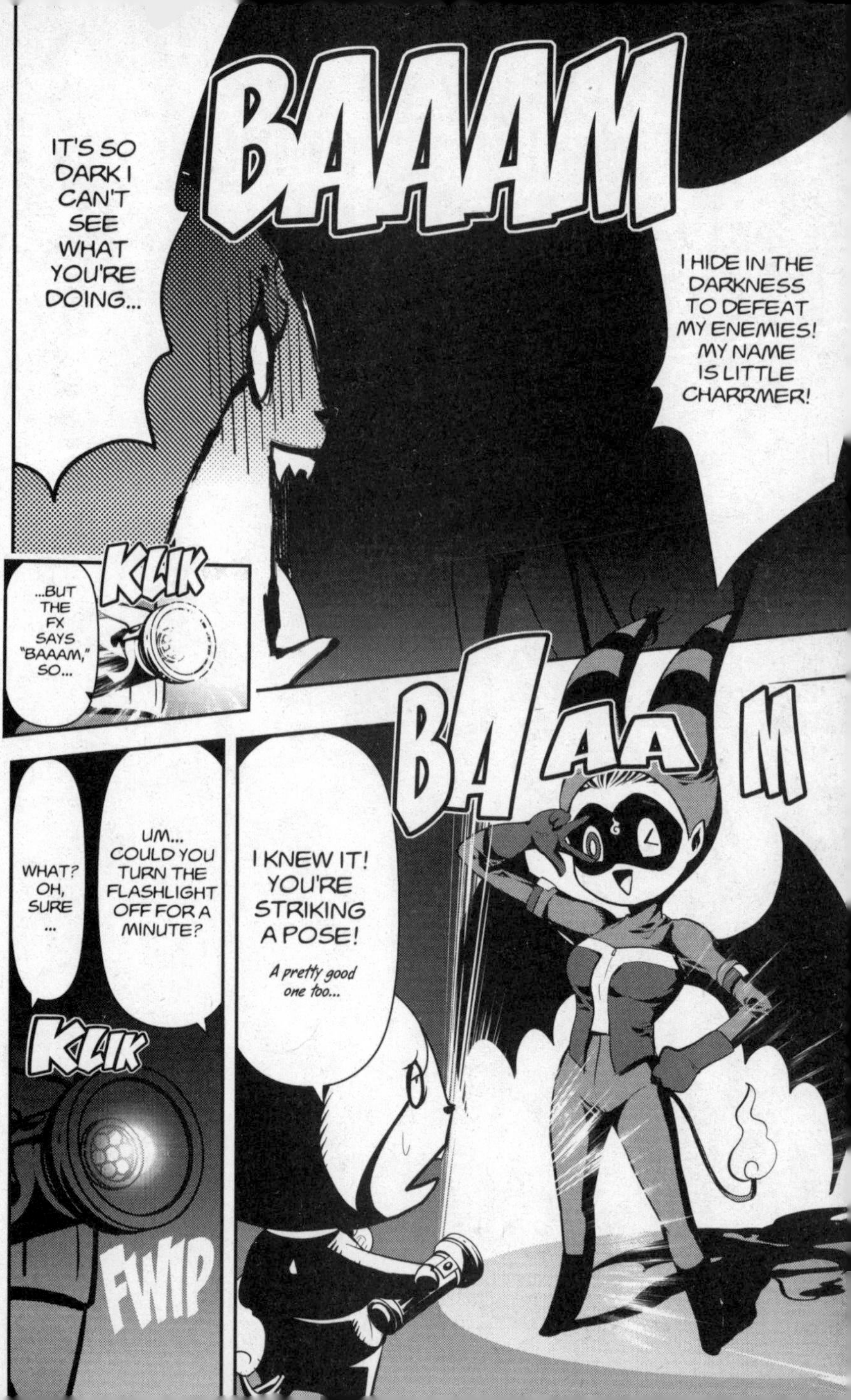
BAAAM
I HIDE IN THE DARKNESS TO DEFEAT MY ENEMIES! MY NAME IS LITTLE CHARRMER!
IT'S SO DARK I CAN'T SEE WHAT YOU'RE DOING...
KLIK
...BUT THE FX SAYS "BAAAM," SO...
BAAAM
I KNEW IT! YOU'RE STRIKING A POSE!
A pretty good one too...
UM... COULD YOU TURN THE FLASHLIGHT OFF FOR A MINUTE?
WHAT? OH, SURE ...
KLIK
FWIP

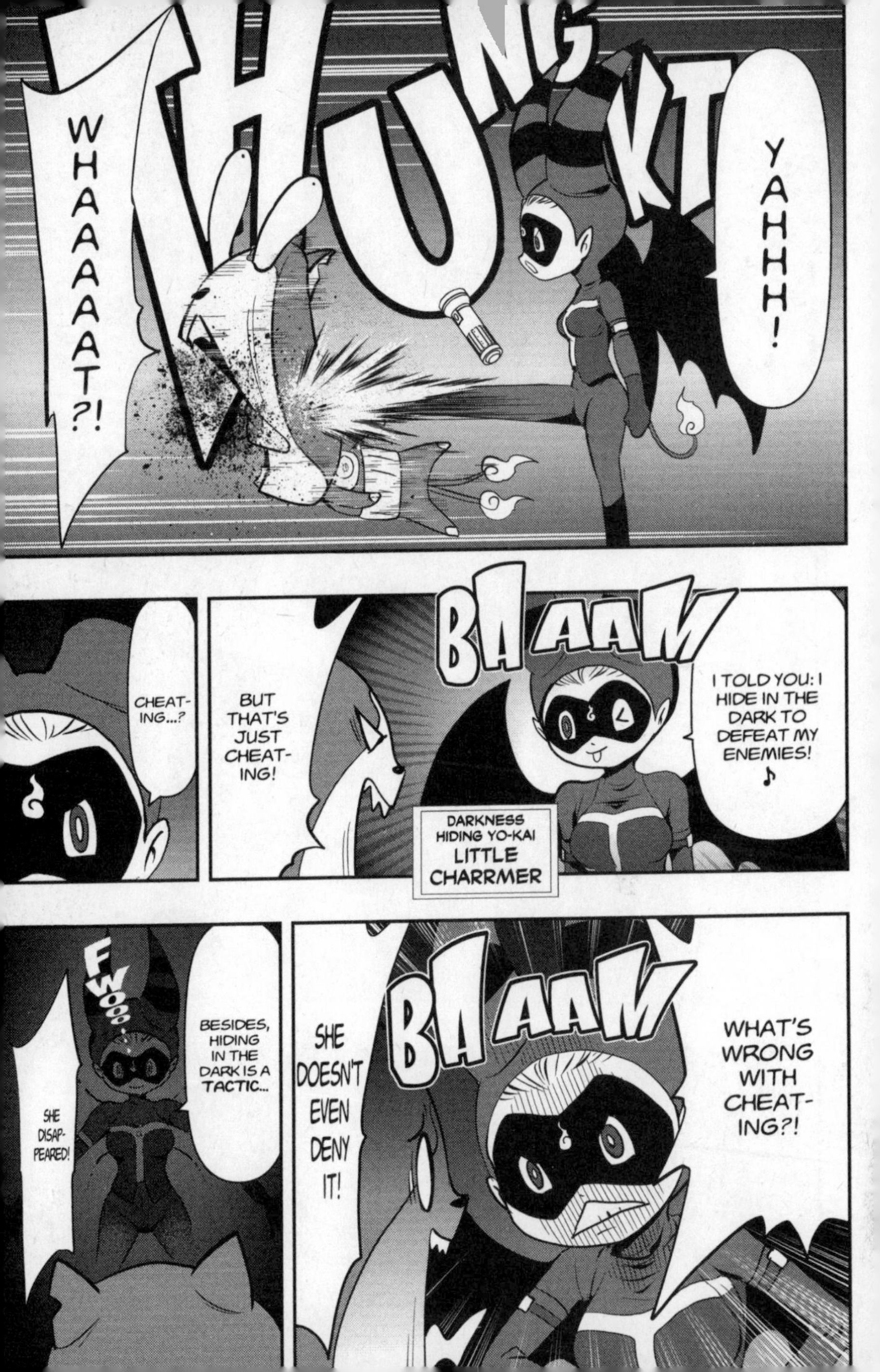
THUNGK
YAHHH!
WHAAAAAAT?!
BAAAM
I TOLD YOU: I HIDE IN THE DARK TO DEFEAT MY ENEMIES! ♪
BUT THAT'S JUST CHEAT-ING!
DARKNESS HIDING YO-KAI LITTLE CHARRMER
CHEAT-ING...?
BAAAM
WHAT'S WRONG WITH CHEAT-ING?!
SHE DOESN'T EVEN DENY IT!
BESIDES, HIDING IN THE DARK IS A TACTIC...
FWOOO
SHE DISAP-PEARED!

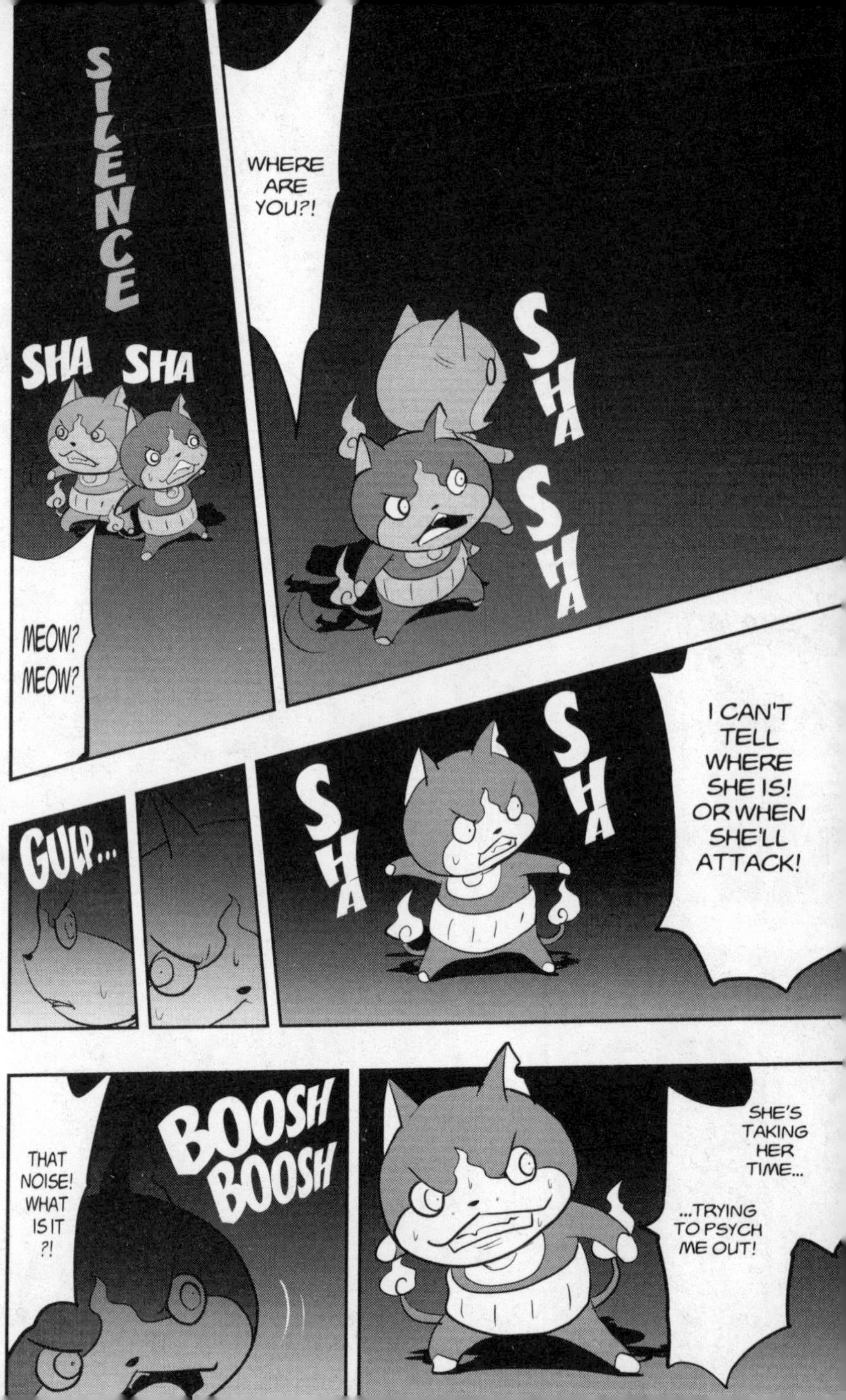
WHERE ARE YOU?!
SHA SHA
SHA SHA
SILENCE
SHA SHA
MEOW? MEOW?
I CAN'T TELL WHERE SHE IS! OR WHEN SHE'LL ATTACK!
SHA SHA
SHA SHA
GULP...
SHE'S TAKING HER TIME...
...TRYING TO PSYCH ME OUT!
BOOSH BOOSH
THAT NOISE! WHAT IS IT ?!

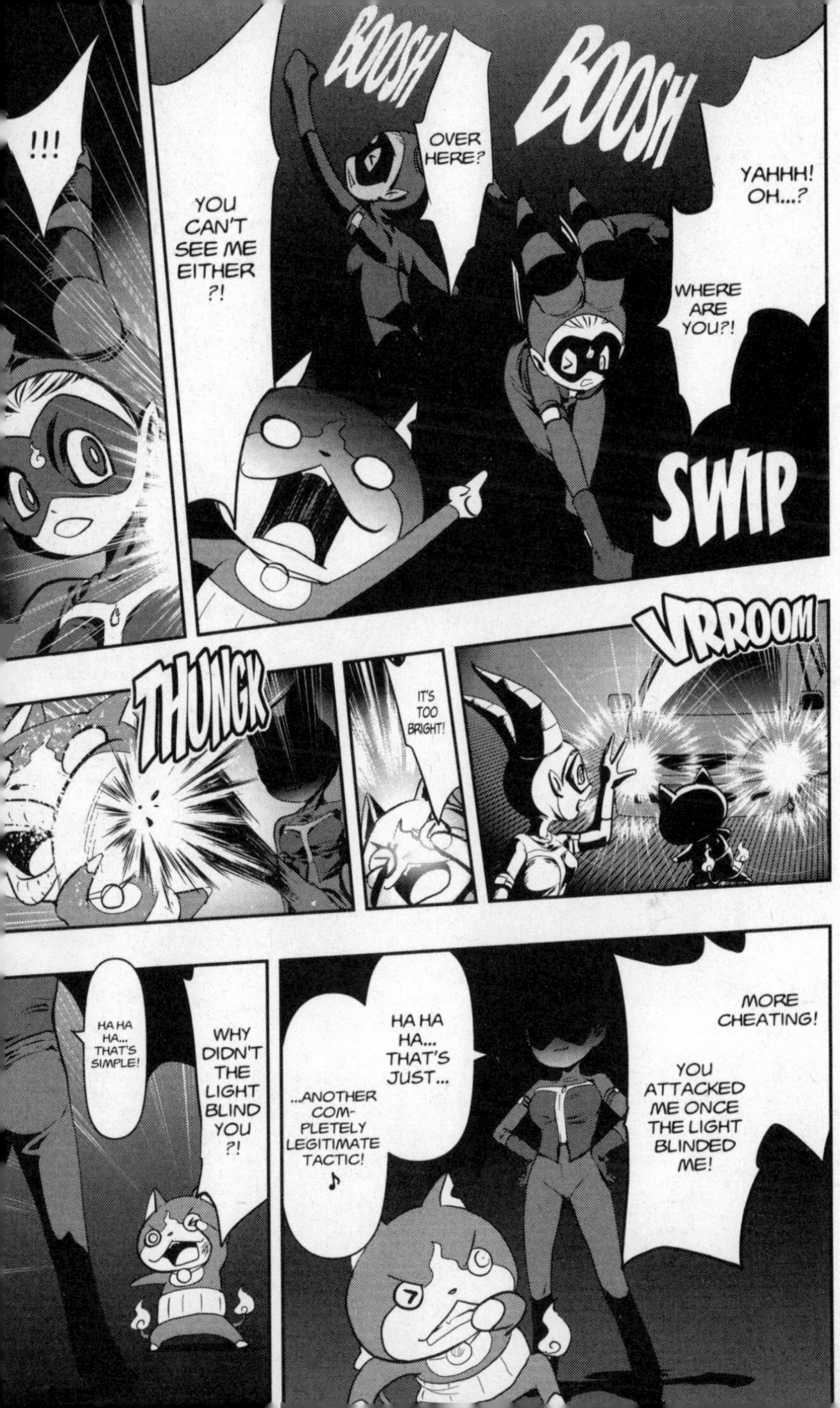
YAHHH! OH...?
BOOSH
BOOSH
OVER HERE?
WHERE ARE YOU?!
SWIP
YOU CAN'T SEE ME EITHER ?!
!!!
VRROOM
IT'S TOO BRIGHT!
THUNGK
MORE CHEATING!
YOU ATTACKED ME ONCE THE LIGHT BLINDED ME!
HA HA HA... THAT'S JUST...
...ANOTHER COM-PLETELY LEGITIMATE TACTIC! ♪
WHY DIDN'T THE LIGHT BLIND YOU ?!
HA HA HA... THAT'S SIMPLE!

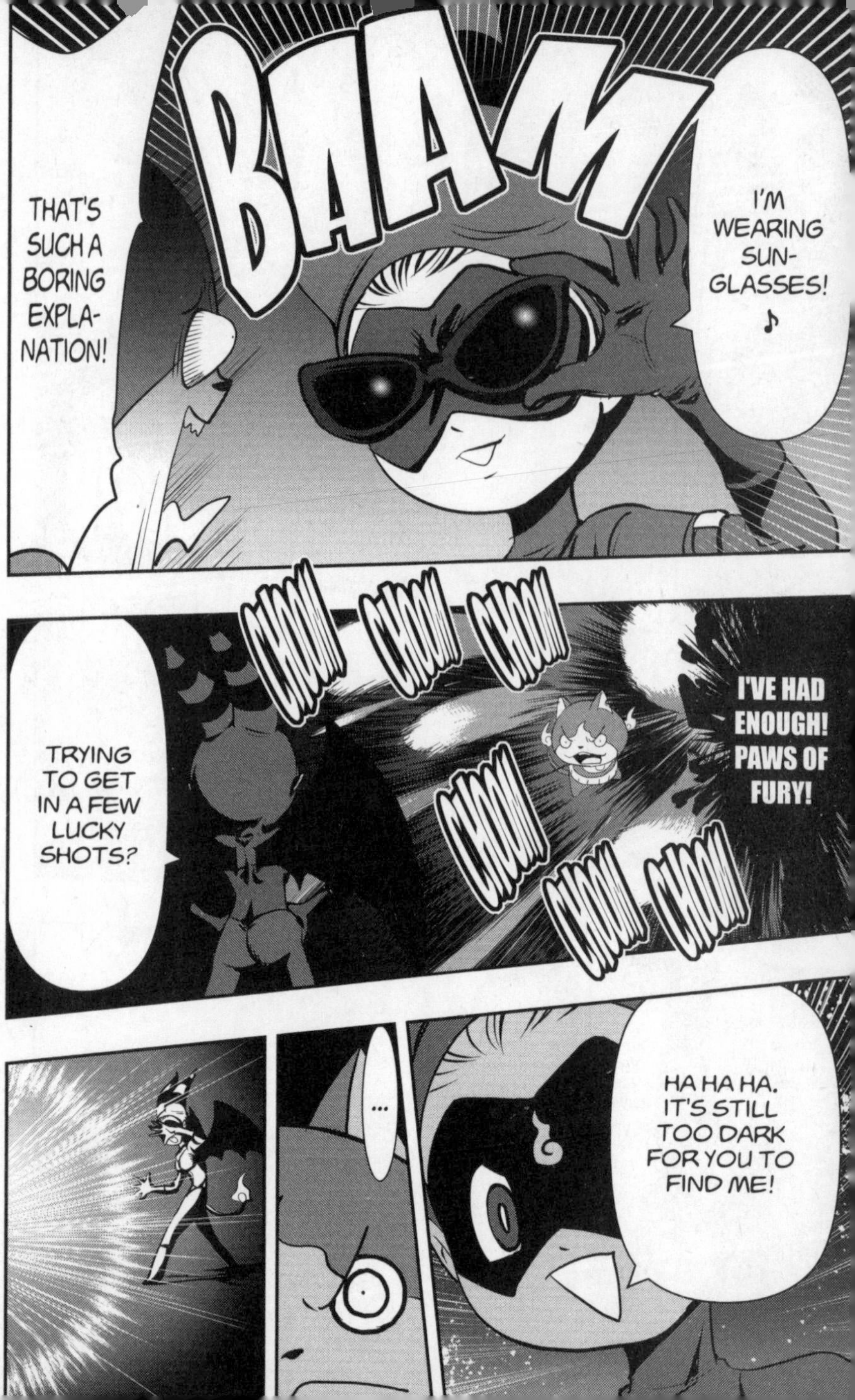
BAAM
I'M WEARING SUN-GLASSES! ♪
THAT'S SUCH A BORING EXPLANATION!
I'VE HAD ENOUGH! PAWS OF FURY!
CHOOM CHOOM CHOOM
CHOOM
CHOOM CHOOM
TRYING TO GET IN A FEW LUCKY SHOTS?
HA HA HA. IT'S STILL TOO DARK FOR YOU TO FIND ME!
...

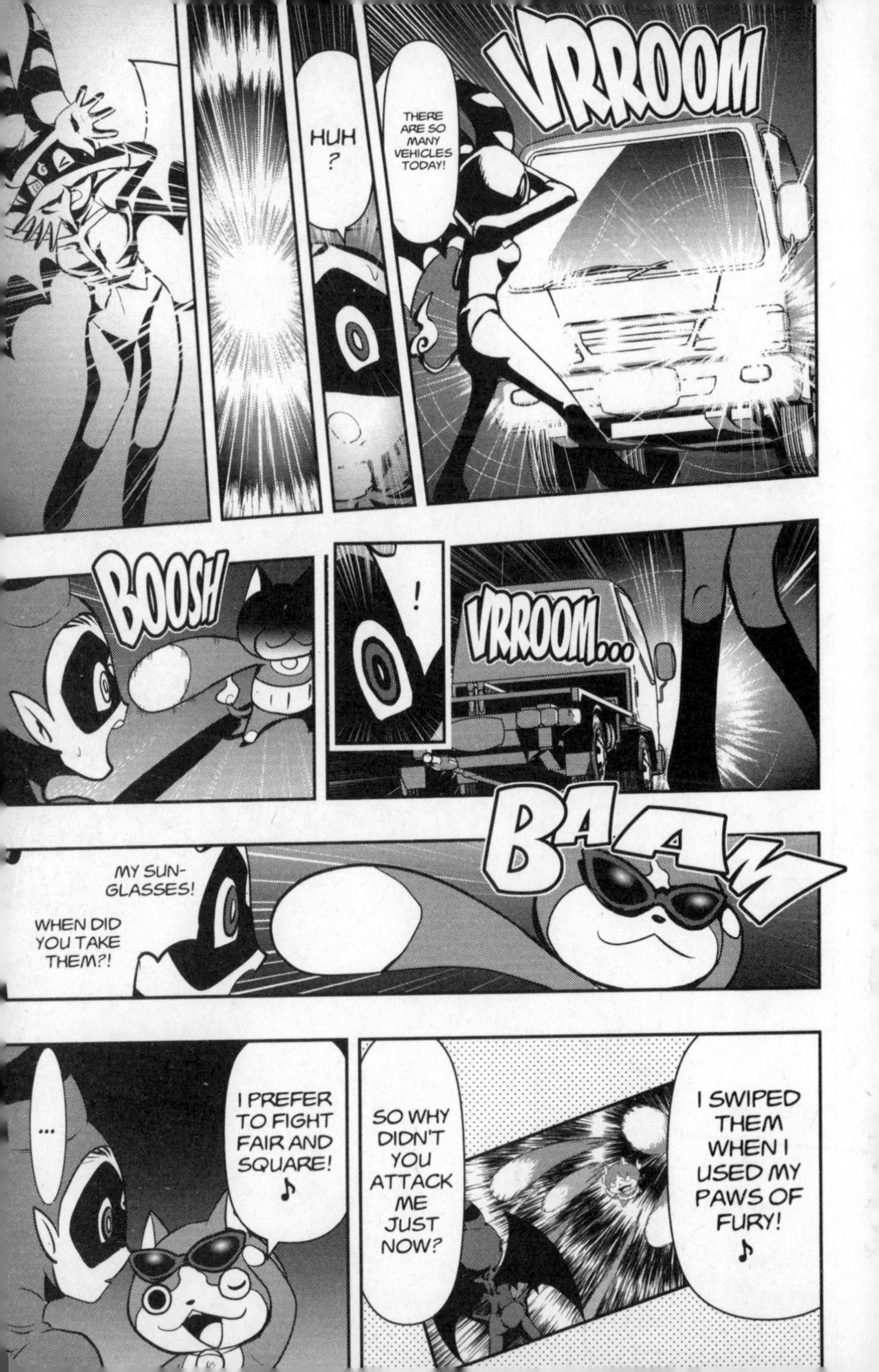
VRROOM
THERE ARE SO MANY VEHICLES TODAY!
HUH ?
VRROOM...
!
BOOSH
BAAM
MY SUN-GLASSES!
WHEN DID YOU TAKE THEM?!
I SWIPED THEM WHEN I USED MY PAWS OF FURY! ♪
SO WHY DIDN'T YOU ATTACK ME JUST NOW?
I PREFER TO FIGHT FAIR AND SQUARE! ♪
...

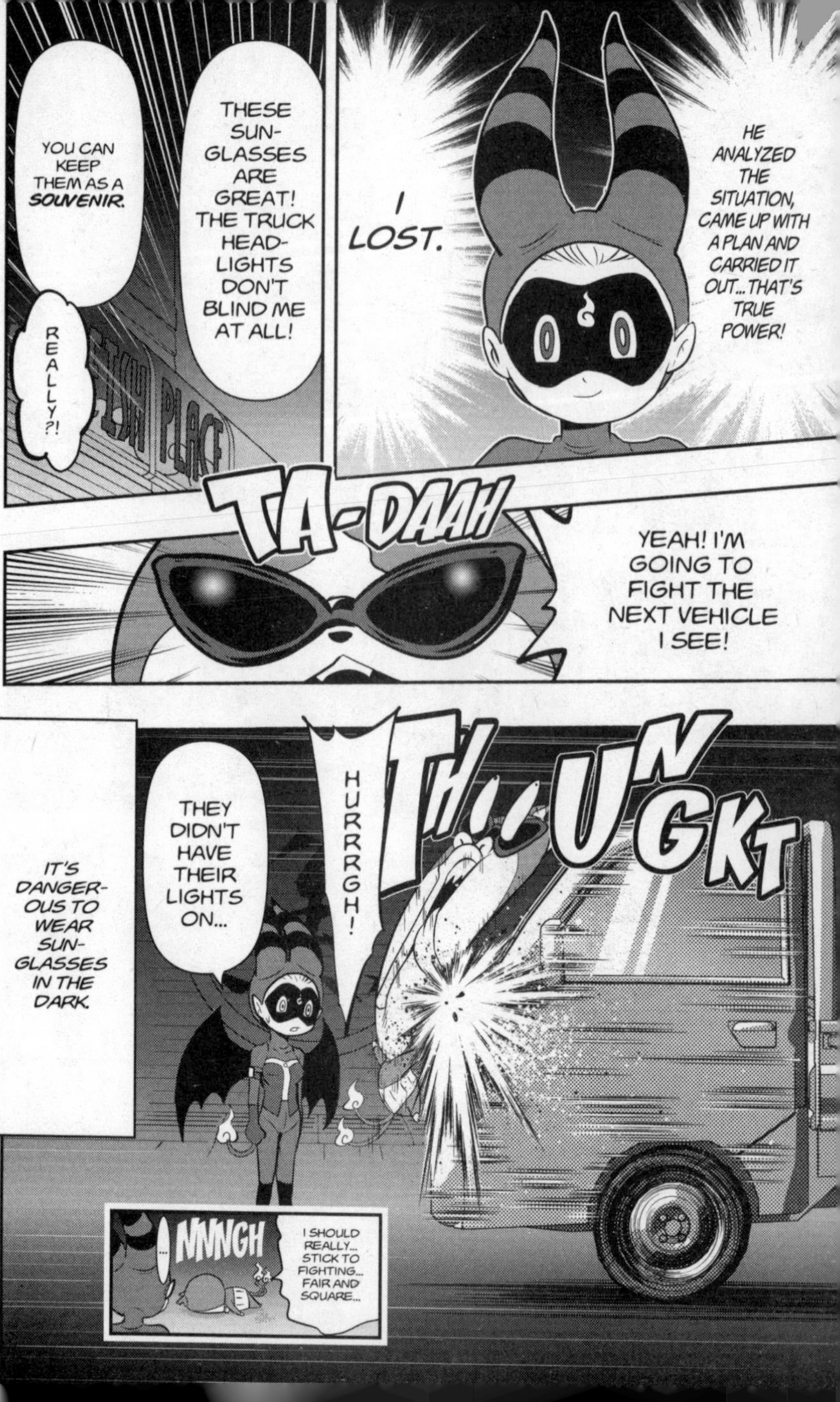
HE ANALYZED THE SITUATION, CAME UP WITH A PLAN AND CARRIED IT OUT...THAT'S TRUE POWER!
I LOST.
THESE SUN-GLASSES ARE GREAT! THE TRUCK HEAD-LIGHTS DON'T BLIND ME AT ALL!
YOU CAN KEEP THEM AS A *SOUVENIR.*
REALLY?!
PLACE
TA-DAAH
YEAH! I'M GOING TO FIGHT THE NEXT VEHICLE I SEE!
THUNGKT
HURRRGH!
THEY DIDN'T HAVE THEIR LIGHTS ON...
IT'S DANGER-OUS TO WEAR SUN-GLASSES IN THE DARK.
I SHOULD REALLY... STICK TO FIGHTING... FAIR AND SQUARE...
NNNGH
...

CHAPTER 155
HUNGRY YO-KAI SUPERSIZE GRAMPS

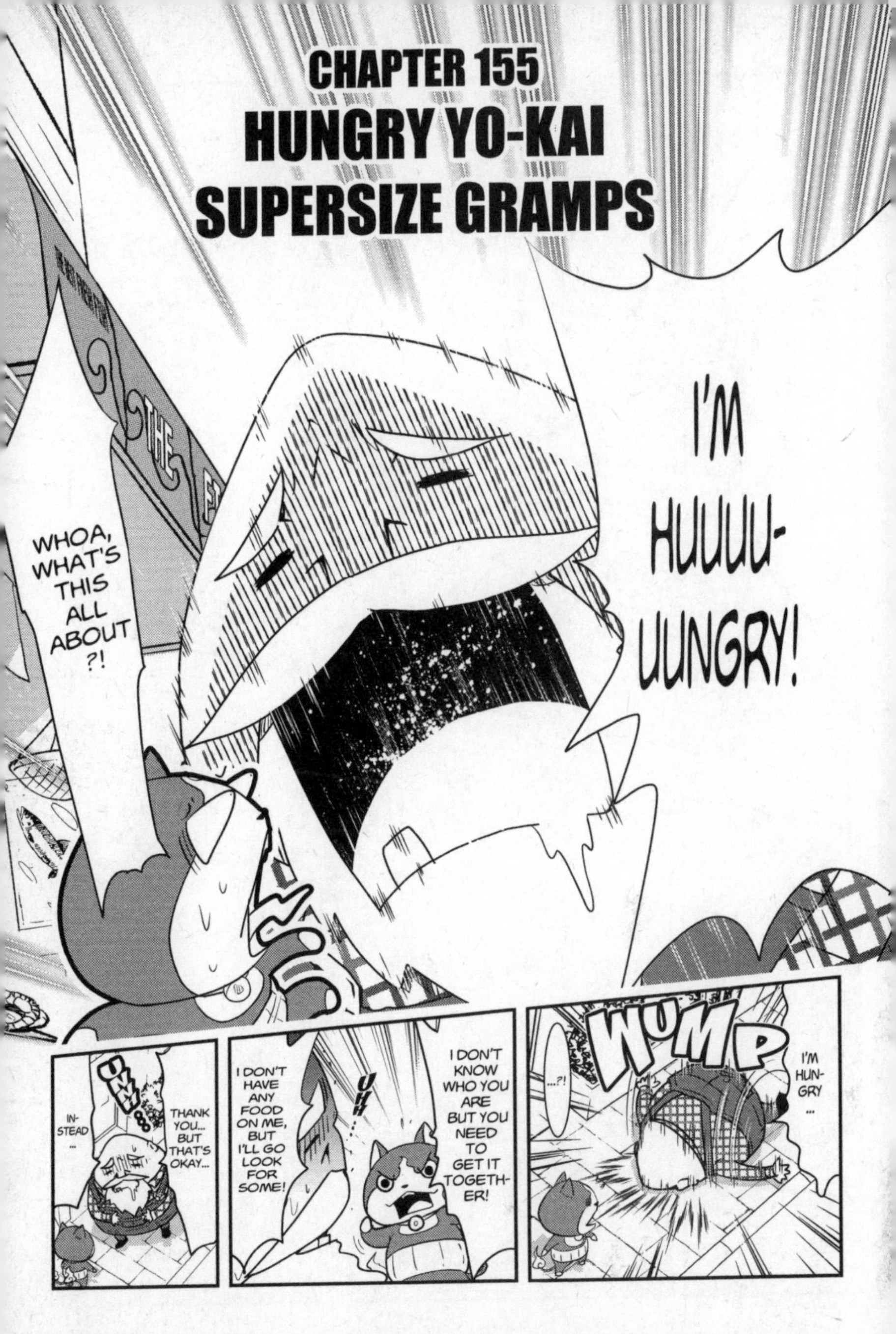
I'M HUUUU-UUNGRY!
WHOA, WHAT'S THIS ALL ABOUT?!
WUMP
I'M HUNGRY...
...?!
I DON'T KNOW WHO YOU ARE BUT YOU NEED TO GET IT TOGETHER!
I DON'T HAVE ANY FOOD ON ME, BUT I'LL GO LOOK FOR SOME!
THANK YOU... BUT THAT'S OKAY...
INSTEAD...

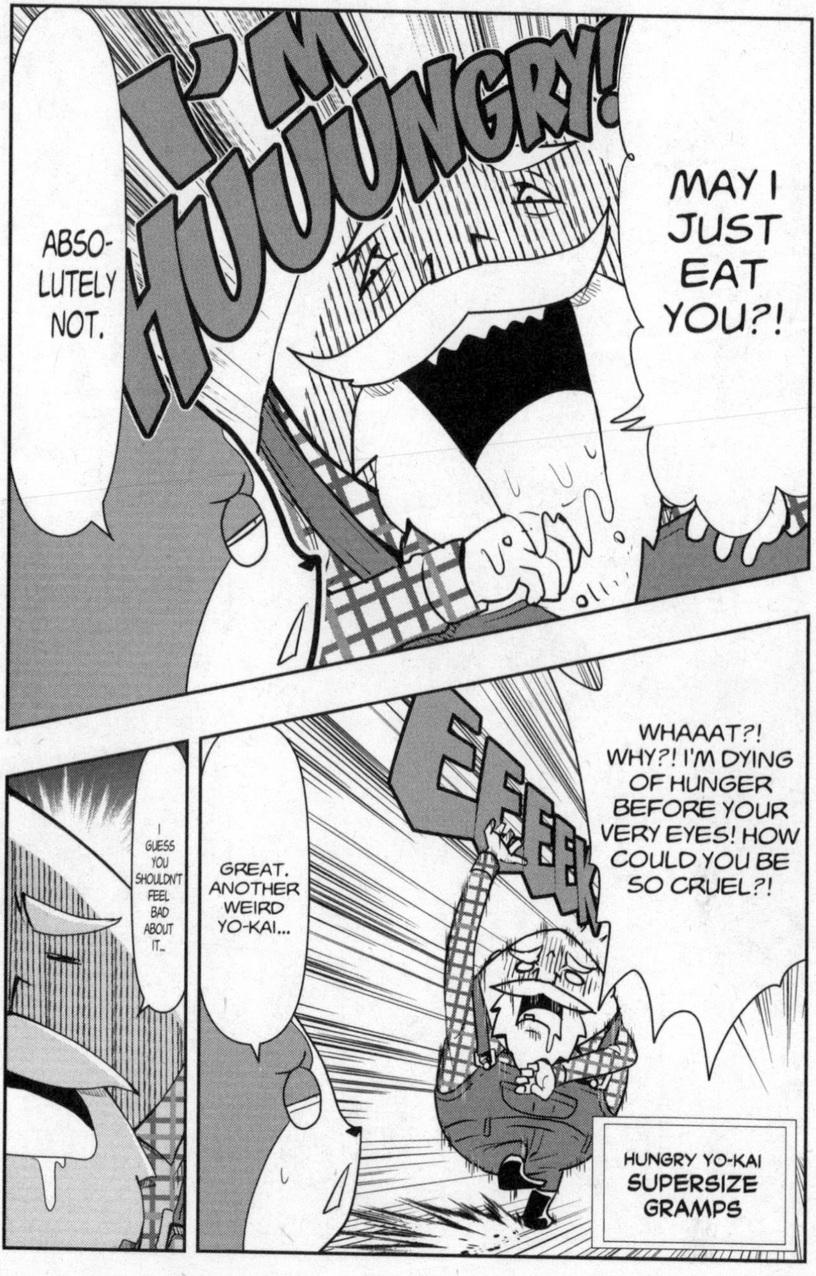
I'M HUUUNGRY!
MAY I JUST EAT YOU?!
ABSO-LUTELY NOT.
EEEEEK
WHAAAT?! WHY?! I'M DYING OF HUNGER BEFORE YOUR VERY EYES! HOW COULD YOU BE SO CRUEL?!
HUNGRY YO-KAI SUPERSIZE GRAMPS
GREAT. ANOTHER WEIRD YO-KAI...
I GUESS YOU SHOULDN'T FEEL BAD ABOUT IT...

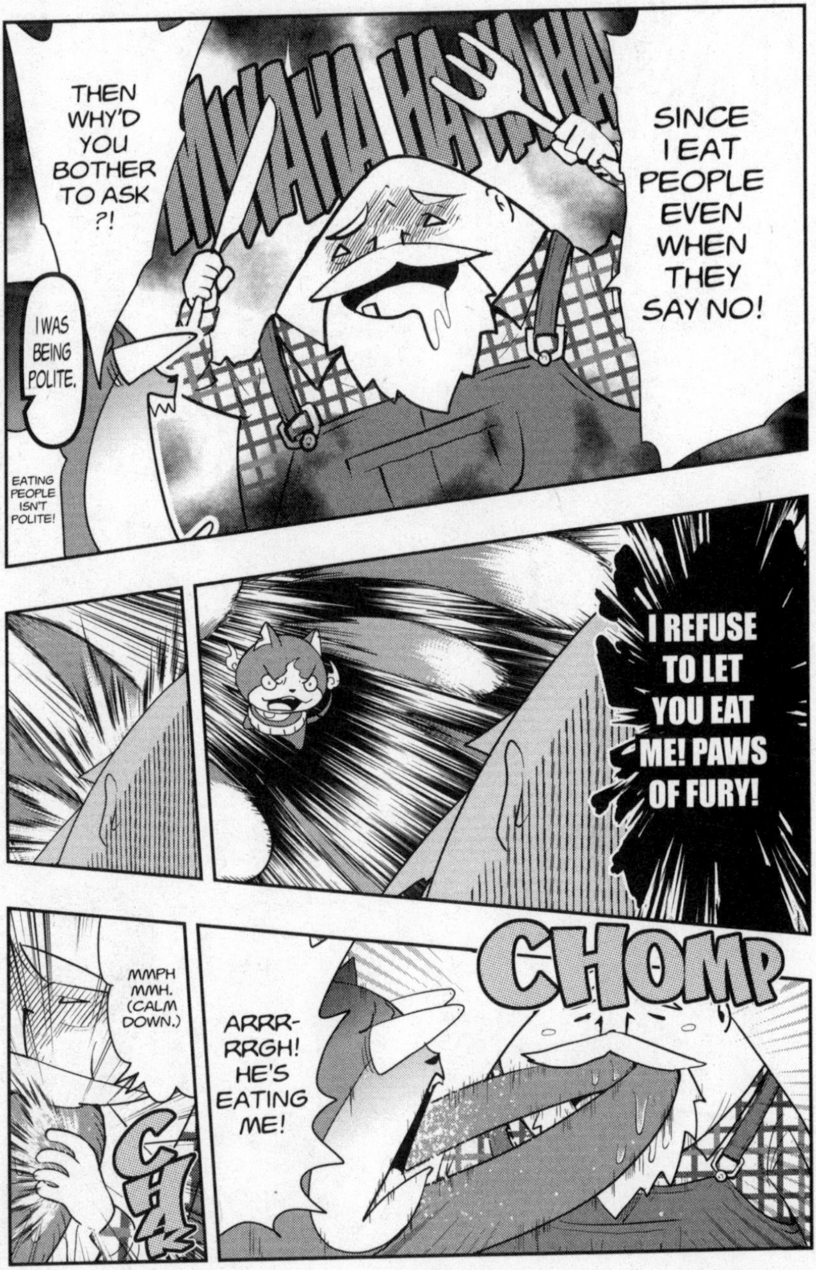
SINCE I EAT PEOPLE EVEN WHEN THEY SAY NO!
THEN WHY'D YOU BOTHER TO ASK ?!
I WAS BEING POLITE.
EATING PEOPLE ISN'T POLITE!
I REFUSE TO LET YOU EAT ME! PAWS OF FURY!
CHOMP
ARRR-RRGH! HE'S EATING ME!
MMPH MMH. (CALM DOWN.)
CHA

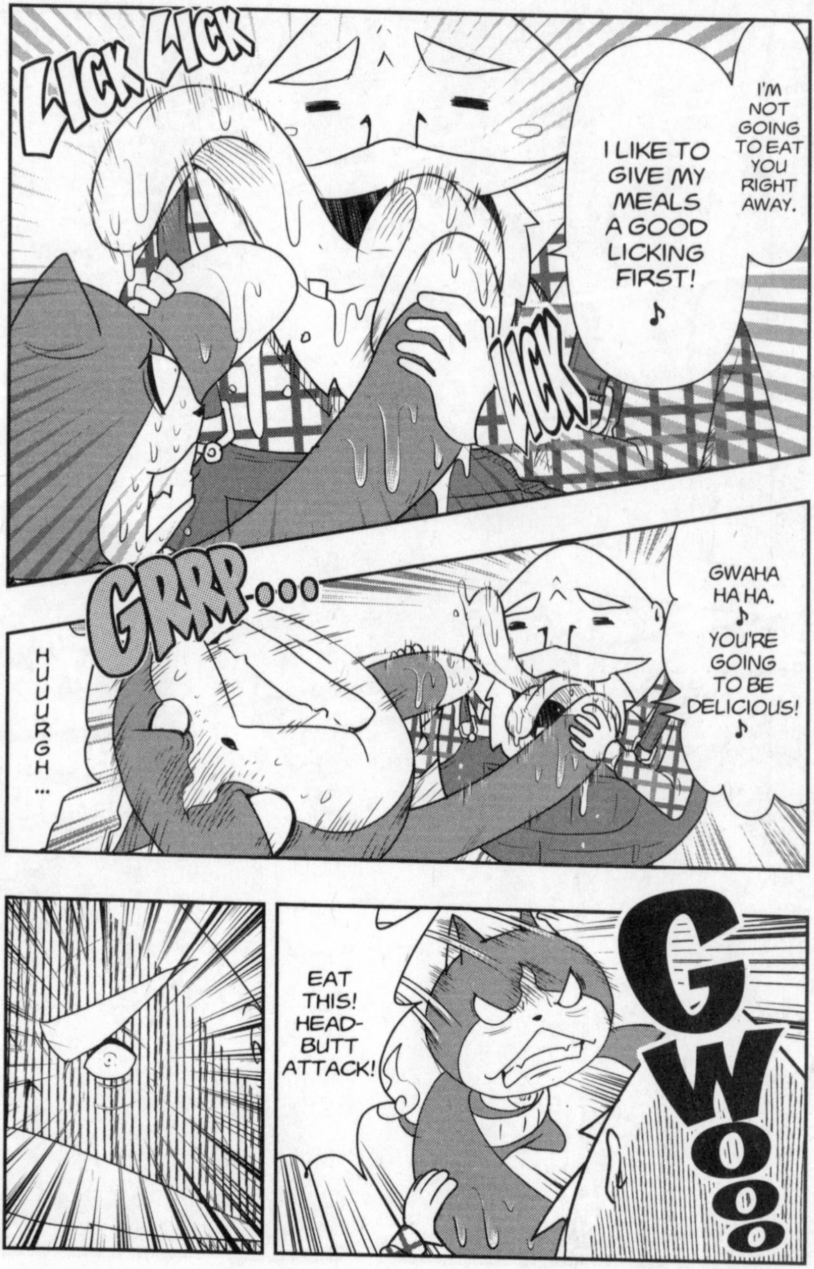
I'M NOT GOING TO EAT YOU RIGHT AWAY.
I LIKE TO GIVE MY MEALS A GOOD LICKING FIRST! ♪
LICK LICK
LICK
GWAHA HA HA. ♪ YOU'RE GOING TO BE DELICIOUS! ♪
GRRP-ooo
HUUURGH...
GWOOO
EAT THIS! HEAD-BUTT ATTACK!

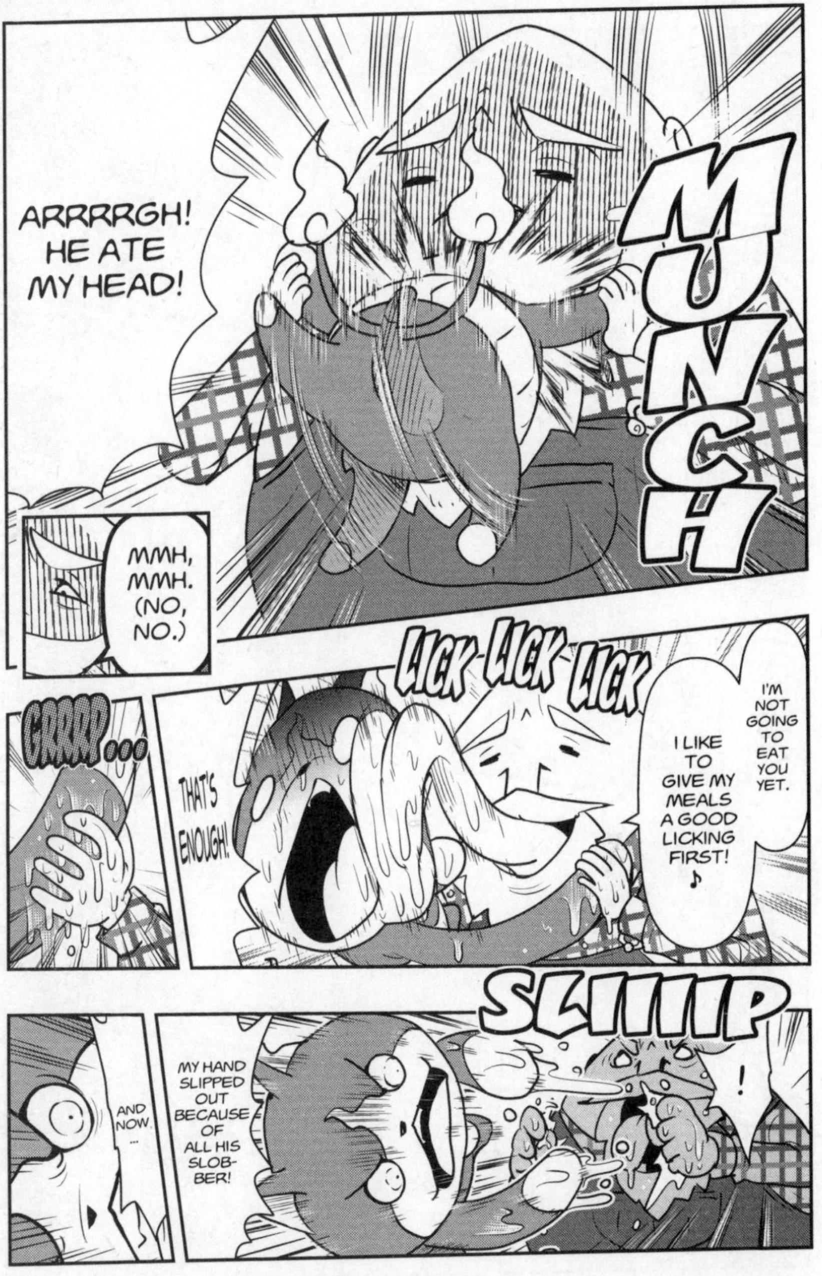
MUNCH
ARRRRGH! HE ATE MY HEAD!
MMH, MMH. (NO, NO.)
LICK LICK LICK
I'M NOT GOING TO EAT YOU YET.
I LIKE TO GIVE MY MEALS A GOOD LICKING FIRST! ♪
THAT'S ENOUGH!
GRRRP...
SLIIIP
!
MY HAND SLIPPED OUT BECAUSE OF ALL HIS SLOB-BER!
AND NOW...

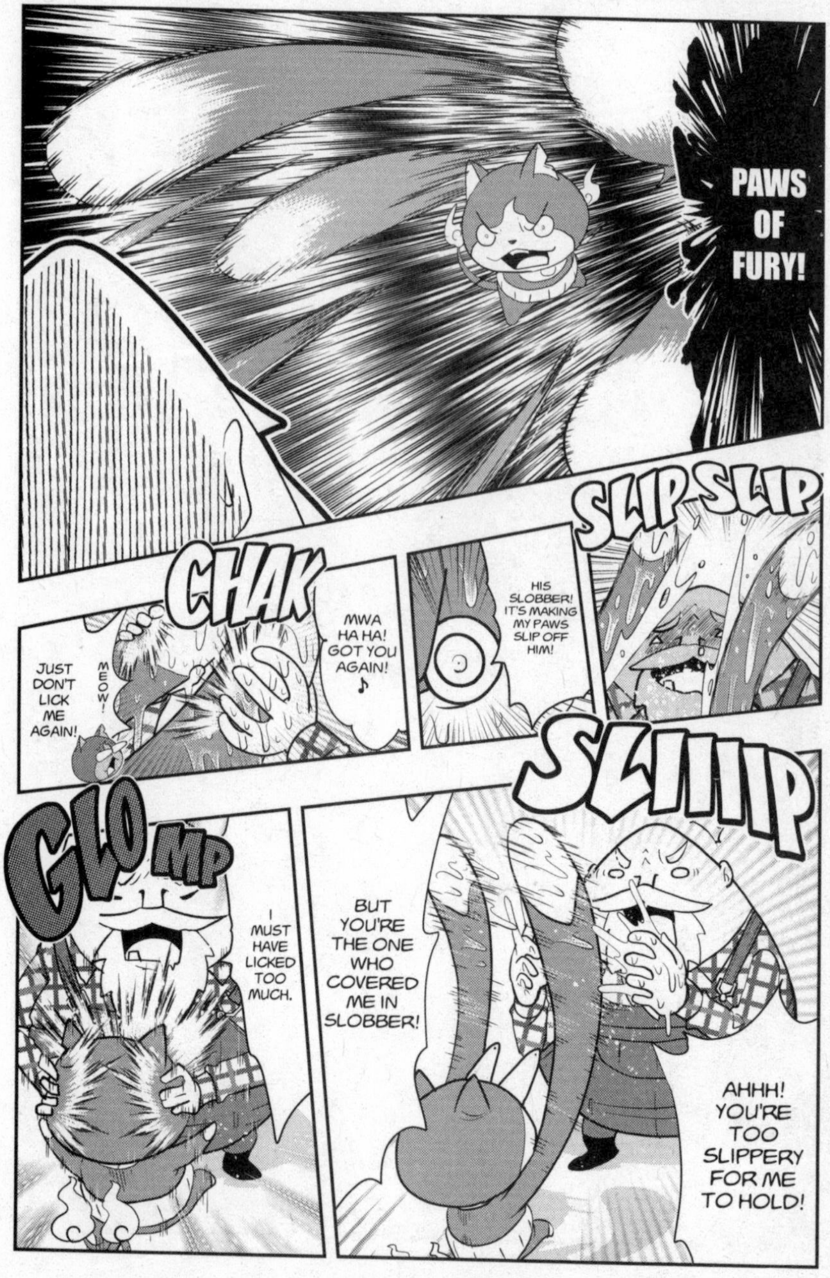
PAWS OF FURY!
SLIP SLIP
HIS SLOBBER! IT'S MAKING MY PAWS SLIP OFF HIM!
CHAK
MWA HA HA! GOT YOU AGAIN! ♪
MEOW!
JUST DON'T LICK ME AGAIN!
SLIIIP
AHHH! YOU'RE TOO SLIPPERY FOR ME TO HOLD!
BUT YOU'RE THE ONE WHO COVERED ME IN SLOBBER!
GLOMP
I MUST HAVE LICKED TOO MUCH.

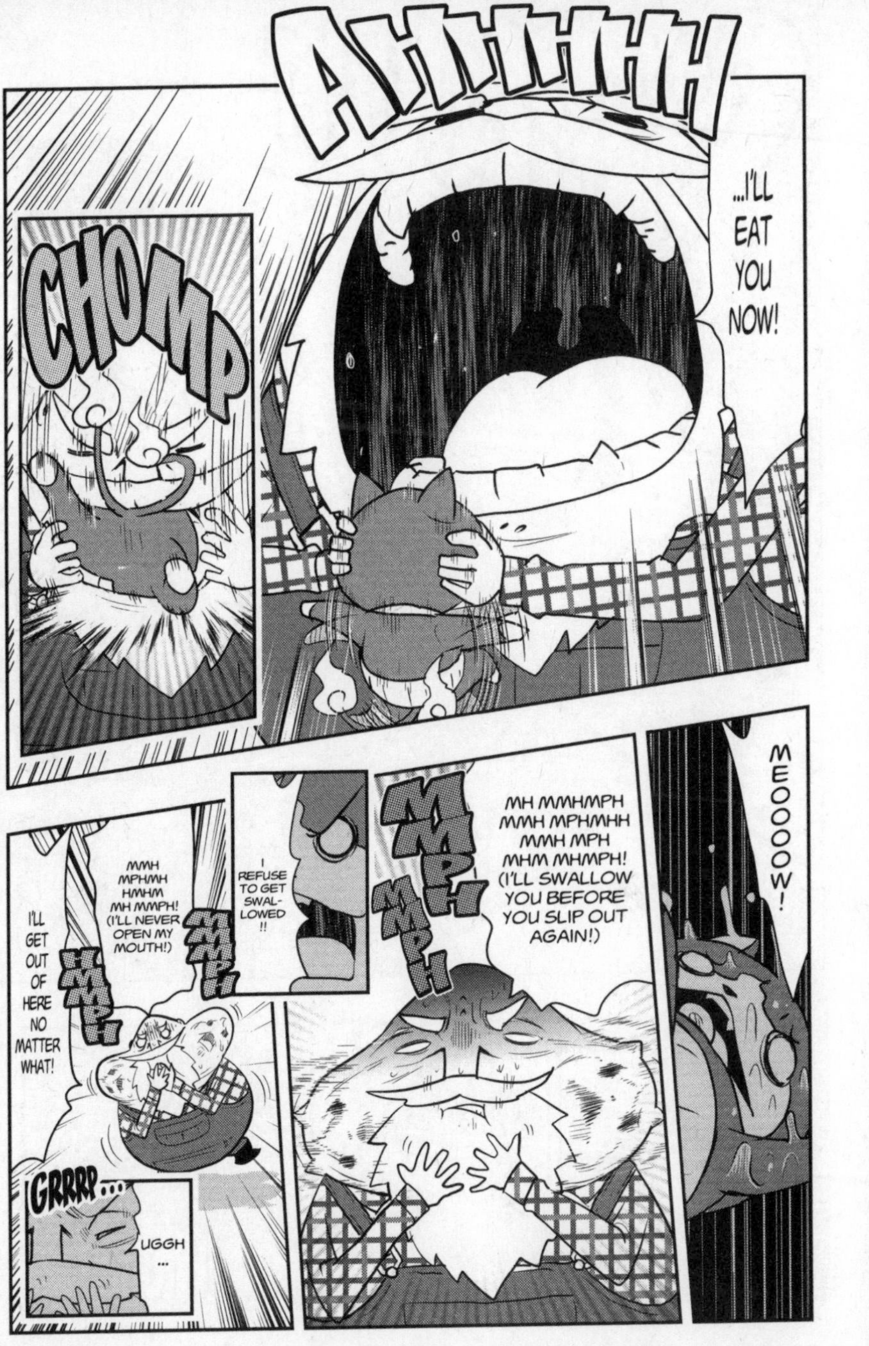
AHHHHHH
...I'LL EAT YOU NOW!
CHOMP
MEOOOOOW!
MPH MMPH
MH MMHMPH MMH MPHMHH MMH MPH MHM MHMPH! (I'LL SWALLOW YOU BEFORE YOU SLIP OUT AGAIN!)
I REFUSE TO GET SWAL-LOWED !!
MMPH!
MMH MPHMH HMHM MH MMPH! (I'LL NEVER OPEN MY MOUTH!)
HMMPH
I'LL GET OUT OF HERE NO MATTER WHAT!
GRRRP...
UGGH ...

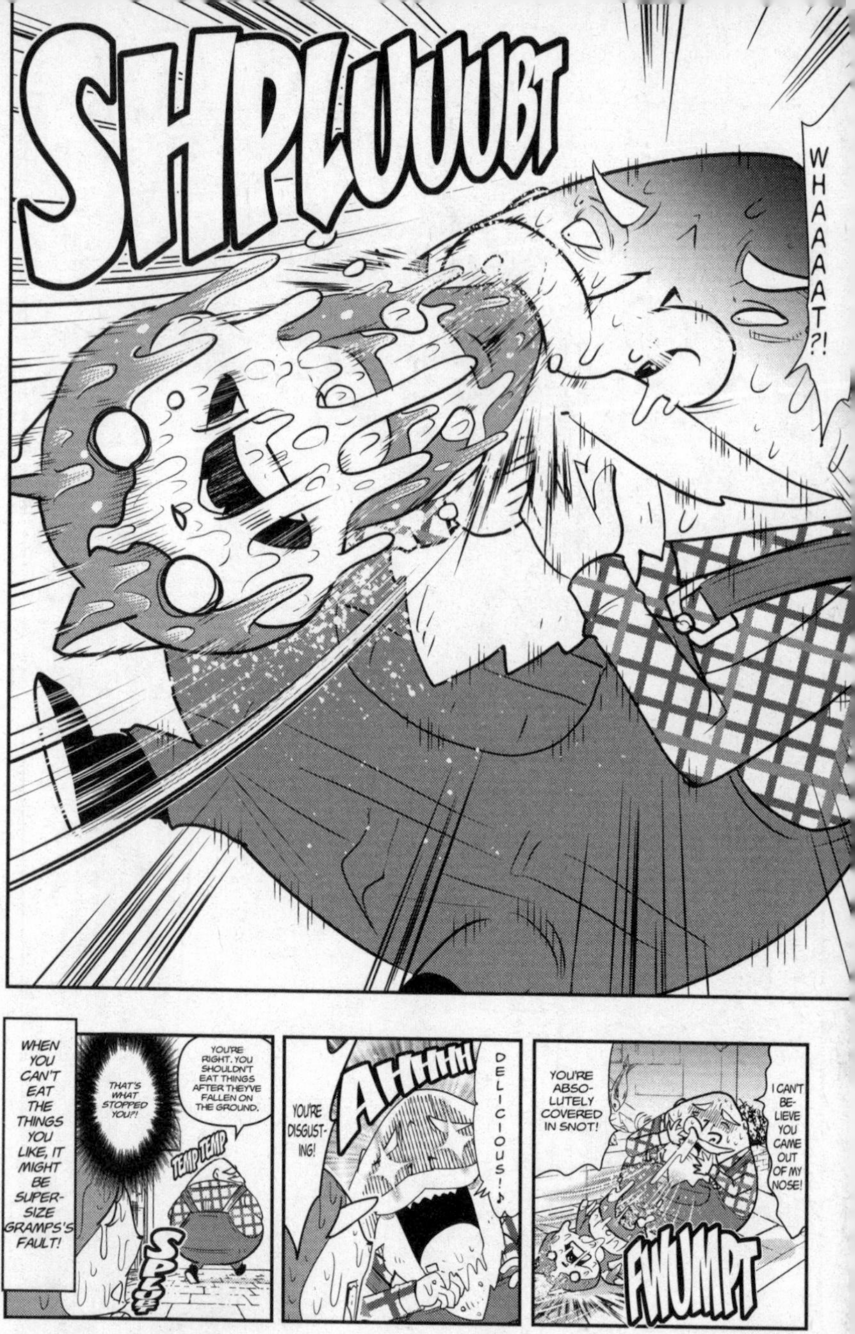
WHAAAAAT?!
SHPLUUUBT
I CAN'T BE-LIEVE YOU CAME OUT OF MY NOSE!
YOU'RE ABSO-LUTELY COVERED IN SNOT!
FWUMPT
DELICIOUS!♪
AHHHH
YOU'RE DISGUST-ING!
YOU'RE RIGHT. YOU SHOULDN'T EAT THINGS AFTER THEY'VE FALLEN ON THE GROUND.
THAT'S WHAT STOPPED YOU?!
WHEN YOU CAN'T EAT THE THINGS YOU LIKE, IT MIGHT BE SUPER-SIZE GRAMPS'S FAULT!
TEMP TEMP
SPLUT

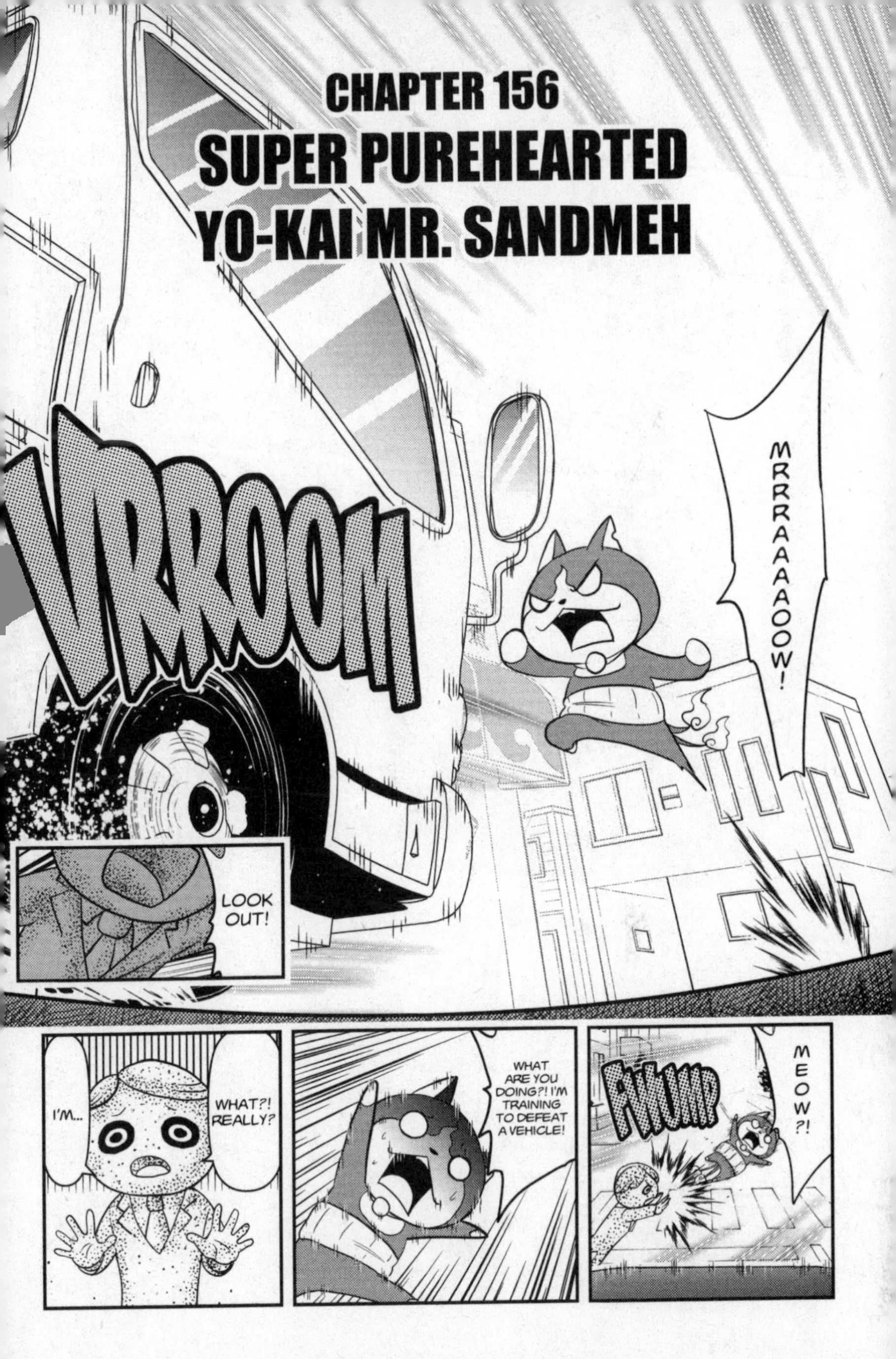

CHAPTER 156
SUPER PUREHEARTED YO-KAI MR. SANDMEH
MRRRAAAAOOW!
VRROOM
LOOK OUT!
PWUMP
MEOW?!
WHAT ARE YOU DOING?! I'M TRAINING TO DEFEAT A VEHICLE!
WHAT?! REALLY?
I'M...

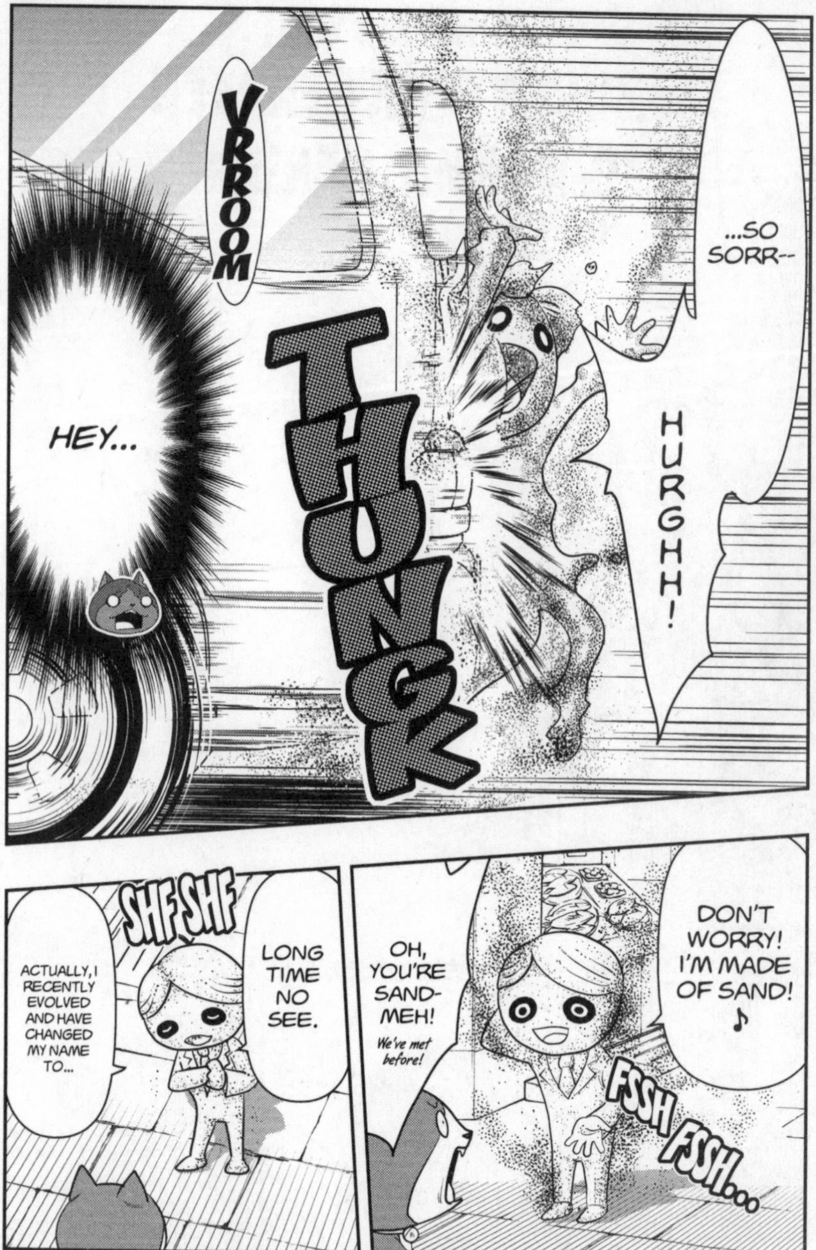
...SO SORR--
VRROOM
HURGH!
THUNGK
HEY...
DON'T WORRY! I'M MADE OF SAND! ♪
OH, YOU'RE SAND-MEH!
We've met before!
FSSH FSSH...
LONG TIME NO SEE.
SHF SHF
ACTUALLY, I RECENTLY EVOLVED AND HAVE CHANGED MY NAME TO...

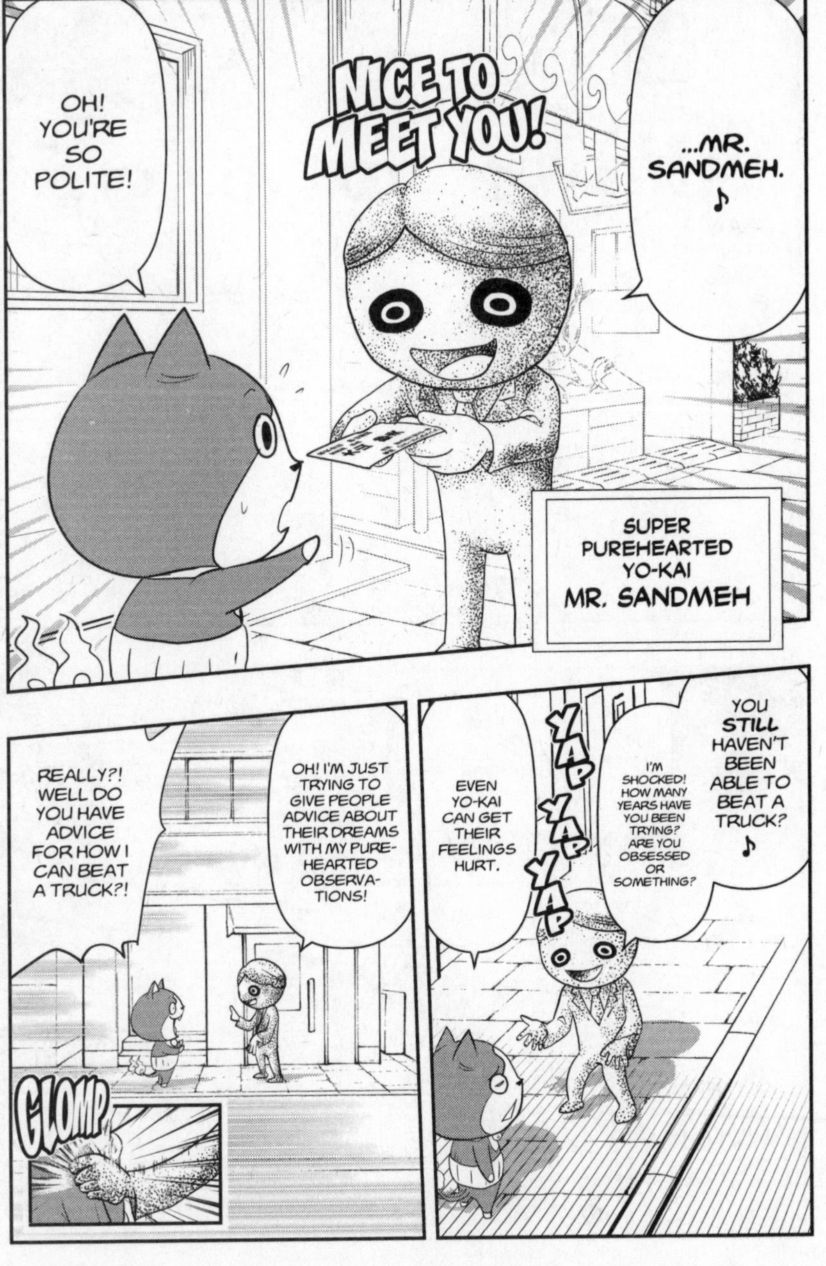
...MR. SANDMEH. ♪
NICE TO MEET YOU!
OH! YOU'RE SO POLITE!
SUPER PUREHEARTED YO-KAI MR. SANDMEH
YOU STILL HAVEN'T BEEN ABLE TO BEAT A TRUCK? ♪
I'M SHOCKED! HOW MANY YEARS HAVE YOU BEEN TRYING? ARE YOU OBSESSED OR SOMETHING?
YAP YAP YAP
EVEN YO-KAI CAN GET THEIR FEELINGS HURT.
OH! I'M JUST TRYING TO GIVE PEOPLE ADVICE ABOUT THEIR DREAMS WITH MY PURE-HEARTED OBSERVA-TIONS!
REALLY?! WELL DO YOU HAVE ADVICE FOR HOW I CAN BEAT A TRUCK?!
GLOMP

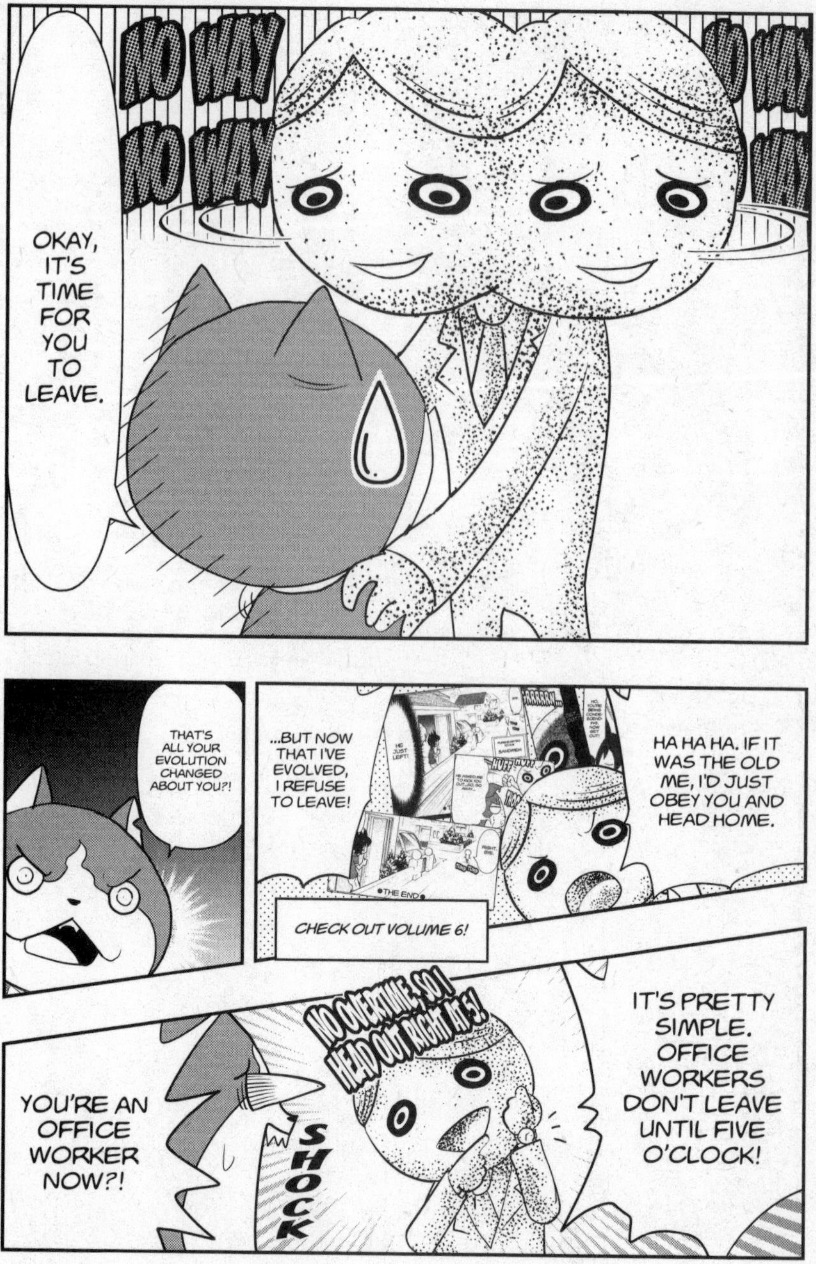
NO WAY NO WAY
OKAY, IT'S TIME FOR YOU TO LEAVE.
HA HA HA. IF IT WAS THE OLD ME, I'D JUST OBEY YOU AND HEAD HOME.
...BUT NOW THAT I'VE EVOLVED, I REFUSE TO LEAVE!
HE JUST LEFT!
●THE END●
CHECK OUT VOLUME 6!
THAT'S ALL YOUR EVOLUTION CHANGED ABOUT YOU?!
IT'S PRETTY SIMPLE. OFFICE WORKERS DON'T LEAVE UNTIL FIVE O'CLOCK!
NO OVERTIME, SO I HEAD OUT RIGHT AT 5!
SHOCK
YOU'RE AN OFFICE WORKER NOW?!

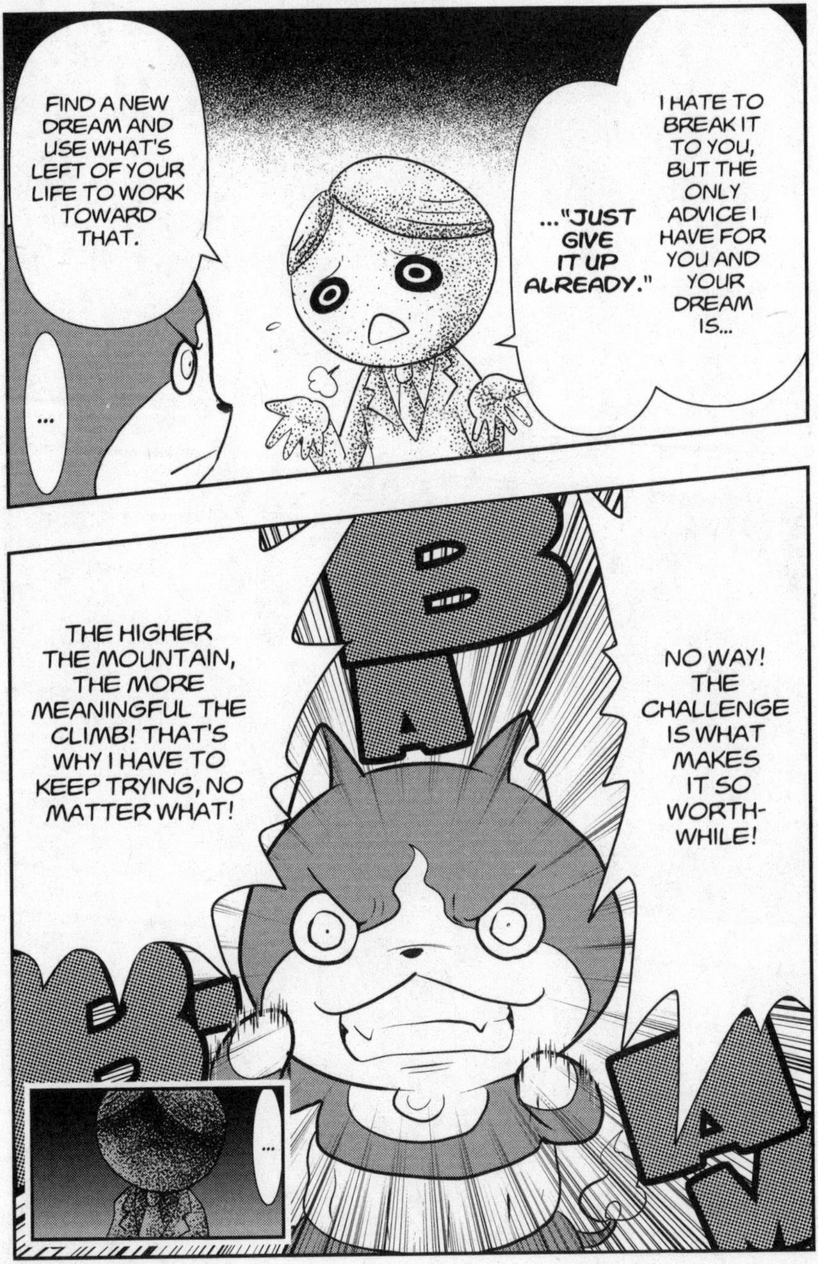

I HATE TO BREAK IT TO YOU, BUT THE ONLY ADVICE I HAVE FOR YOU AND YOUR DREAM IS...
..."JUST GIVE IT UP ALREADY."
FIND A NEW DREAM AND USE WHAT'S LEFT OF YOUR LIFE TO WORK TOWARD THAT.
...
NO WAY! THE CHALLENGE IS WHAT MAKES IT SO WORTH-WHILE!
THE HIGHER THE MOUNTAIN, THE MORE MEANINGFUL THE CLIMB! THAT'S WHY I HAVE TO KEEP TRYING, NO MATTER WHAT!
...

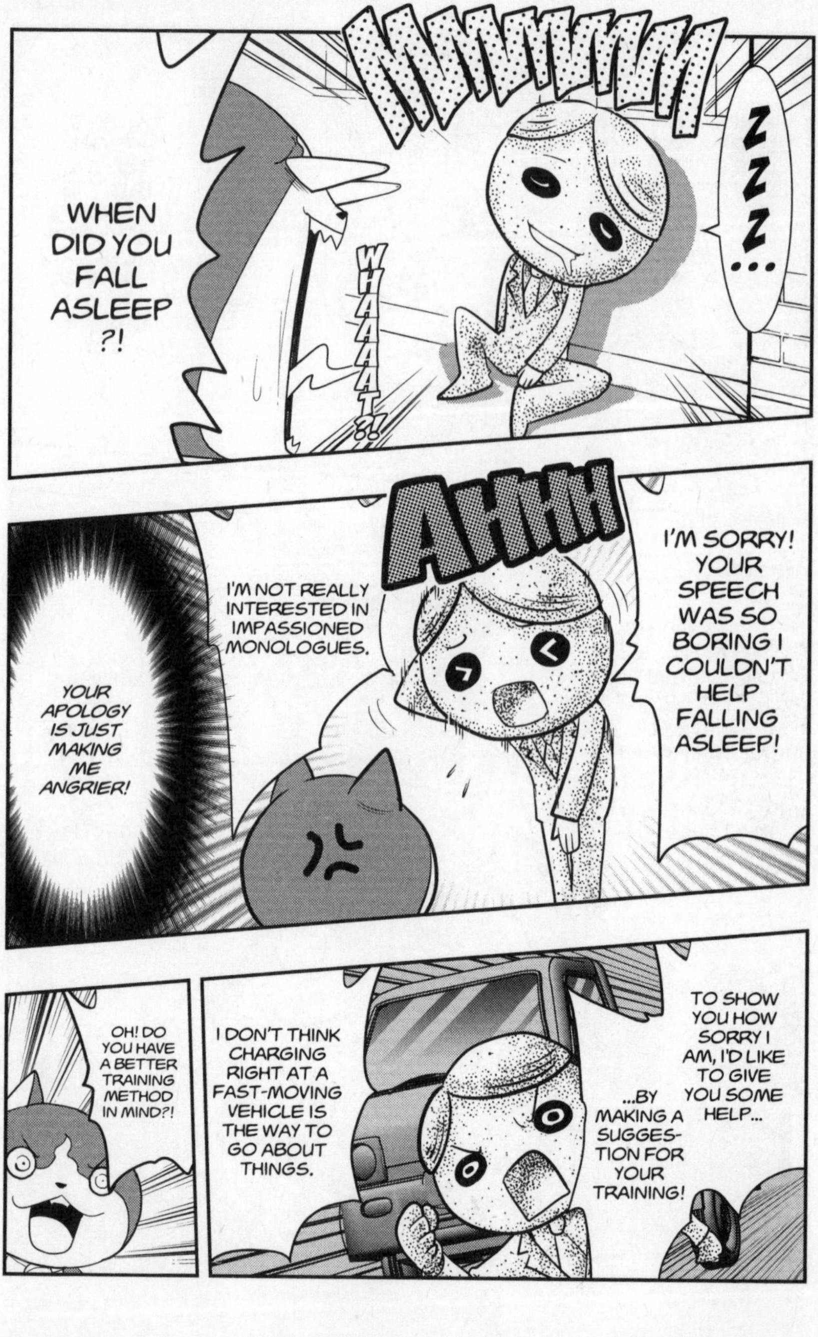
MMMMM
ZZZ...
WHAAAAAT?!
WHEN DID YOU FALL ASLEEP?!
AHHH
I'M SORRY! YOUR SPEECH WAS SO BORING I COULDN'T HELP FALLING ASLEEP!
I'M NOT REALLY INTERESTED IN IMPASSIONED MONOLOGUES.
YOUR APOLOGY IS JUST MAKING ME ANGRIER!
TO SHOW YOU HOW SORRY I AM, I'D LIKE TO GIVE YOU SOME HELP...
...BY MAKING A SUGGES-TION FOR YOUR TRAINING!
I DON'T THINK CHARGING RIGHT AT A FAST-MOVING VEHICLE IS THE WAY TO GO ABOUT THINGS.
OH! DO YOU HAVE A BETTER TRAINING METHOD IN MIND?!

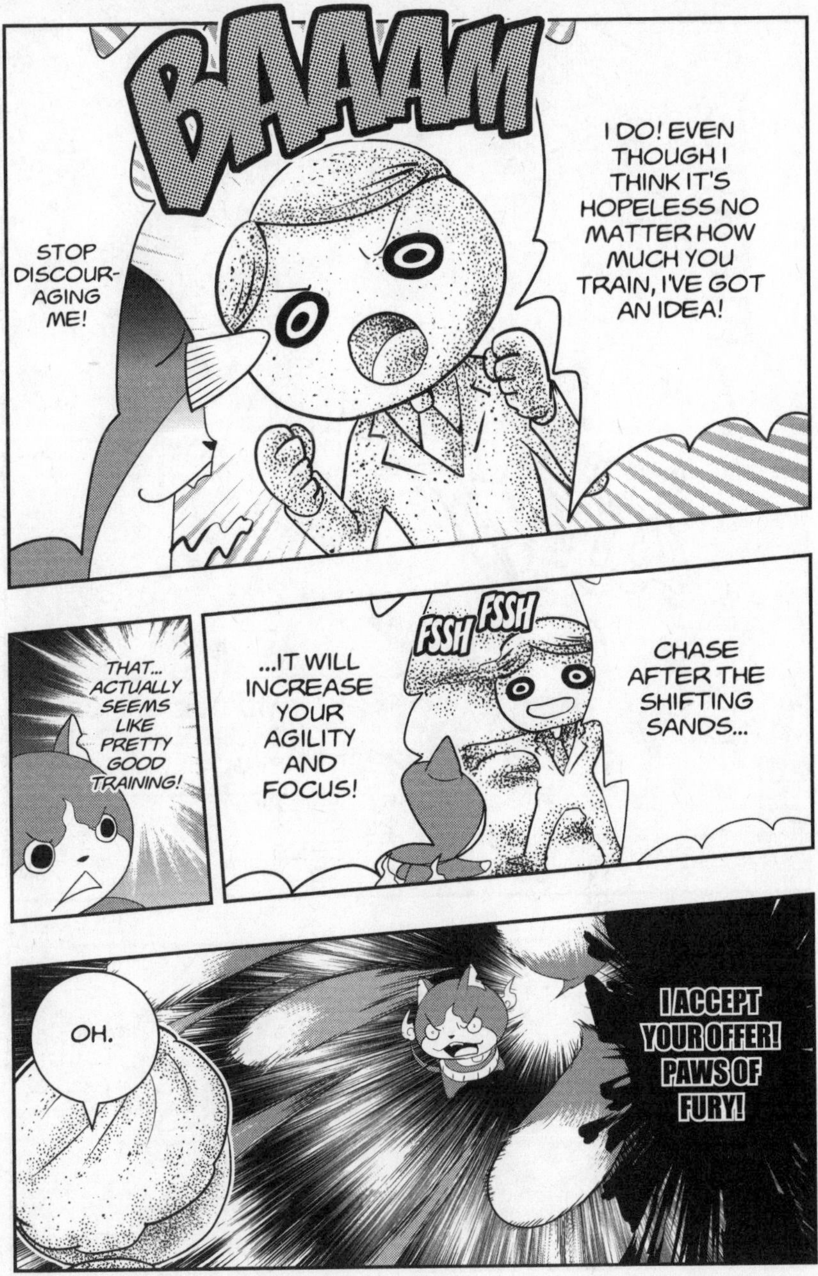
BAAAM
I DO! EVEN THOUGH I THINK IT'S HOPELESS NO MATTER HOW MUCH YOU TRAIN, I'VE GOT AN IDEA!
STOP DISCOUR-AGING ME!
FSSH
FSSH
CHASE AFTER THE SHIFTING SANDS...
...IT WILL INCREASE YOUR AGILITY AND FOCUS!
THAT... ACTUALLY SEEMS LIKE PRETTY GOOD TRAINING!
I ACCEPT YOUR OFFER! PAWS OF FURY!
OH.

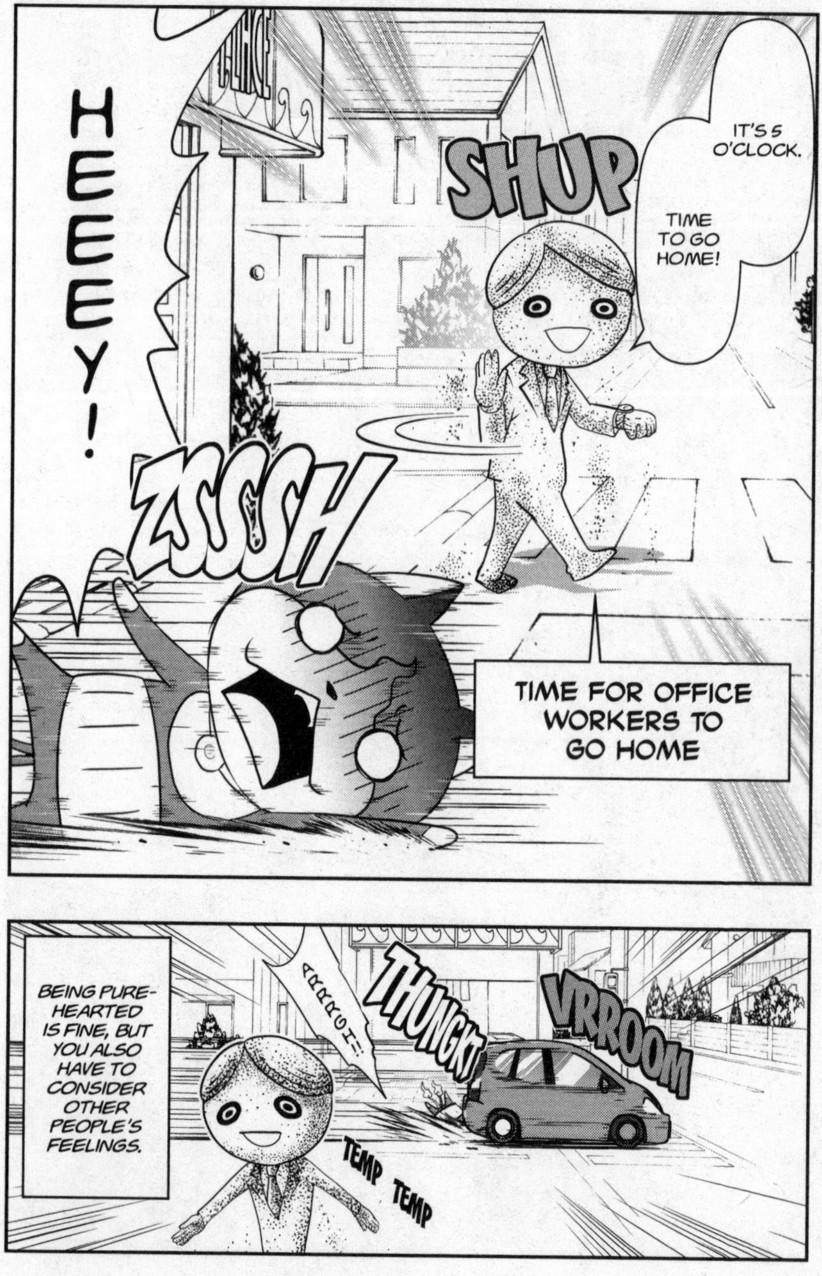
IT'S 5 O'CLOCK.
TIME TO GO HOME!
SHUP
TIME FOR OFFICE WORKERS TO GO HOME
ZSCSH
HEEEY!
VRROOM
THUNGK!
ARRRGH!!
BEING PURE-HEARTED IS FINE, BUT YOU ALSO HAVE TO CONSIDER OTHER PEOPLE'S FEELINGS.
TEMP TEMP

CHAPTER 157
SMOKE YO-KAI SMOGLING

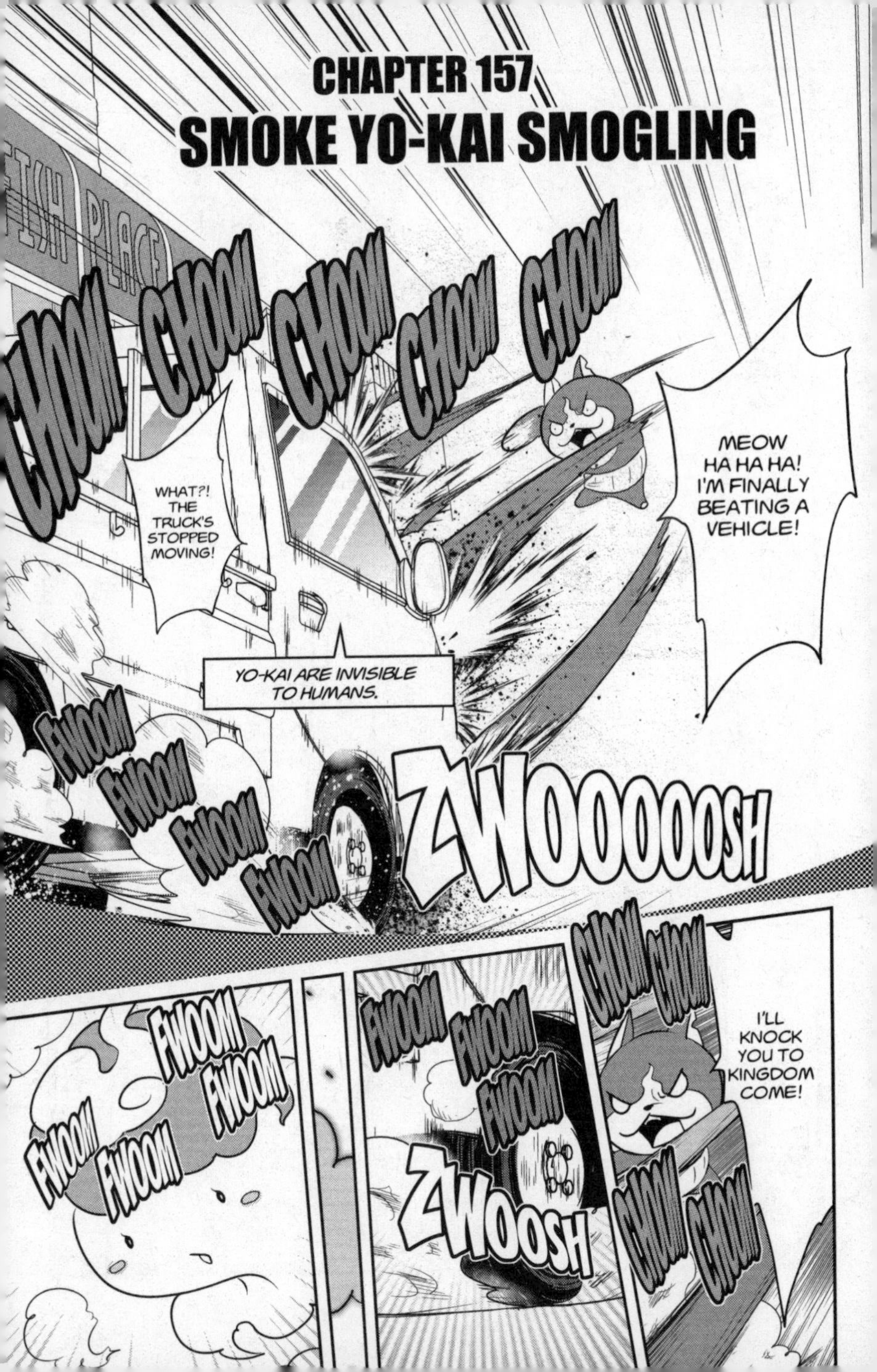
MEOW HA HA HA! I'M FINALLY BEATING A VEHICLE!
CHOOM CHOOM CHOOM CHOOM CHOOM
WHAT?! THE TRUCK'S STOPPED MOVING!
YO-KAI ARE INVISIBLE TO HUMANS.
ZWOOOOOOSH
FWOOM FWOOM FWOOM FWOOM
CHOOM CHOOM
I'LL KNOCK YOU TO KINGDOM COME!
CHOOM CHOOM
FWOOM FWOOM FWOOM
ZWOOSH
FWOOM FWOOM FWOOM FWOOM FWOOM

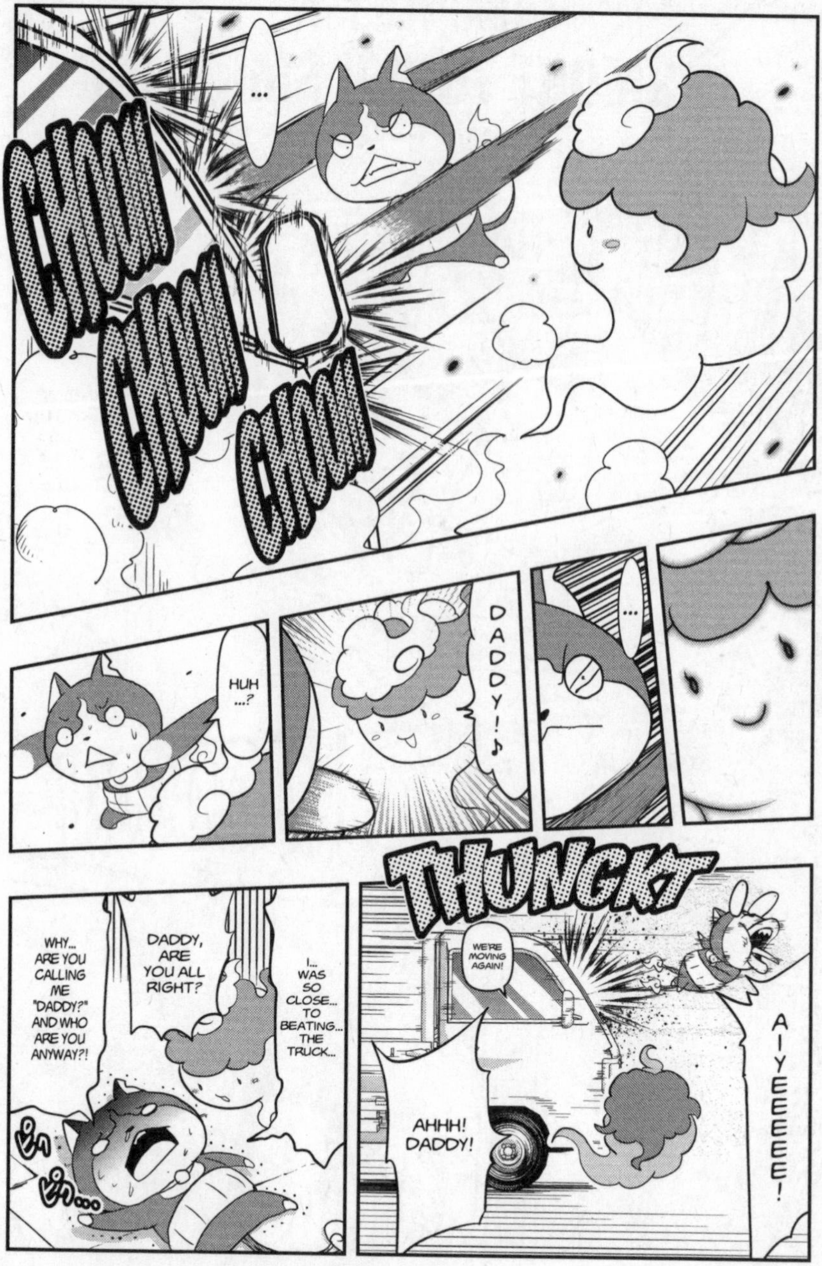
...
CHOMM
CHOMM
CHOMM
...
DADDY!♪
HUH ...?
THUNCK!
AIYEEEEEE!
WE'RE MOVING AGAIN!
AHHH! DADDY!
I... WAS SO CLOSE... TO BEATING... THE TRUCK...
DADDY, ARE YOU ALL RIGHT?
WHY... ARE YOU CALLING ME "DADDY?" AND WHO ARE YOU ANYWAY?!

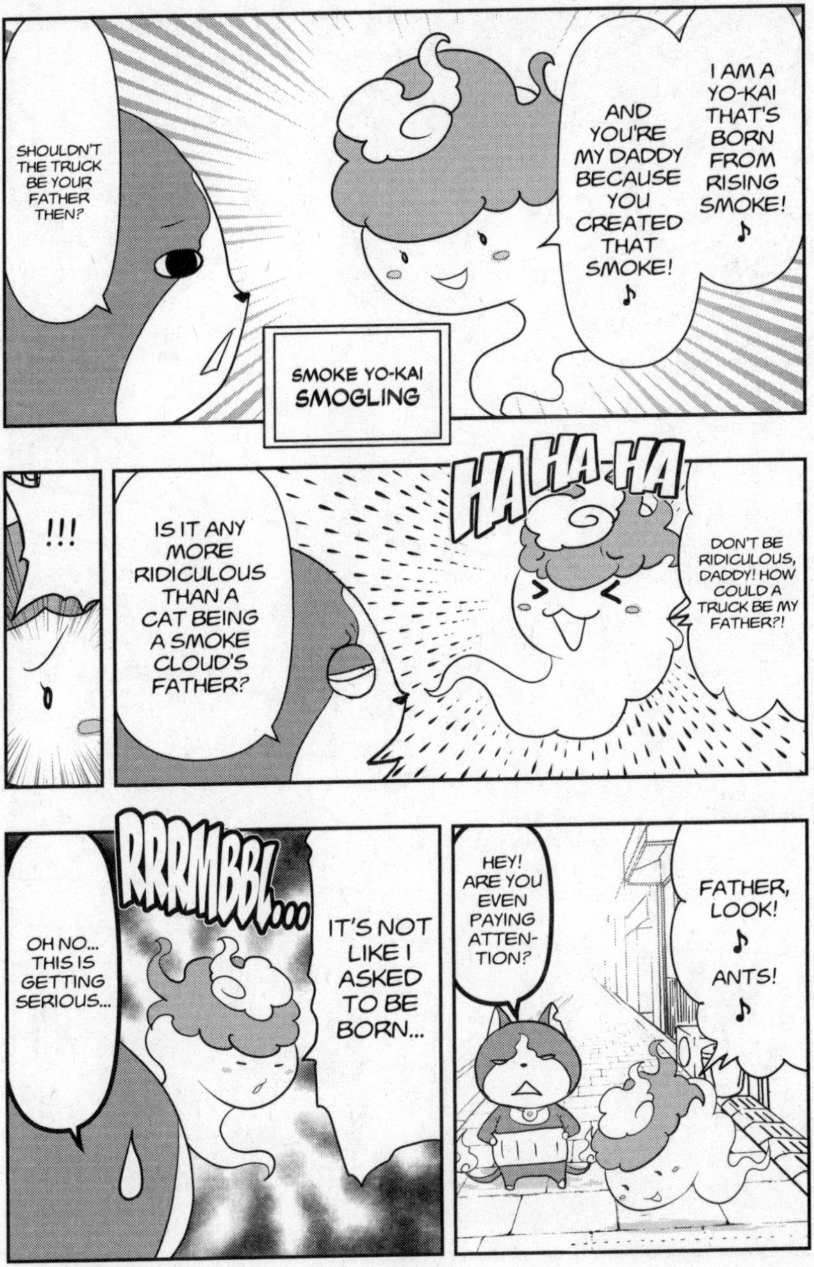
I AM A YO-KAI THAT'S BORN FROM RISING SMOKE! ♪
AND YOU'RE MY DADDY BECAUSE YOU CREATED THAT SMOKE! ♪
SMOKE YO-KAI SMOGLING
SHOULDN'T THE TRUCK BE YOUR FATHER THEN?
HAHA-HA
DON'T BE RIDICULOUS, DADDY! HOW COULD A TRUCK BE MY FATHER?!
IS IT ANY MORE RIDICULOUS THAN A CAT BEING A SMOKE CLOUD'S FATHER?
!!!
FATHER, LOOK! ♪
ANTS! ♪
HEY! ARE YOU EVEN PAYING ATTEN-TION?
RRRMBBL...
IT'S NOT LIKE I ASKED TO BE BORN...
OH NO... THIS IS GETTING SERIOUS...

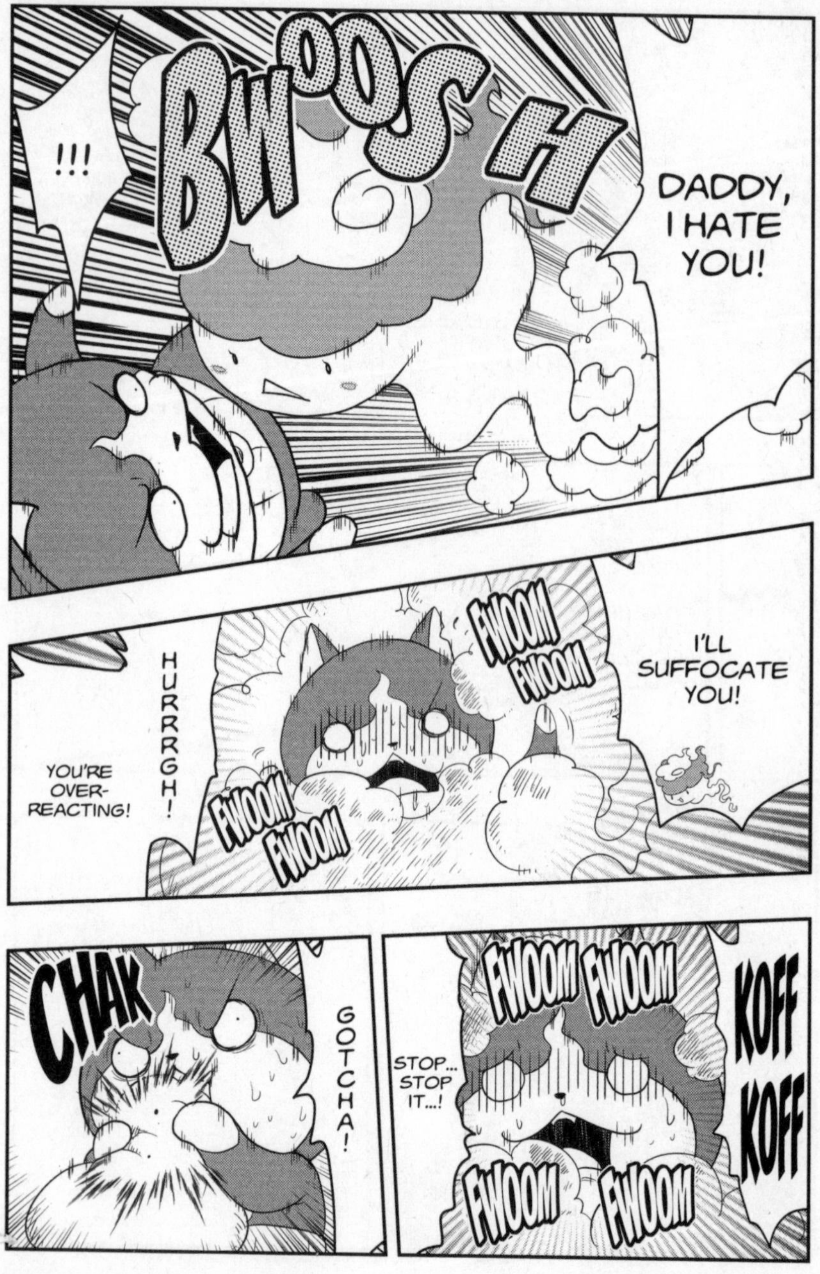
DADDY, I HATE YOU!
BWOOSH
!!!
I'LL SUFFOCATE YOU!
FWOOM FWOOM
FWOOM FWOOM
HURRRGH!
YOU'RE OVER-REACTING!
KOFF KOFF
FWOOM FWOOM
STOP... STOP IT...!
FWOOM FWOOM
GOTCHA!
CHAK

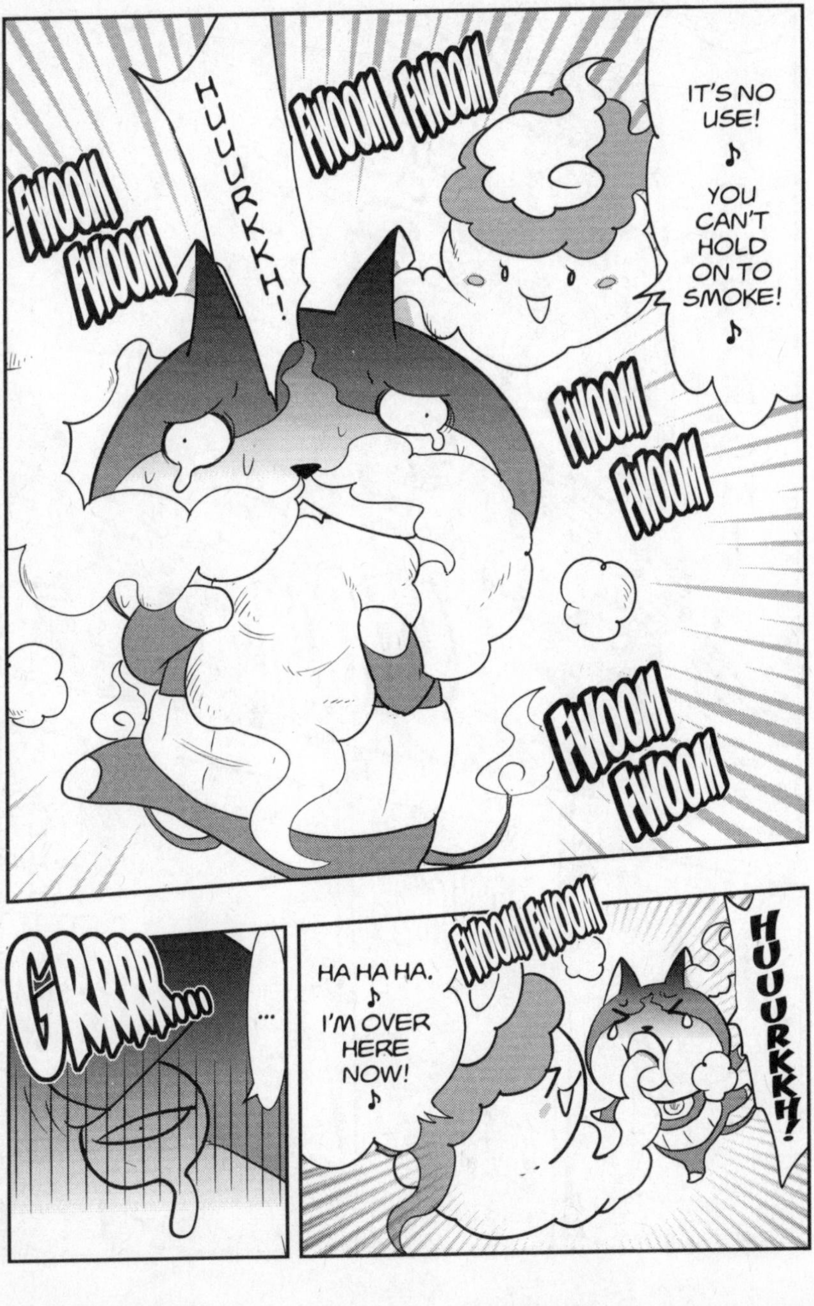
IT'S NO USE! ♪ YOU CAN'T HOLD ON TO SMOKE! ♪
FWOOM FWOOM
HUUURKKH!
FWOOM FWOOM
FWOOM FWOOM
FWOOM FWOOM
HUUURKKH!
FWOOM FWOOM
HA HA HA. ♪ I'M OVER HERE NOW! ♪
...
GRRRR...

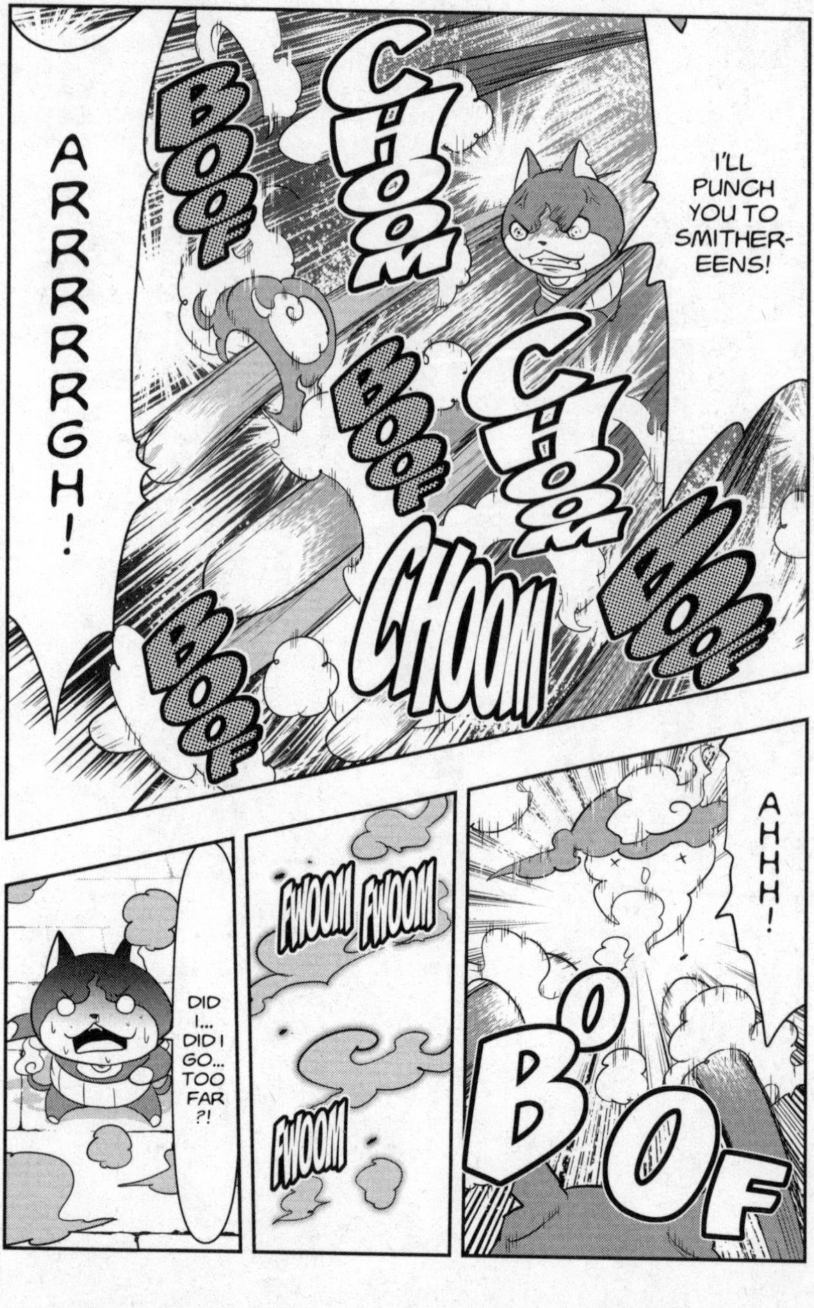
I'LL PUNCH YOU TO SMITHER-EENS!
CHOOM
BOOF
CHOOM
BOOF
BOOF
CHOOM
BOOF
ARRRRRRGH!
AHHH!
BOOF
FWOOM FWOOM
FWOOM
DID I... DID I GO... TOO FAR?!

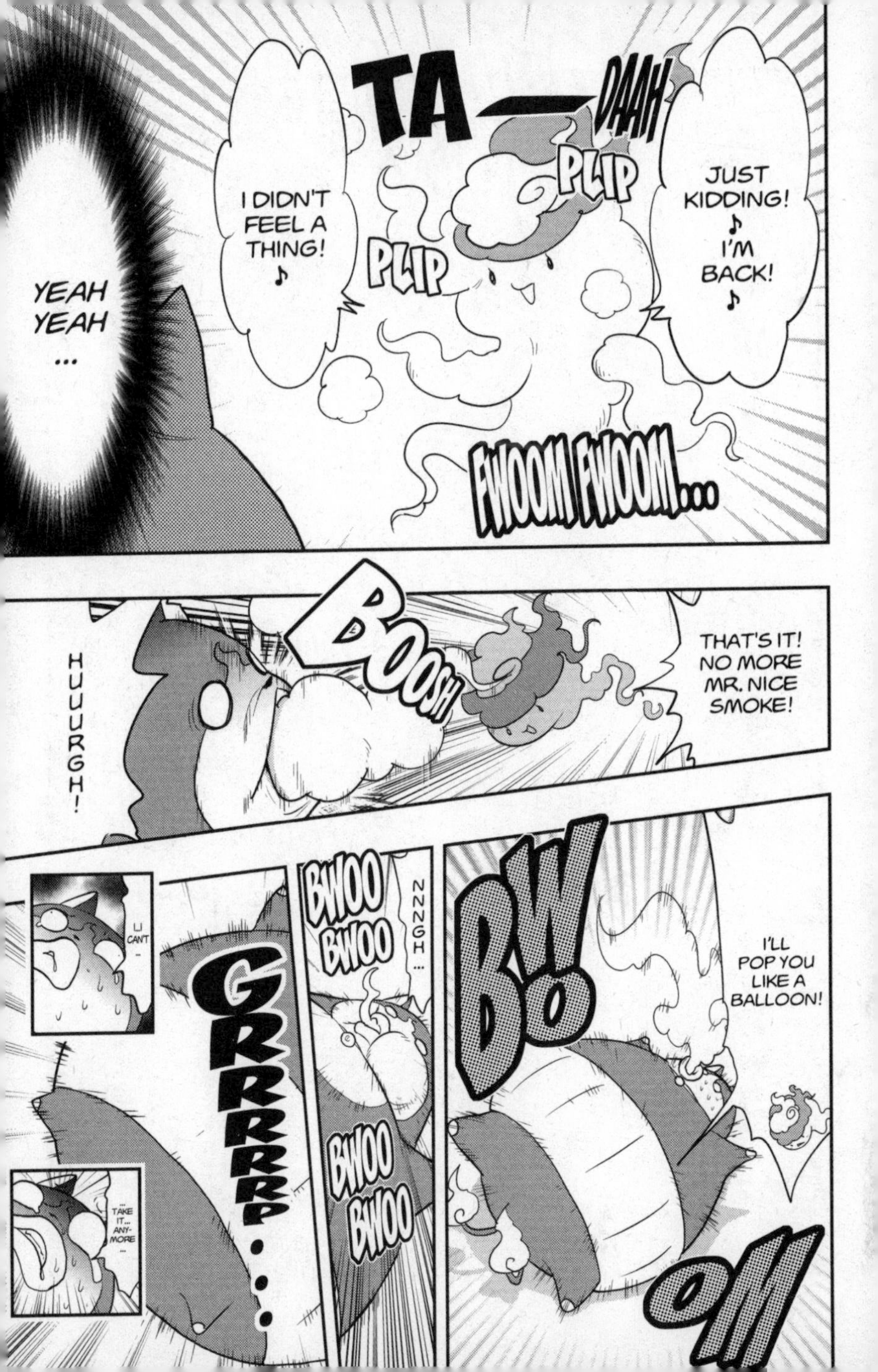
JUST KIDDING! ♪ I'M BACK! ♪
TA—DAAH
PLIP
PLIP
I DIDN'T FEEL A THING! ♪
FWOOM FWOOM...
YEAH YEAH ...
THAT'S IT! NO MORE MR. NICE SMOKE!
BOOSH
HUUURGH!
I'LL POP YOU LIKE A BALLOON!
BWOOM
BWOO BWOO
NNNGH ...
BWOO BWOO
GRRRRP...
I CAN'T ...
... TAKE IT... ANYMORE ...

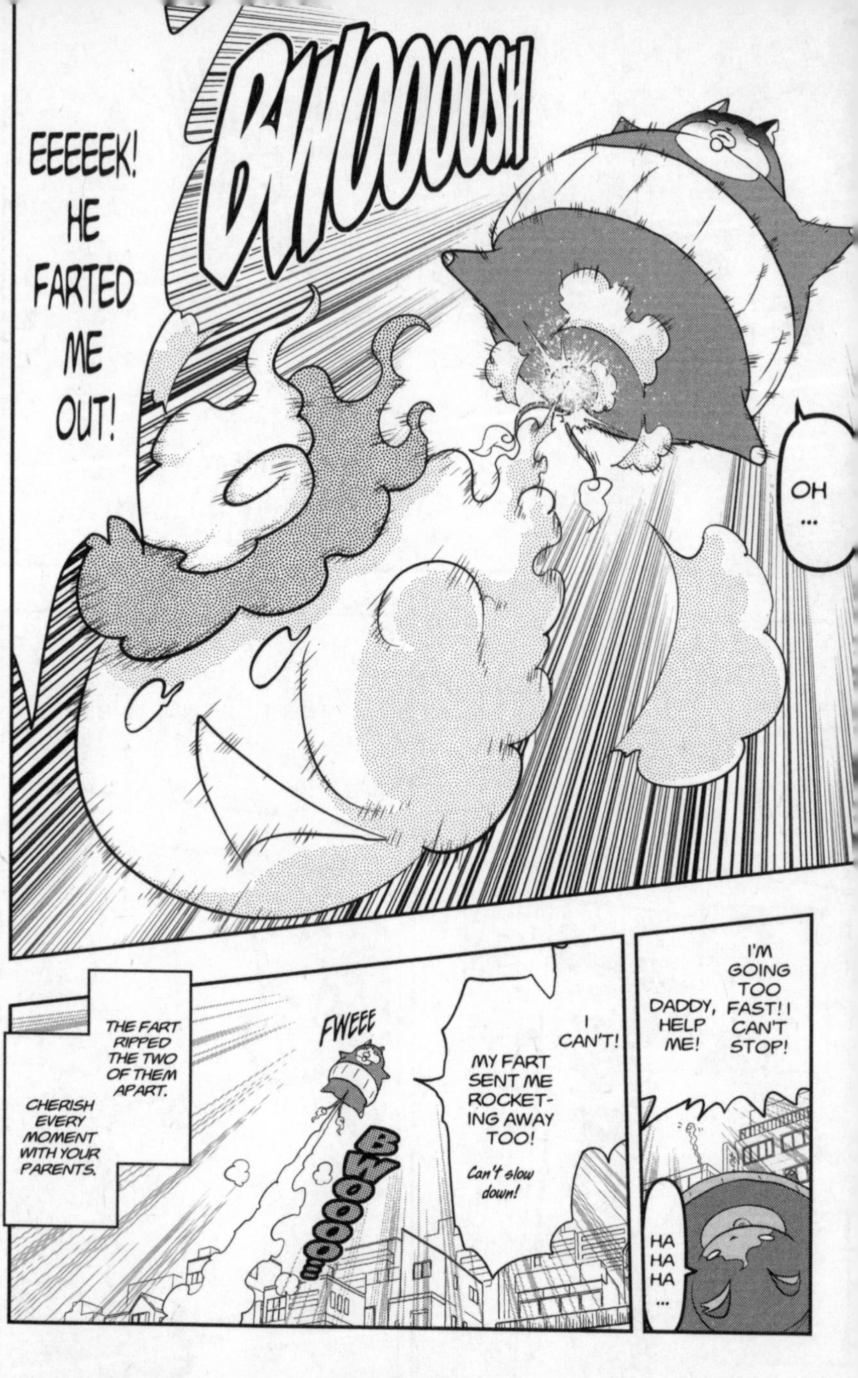
BWOOOOOSH
OH ...
EEEEEK! HE FARTED ME OUT!
I'M GOING TOO FAST! I CAN'T STOP!
DADDY, HELP ME!
HA HA HA ...
I CAN'T!
MY FART SENT ME ROCKETING AWAY TOO!
Can't slow down!
FWEEE
BWOOOOO...
THE FART RIPPED THE TWO OF THEM APART.
CHERISH EVERY MOMENT WITH YOUR PARENTS.

CHAPTER 158
ABSORBING YO-KAI URNFULFILLED

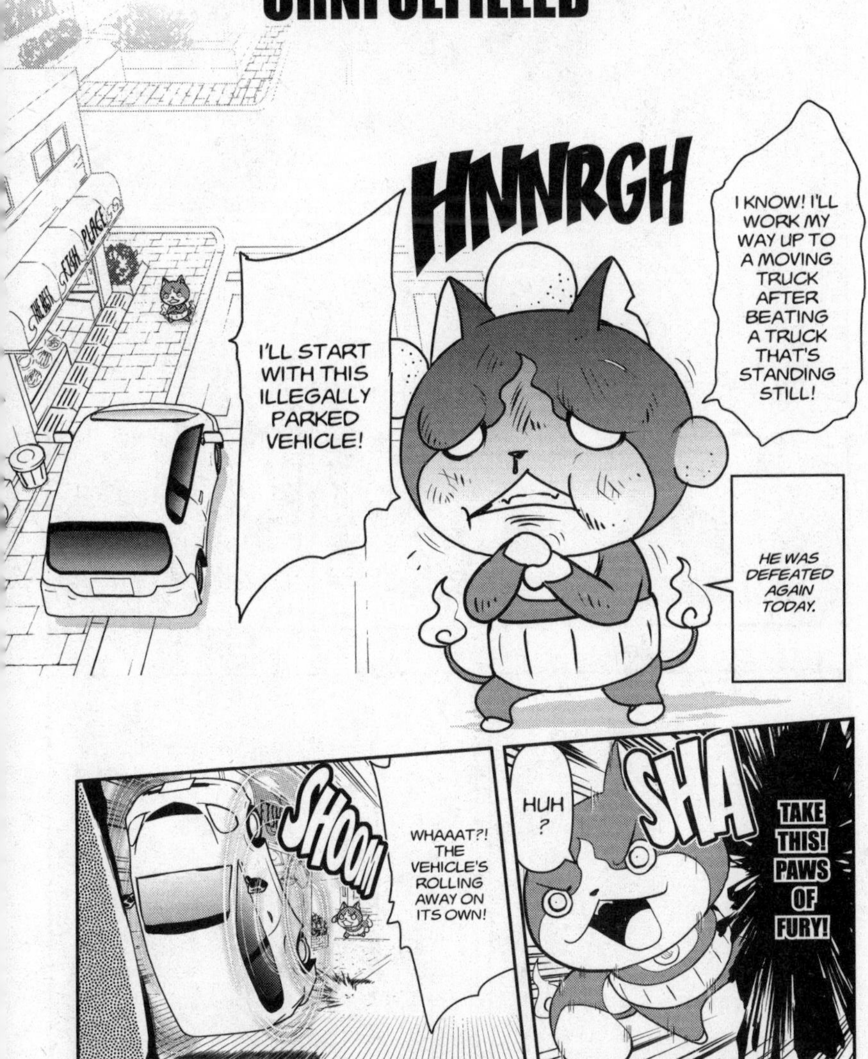

I KNOW! I'LL WORK MY WAY UP TO A MOVING TRUCK AFTER BEATING A TRUCK THAT'S STANDING STILL!
HNNRGH
HE WAS DEFEATED AGAIN TODAY.
I'LL START WITH THIS ILLEGALLY PARKED VEHICLE!
TAKE THIS! PAWS OF FURY!
SHA
HUH?
SHOOM
WHAAAT?! THE VEHICLE'S ROLLING AWAY ON ITS OWN!

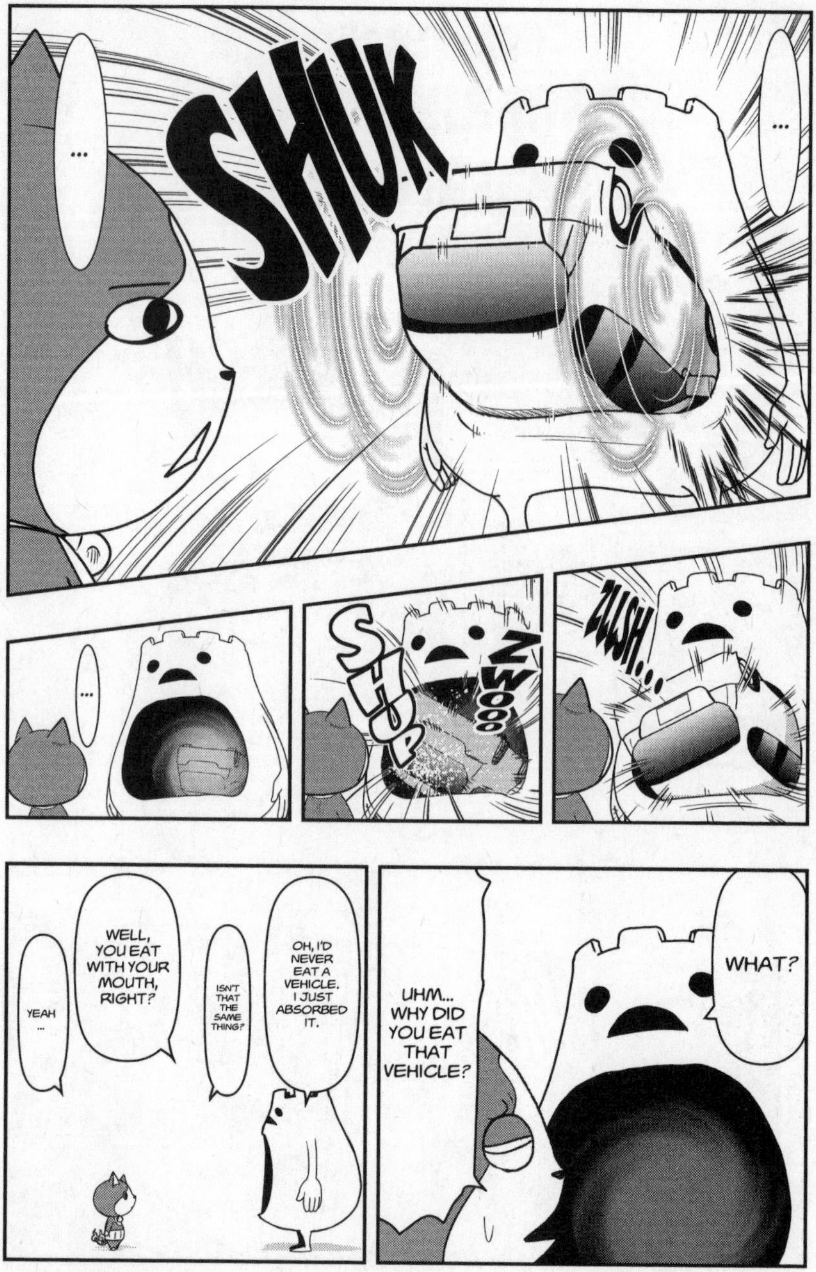
...
SHUK
...
ZLLSH...
SHUP
ZWOOO
...
WHAT?
UHM... WHY DID YOU EAT THAT VEHICLE?
OH, I'D NEVER EAT A VEHICLE. I JUST ABSORBED IT.
ISN'T THAT THE SAME THING?
WELL, YOU EAT WITH YOUR MOUTH, RIGHT?
YEAH ...

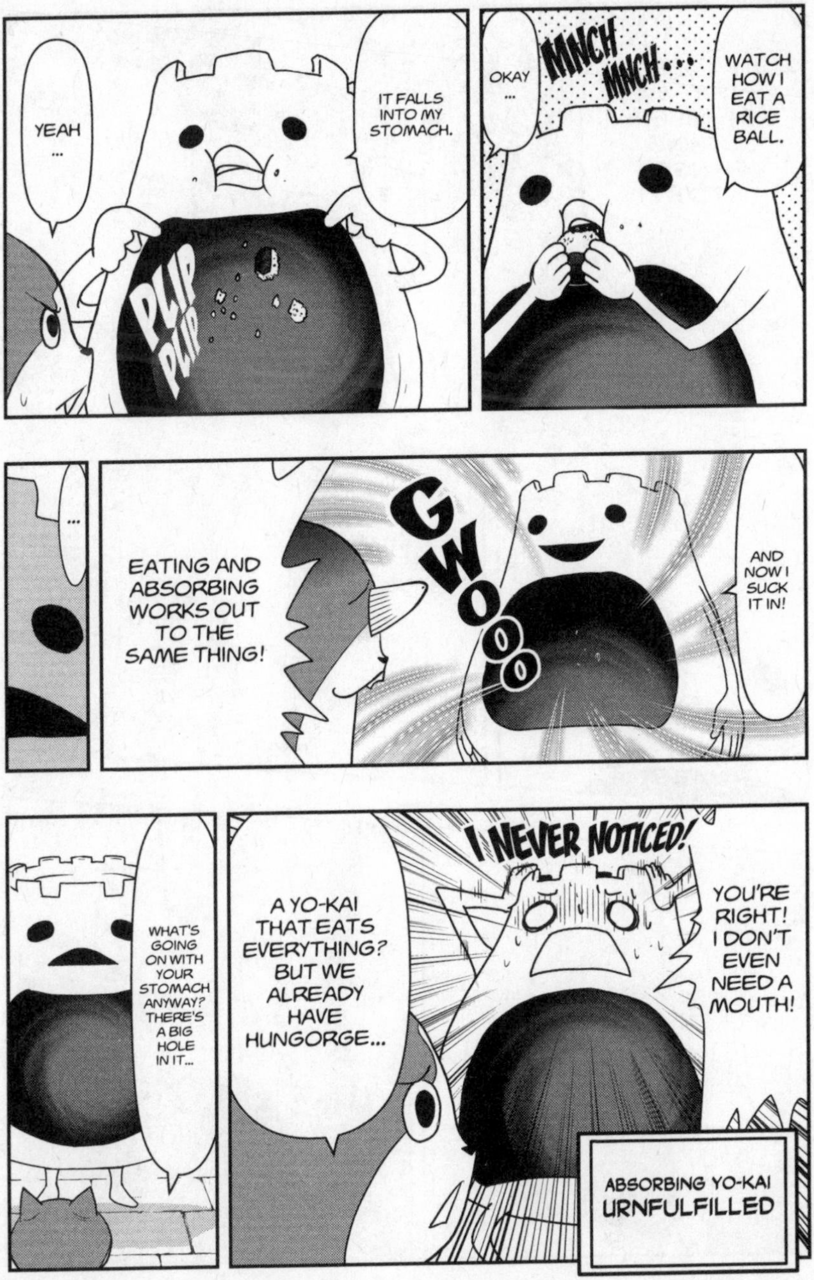
WATCH HOW I EAT A RICE BALL.
MNCH MNCH...
OKAY ...
IT FALLS INTO MY STOMACH.
PLIP PLIP
YEAH ...
AND NOW I SUCK IT IN!
GWOOO
EATING AND ABSORBING WORKS OUT TO THE SAME THING!
...
I NEVER NOTICED!
YOU'RE RIGHT! I DON'T EVEN NEED A MOUTH!
A YO-KAI THAT EATS EVERYTHING? BUT WE ALREADY HAVE HUNGORGE...
ABSORBING YO-KAI URNFULFILLED
WHAT'S GOING ON WITH YOUR STOMACH ANYWAY? THERE'S A BIG HOLE IN IT...

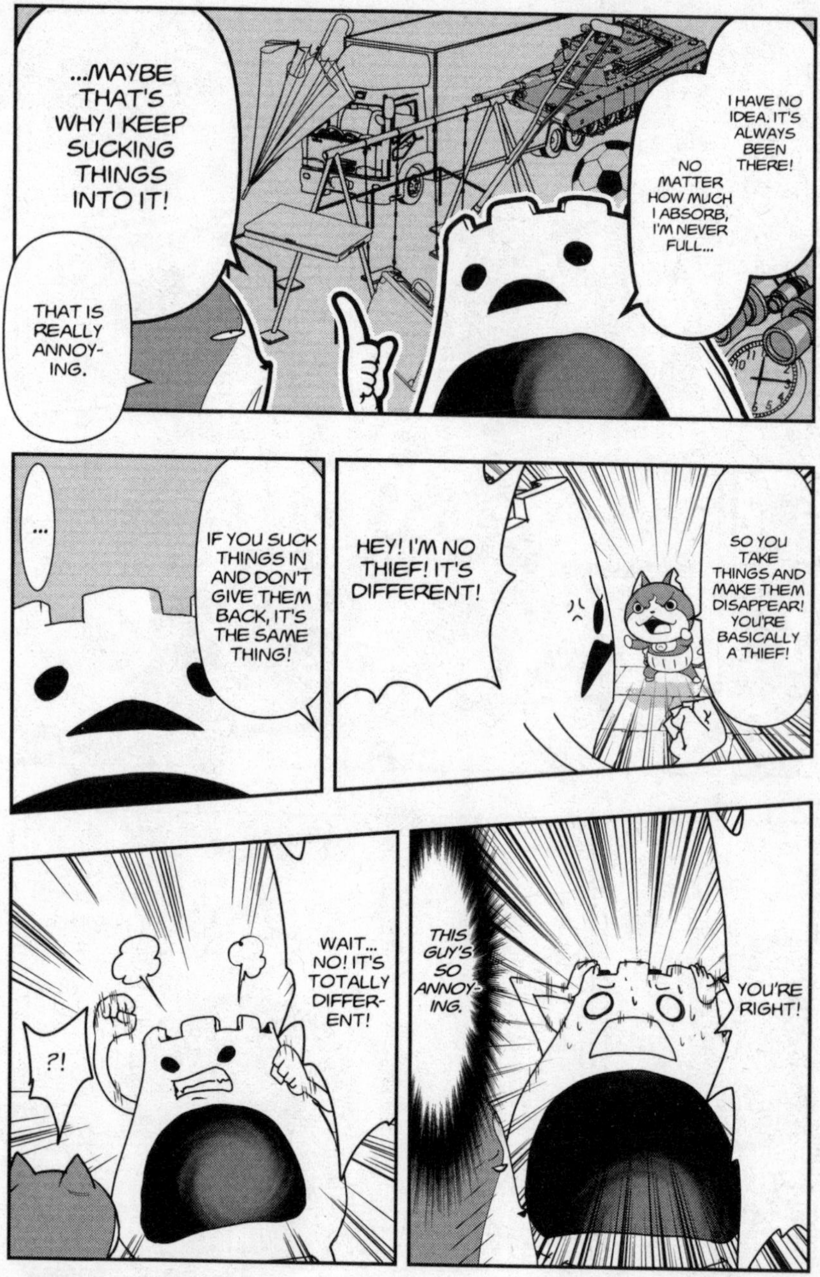
I HAVE NO IDEA. IT'S ALWAYS BEEN THERE!
NO MATTER HOW MUCH I ABSORB, I'M NEVER FULL...
...MAYBE THAT'S WHY I KEEP SUCKING THINGS INTO IT!
THAT IS REALLY ANNOY-ING.
SO YOU TAKE THINGS AND MAKE THEM DISAPPEAR! YOU'RE BASICALLY A THIEF!
HEY! I'M NO THIEF! IT'S DIFFERENT!
IF YOU SUCK THINGS IN AND DON'T GIVE THEM BACK, IT'S THE SAME THING!
...
YOU'RE RIGHT!
THIS GUY'S SO ANNOY-ING.
WAIT... NO! IT'S TOTALLY DIFFER-ENT!
?!

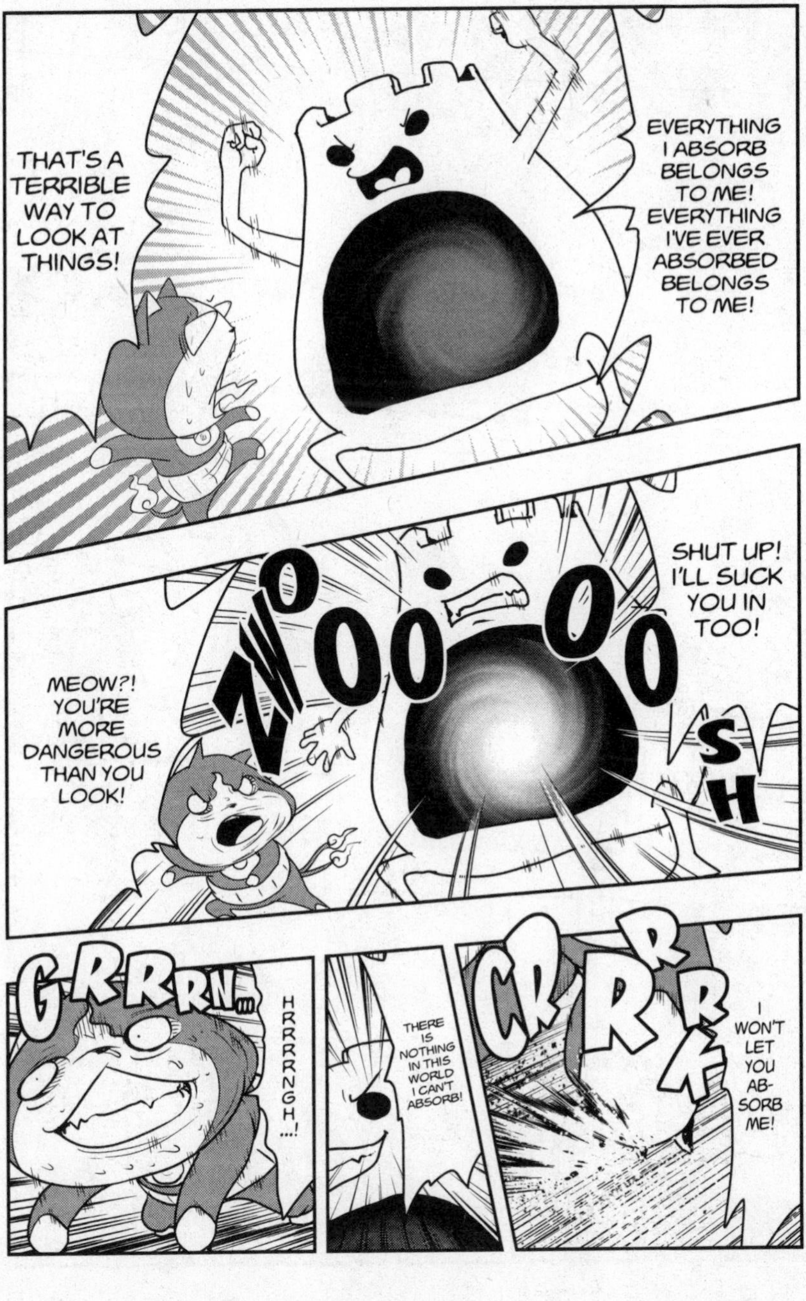
EVERYTHING I ABSORB BELONGS TO ME! EVERYTHING I'VE EVER ABSORBED BELONGS TO ME!
THAT'S A TERRIBLE WAY TO LOOK AT THINGS!
SHUT UP! I'LL SUCK YOU IN TOO!
ZWOOOOOSH
MEOW?! YOU'RE MORE DANGEROUS THAN YOU LOOK!
CRRRRK
I WON'T LET YOU AB-SORB ME!
THERE IS NOTHING IN THIS WORLD I CAN'T ABSORB!
GRRRN...
HRRRRNGH...!

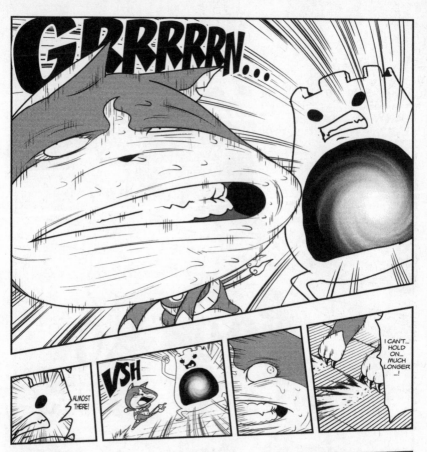

GRRRRN...

ALMOST THERE!

VSH

I CAN'T... HOLD ON... MUCH LONGER...!

!!!

PAWS OF...

BOOSH

BEFORE YOU ABSORB ME, I'M GONNA BEAT THE LIVING DAYLIGHTS OUT OF YOU!

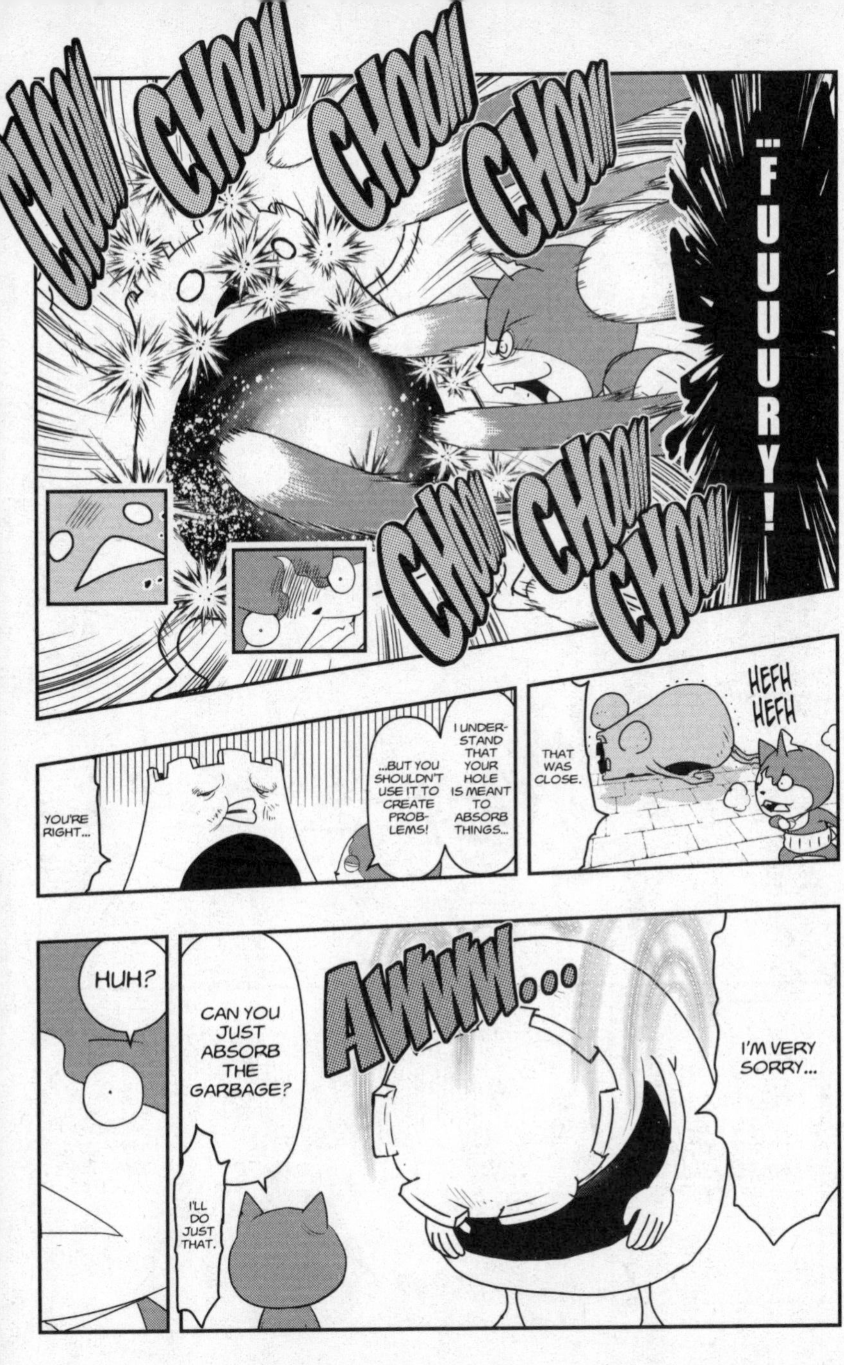
...FUUUURY!
CHOOM CHOOM CHOOM CHOOM
CHOOM CHOOM CHOOM
HEFH HEFH
THAT WAS CLOSE.
I UNDER-STAND THAT YOUR HOLE IS MEANT TO ABSORB THINGS...
...BUT YOU SHOULDN'T USE IT TO CREATE PROB-LEMS!
YOU'RE RIGHT...
I'M VERY SORRY...
AWWW...
CAN YOU JUST ABSORB THE GARBAGE?
I'LL DO JUST THAT.
HUH?

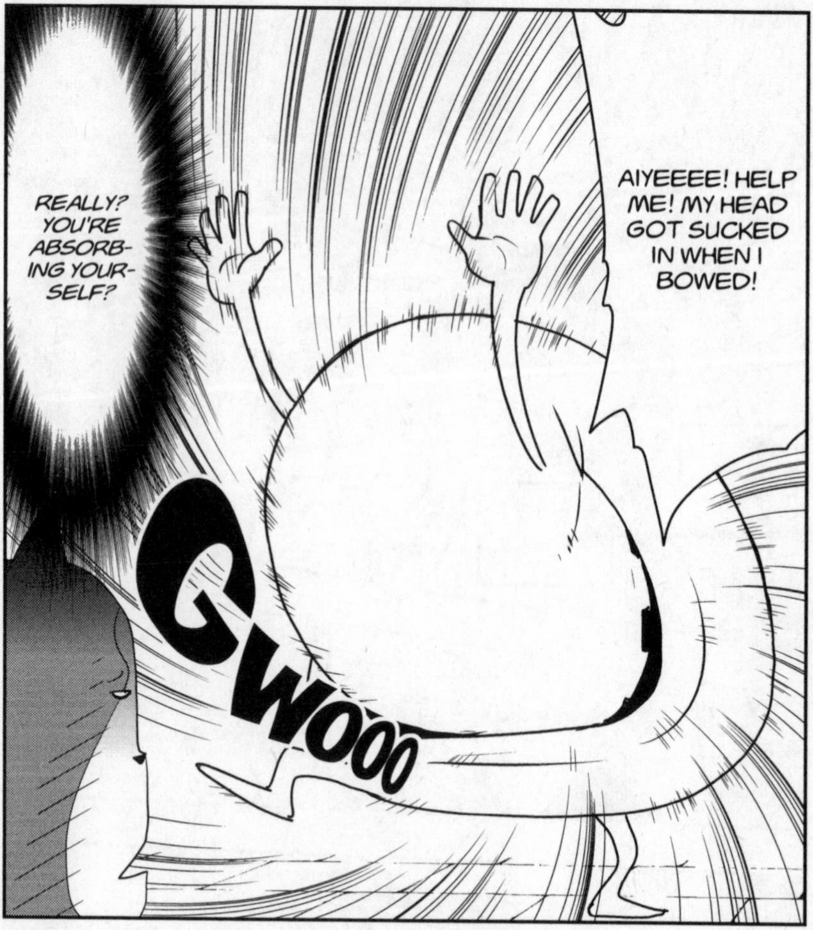
AIYEEEE! HELP ME! MY HEAD GOT SUCKED IN WHEN I BOWED!
REALLY? YOU'RE ABSORB-ING YOUR-SELF?
GWOOO
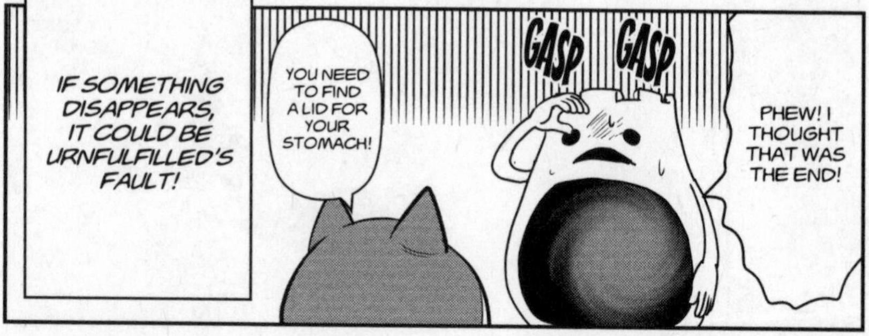
PHEW! I THOUGHT THAT WAS THE END!
GASP GASP
YOU NEED TO FIND A LID FOR YOUR STOMACH!
IF SOMETHING DISAPPEARS, IT COULD BE URNFULFILLED'S FAULT!

CHAPTER 159
NINJA YO-KAI SHURIKENNY

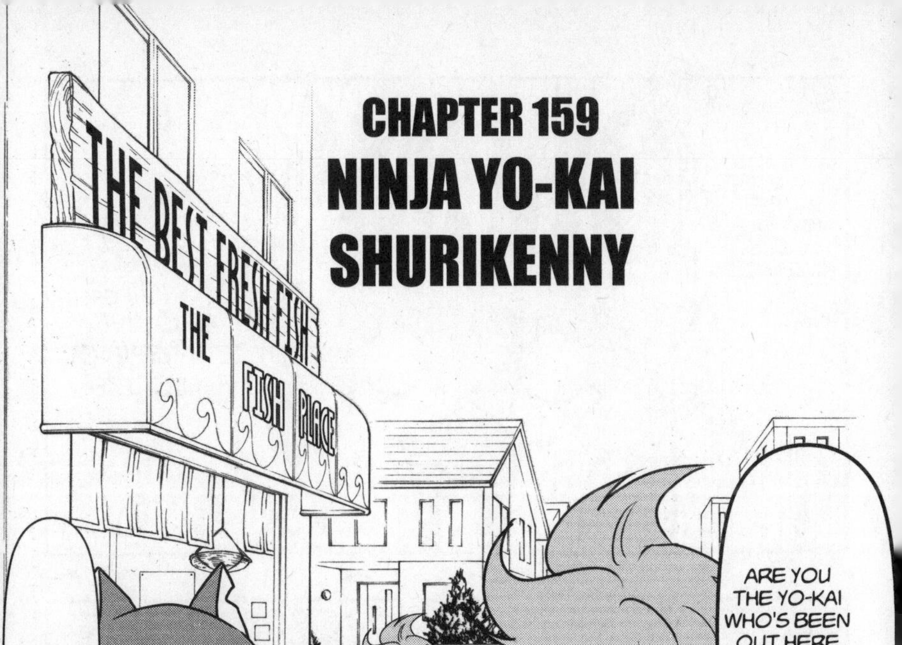
THE BEST FRESH FISH
THE FISH PLACE
ARE YOU THE YO-KAI WHO'S BEEN OUT HERE PUNCHING VEHICLES?
MEOW?! WHO ARE YOU?!

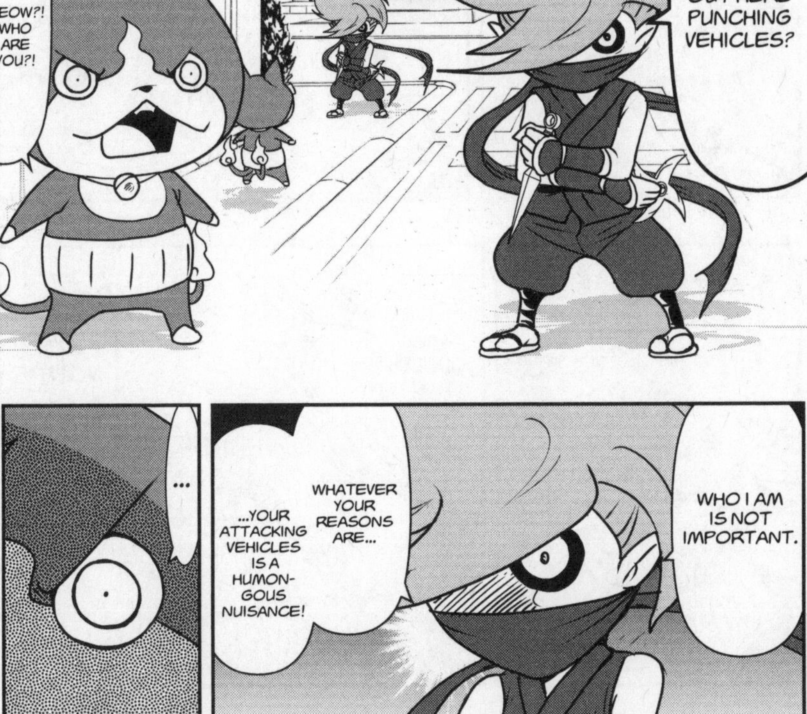
WHO I AM IS NOT IMPORTANT.
WHATEVER YOUR REASONS ARE...
...YOUR ATTACKING VEHICLES IS A HUMON-GOUS NUISANCE!
...

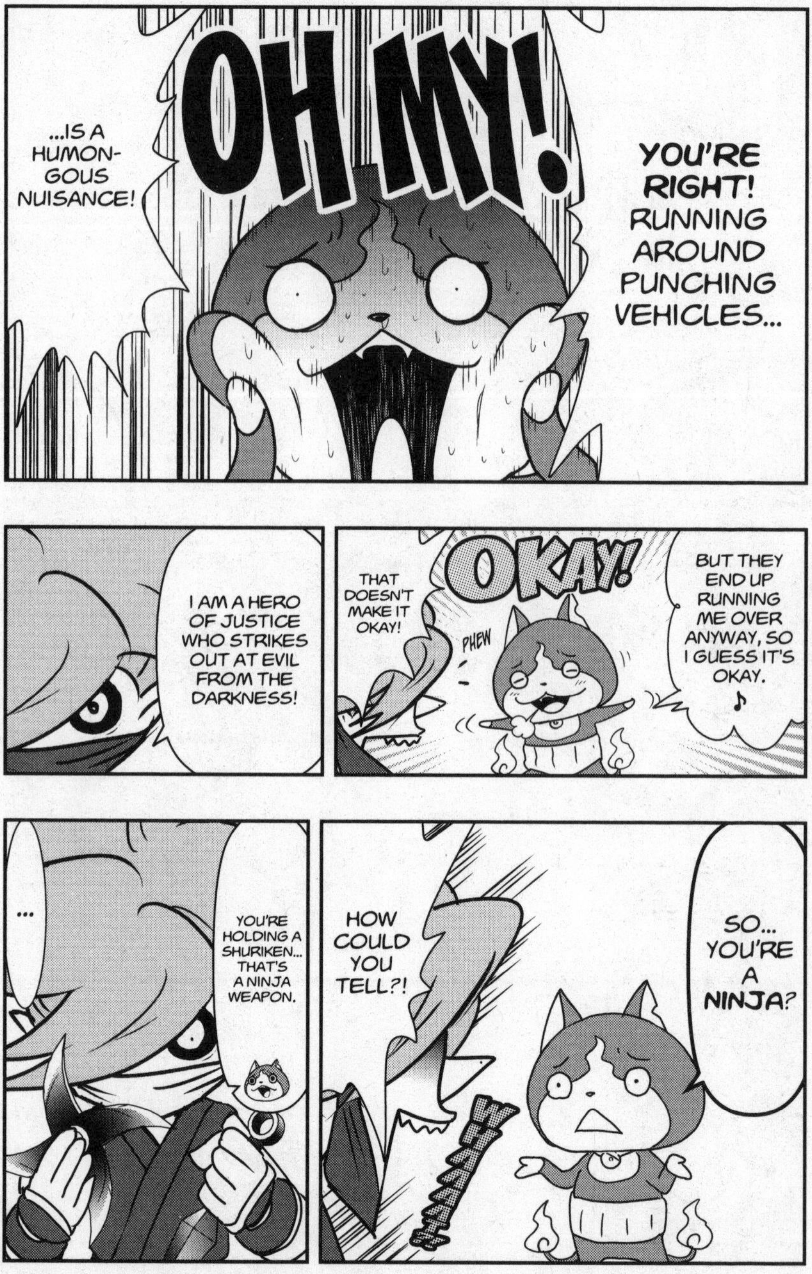
YOU'RE RIGHT! RUNNING AROUND PUNCHING VEHICLES...
OH MY!
...IS A HUMON-GOUS NUISANCE!
BUT THEY END UP RUNNING ME OVER ANYWAY, SO I GUESS IT'S OKAY. ♪
OKAY!
PHEW
THAT DOESN'T MAKE IT OKAY!
I AM A HERO OF JUSTICE WHO STRIKES OUT AT EVIL FROM THE DARKNESS!
SO... YOU'RE A NINJA?
HOW COULD YOU TELL?!
YOU'RE HOLDING A SHURIKEN... THAT'S A NINJA WEAPON.
...

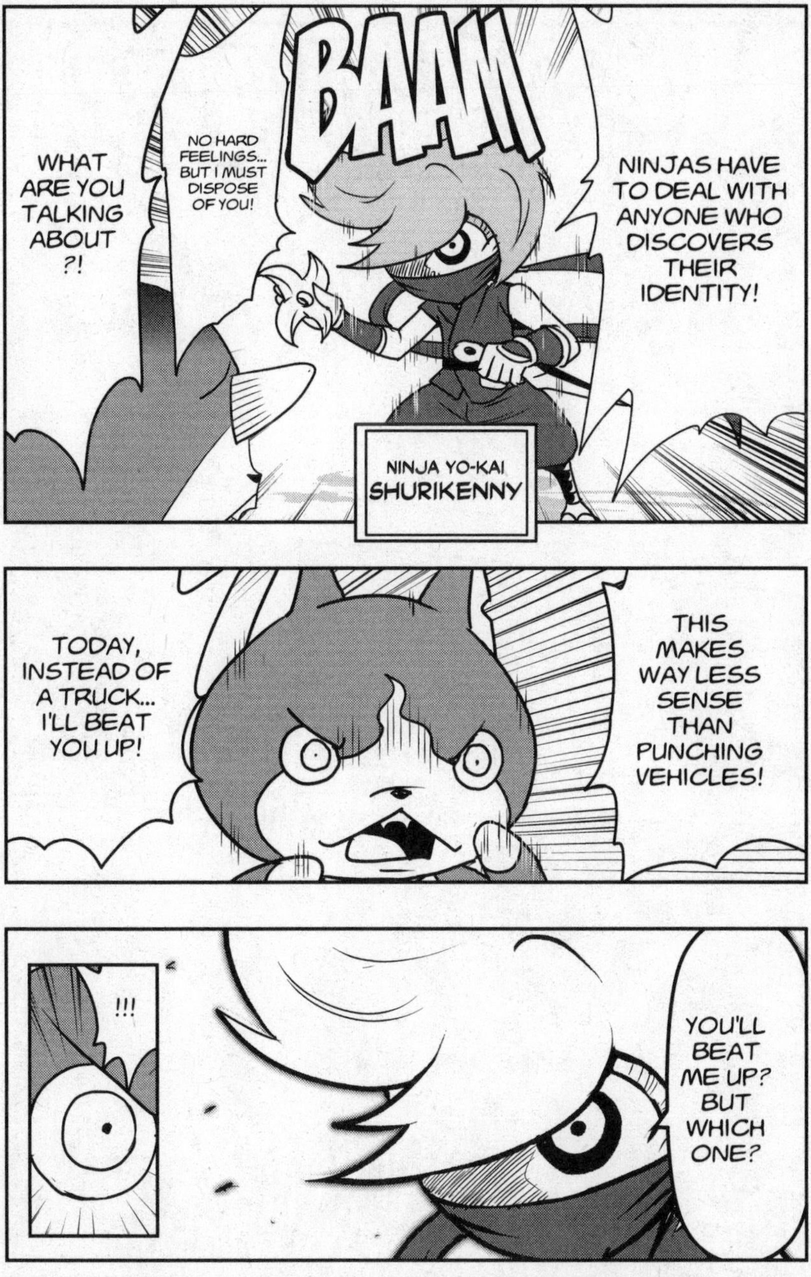
NINJAS HAVE TO DEAL WITH ANYONE WHO DISCOVERS THEIR IDENTITY!
BAAM
NO HARD FEELINGS... BUT I MUST DISPOSE OF YOU!
WHAT ARE YOU TALKING ABOUT ?!
NINJA YO-KAI SHURIKENNY
THIS MAKES WAY LESS SENSE THAN PUNCHING VEHICLES!
TODAY, INSTEAD OF A TRUCK... I'LL BEAT YOU UP!
YOU'LL BEAT ME UP? BUT WHICH ONE?
!!!

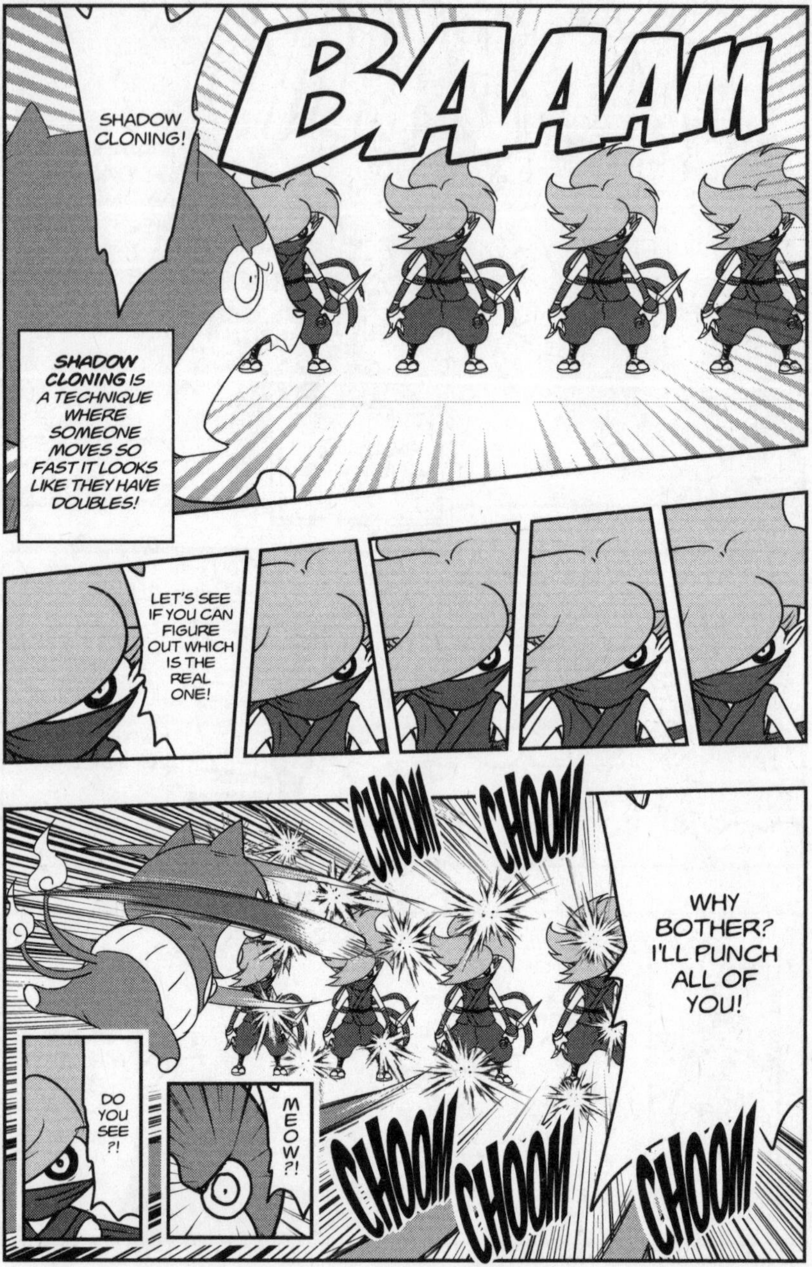
BAAAM
SHADOW CLONING!
SHADOW CLONING IS A TECHNIQUE WHERE SOMEONE MOVES SO FAST IT LOOKS LIKE THEY HAVE DOUBLES!
LET'S SEE IF YOU CAN FIGURE OUT WHICH IS THE REAL ONE!
CHOOM CHOOM
WHY BOTHER? I'LL PUNCH ALL OF YOU!
CHOOM CHOOM CHOOM
MEOW?!
DO YOU SEE?!

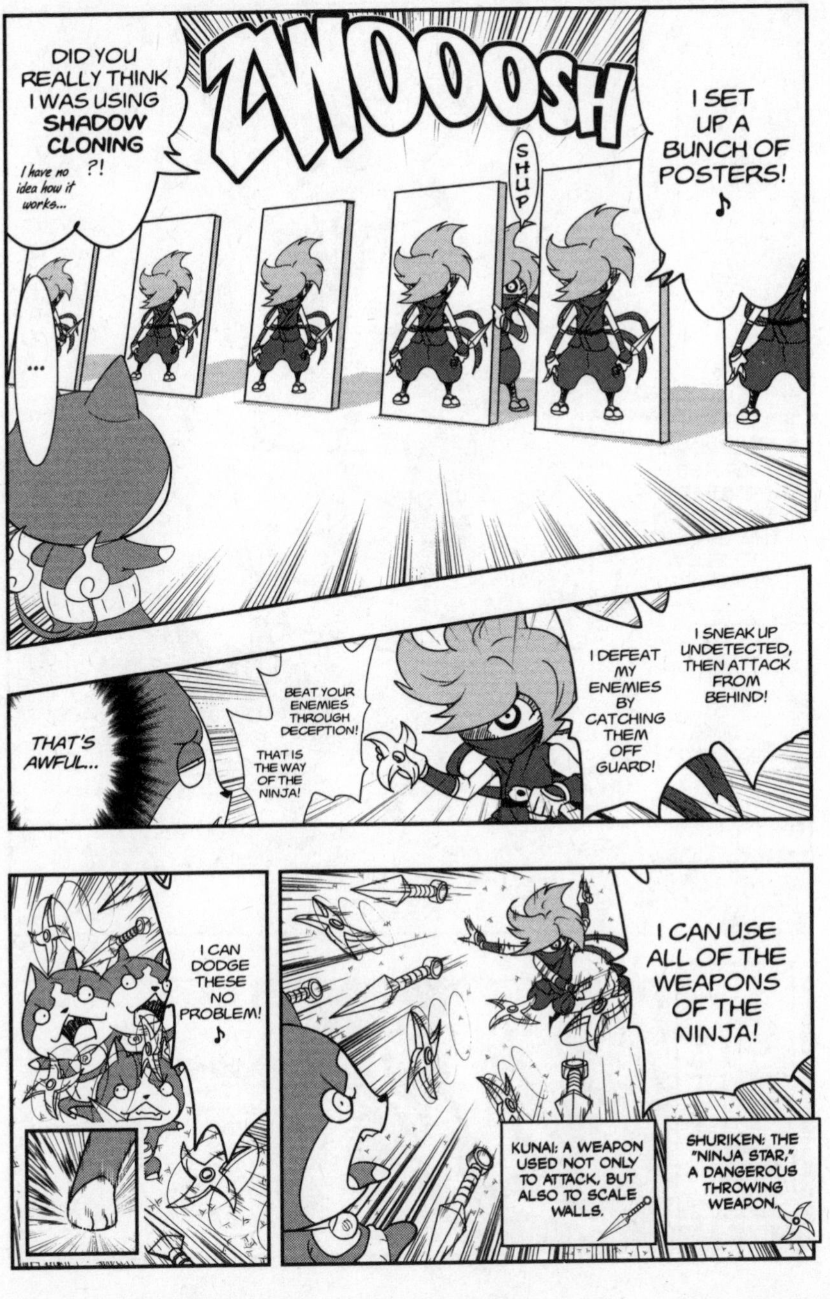
ZWOOOSH
I SET UP A BUNCH OF POSTERS! ♪
SHUP
DID YOU REALLY THINK I WAS USING SHADOW CLONING ?!
I have no idea how it works...
...
I SNEAK UP UNDETECTED, THEN ATTACK FROM BEHIND!
I DEFEAT MY ENEMIES BY CATCHING THEM OFF GUARD!
BEAT YOUR ENEMIES THROUGH DECEPTION!
THAT IS THE WAY OF THE NINJA!
THAT'S AWFUL...
I CAN USE ALL OF THE WEAPONS OF THE NINJA!
SHURIKEN: THE "NINJA STAR," A DANGEROUS THROWING WEAPON.
KUNAI: A WEAPON USED NOT ONLY TO ATTACK, BUT ALSO TO SCALE WALLS.
I CAN DODGE THESE NO PROBLEM! ♪

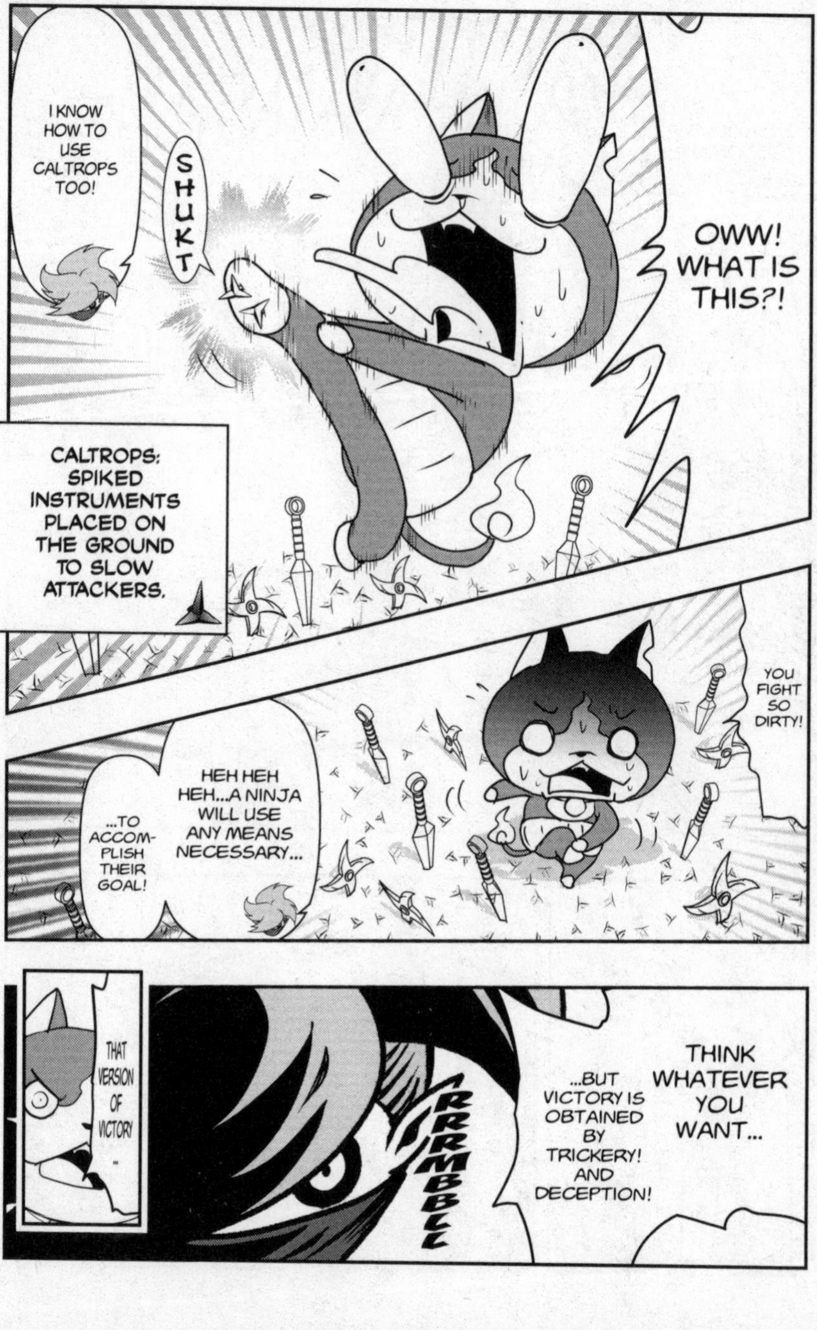
OWW! WHAT IS THIS?!
SHUKT
I KNOW HOW TO USE CALTROPS TOO!
CALTROPS: SPIKED INSTRUMENTS PLACED ON THE GROUND TO SLOW ATTACKERS.
YOU FIGHT SO DIRTY!
HEH HEH HEH...A NINJA WILL USE ANY MEANS NECESSARY...
...TO ACCOMPLISH THEIR GOAL!
THINK WHATEVER YOU WANT...
...BUT VICTORY IS OBTAINED BY TRICKERY! AND DECEPTION!
RRRMBBLL
THAT VERSION OF VICTORY ...

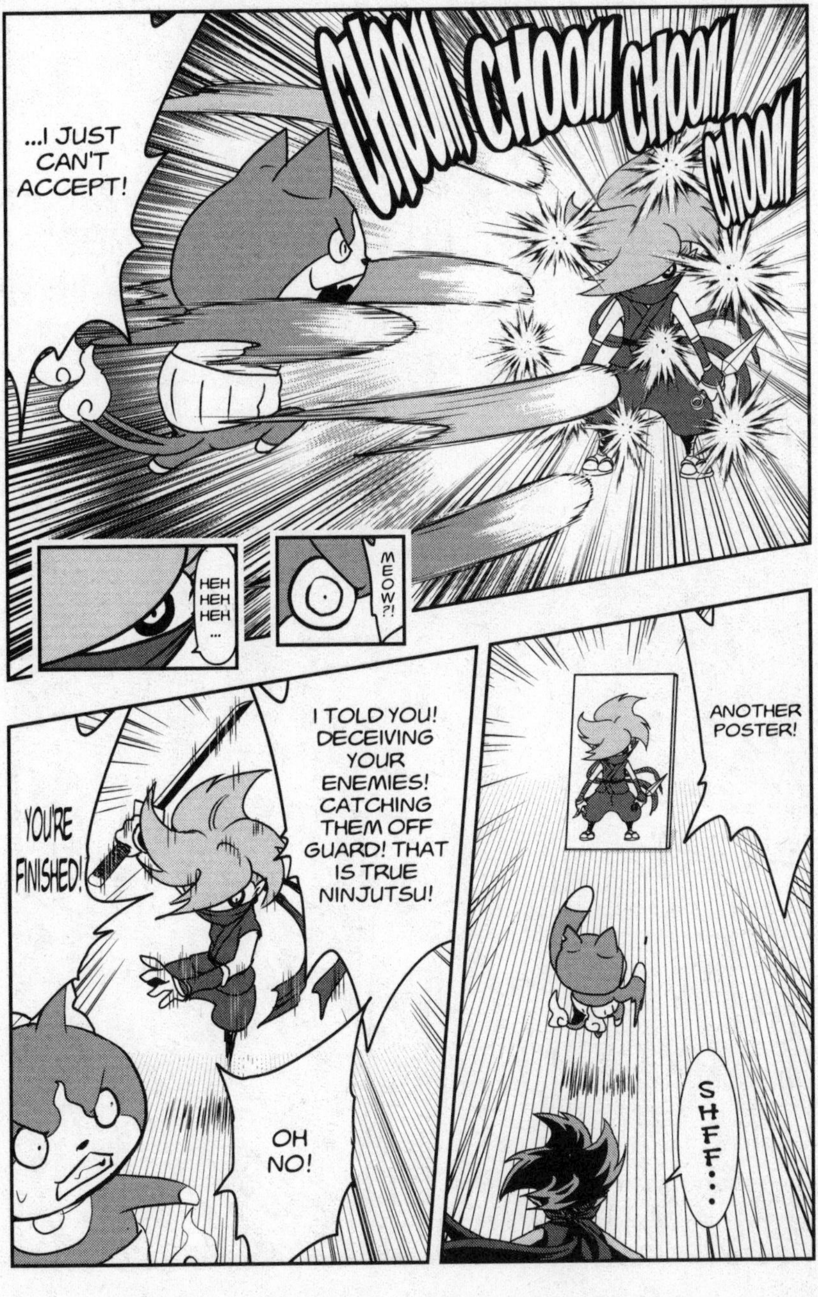
CHOOM CHOOM CHOOM CHOOM
...I JUST CAN'T ACCEPT!
MEOW?!
HEH HEH HEH ...
ANOTHER POSTER!
SHFF...
I TOLD YOU! DECEIVING YOUR ENEMIES! CATCHING THEM OFF GUARD! THAT IS TRUE NINJUTSU!
YOU'RE FINISHED!
OH NO!

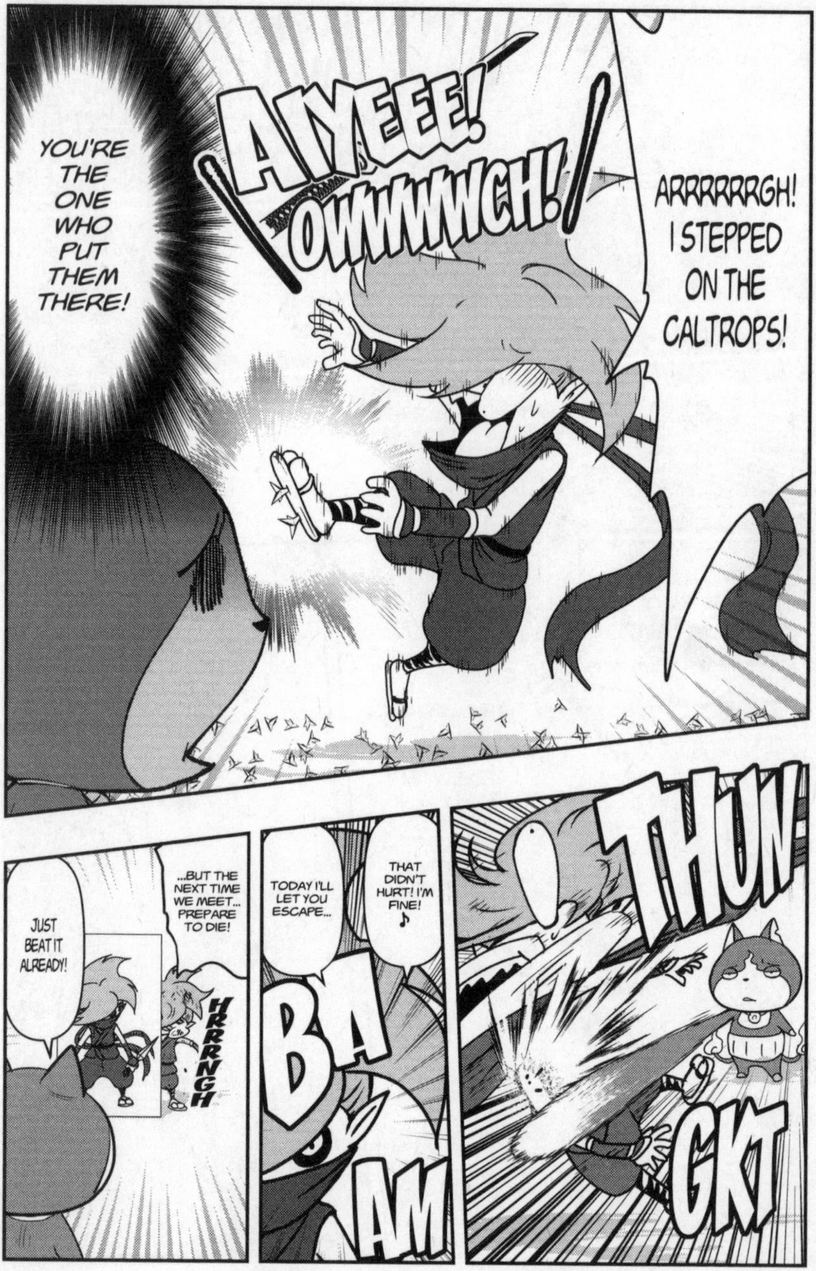
AIYEEE!
OWWWWCH!
ARRRRRRGH! I STEPPED ON THE CALTROPS!
YOU'RE THE ONE WHO PUT THEM THERE!
THUN
GKT
THAT DIDN'T HURT! I'M FINE! ♪
TODAY I'LL LET YOU ESCAPE...
BA
AM
...BUT THE NEXT TIME WE MEET... PREPARE TO DIE!
HRRRNGH
JUST BEAT IT ALREADY!

CHAPTER 160
PROCRASTINATION YO-KAI PROCRASTINOCCHIO

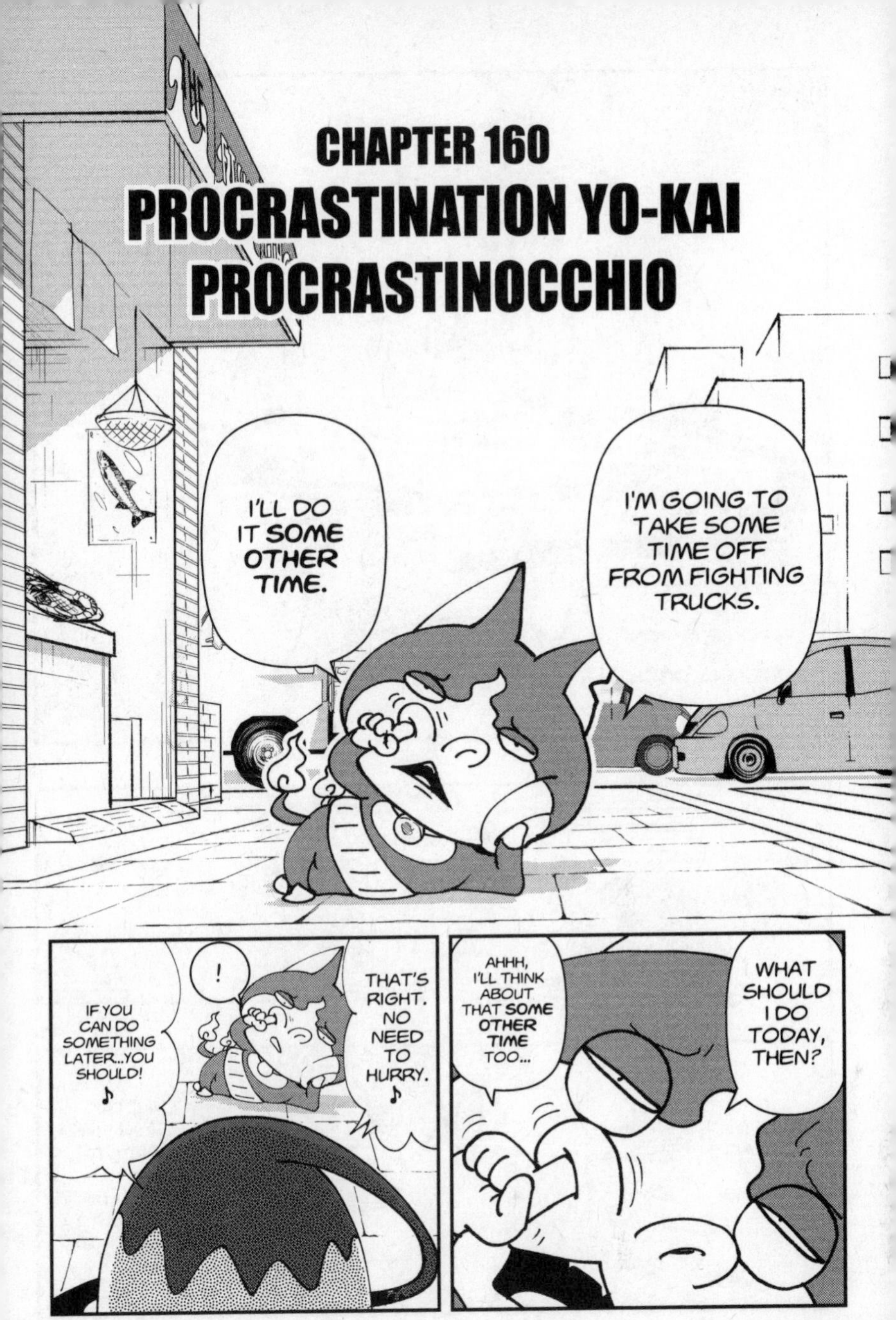

I'M GOING TO TAKE SOME TIME OFF FROM FIGHTING TRUCKS.
I'LL DO IT SOME OTHER TIME.
WHAT SHOULD I DO TODAY, THEN?
AHHH, I'LL THINK ABOUT THAT SOME OTHER TIME TOO...
THAT'S RIGHT. NO NEED TO HURRY. ♪
!
IF YOU CAN DO SOMETHING LATER...YOU SHOULD! ♪

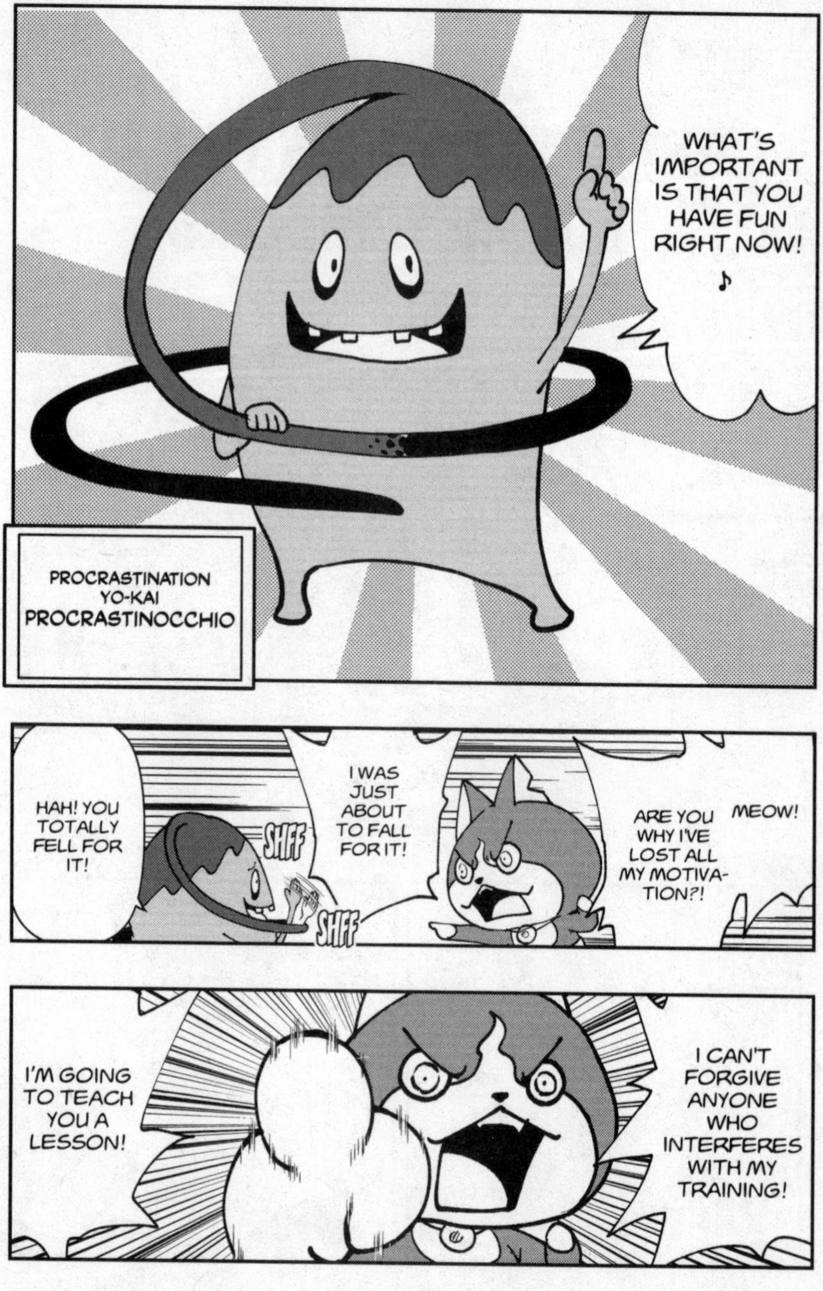
WHAT'S IMPORTANT IS THAT YOU HAVE FUN RIGHT NOW! ♪
PROCRASTINATION YO-KAI PROCRASTINOCCHIO
MEOW!
ARE YOU WHY I'VE LOST ALL MY MOTIVA-TION?!
I WAS JUST ABOUT TO FALL FOR IT!
SHFF
SHFF
HAH! YOU TOTALLY FELL FOR IT!
I CAN'T FORGIVE ANYONE WHO INTERFERES WITH MY TRAINING!
I'M GOING TO TEACH YOU A LESSON!

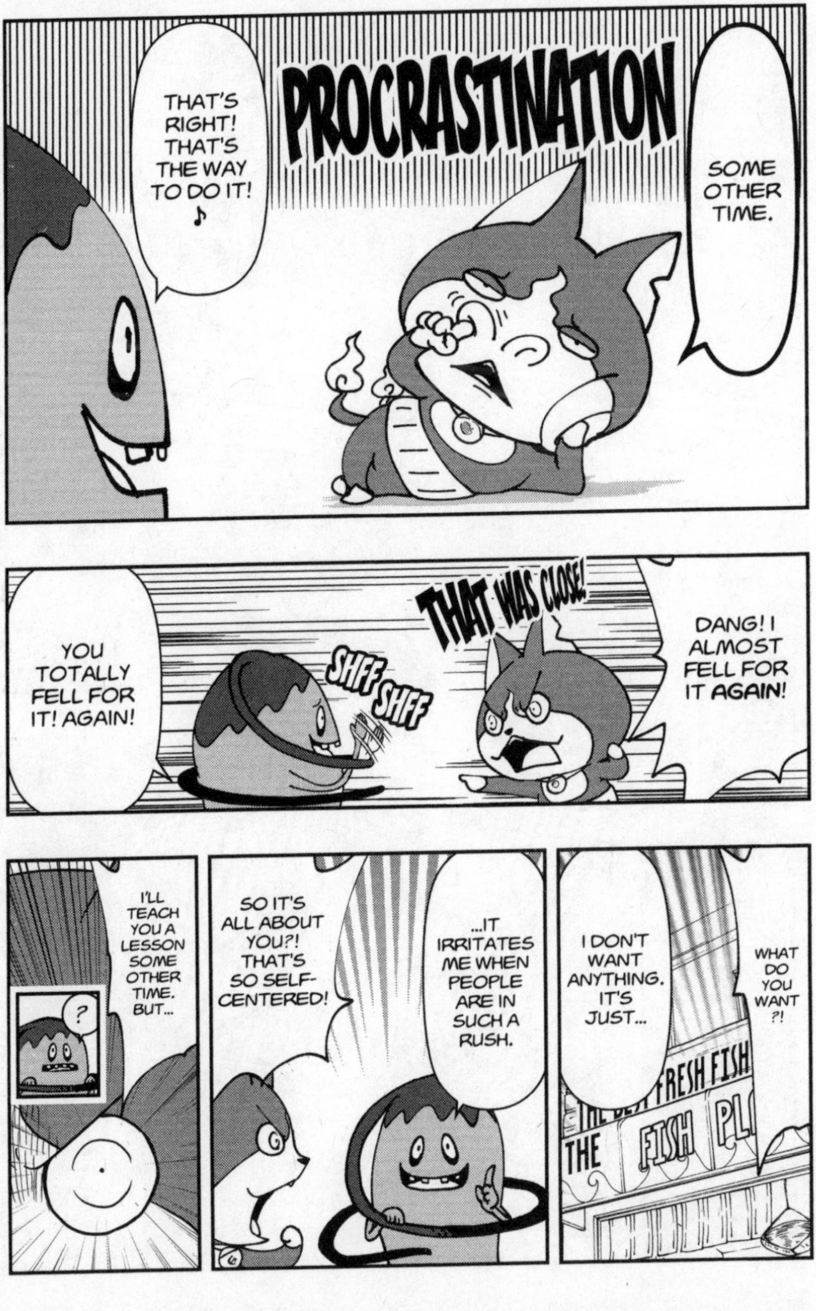
SOME OTHER TIME.
PROCRASTINATION
THAT'S RIGHT! THAT'S THE WAY TO DO IT! ♪
DANG! I ALMOST FELL FOR IT AGAIN!
THAT WAS CLOSE!
SHFF SHFF
YOU TOTALLY FELL FOR IT! AGAIN!
WHAT DO YOU WANT?!
I DON'T WANT ANYTHING. IT'S JUST...
FRESH FISH
THE FISH
...IT IRRITATES ME WHEN PEOPLE ARE IN SUCH A RUSH.
SO IT'S ALL ABOUT YOU?! THAT'S SO SELF-CENTERED!
?
I'LL TEACH YOU A LESSON SOME OTHER TIME. BUT...

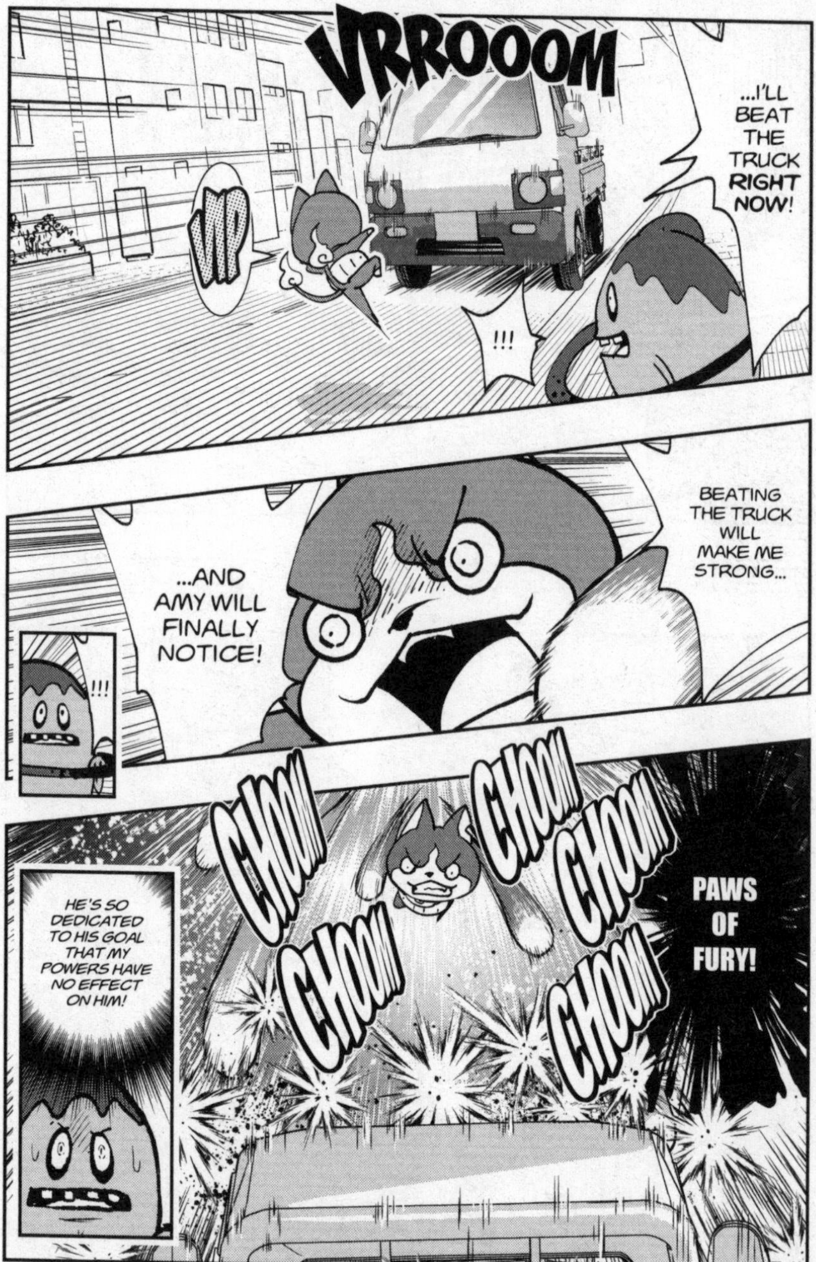
VRROOM
...I'LL BEAT THE TRUCK RIGHT NOW!
!!!
VIP
BEATING THE TRUCK WILL MAKE ME STRONG...
...AND AMY WILL FINALLY NOTICE!
!!!
PAWS OF FURY!
CHOOM
CHOOM
CHOOM
CHOOM
CHOOM
CHOOM
HE'S SO DEDICATED TO HIS GOAL THAT MY POWERS HAVE NO EFFECT ON HIM!

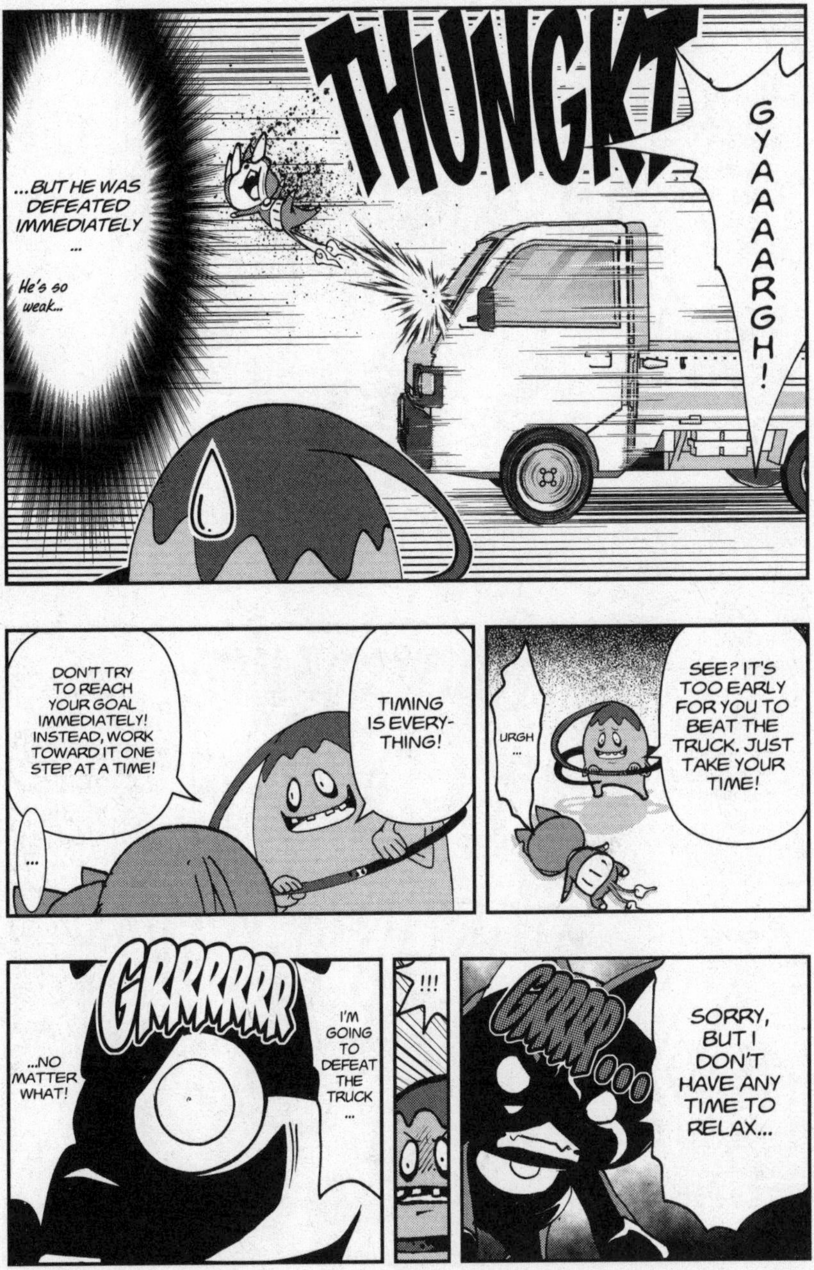
GYAAAAARGH!
THUNK!!
...BUT HE WAS DEFEATED IMMEDIATELY ...
He's so weak...
SEE? IT'S TOO EARLY FOR YOU TO BEAT THE TRUCK. JUST TAKE YOUR TIME!
URGH ...
TIMING IS EVERY-THING!
DON'T TRY TO REACH YOUR GOAL IMMEDIATELY! INSTEAD, WORK TOWARD IT ONE STEP AT A TIME!
...
SORRY, BUT I DON'T HAVE ANY TIME TO RELAX...
GRRRR...
!!!
GRRRRRR
I'M GOING TO DEFEAT THE TRUCK ...
...NO MATTER WHAT!

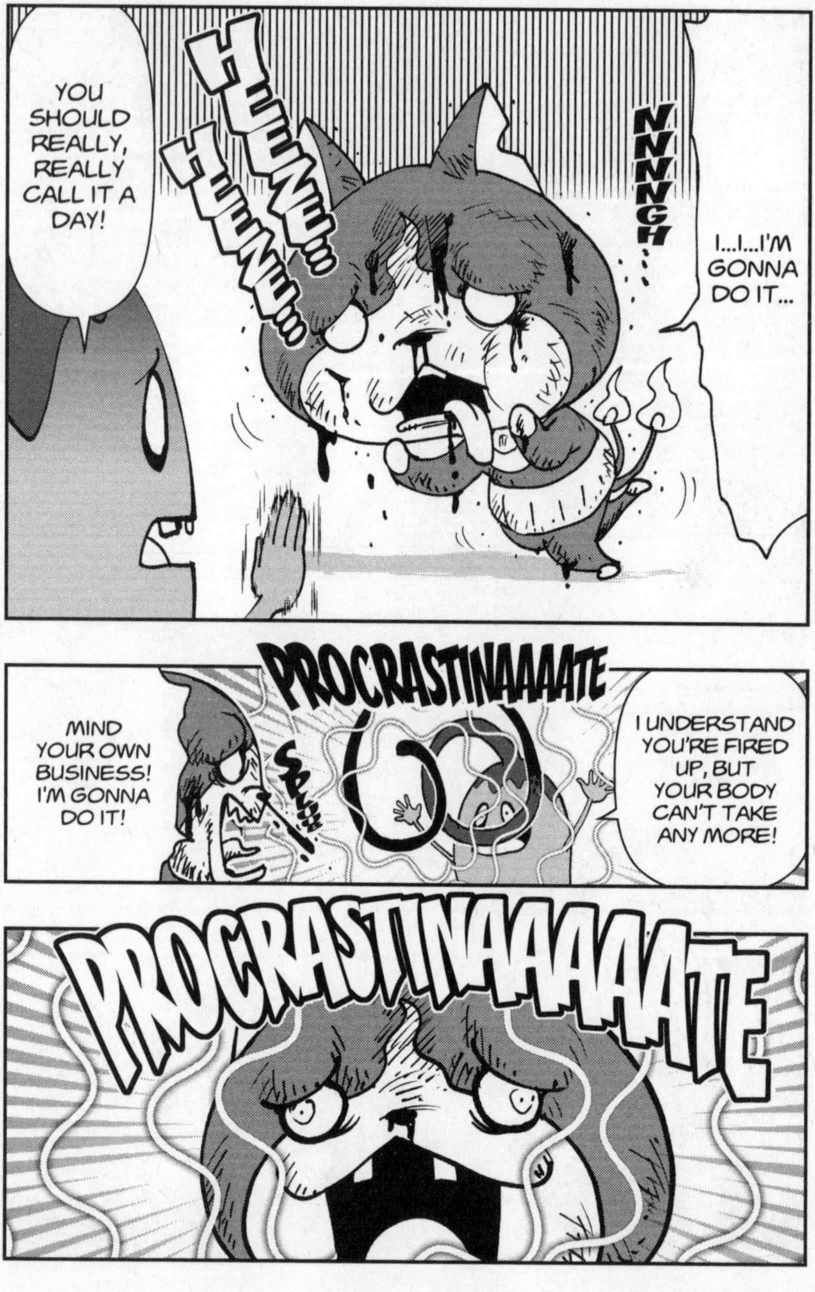
I...I...I'M GONNA DO IT...
NNNNGH...
HEENE... HEENE...
YOU SHOULD REALLY, REALLY CALL IT A DAY!
I UNDERSTAND YOU'RE FIRED UP, BUT YOUR BODY CAN'T TAKE ANY MORE!
PROCRASTINAAAATE
MIND YOUR OWN BUSINESS! I'M GONNA DO IT!
PROCRASTINAAAAATE

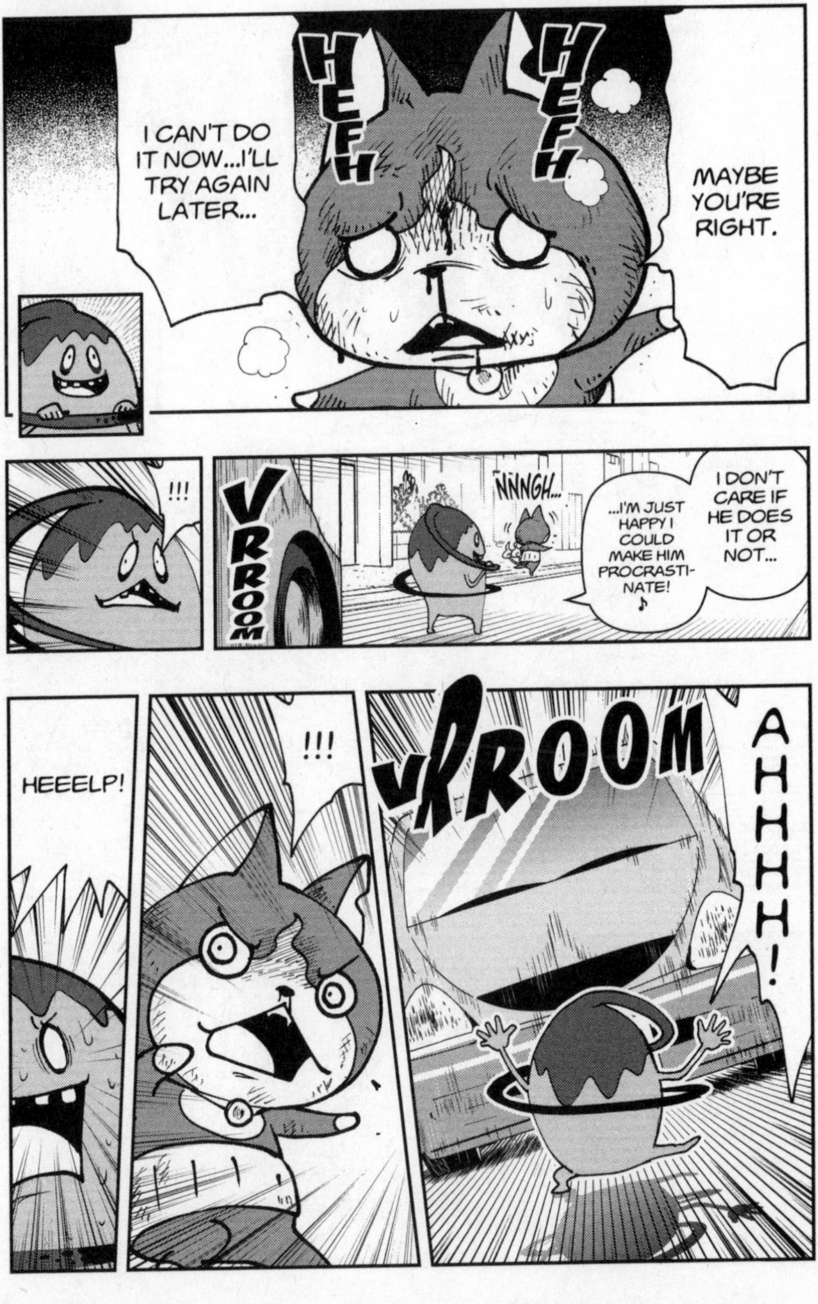
MAYBE YOU'RE RIGHT.
HEFH
HEFH
I CAN'T DO IT NOW...I'LL TRY AGAIN LATER...
I DON'T CARE IF HE DOES IT OR NOT...
...I'M JUST HAPPY I COULD MAKE HIM PROCRASTI-NATE! ♪
NNNGH...
VRROOM
!!!
AHHHH!
VRROOM
!!!
HEEELP!

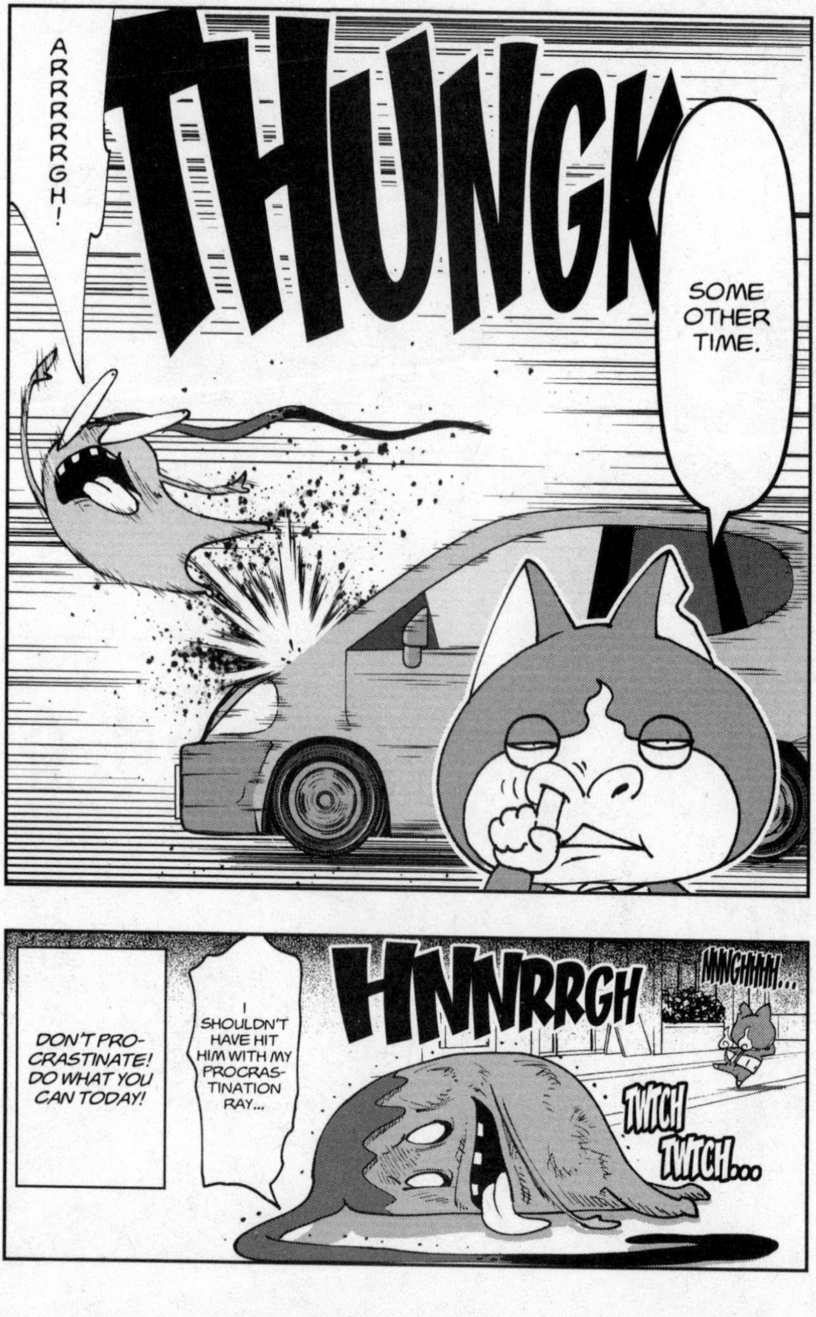
SOME OTHER TIME.
THUNK
ARRRRRGH!
MNGHHHH...
TWITCH TWITCH...
HNNRRGH
I SHOULDN'T HAVE HIT HIM WITH MY PROCRAS-TINATION RAY...
DON'T PRO-CRASTINATE! DO WHAT YOU CAN TODAY!

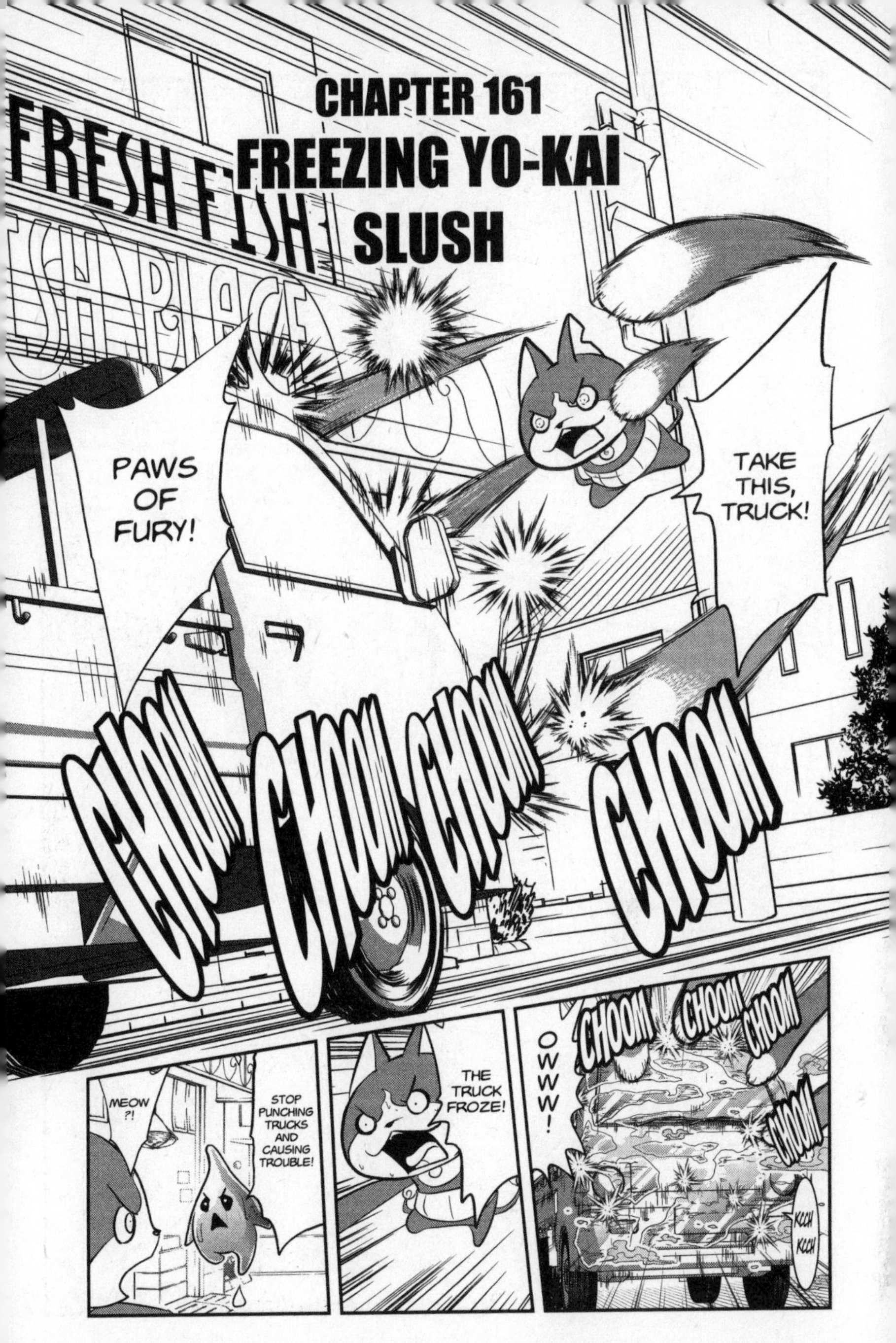
CHAPTER 161
FREEZING YO-KAI SLUSH
FRESH FISH
TAKE THIS, TRUCK!
PAWS OF FURY!
CHOOM
CHOOM
CHOOM
CHOOM
CHOOM
CHOOM
CHOOM
CHOOM
OWWW!
KCCH KCCH
THE TRUCK FROZE!
STOP PUNCHING TRUCKS AND CAUSING TROUBLE!
MEOW?!

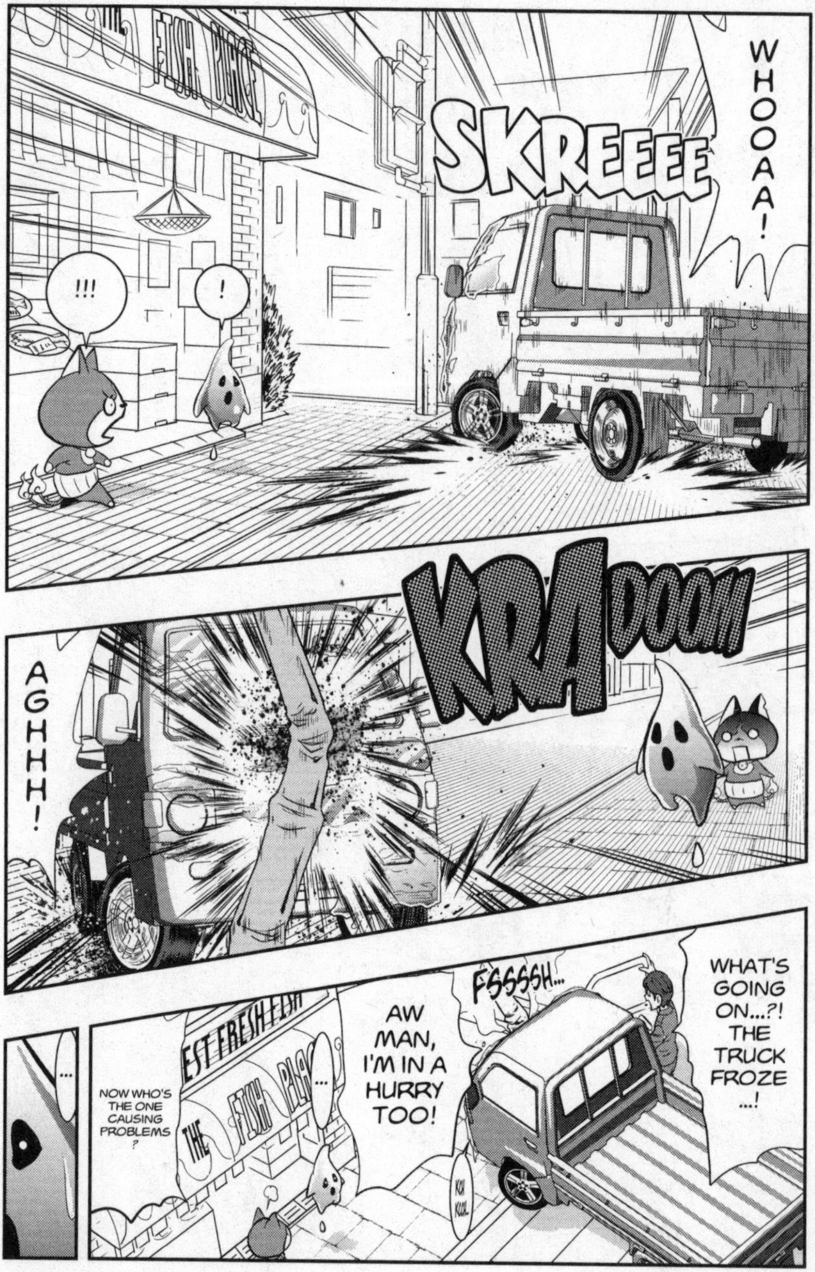
WHOOAAA!
SKREEEE
!
!!!
KRADOOM
AGHHH!
WHAT'S GOING ON...?! THE TRUCK FROZE ...!
FSSSSH...
AW MAN, I'M IN A HURRY TOO!
...
NOW WHO'S THE ONE CAUSING PROBLEMS ?
...

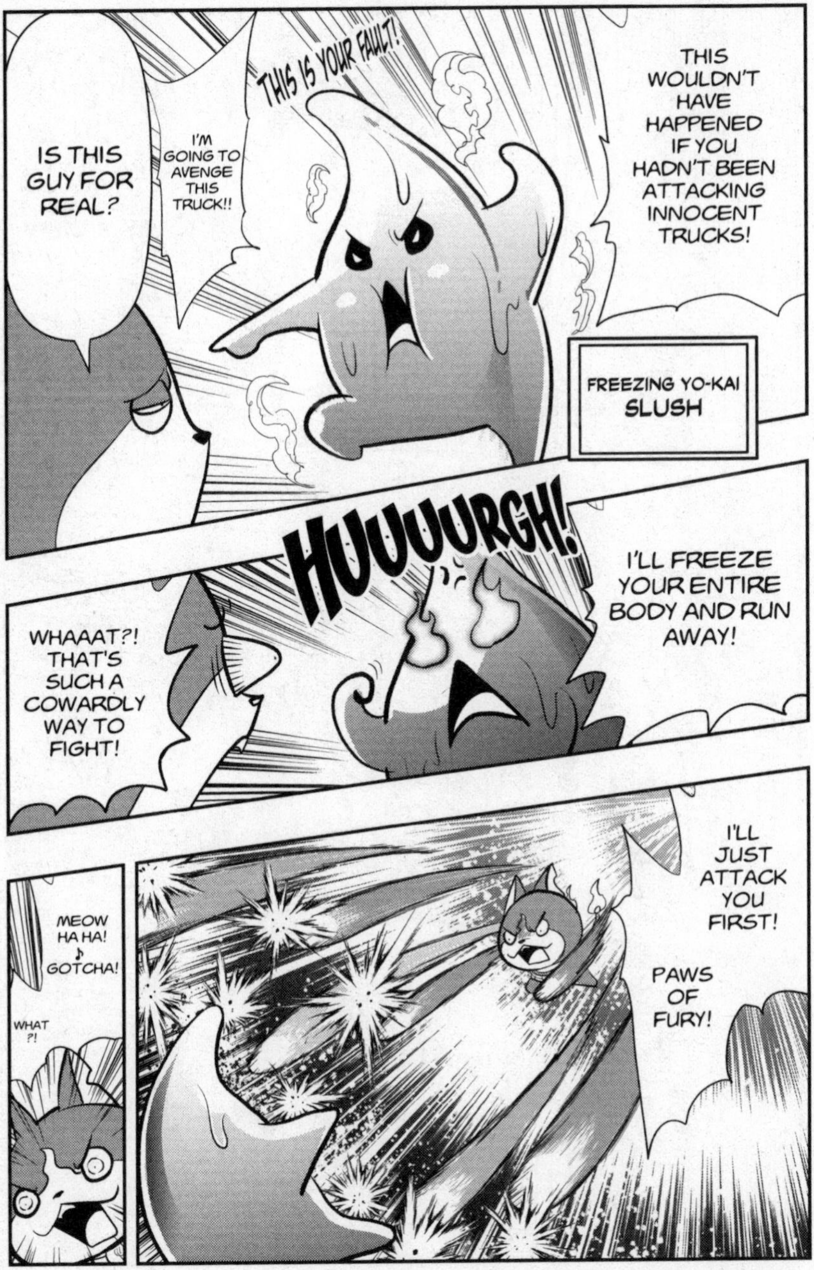
THIS WOULDN'T HAVE HAPPENED IF YOU HADN'T BEEN ATTACKING INNOCENT TRUCKS!
THIS IS YOUR FAULT!
FREEZING YO-KAI SLUSH
I'M GOING TO AVENGE THIS TRUCK!!
IS THIS GUY FOR REAL?
HUUUURGH!
I'LL FREEZE YOUR ENTIRE BODY AND RUN AWAY!
WHAAAT?! THAT'S SUCH A COWARDLY WAY TO FIGHT!
I'LL JUST ATTACK YOU FIRST!
PAWS OF FURY!
MEOW HA HA! ♪ GOTCHA!
WHAT?!

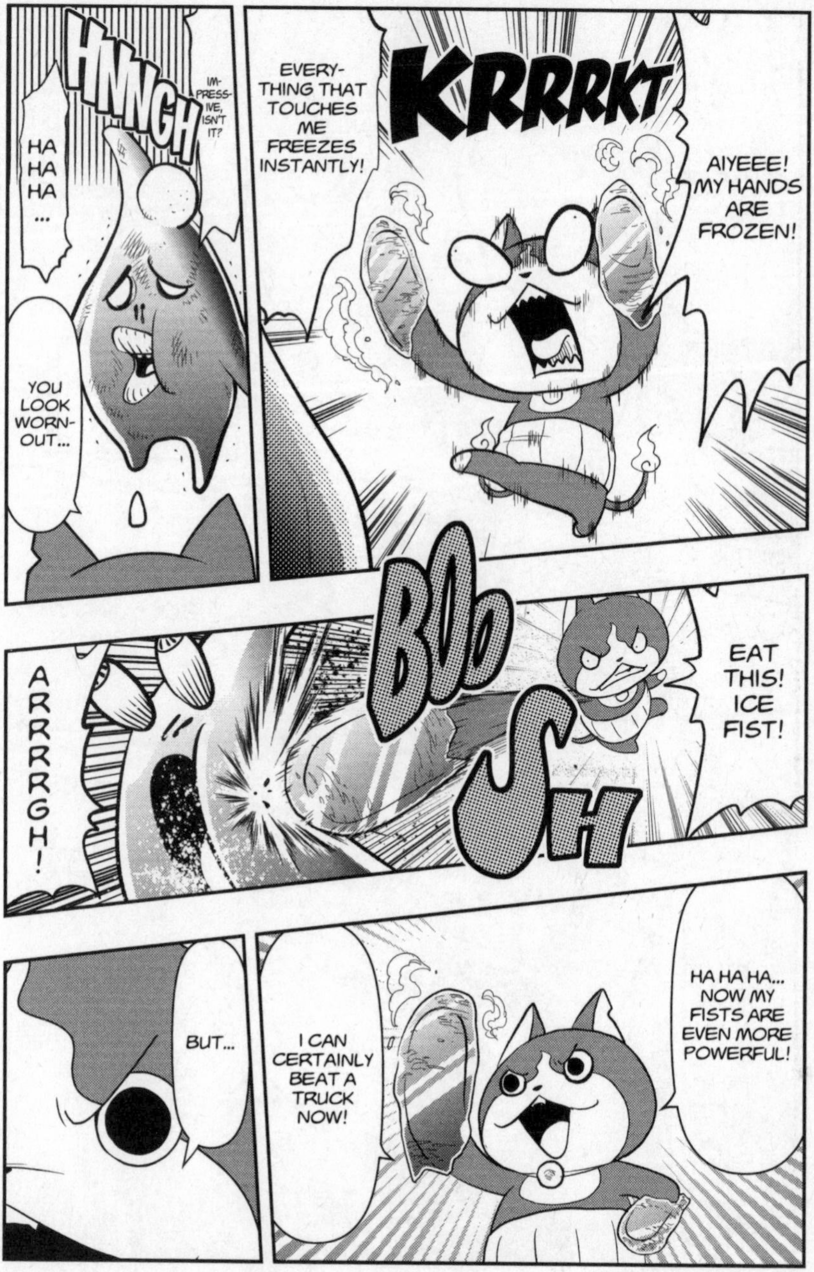
KRRRKT
AIYEEE! MY HANDS ARE FROZEN!
EVERY-THING THAT TOUCHES ME FREEZES INSTANTLY!
IM-PRESS-IVE, ISN'T IT?
HNNGH
HA HA HA ...
YOU LOOK WORN-OUT...
EAT THIS! ICE FIST!
BOOSH
ARRRRGH!
HA HA HA... NOW MY FISTS ARE EVEN MORE POWERFUL!
I CAN CERTAINLY BEAT A TRUCK NOW!
BUT...

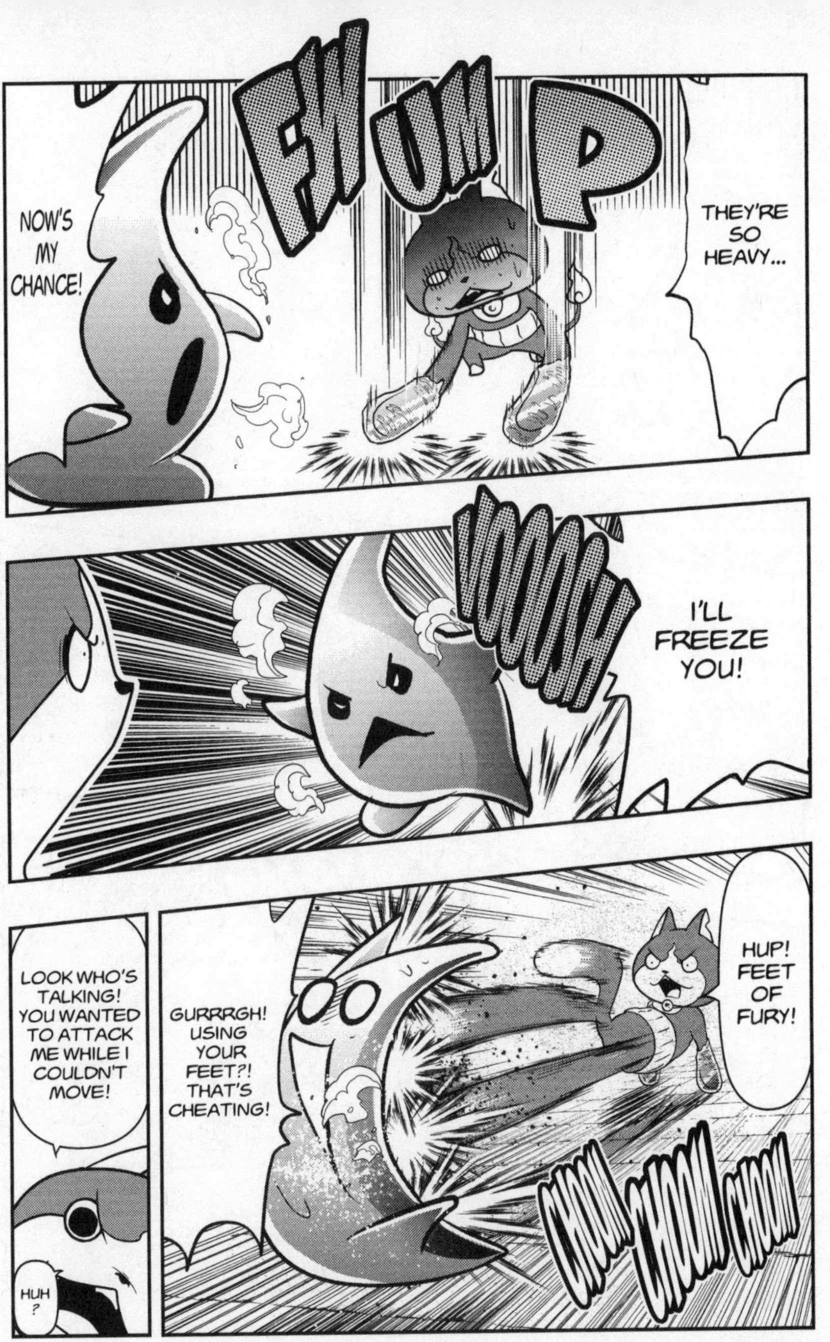
THEY'RE SO HEAVY...
FWUMP
NOW'S MY CHANCE!
I'LL FREEZE YOU!
WOOOSH
HUP! FEET OF FURY!
CHOOM CHOOM CHOOM
GURRRGH! USING YOUR FEET?! THAT'S CHEATING!
LOOK WHO'S TALKING! YOU WANTED TO ATTACK ME WHILE I COULDN'T MOVE!
HUH?

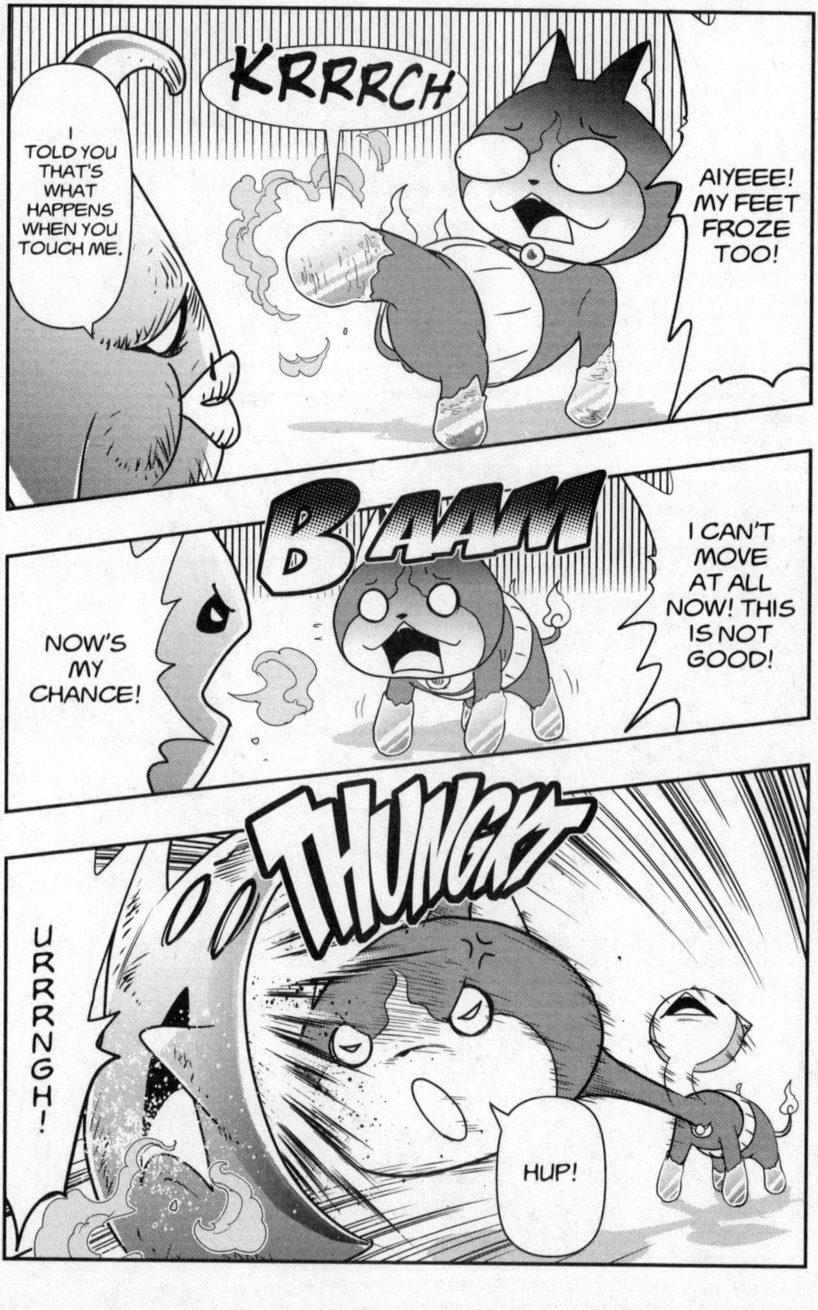
KRRRCH
AIYEEE! MY FEET FROZE TOO!
I TOLD YOU THAT'S WHAT HAPPENS WHEN YOU TOUCH ME.
BAAM
I CAN'T MOVE AT ALL NOW! THIS IS NOT GOOD!
NOW'S MY CHANCE!
THUNGK
HUP!
URRRNGH!

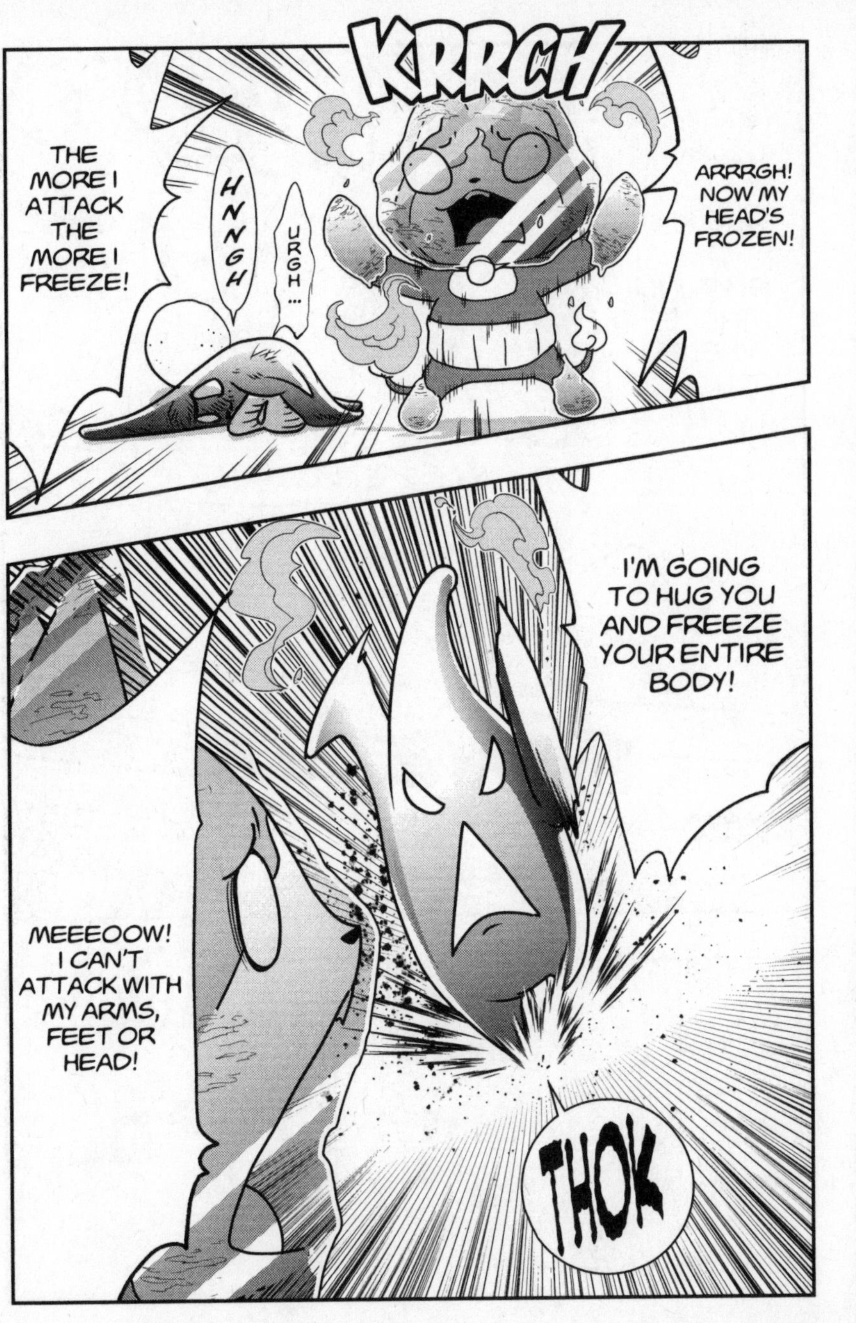
KRRCH
ARRRGH! NOW MY HEAD'S FROZEN!
URGH...
HNNGH
THE MORE I ATTACK THE MORE I FREEZE!
I'M GOING TO HUG YOU AND FREEZE YOUR ENTIRE BODY!
THOK
MEEEOOW! I CAN'T ATTACK WITH MY ARMS, FEET OR HEAD!

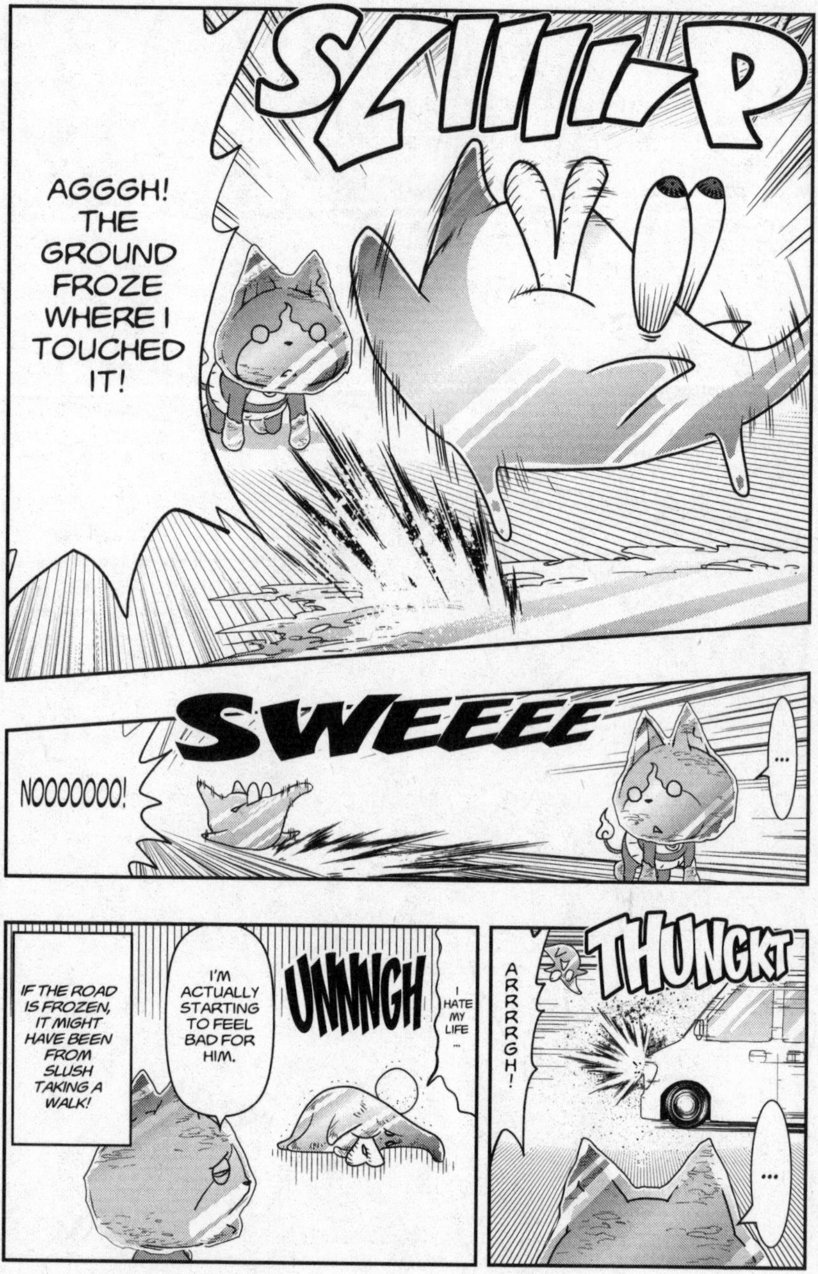
SZIII-P
AGGGH! THE GROUND FROZE WHERE I TOUCHED IT!
...
SWEEEE
NOOOOOOO!
THUNGKT
ARRRRGH!
...
I HATE MY LIFE...
UNNNGH
I'M ACTUALLY STARTING TO FEEL BAD FOR HIM.
IF THE ROAD IS FROZEN, IT MIGHT HAVE BEEN FROM SLUSH TAKING A WALK!

CHAPTER 162
LUMBERJACK YO-KAI BUMBLEJACK

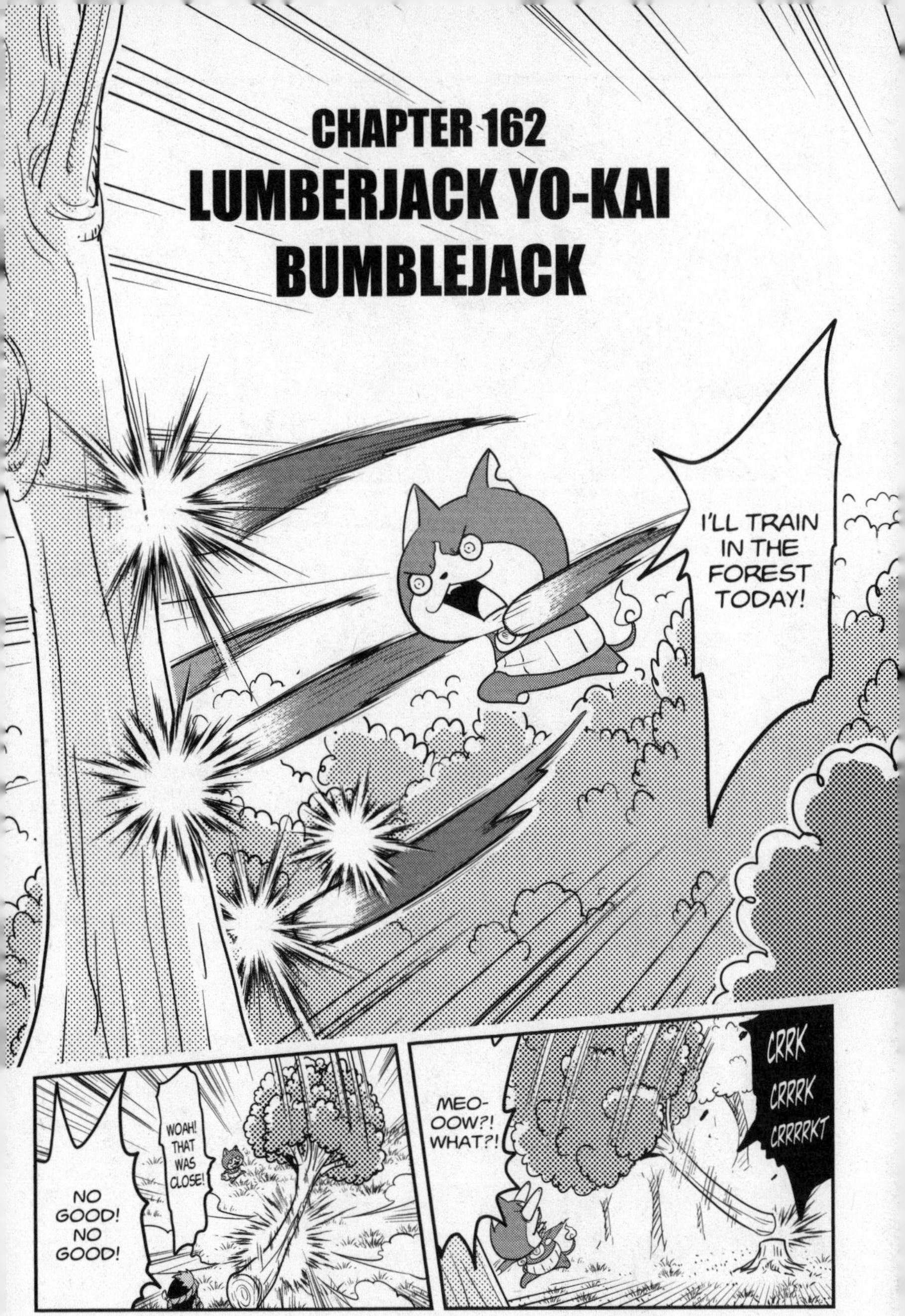
I'LL TRAIN IN THE FOREST TODAY!
MEO-OOW?! WHAT?!
CRRK CRRRK CRRRRKT
WOAH! THAT WAS CLOSE!
NO GOOD! NO GOOD!

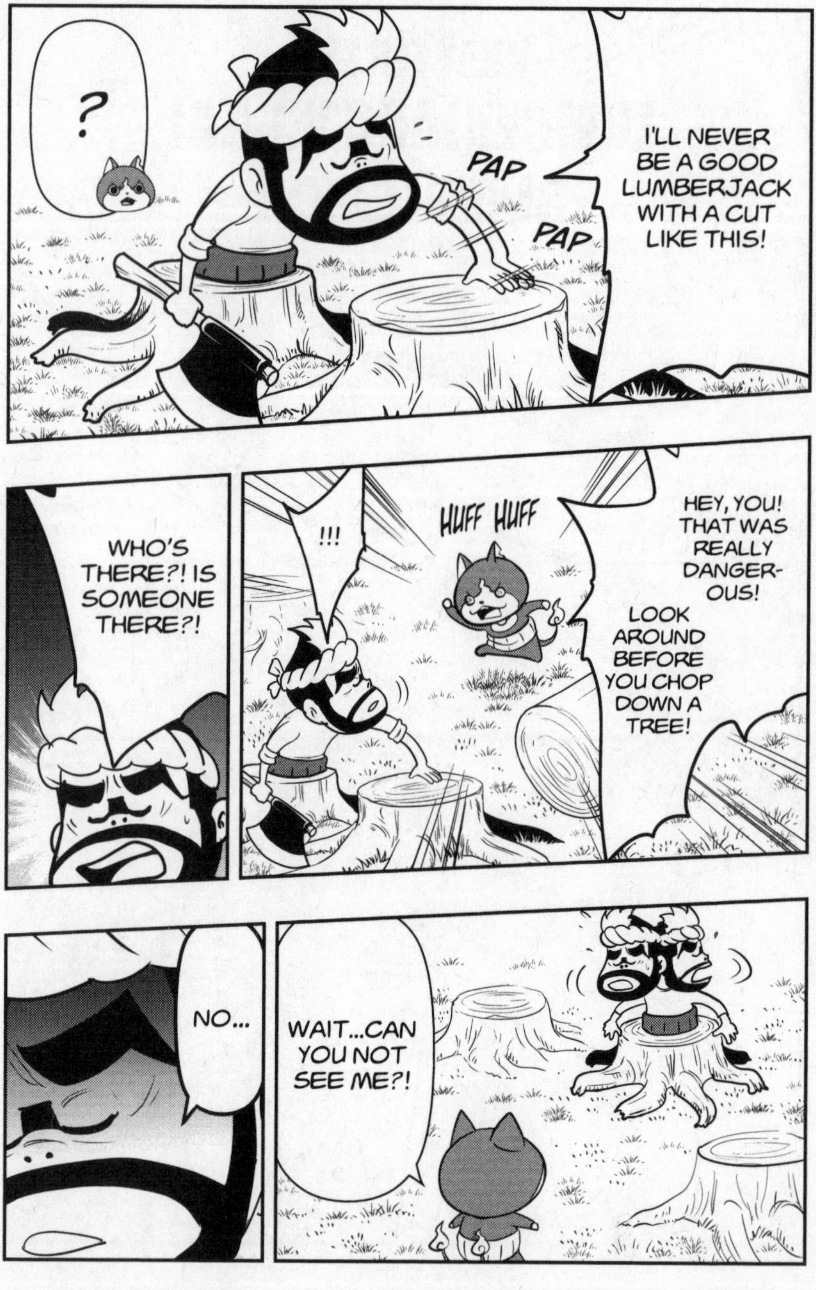
I'LL NEVER BE A GOOD LUMBERJACK WITH A CUT LIKE THIS!
PAP
PAP
?
HEY, YOU! THAT WAS REALLY DANGER-OUS!
LOOK AROUND BEFORE YOU CHOP DOWN A TREE!
HUFF HUFF
!!!
WHO'S THERE?! IS SOMEONE THERE?!
WAIT...CAN YOU NOT SEE ME?!
NO...

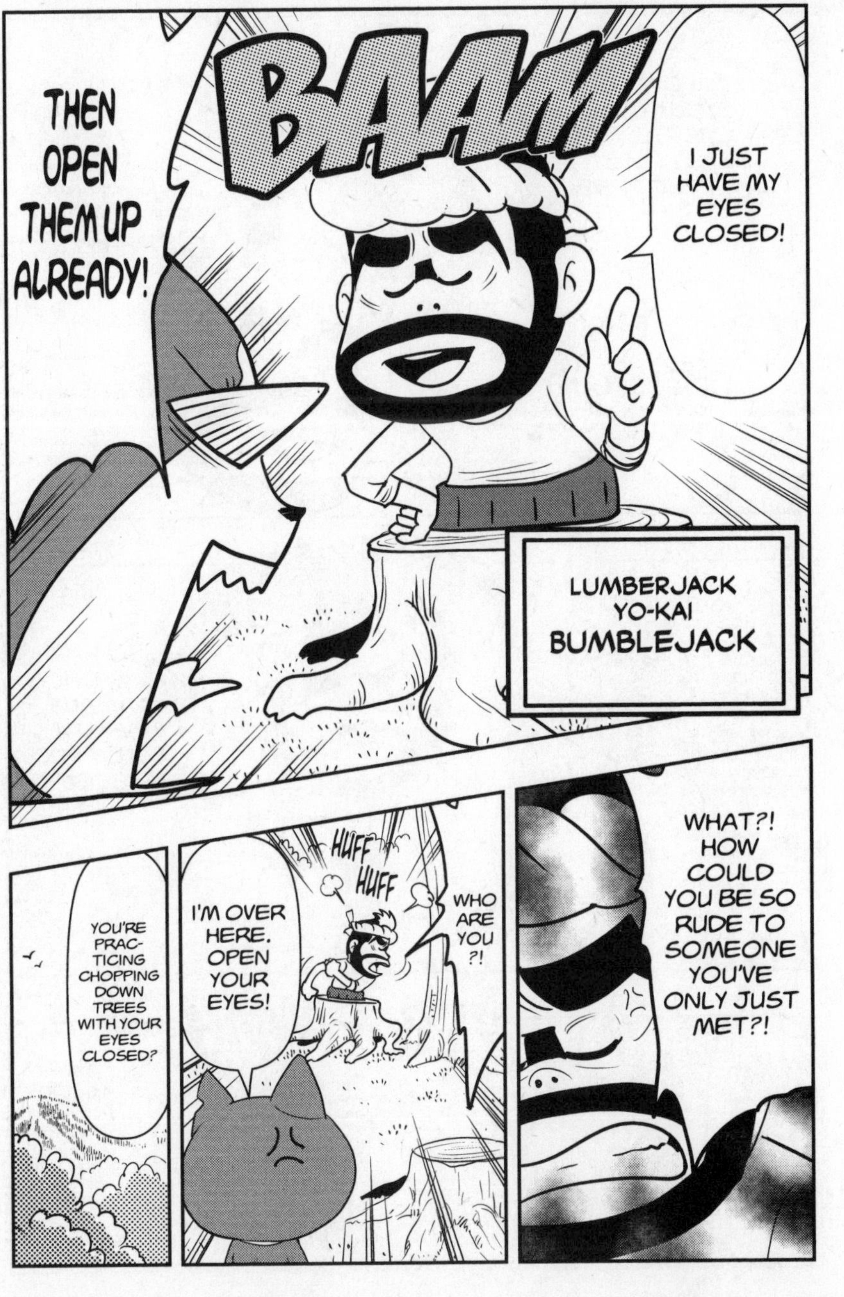
I JUST HAVE MY EYES CLOSED!
BAAM
THEN OPEN THEM UP ALREADY!
LUMBERJACK YO-KAI BUMBLEJACK
WHAT?! HOW COULD YOU BE SO RUDE TO SOMEONE YOU'VE ONLY JUST MET?!
HUFF HUFF
WHO ARE YOU?!
I'M OVER HERE. OPEN YOUR EYES!
YOU'RE PRACTICING CHOPPING DOWN TREES WITH YOUR EYES CLOSED?

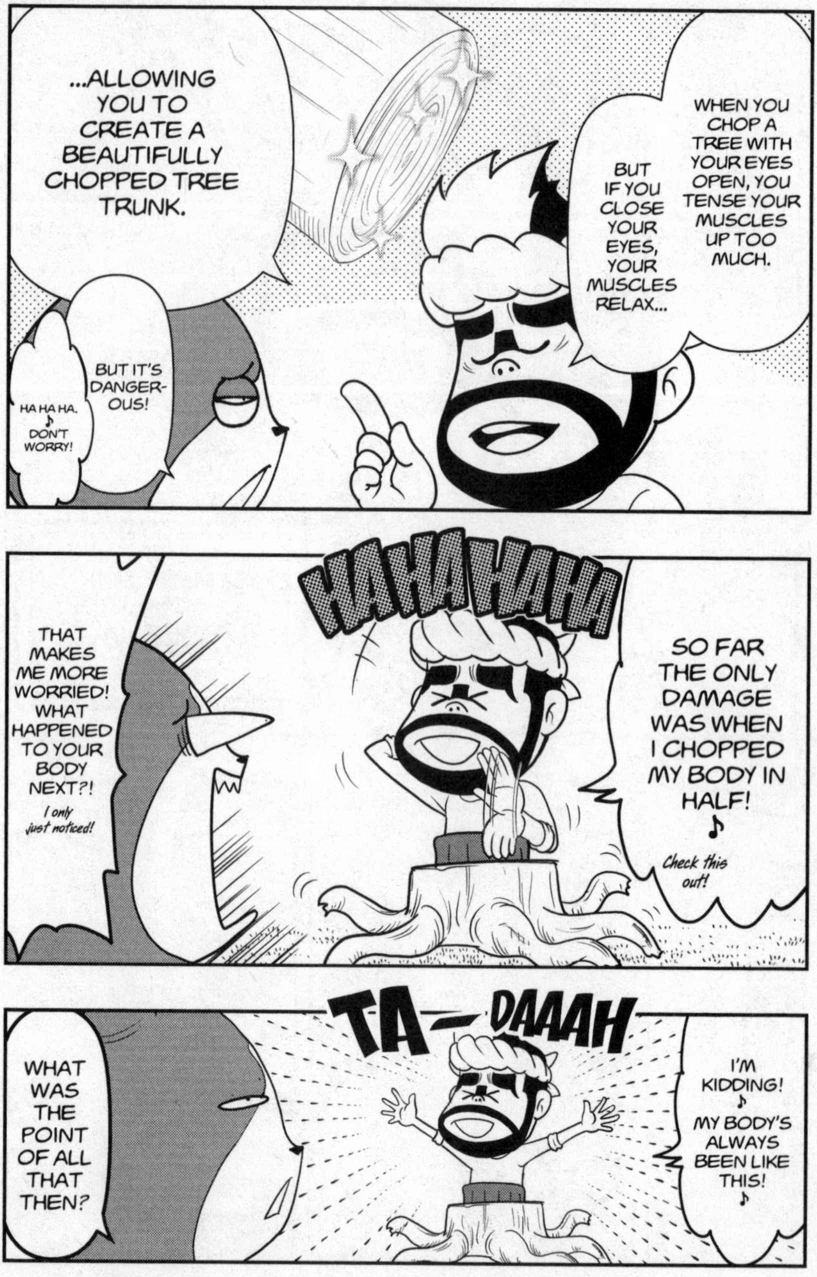
WHEN YOU CHOP A TREE WITH YOUR EYES OPEN, YOU TENSE YOUR MUSCLES UP TOO MUCH.
BUT IF YOU CLOSE YOUR EYES, YOUR MUSCLES RELAX...
...ALLOWING YOU TO CREATE A BEAUTIFULLY CHOPPED TREE TRUNK.
BUT IT'S DANGER-OUS!
HA HA HA. ♪ DON'T WORRY!
HAHAHAHA
SO FAR THE ONLY DAMAGE WAS WHEN I CHOPPED MY BODY IN HALF! ♪
Check this out!
THAT MAKES ME MORE WORRIED! WHAT HAPPENED TO YOUR BODY NEXT?!
I only just noticed!
TA-DAAAH
I'M KIDDING! ♪ MY BODY'S ALWAYS BEEN LIKE THIS! ♪
WHAT WAS THE POINT OF ALL THAT THEN?

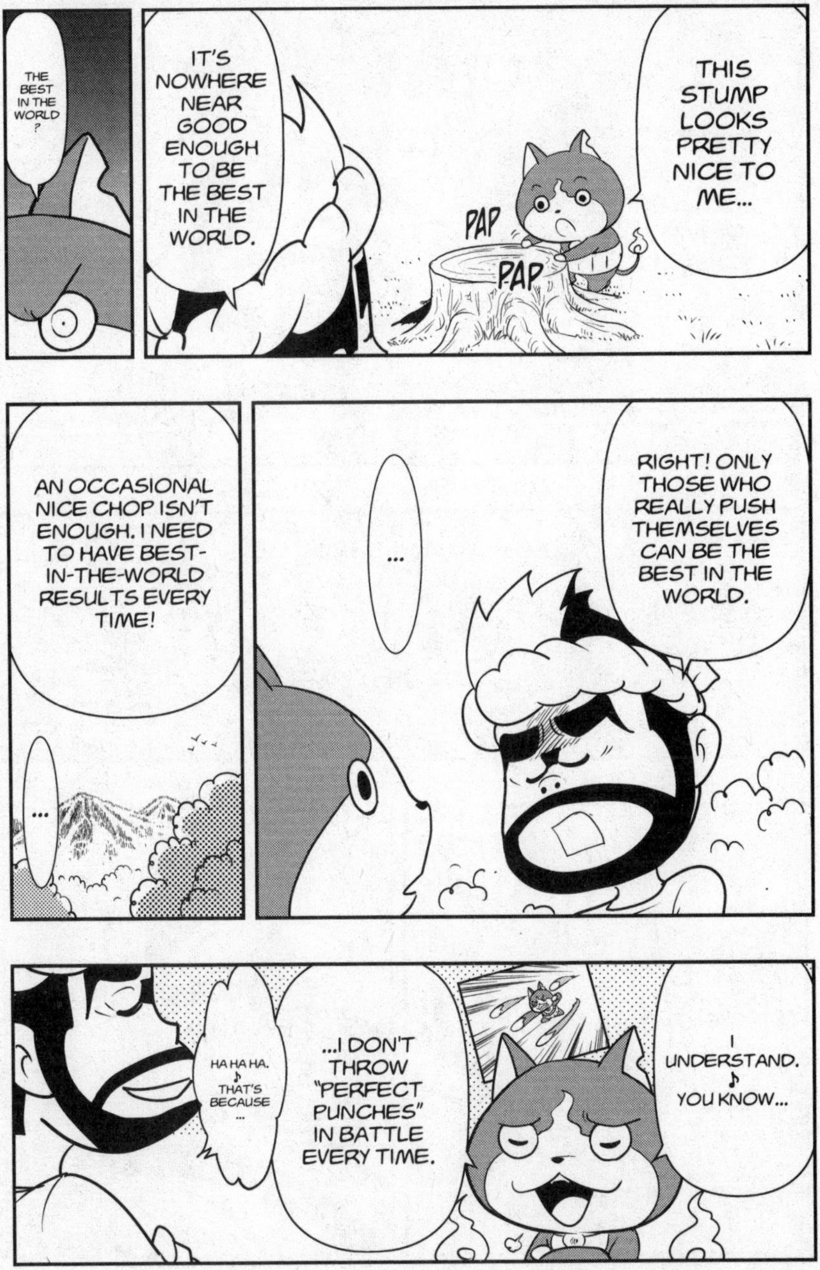
THIS STUMP LOOKS PRETTY NICE TO ME...
PAP
PAP
IT'S NOWHERE NEAR GOOD ENOUGH TO BE THE BEST IN THE WORLD.
THE BEST IN THE WORLD?
RIGHT! ONLY THOSE WHO REALLY PUSH THEMSELVES CAN BE THE BEST IN THE WORLD.
...
AN OCCASIONAL NICE CHOP ISN'T ENOUGH. I NEED TO HAVE BEST-IN-THE-WORLD RESULTS EVERY TIME!
...
I UNDERSTAND. ♪ YOU KNOW...
...I DON'T THROW "PERFECT PUNCHES" IN BATTLE EVERY TIME.
HA HA HA. ♪ THAT'S BECAUSE ...

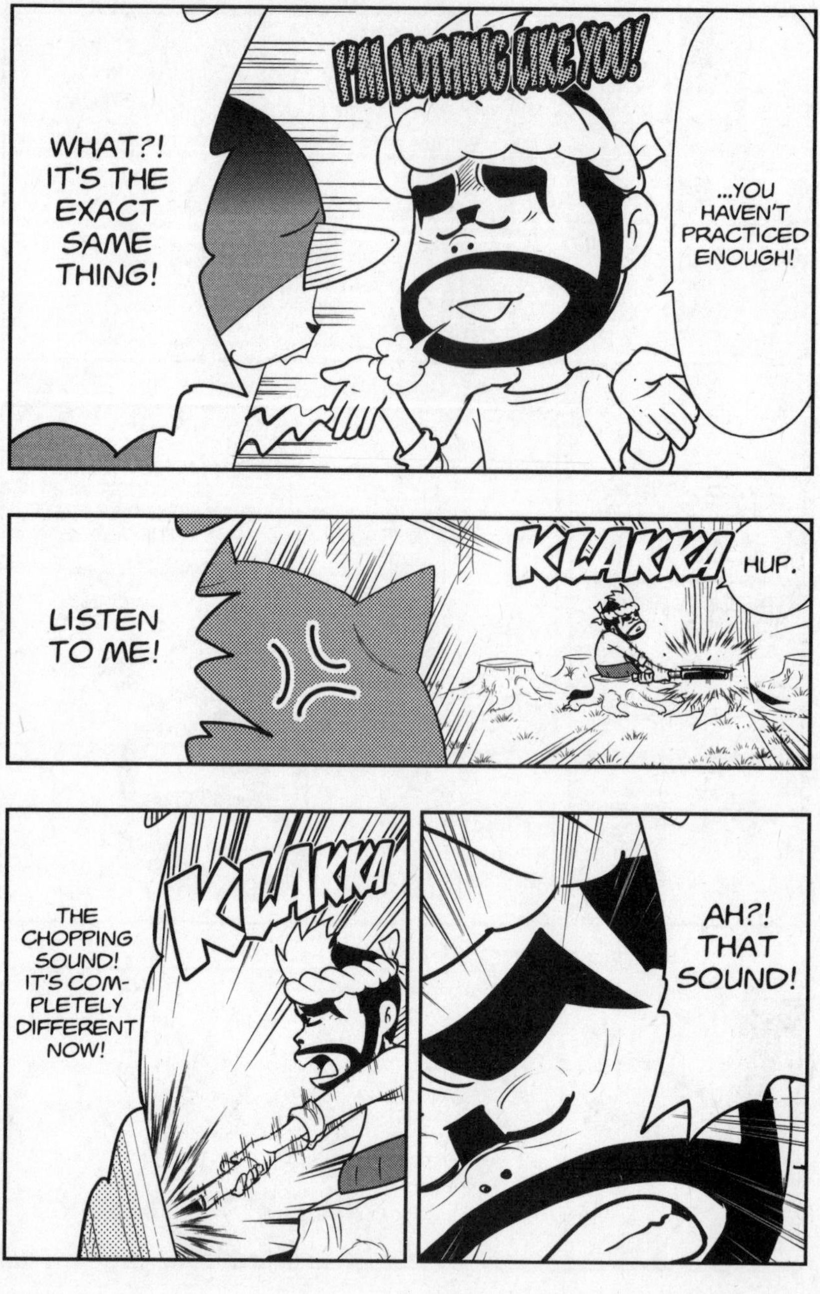
I'M NOTHING LIKE YOU!
...YOU HAVEN'T PRACTICED ENOUGH!
WHAT?! IT'S THE EXACT SAME THING!
HUP.
KLAKKA
LISTEN TO ME!
AH?! THAT SOUND!
KLAKKA
THE CHOPPING SOUND! IT'S COMPLETELY DIFFERENT NOW!

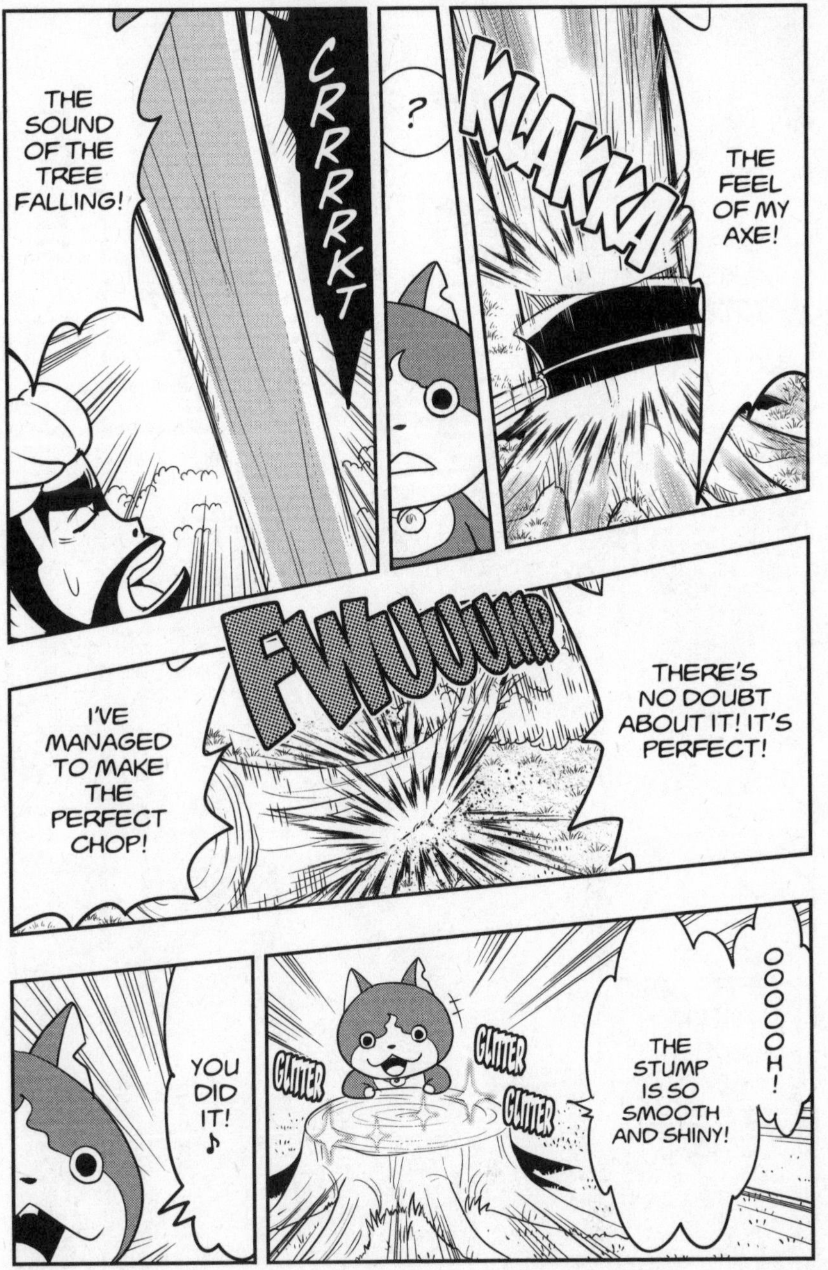
KLAKKA
THE FEEL OF MY AXE!
?
CRRRRRKT
THE SOUND OF THE TREE FALLING!
FWUUUMP
THERE'S NO DOUBT ABOUT IT! IT'S PERFECT!
I'VE MANAGED TO MAKE THE PERFECT CHOP!
OOOOOOH!
THE STUMP IS SO SMOOTH AND SHINY!
GLITTER
GLITTER
GLITTER
YOU DID IT! ♪

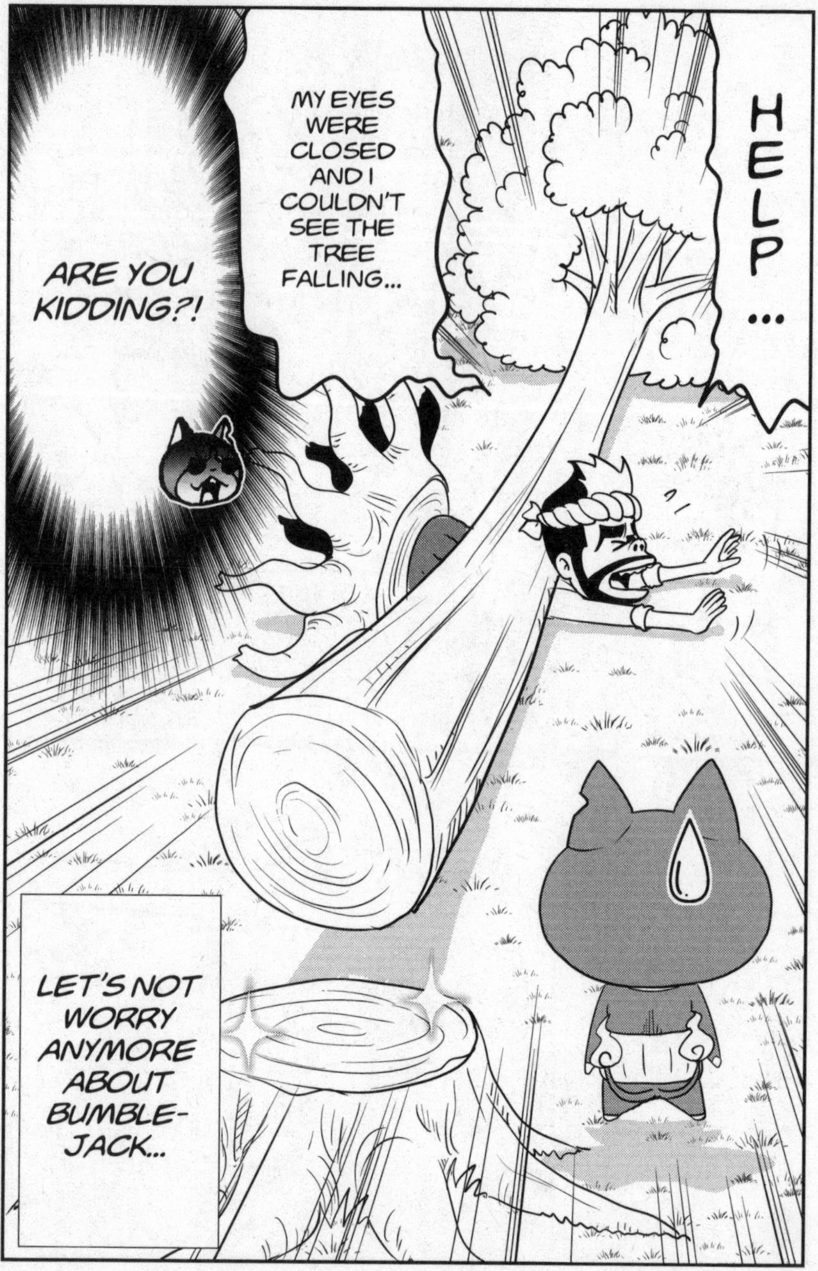
HELP...
MY EYES WERE CLOSED AND I COULDN'T SEE THE TREE FALLING...
ARE YOU KIDDING?!
LET'S NOT WORRY ANYMORE ABOUT BUMBLE-JACK...

CHAPTER 163
DUMB YO-KAI DUMMKAP

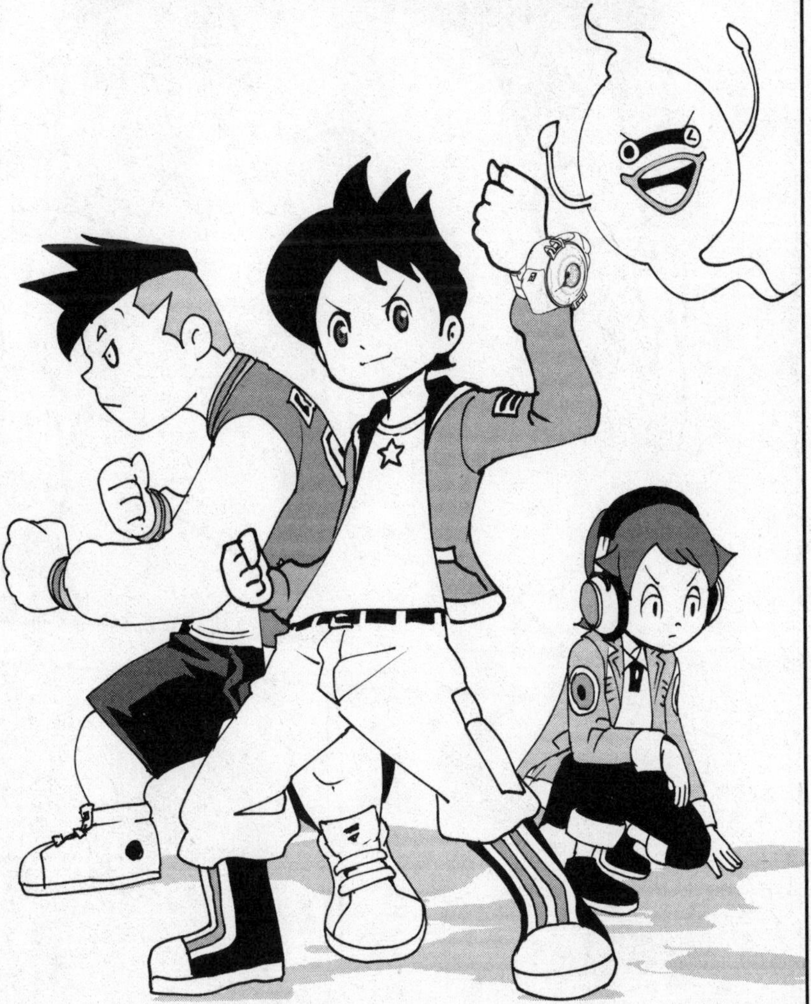

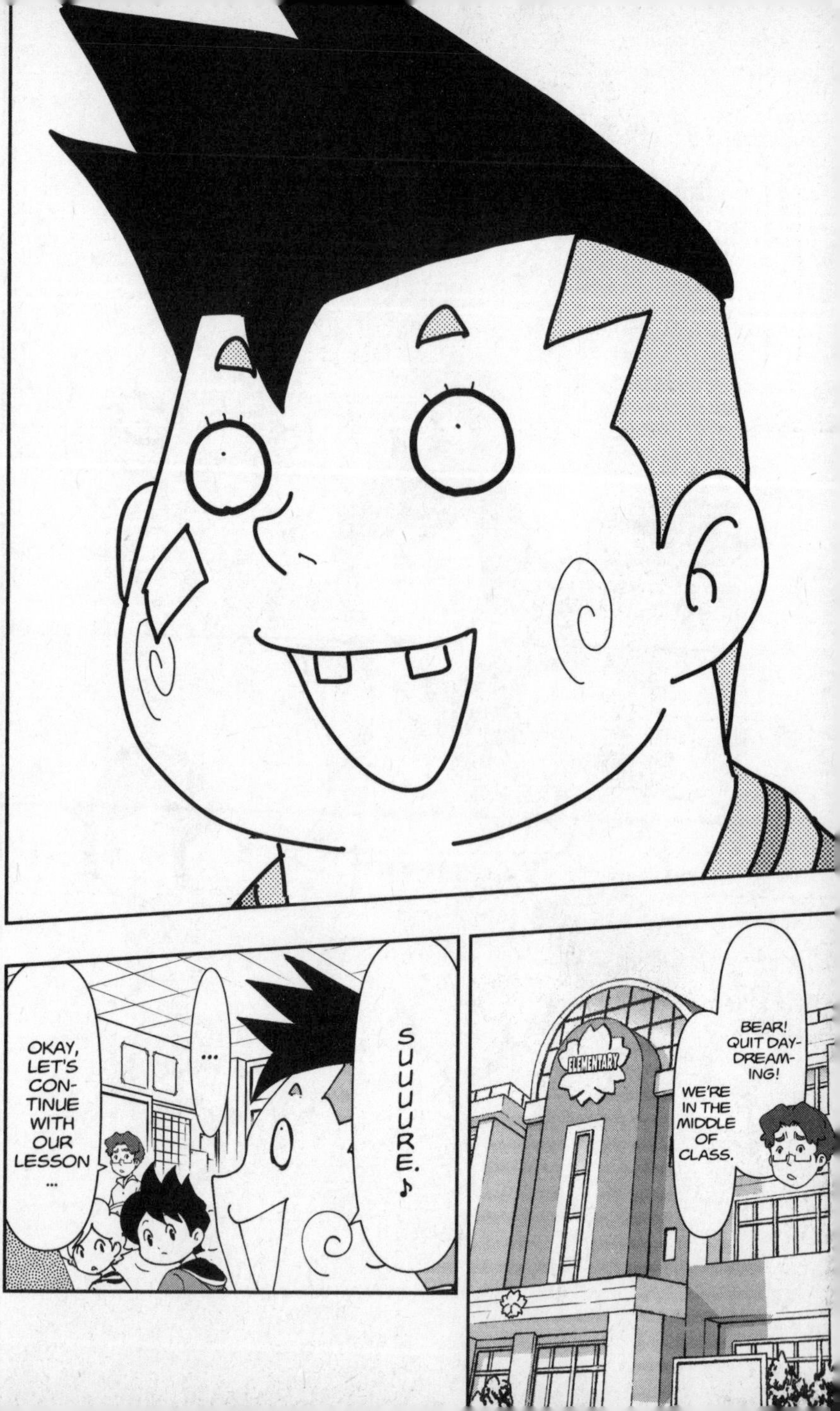
ELEMENTARY
BEAR! QUIT DAY-DREAM-ING!
WE'RE IN THE MIDDLE OF CLASS.
SUUUURE.♪
...
OKAY, LET'S CON-TINUE WITH OUR LESSON ...

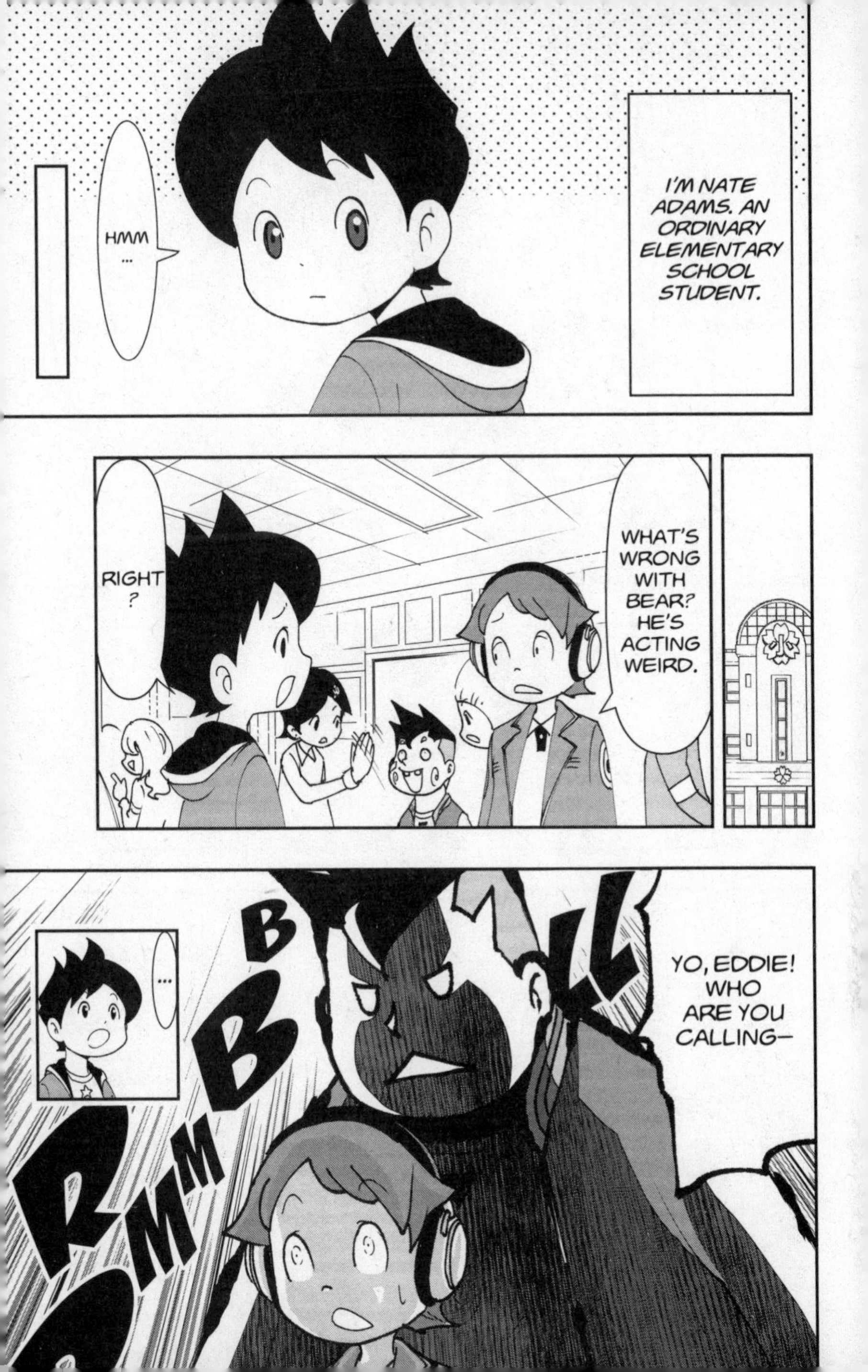
I'M NATE ADAMS. AN ORDINARY ELEMENTARY SCHOOL STUDENT.
HMM ...
WHAT'S WRONG WITH BEAR? HE'S ACTING WEIRD.
RIGHT?
YO, EDDIE! WHO ARE YOU CALLING—
RMMBB
...

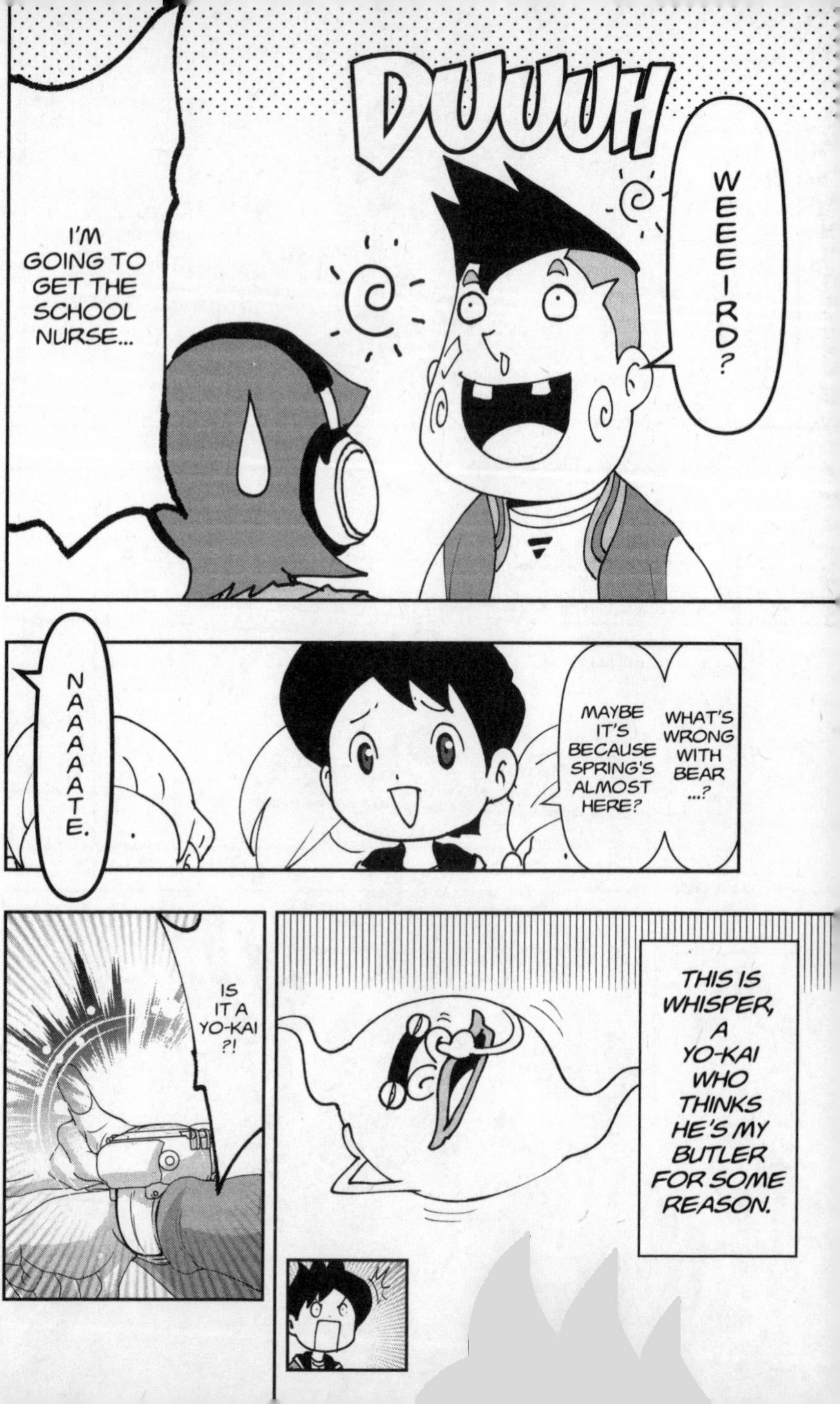
DUUUH
WEEEIRD?
I'M GOING TO GET THE SCHOOL NURSE...
WHAT'S WRONG WITH BEAR ...?
MAYBE IT'S BECAUSE SPRING'S ALMOST HERE?
NAAAAAATE.
THIS IS WHISPER, A YO-KAI WHO THINKS HE'S MY BUTLER FOR SOME REASON.
IS IT A YO-KAI ?!

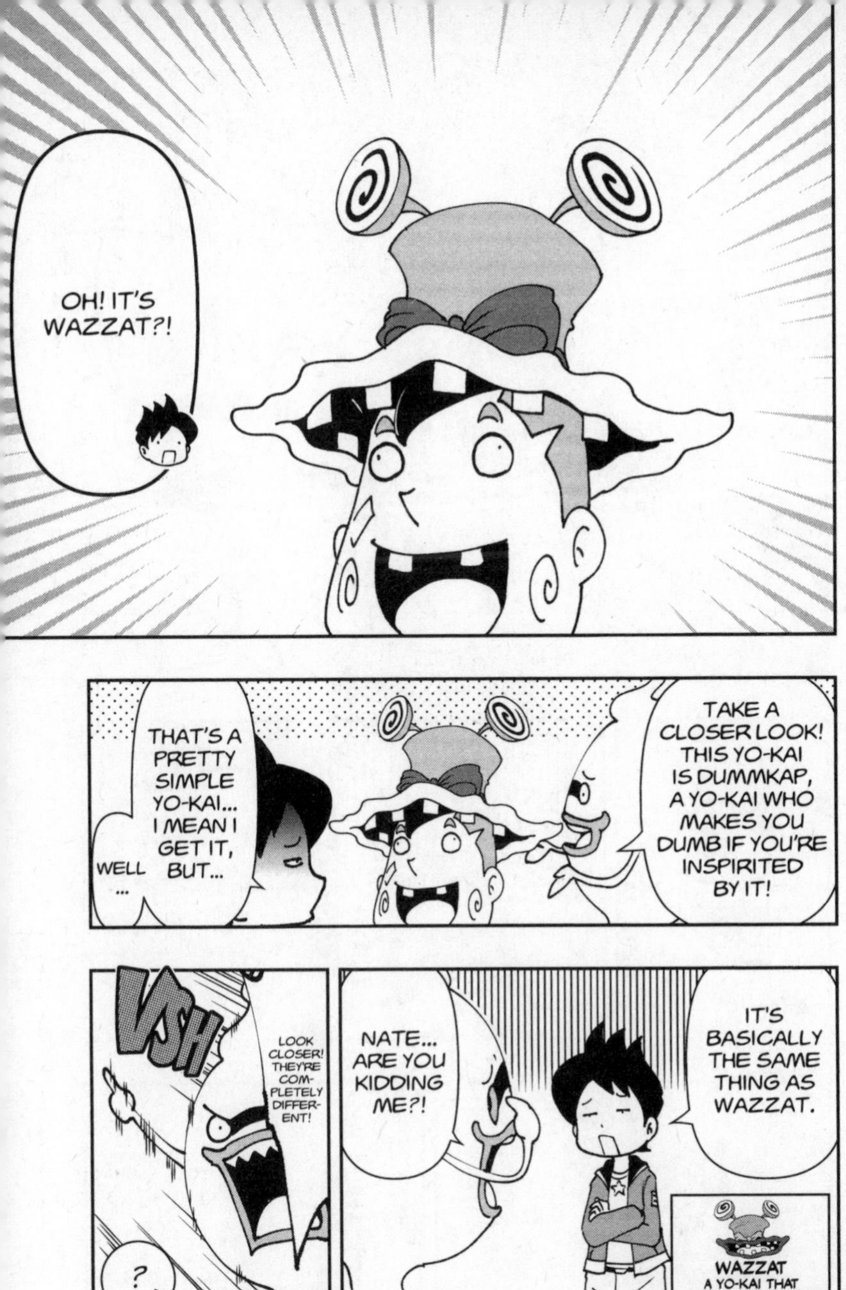
OH! IT'S WAZZAT?!
TAKE A CLOSER LOOK! THIS YO-KAI IS DUMMKAP, A YO-KAI WHO MAKES YOU DUMB IF YOU'RE INSPIRITED BY IT!
WELL...
THAT'S A PRETTY SIMPLE YO-KAI... I MEAN I GET IT, BUT...
IT'S BASICALLY THE SAME THING AS WAZZAT.
NATE... ARE YOU KIDDING ME?!
WAZZAT
A YO-KAI THAT MAKES YOU FORGET THINGS.
VSH
LOOK CLOSER! THEY'RE COM-PLETELY DIFFER-ENT!
?

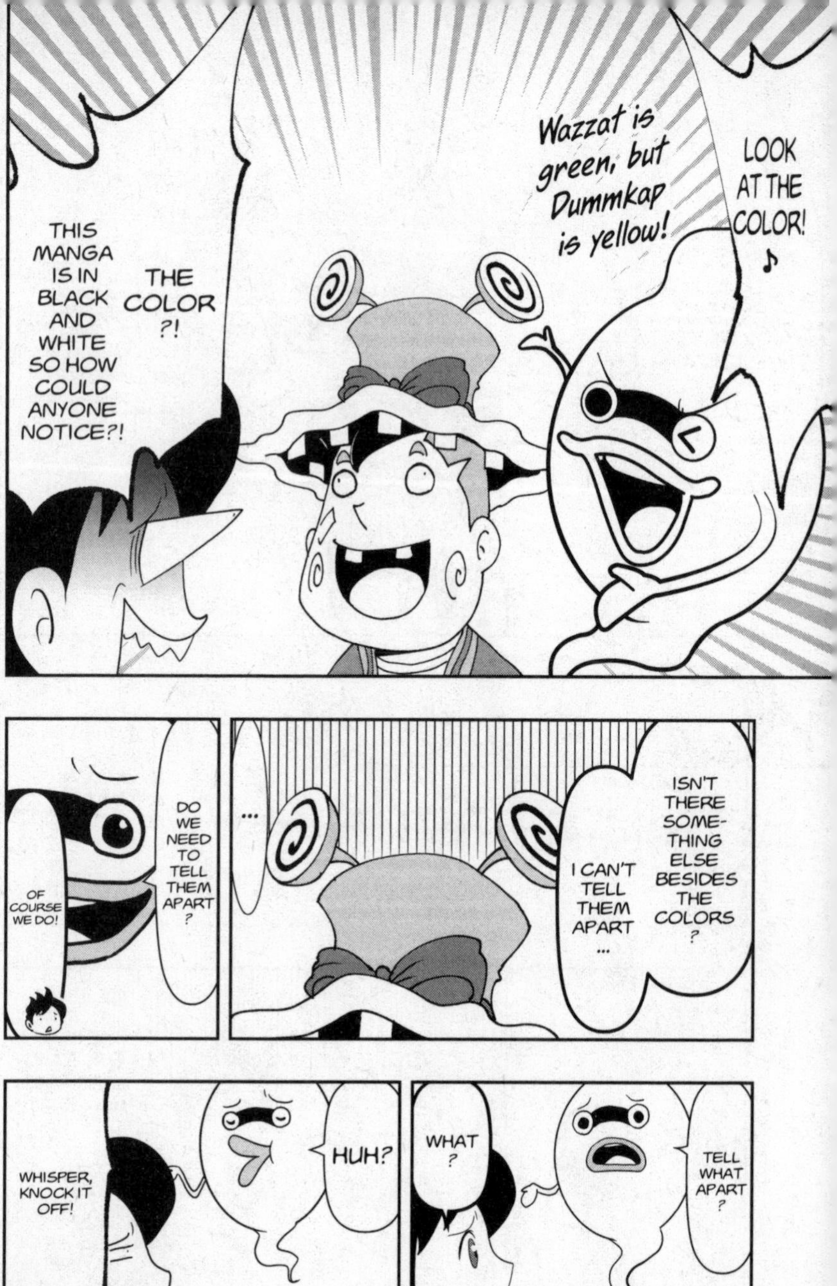
LOOK AT THE COLOR! ♪
Wazzat is green, but Dummkap is yellow!
THE COLOR?!
THIS MANGA IS IN BLACK AND WHITE SO HOW COULD ANYONE NOTICE?!
ISN'T THERE SOME-THING ELSE BESIDES THE COLORS?
I CAN'T TELL THEM APART...
...
DO WE NEED TO TELL THEM APART?
OF COURSE WE DO!
TELL WHAT APART?
WHAT?
HUH?
WHISPER, KNOCK IT OFF!

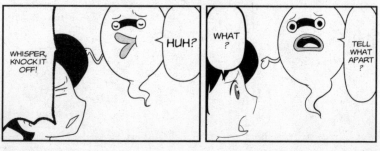

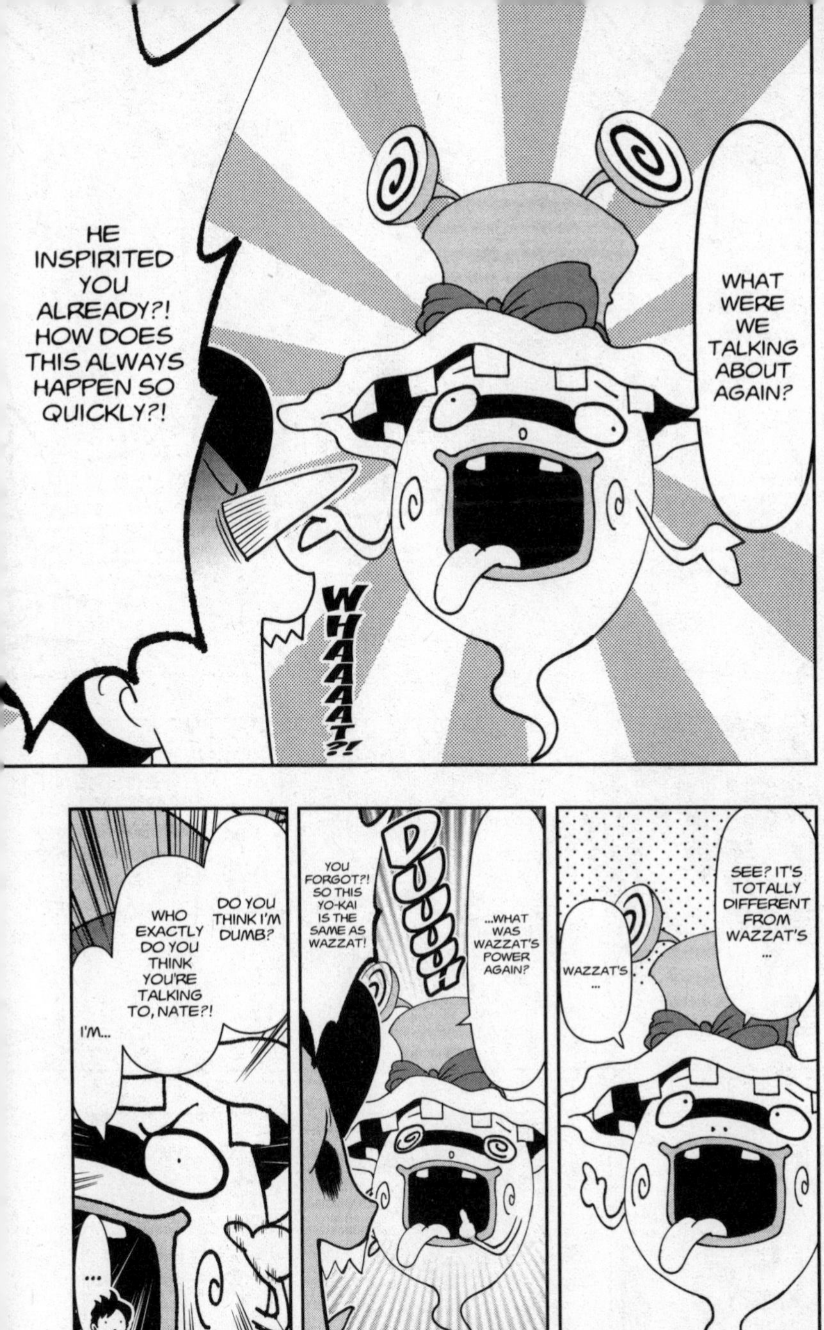
WHAT WERE WE TALKING ABOUT AGAIN?
HE INSPIRITED YOU ALREADY?! HOW DOES THIS ALWAYS HAPPEN SO QUICKLY?!
WHAAAAAT?!
SEE? IT'S TOTALLY DIFFERENT FROM WAZZAT'S ...
WAZZAT'S ...
...WHAT WAS WAZZAT'S POWER AGAIN?
DUUUUH
YOU FORGOT?! SO THIS YO-KAI IS THE SAME AS WAZZAT!
DO YOU THINK I'M DUMB?
WHO EXACTLY DO YOU THINK YOU'RE TALKING TO, NATE?!
I'M...
...

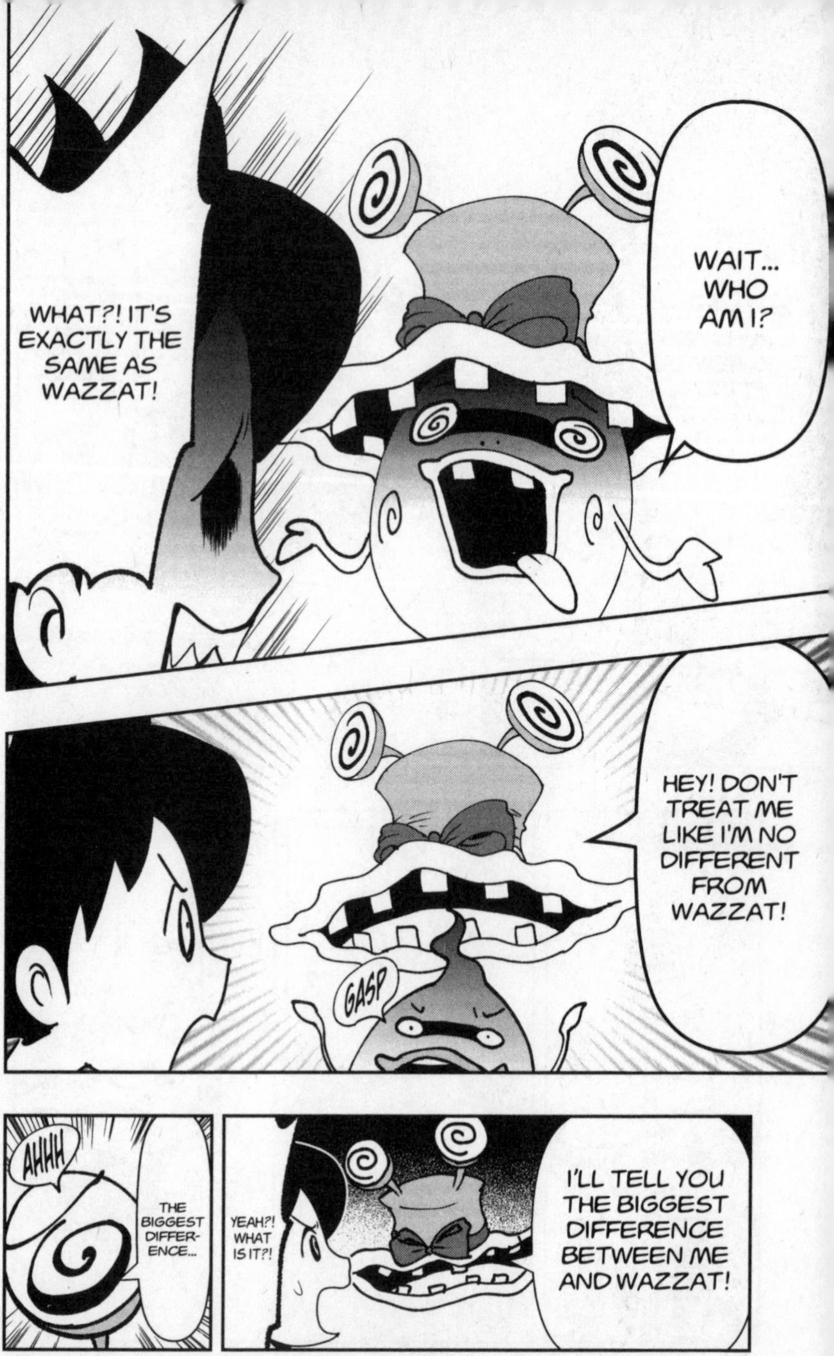
WAIT... WHO AM I?
WHAT?! IT'S EXACTLY THE SAME AS WAZZAT!
HEY! DON'T TREAT ME LIKE I'M NO DIFFERENT FROM WAZZAT!
GASP
I'LL TELL YOU THE BIGGEST DIFFERENCE BETWEEN ME AND WAZZAT!
YEAH?! WHAT IS IT?!
THE BIGGEST DIFFER-ENCE...
AHHH

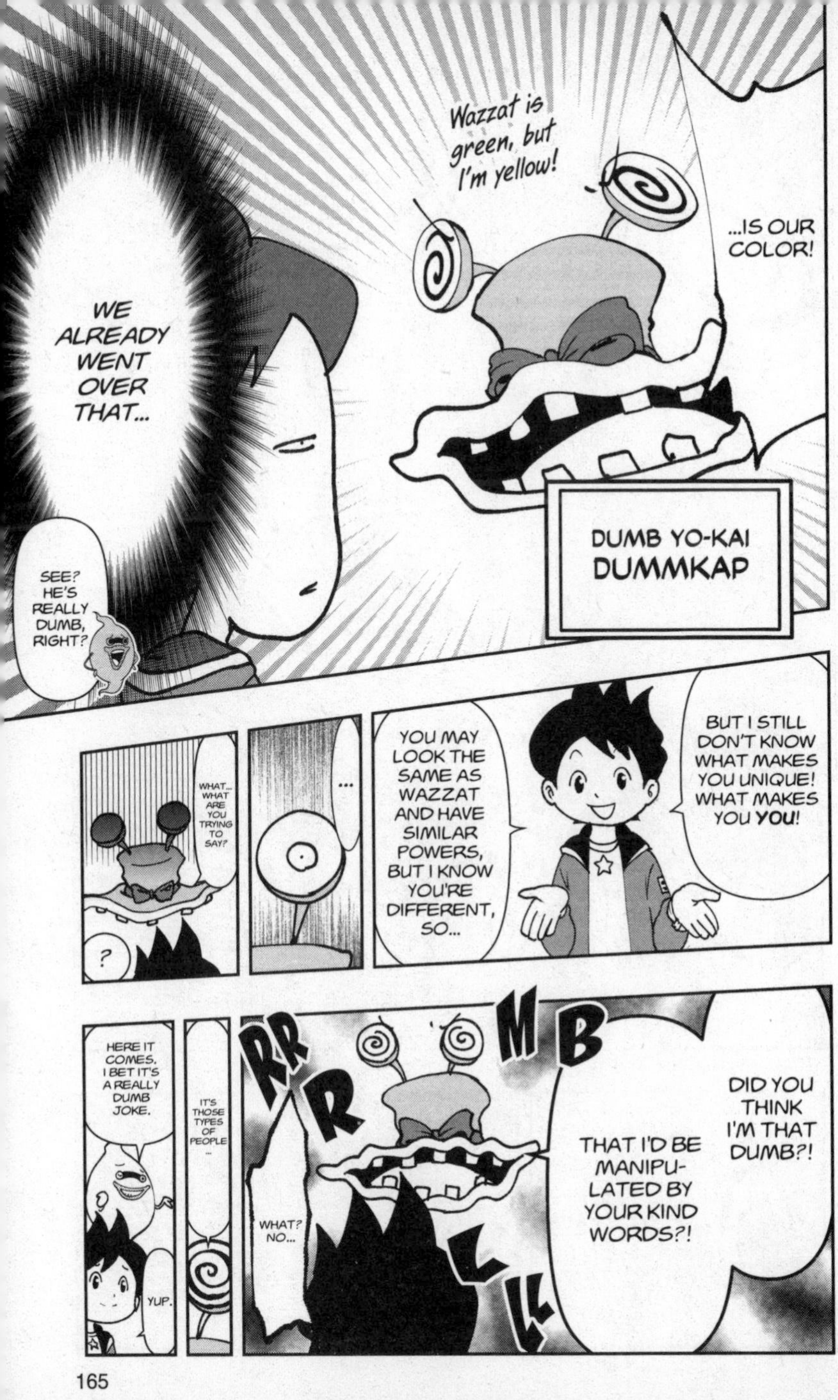
...IS OUR COLOR!
Wazzat is green, but I'm yellow!
DUMB YO-KAI DUMMKAP
WE ALREADY WENT OVER THAT...
SEE? HE'S REALLY DUMB, RIGHT?
BUT I STILL DON'T KNOW WHAT MAKES YOU UNIQUE! WHAT MAKES YOU **YOU**!
YOU MAY LOOK THE SAME AS WAZZAT AND HAVE SIMILAR POWERS, BUT I KNOW YOU'RE DIFFERENT, SO...
...
WHAT... WHAT ARE YOU TRYING TO SAY?
?
DID YOU THINK I'M THAT DUMB?!
THAT I'D BE MANIPULATED BY YOUR KIND WORDS?!
RRRMBLL!
WHAT? NO...
IT'S THOSE TYPES OF PEOPLE...
HERE IT COMES. I BET IT'S A REALLY DUMB JOKE.
YUP.

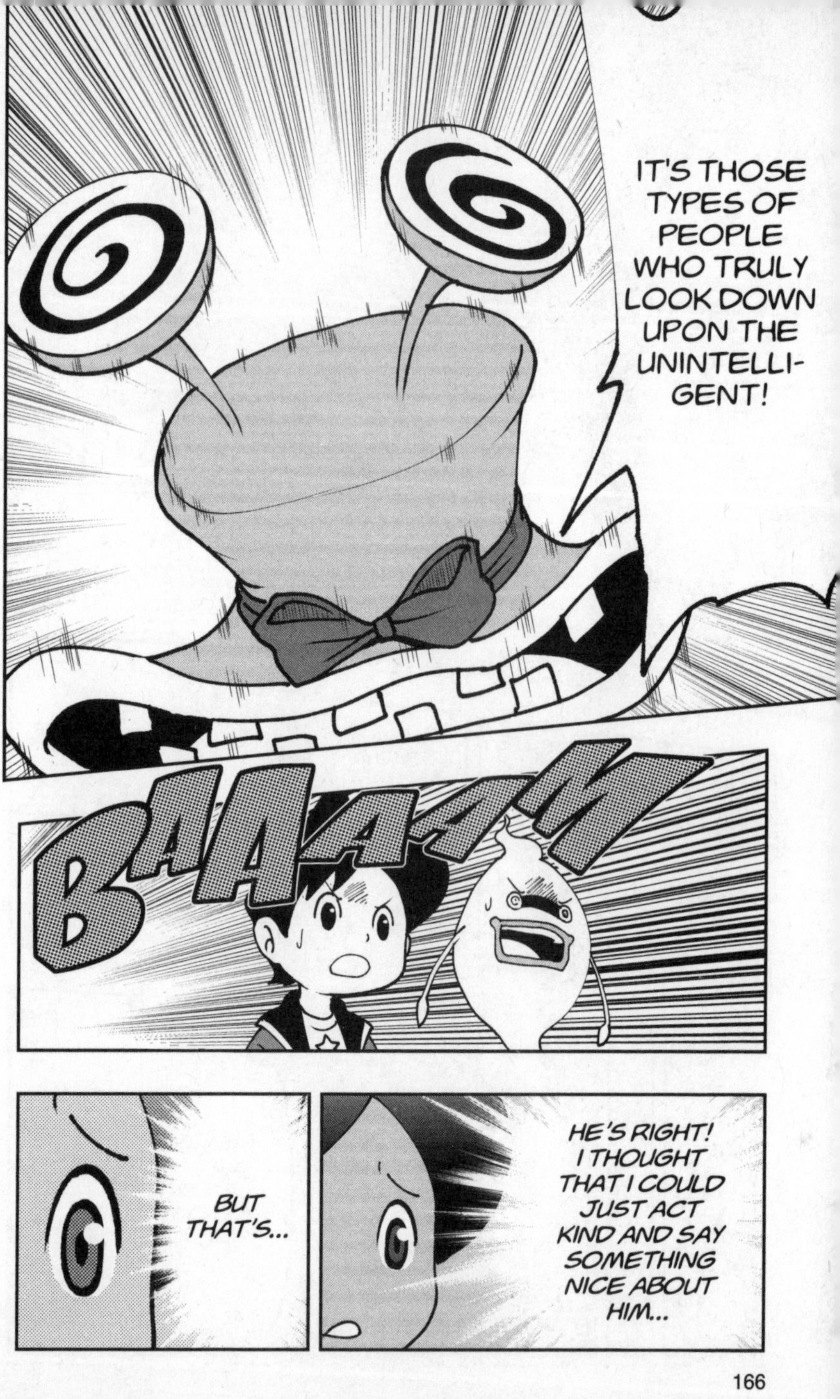
IT'S THOSE TYPES OF PEOPLE WHO TRULY LOOK DOWN UPON THE UNINTELLI-GENT!
BAAAAM
HE'S RIGHT! I THOUGHT THAT I COULD JUST ACT KIND AND SAY SOMETHING NICE ABOUT HIM...
BUT THAT'S...

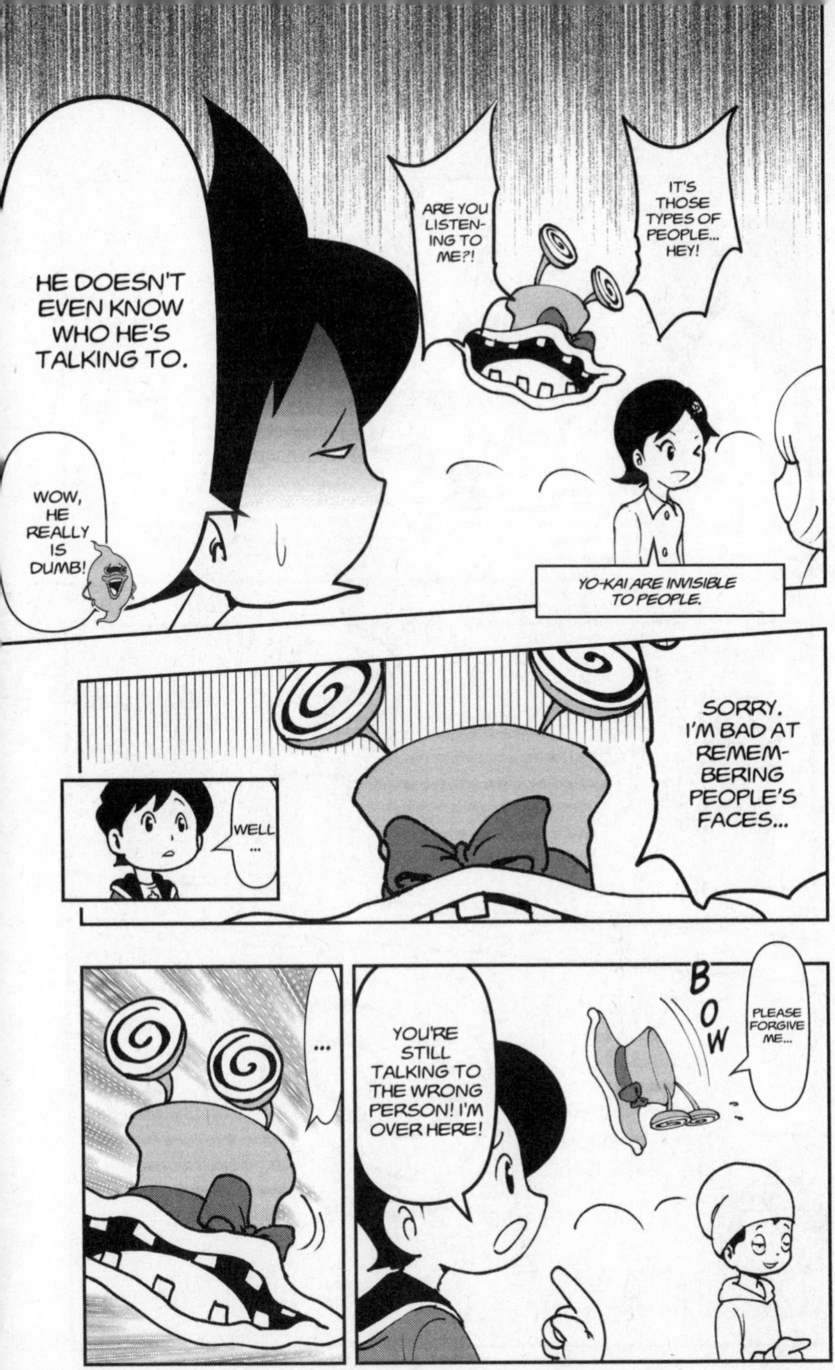
IT'S THOSE TYPES OF PEOPLE... HEY!
ARE YOU LISTENING TO ME?!
HE DOESN'T EVEN KNOW WHO HE'S TALKING TO.
YO-KAI ARE INVISIBLE TO PEOPLE.
WOW, HE REALLY IS DUMB!
SORRY. I'M BAD AT REMEMBERING PEOPLE'S FACES...
WELL ...
BOW
PLEASE FORGIVE ME...
YOU'RE STILL TALKING TO THE WRONG PERSON! I'M OVER HERE!
...

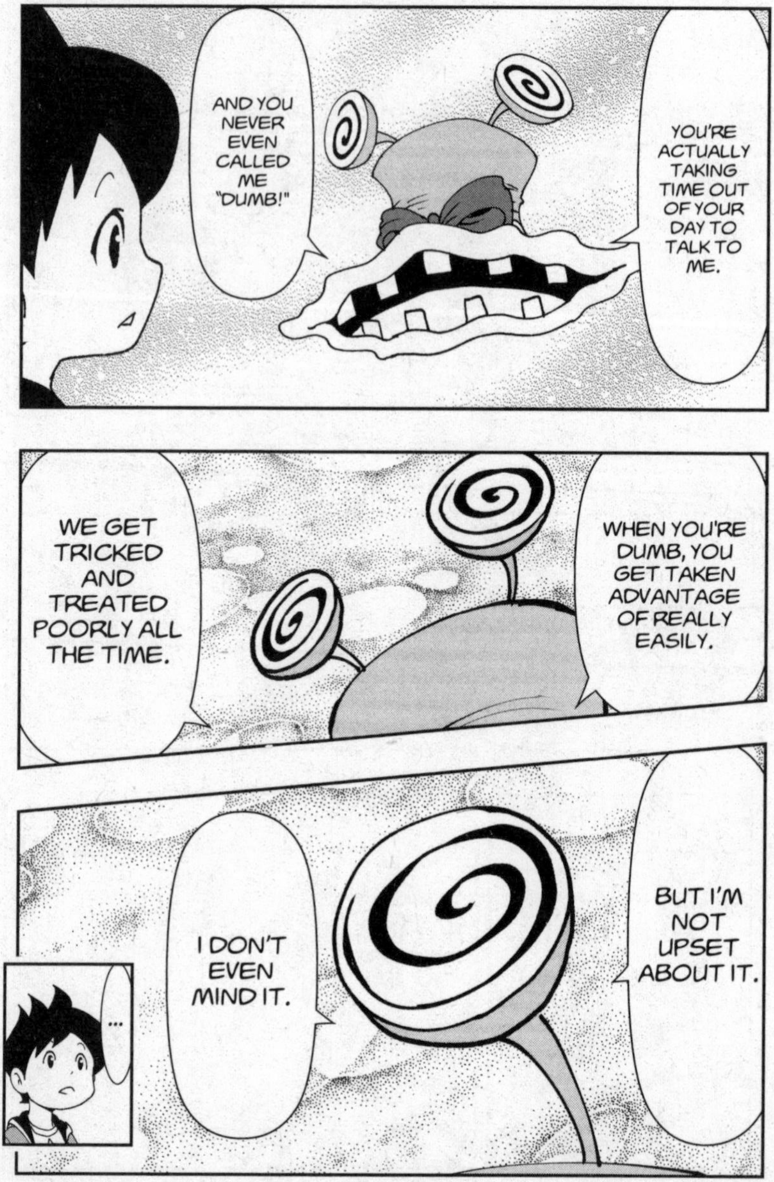
YOU'RE ACTUALLY TAKING TIME OUT OF YOUR DAY TO TALK TO ME.
AND YOU NEVER EVEN CALLED ME "DUMB!"
WHEN YOU'RE DUMB, YOU GET TAKEN ADVANTAGE OF REALLY EASILY.
WE GET TRICKED AND TREATED POORLY ALL THE TIME.
BUT I'M NOT UPSET ABOUT IT.
I DON'T EVEN MIND IT.
...

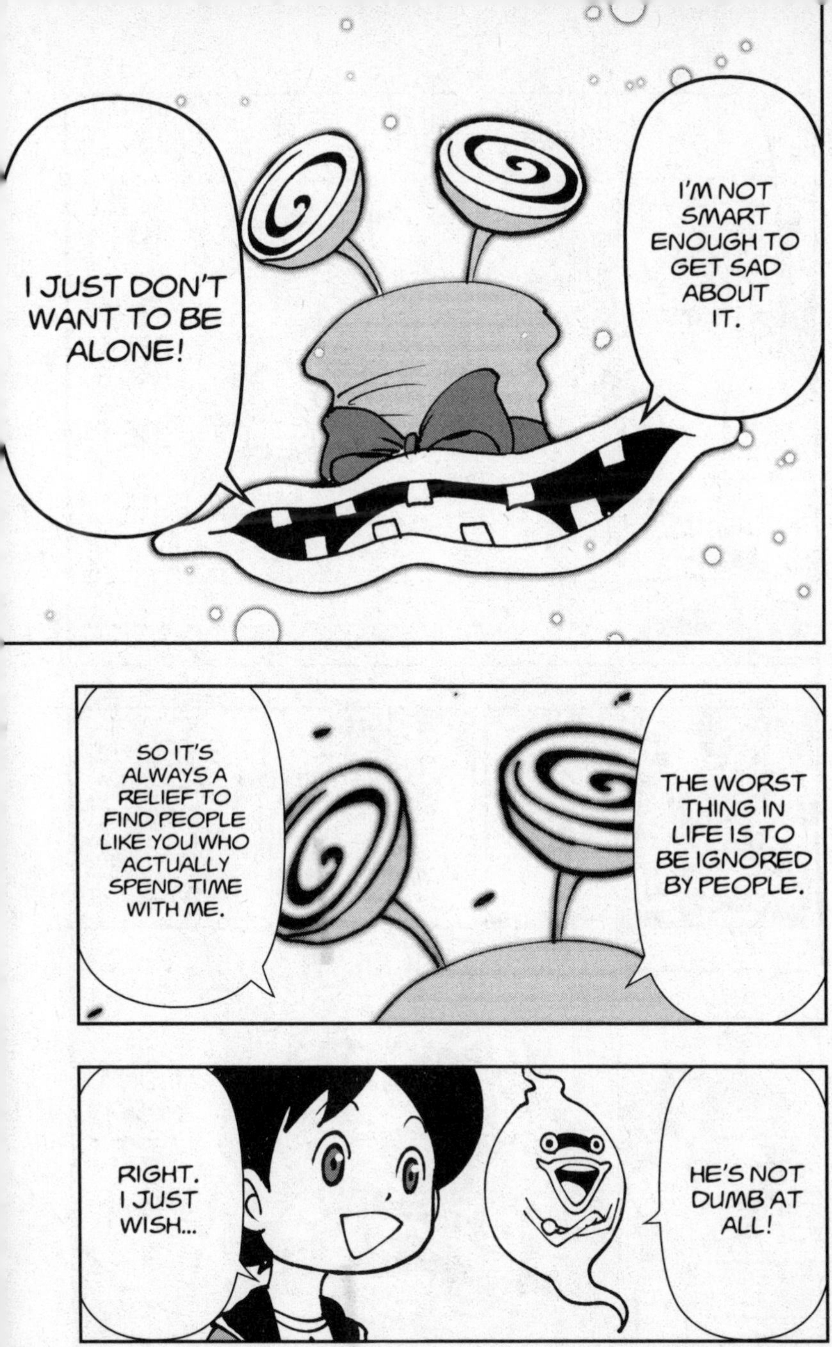
I'M NOT SMART ENOUGH TO GET SAD ABOUT IT.
I JUST DON'T WANT TO BE ALONE!
THE WORST THING IN LIFE IS TO BE IGNORED BY PEOPLE.
SO IT'S ALWAYS A RELIEF TO FIND PEOPLE LIKE YOU WHO ACTUALLY SPEND TIME WITH ME.
HE'S NOT DUMB AT ALL!
RIGHT. I JUST WISH...

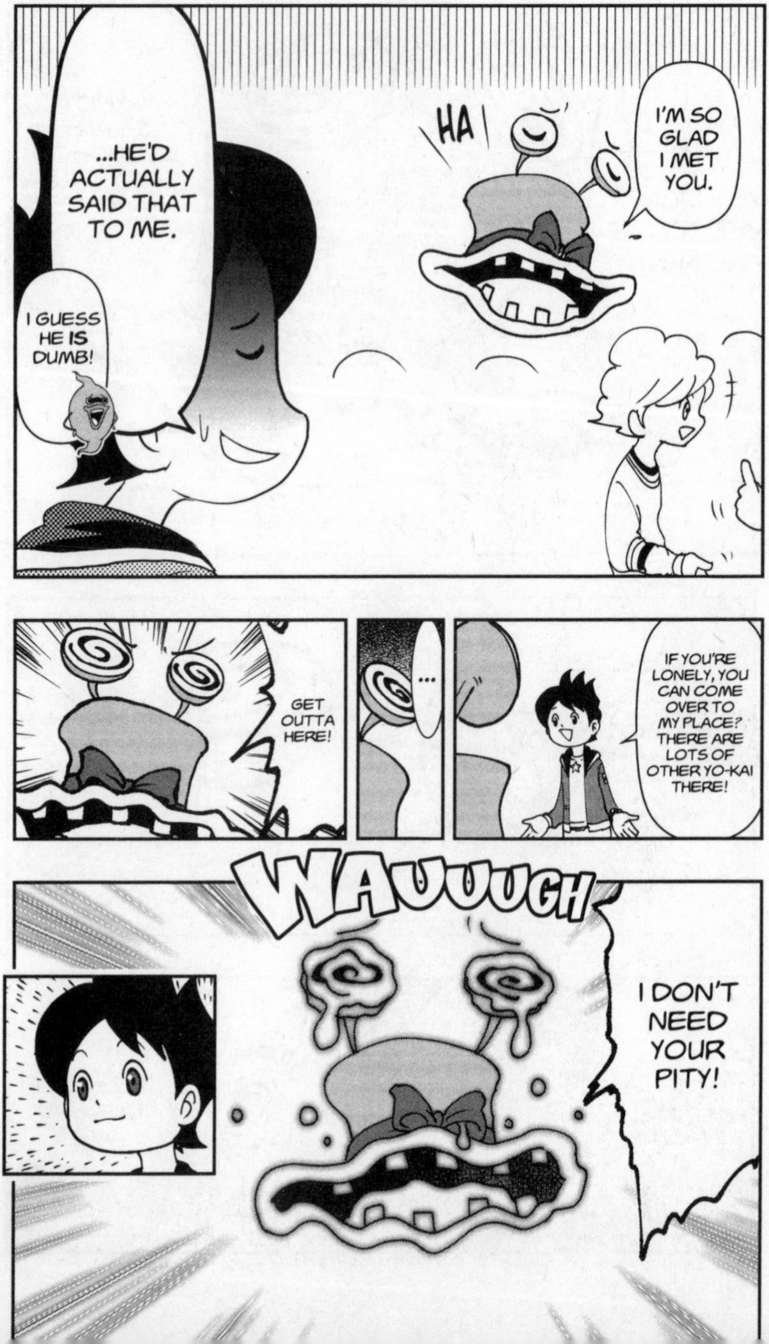
HA
I'M SO GLAD I MET YOU.
...HE'D ACTUALLY SAID THAT TO ME.
I GUESS HE IS DUMB!
IF YOU'RE LONELY, YOU CAN COME OVER TO MY PLACE? THERE ARE LOTS OF OTHER YO-KAI THERE!
...
GET OUTTA HERE!
WAUUUGH
I DON'T NEED YOUR PITY!

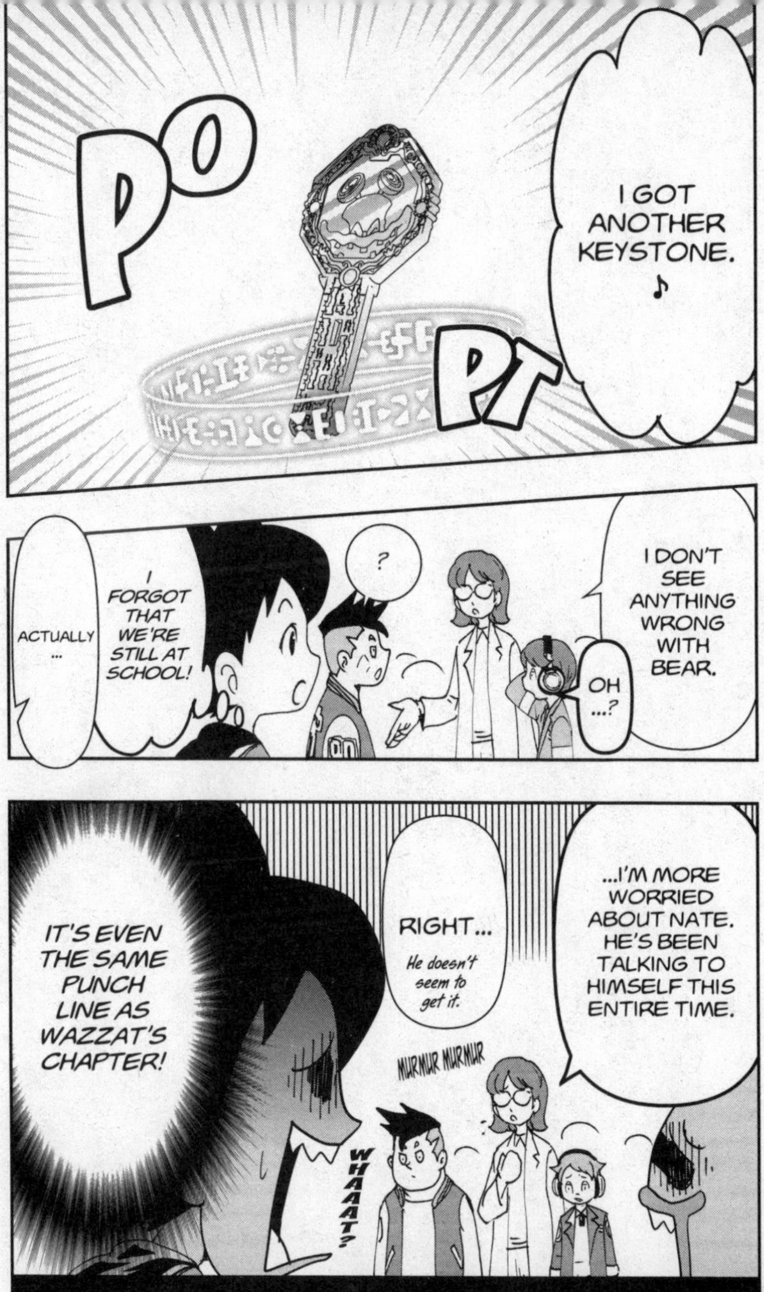
I GOT ANOTHER KEYSTONE. ♪
POPT
I DON'T SEE ANYTHING WRONG WITH BEAR.
OH ...?
?
I FORGOT THAT WE'RE STILL AT SCHOOL!
ACTUALLY ...
...I'M MORE WORRIED ABOUT NATE. HE'S BEEN TALKING TO HIMSELF THIS ENTIRE TIME.
RIGHT...
He doesn't seem to get it.
MURMUR MURMUR
WHAAAAT?
IT'S EVEN THE SAME PUNCH LINE AS WAZZAT'S CHAPTER!
NATE ADAMS'S CURRENT NUMBER OF YO-KAI FRIENDS: 79

HOW TO USE THE YO-KAI WATCH ARCANE

DUUUUH...
IT'S SO HOT ...
RIGHT ...
SIZZLE...
SIZZLE...
I KNOW! MAYBE WE CAN USE THIS TO COOL OUR-SELVES?!
SHUP
WHAT? WHICH YO-KAI IS IT?
FWIP FWIP
KCH KCH
?
PHEEW, THAT FEELS COOL...
YOU'RE OPENING AND CLOS-ING THE LID TO CREATE A BREEZE ?!
FWIP FWIP

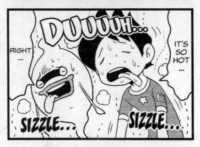

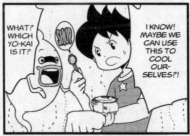

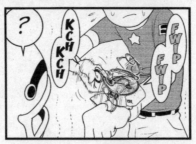

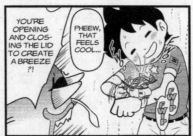

AUTHOR BIO

Nate is back with a brand new Yo-kai Watch! Find out how he uses it, along with the Yo-kai Keystones, to meet and make even more Yo-kai friends!

Noriyuki Konishi hails from Shimabara City in Nagasaki Prefecture, Japan. He debuted with the one-shot *E-CUFF* in *Monthly Shonen Jump Original* in 1997. He is known in Japan for writing manga adaptations of *AM Driver* and *Mushiking: King of the Beetles*, along with *Saiyuki Hiro Go-Kū Den!*, *Chōhenshin Gag Gaiden!! Card Warrior Kamen Riders*, *Go-Go-Go Saiyuki: Shin Gokūden* and more. Konishi was the recipient of the 38th Kodansha manga award in 2014 and the 60th Shogakukan manga award in 2015.

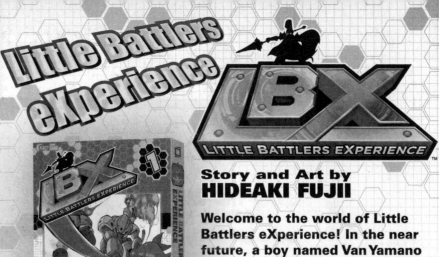

THIS IS THE END OF
THIS GRAPHIC NOVEL.

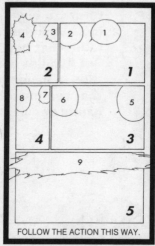

FOLLOW THE ACTION THIS WAY.

**To properly enjoy this graphic novel,
please turn it around and begin
reading from right to left.**